BARTENDER,
I'LL HAVE ANOTHER
MURDER

DICK & LISA LYNN BACKUS

BARTENDER,
I'LL HAVE ANOTHER
MURDER

1

The industrial-strength vacuum was emitting a high-pitched whine, much like the revelers had a few hours earlier. Sucking up confetti, feathers, glittery cardboard and plastic noisemakers, shards of broken dishware and glasses, and assorted confectionary remnants. These folks had partied hearty, and with unconstrained messiness.

Josh Wheeler, manning the 'Carpet Zamboni,' as he called it, didn't much care. To him, it was all in a day's work. He even felt a certain pride that his employer's equipment was making quick work of the colossal clutter its guests had uncaringly strewn about. But he was shocked – damn near vomited, in fact – as he spotted what looked like a human body part in the path of his Irving Accumulator II. Hastily, he hit the kill switch and the whine of the machine ground to a halt. The hustle and bustle of those in the large banquet room going about their prescribed chores could again be heard.

Wheeler unseated himself and scurried around the front of the motorized vacuum. Bending down, he confirmed his suspicions. It sure looked like a human hand – a fist with its middle digit pointing straight up – but he couldn't be sure and didn't want to spend a lot of time examining the gruesome appendage. He looked up and caught the eye of Alfredo Suarez, one of the banquet servers who'd stayed on overtime to assist with clean-up, beckoning him over.

"Hey Alf, who's the on-site MOD?"

"I think Charlie. Anything I can help you with?" asked Alfredo as he approached.

Josh motioned toward the hand. "Not unless you wanna take care of this, and all the questions that are gonna come with it."

Alfredo turned pale, backed away a few feet and exclaimed, "C-c-call Charlie, man!" Then he did what Josh had nearly done – he puked. Right there on the carpet, about four feet from the severed fist that seemed to be saying *f- - - off* to someone."

Activity at the lobby bar carried on much like any other late night, with everyone oblivious to the happenings upstairs in the Fascination Ballroom. People came, people went. Drinks were poured and consumed, and for the most part nobody was all that excited about the arrival of a new year. Big deal. 2016 had kinda sucked; what reason was there to expect that 2017 would be a big improvement? At least there'd be no election to deal with, so maybe that was a small consolation. But then there'd be the tedium of dealing with those who'd gotten themselves elected – not an attractive array of characters, for the most part. That seemed to be the consensus.

Signage identified the bar as Libations on the Lobby, but staff referred to it simply – and ironically – as 'LOL'. Head bartender Grayson Moore was an affable dude who thrived on conversation. Dialogue often translated to repeat customers, which meant good tips. But he steadfastly refused to discuss politics; it only resulted in someone getting bent out of shape – often-times himself – and there were too many other topics to talk about. Sports was his favorite, but he tried to stay abreast of local shows and happenings, the music scene, good dining choices, travel destinations, books and movies. There was so much – but please, not politics!

Gray, as most knew him — who usually worked days at the LOL, but drew a double shift for the holiday — was happy to see the crowd finally diminish. He'd sent Tapper home an hour after midnight, as she was dog tired from being on her feet for thirteen hours straight. It'd been a lively place earlier, hence the double staffing. It had been one of those nights that made him think of *At the Zoo* by Simon & Garfunkel. His friend Charlie had taught him the practice of translating life experiences into music, and the LOL's diverse clientele fit the song perfectly.

Now he was winding down, set to close at 3 a.m., but he sure wouldn't mind if he could make it even earlier. It was mostly stragglers now. The regulars (and decent tippers) were long since inebriated and gone.

All except Maryland. She was a perpetual hanger-onner, but there was nothing left in it for her at this godforsaken hour. She'd chatted a while with some pointy-faced youngster, but he seemed preoccupied with a video game he was playing with an unseen adversary in Singapore. Kid finally departed about 1:45, leaving most of his third Vod-bomb on the table. No loss, conversationwise. Maryland was a little chagrined that her friend Charlie hadn't stopped by once all evening, though Charlie had mentioned the burdensome MOD assignment.

As she pondered her lot in life, she thought of her upcoming trip, which lifted her spirits. She pulled out her phone and rechecked the forecasts for Baltimore and Raleigh-Durham. Not particularly pleasant, but what can you expect in January. At least it had given her a clue as to what she should pack.

Gray sensed that Maryland was off in another world. He comped her a final Brandy Alexander and told her to scram in ten.

She snickered, smirked and sneered all at once. "Ten'll get ya ten, Moore," she finally said, throwing a crisp Hamilton in his direction. "See ya, sonny boy."

"Happy New Year!" he called out, but she was gone, acting as if she owned the place and carrying the fresh cocktail with her.

What exactly is her story? Grayson Moore wondered that about Maryland Burfurd every time he encountered her.

Someday, perhaps, he'd get to the bottom of it.

But it might take Charlie's help.

2

Charlie here, and that's me everyone's talking about.

Being MOD – Manager on Duty – is no picnic, but we've all gotta do it from time to time. Working for a big hotel, you periodically get to be in charge of the whole operation for a tour of duty—generally overnight or for a whole weekend. Lots of authority, and for some it's an ego booster. To me, the headaches outweigh whatever glory there might be. That's how it usually went, and this tour was no exception.

My 'day job' is Senior Catering & Convention Services Manager at the Paradise Spectacular Resort Hotel and Casino. I'd been the natural choice for this particular MOD assignment, since New Year's Eve and New Year's Day were my big events and I had to be on-site anyway. So here I was, at 2:48 a.m. on January 1st, looking over early reports from December 31st. Everything was running smoothly, just like my big NYE bash that had just wound down. That event was for high rollers — 900+ attendees was the guarantee — who'd been invited to celebrate the coming of 2017 as guests of The ParaSpec, as our property was affectionately known. After feasting on a gourmet five-course meal, we counted on them to bring their bankrolls and leave a substantial chunk on our tables and in our slots.

Here's the theory: Meal ends at 9 p.m., celebrity entertainment starts at 11:30. In that 2½-hour interval, they can (and collectively will) drop a bundle. The 90-minute showbiz extravaganza rejuvenates them, makes them forget their earlier losses, and sends them back to the tables of their choice by 1 a.m. or so. Of course, the house loves those who stay at it till dawn.

That's the plan anyway. But here's the reality this morning: At 2:52 a.m., a khaki-clad guy with a neatly-trimmed beard burst into my office and breathlessly uttered, "I've just been given the finger!"

After the evidence — that is, the fist with extended finger — was photographed, bagged and removed by the police and Medical Examiner, I received a visit from a uniformed officer whose name, according to his badge, was Ainsworth.

I gave the thirtyish cop the rundown on what had happened, though I had little substance to add to what Josh Wheeler had already told him. I explained the dual capacities I was fulfilling for the resort at that moment, adding that I was acting as MOD only from 9 a.m. Saturday until 9 p.m. Sunday. Ainsworth looked questioningly at me, and I explained that I had a mini-suite at my disposal since I couldn't be expected to stay on my feet for 36 hours straight. He gave me a sardonic smile, almost like he thought this suite was a perk I'd maybe wheedled out of my employer through some form of subterfuge.

I put that crazy notion to rest. "Believe me, I'd rather be home with my husband and pets. Being MOD is not a treat, it just comes with the territory."

"And your usual job function is?"

I handed him a business card, which spelled out the whole thing: Senior Catering and Convention Services Manager. "CCSM for short."

"And your name?"

"Charlie Champagne. It's right there on the card."

"No, I mean your proper name."

"What, you feel it's improper that a woman could be named Charlie?"

"It's a bit unusual, but—"

"You want a feminine sounding name, is that it? Well, I'm afraid Charlie's as close as we're gonna get. Blame my parents."

Officer Ainsworth, looking sheepish, said, "Look, I'm sorry to be so particular, Ms. Champagne. It's just that my witness interview form requires a legal given name. No nicknames."

I couldn't keep from chuckling, "You asked for it. Try Charlemagne Carlotta Chardonnay hyphen Champagne. Got room for that on your form?"

The officer looked dazed. "I think maybe I'll make an exception and stick with Charlie."

I smiled, said nothing. We exchanged a few more words and he gave me his business card before departing. I looked at it and had to stifle a snigger. "Officer Rob Ainsworth, is it? Card didn't have room for Robert, I guess."

"It's Robin, not Robert," he explained, blushing slightly.

Yeah, when I'm not playing MOD, I'm a Senior Catering & Convention Services Manager. That's quite a mouthful, thus the CCSM acronym. The 'Senior' part just means I've been around a little longer and earn a few more bucks than the other guys and gals I work with, and I'm sorta seen as a straw boss. I kinda like it, having a little clout but no major managerial responsibilities and budgetary headaches to contend with.

What I didn't particularly care for was being told by a fellow employee that he'd been given the finger and that the finger was no longer attached to its original owner. That's what Josh Wheeler – nice guy, from what little I knew of him – had finally spit out after blathering incoherently for a while when he'd charged into my office at eight minutes to three on this first morning of 2017. By 3:00 I'd followed him to the banquet room floor so we could survey the situation together. A small crowd had gathered by then, with onlookers craning their necks to sneak a peek at what we all quickly dubbed the 'crime scene.'

Josh, smart guy that he was, had called Security before coming to see me, and they arrived at 3:05. No shortage of happenings on a night (morning?) like this to keep the security staff hopping! Now that they were here and inspecting the evidence, they too decided it was a 'crime scene.' This gave me a small measure of satisfaction, as I fancied myself the 'pseudo-sleuth du jour' of the Paradise Spectacular Resort. Security called the Metro PD and happily (I would imagine) turned the matter over to a bona fide law enforcement team.

At that moment, the first verse of *Auld Lang Syne* came like a tidal wave flooding my thoughts. I always seem to have a song bouncing around in my prefrontal cortex, and I suppose that was a natural for this occasion.

Before the morning was out, the authorities had matched a body to the finger and a name to the body. Ben Pierce, age 41, male Caucasian from Shaker Heights, Ohio. He was a high roller who'd been one of the honored 900+ guests at our New Year's Eve shindig, along with his 38-year-old wife, Stella. The Pierces were the youngest generation of a family of plumbing supply magnates that dominated the East and Midwest market in high-end bathroom and kitchen fixtures.

By now, our Director of Security was on the scene and running roughshod over the proceedings. Gunnar Block was a massive Swedish guy in his early 50s with an ego to match his bulk. To him, the ParaSpec was *his* hotel and *he alone* would be the hotel's point of contact when dealing with the official local police force. He was brash and offered no apologies for it. It was he who introduced a Detective Lieutenant Rex Scharffenberger, who informed us all that Mr. Pierce's time of death was estimated to be about midnight, but I knew it had to be sometime after that because I recalled seeing him and Mrs.

Pierce pressing lips as the broadcast of the fireworks outside played across the multiple big screens in our ballroom.

I could tell that Detective Scharffenberger was a bit taken aback by DOS Block's intractable manner. At one point, he gave me a sideways glance and a roll of the eyeballs, to which I responded with a pursing of my lips and a shrug of my shoulders. With that momentary exchange was born a special bond between us, one that would serve us well through the coming weeks of his investigation, one that silently said we will solve this crime together, and without the bureaucratic interference that Block the Blockhead (one of his popular nicknames around the hotel) wanted to inject into the process.

Ben and Stella Pierce were among the few guests of the Paradise Spectacular with whom I'd become personally friendly. Yeah, it happens now and then … a bride and groom who somehow click with me, conventioneers who share one of my personal interests – like maybe they're wine connoisseurs who've visited one of my favorite NorCal wineries, or maybe they're fanatical Parrotheads, or whatever. A lotta things can capture my attention these days.

Fact is, I can't recall what it was that put Ben and Stella into that small group … oh wait, now I *do* remember! Mason – that's my hubby – had popped into the hotel on the 4th of July in 2014 because some group was having a 'M*A*S*H-fest' evening with marathon showings of highlights from the old '70s classic TV show. My Mase is a diehard fan if ever there was one, and he planned to stand on the sidelines and partake in the laughs. Anyway, the 4th was also one of our big high roller events, and Mr. & Mrs. Pierce were invited guests for that. So Mr. Pierce – Ben, that is – walked by and happened to catch a glimpse of one of the videos and stopped to watch, and in so doing sloshed a wave of Siduri Pinot from his glass onto Mase's shirt. Mase was largely unfazed, as he was engrossed in a classic gin-brewing scene from 'The Swamp,' but Ben apologized profusely and offered to replace the stained shirt (which, as luck would have it, was snow white before the dark red tsunami had attacked it!). Chit chat followed and the two became sudden chums. M*A*S*H lovers, wine buffs, aficionados of beautiful brunettes (yeah, me and Stel). Two or three times a year we'd enjoyed seeing them.

Oh shit, Mase was gonna take Ben's death very hard.

I'd managed only two hours of shut-eye earlier, just before sunrise, and now as noon approached I was dragging again. I'd been busy as a bee with final arrangements for the New Year's Day high rollers' brunch, coupled with a swarm of other issues. A pair of planners from an Israeli industrialists' group were on my doorstep at 8 a.m. sharp – holiday notwithstanding – and wanted to make changes to their awards banquet scheduled for January 8th, a week out. Not bad enough that they failed to respect my closed door and overwrought status, but then they started disagreeing with each other. First in English and then in what I assumed was Hebrew. That was the last straw.

"Ladies, please stop!" I finally exclaimed, in clear and concise English (my one and only language). "If you must argue in your native tongue, please do not do it my office! And I know Sunday is not your Sabbath, and I'm not even sure it's mine since I work seven days a week so often that I'd have no time to worship if I wanted to. But today *is* a holiday for me, and so far as I know, your country also follows the Gregorian calendar and recognizes the same."

"It's just that we need to—"

"I understand. You need to *make sure* the salmon for the banquet is properly blessed by a rabbi. I assure you, I have a good relationship with our local rabbi, Rabbi Schulmann, and will contact him first thing tomorrow. Now if you'll excuse me, I've got a ton of work to do regarding *today's* program."

The women retracted and begrudgingly left. I hoped I hadn't been too hard on them. After all, Jewish events are among my favorite to manage – I think it's the importance they attach to the celebration of their faith, family and community. These two were a pushy pair and I knew it'd take a lot more than my abruptness to throw them off their quest for the perfect finale event for their group of 1200 people.

Truth was, it was only Ben Pierce's severed hand that had been found in my Fascination Ballroom, and the police were still puzzled about how it had made its way there. The rest of poor Ben had been found behind a stack of shipping pallets on the fresh food dock of our 30-story, 4-restaurant hotel. The bloodied stump of his right arm, severed at the wrist, was wrapped in a white cloth secured with a heavy-duty blue rubber band. The rubber band had "Produce of Mexico #4080" in bold black lettering, which the detectives quickly deduced was nothing more than a band placed around a bunch of Mexican-grown green asparagus. The price look-up code (PLU) identified it, but I could've saved them the trouble. We'd had oodles of asparagus coming in lately, and in fact our friends from Tel Aviv would be using a couple hundred bunches for their kosher Sunday banquet. I had a lot of the wide blue rubber bands in my desk, as they were sturdy and good for bundling up fat stacks of customer-signed BEOs (Banquet Event Orders). The loading dock and kitchen prep areas were often littered with them, and every once in a while I picked up another bunch. As for the blood-soaked cloth, it proved to instead be two identical hotel washrags, each embroidered with the logo of the Paradise Spectacular Resort. Regulation stuff, available in every one of our 2105 guest rooms and 100+ suites.

So the only potential clues were the guest-room washrags, rubber band and the bloody scene on the loading dock. It wasn't a lot to go on.

Shortly after the Jewish women departed, another head popped in my doorway. "Hey kiddo, I'm goin' to grab a bite. Wanna join me?"

It was Maris Kean, my go-to gal. Second in charge in the office.

Funny, I'd been thinking about her not more than thirty minutes earlier. But I sure didn't expect to see her in the flesh on this holiday morning.

"Thanks, Mare, but I'm swamped. Hey, get this – I was just having a vision of you and Jameson in bold-colored costumes, dancing the flamenco up on some stage. Am I crazy or what?"

"Or what," she answered with a sarcastic smirk. Nothing further.

"So what on earth are you doing here?" I asked, skipping over the veiled meaning – if there was one – of her response. "I thought you'd be home watching parades and football, or maybe ironing your kilts."

Her face and voice hardened. "Hell-fuckin'-no! Dyvan has taken control of my damn life from here till whenever they pack up and leave. 16th, 18th, 19th, I fuckin' can't even remember now. But shit, they keep changing things, so they'll probably change their fuckin' breakdown date too."

I figured it out then: Maris had finally cracked.

She'd clearly been hibernating in her office doing BEOs for a gathering of big pharma folks later in the month. Dyvan Health, Limited. For how long she'd been in there, I had no idea. Several hours at least. *Dyvan 2017* was a complex program requiring diligent planning, and I was glad Mare was my staffer working it. Her attention to detail was unparalleled.

But when the client starts throwing curveballs daily – sometimes even hourly – the pressure becomes so much that one begins to crack. I know, I've been there a few times myself. I could definitely see Maris cracking this morning. The sweet lady was stressed close to her limit. She rarely cussed aloud, for *any* reason, and here she was spouting off three *fuckin's*, one *hell*, one *damn* and one *shit* in a rapid-fire salvo that belied her normal laid-back demeanor.

"Can you just bring me a coffee on your way back?" I asked, trying not to feed off her aggravation. Let it lie, maybe it'd smooth itself out.

"Got it," she said, and let the door swing shut.

I went back to my number crunching, but Maris was not fully erased from my mind. She was a jewel and I had to keep her content doing what she did best. Which was, among other things, keeping my ass out of the wringer.

I was still juggling a bunch of crap in my mind when Maris bounded back in and plopped a steaming Caffè Grande on my desk. She looked at me with puzzlement.

"So how'd you know?" she blurted.

"Know what?"

"That we'd changed our plans."

"Changed your plans? All I know is you're gonna fly off soon to spend ten days in Scotland and Ireland, looking for hubby's roots. Sounds like some pretty good plans to me."

"Spain," Maris said flatly.

"Huh?"

"Spain is where we're going. New plans. Jameson says the Isles are too cold to dig in this time of year. We'll go in six months if my sweet boss wants to give me some more PTO. But I asked how you knew."

"You must've told me. I try to remember things—"

"The hell I did! Our plans changed last night, about 20 minutes to midnight. Up until then, it *was* Scotland and Ireland."

I rationalized. No way I could've known, not given those timing details.

"Just another psychic moment, I guess."

I said it as casually as possible, not wanting to burden Maris with direct knowledge of my gift – or my affliction, depending on one's viewpoint. But there was no avoiding it this time.

I could suddenly hear Smash Mouth singing *Sister Psychic*. Hey, I welcomed the intrusion. It served to kick that annoying *Auld Lang Syne* out of my brain trap.

That's another of my quirks. These songs in my head often seem to accompany one of my psychic events.

Maris looked at me suspiciously, but was anxious to return to her office and unravel the latest of the Dyvan program revisions in privacy, so she left.

"Hang in there, girl!" I shouted after her. "I hear they're good tippers."

I returned to my keyboard, but within seconds was interrupted by my cellphone. The caller ID told me that my loving husband was calling.

3

Not all days are created equal, and New Year's Day 2017 was one of those days. For poor Ben Pierce, it lasted about 30 minutes before the curtain fell. For the Spakisumar family, it was destined to drag on for 37 hours and 30 minutes, thanks to the joys of trans-global travel. Their January 1st had begun long before Ben and Stella Pierce had consumed their December 31st dinner and lasted long after Ben's blood was cleansed from the ParaSpec's loading dock.

Dr. Samir Spakisumar – Sammy for short – was returning with his family from a three-week long holiday in their native India. As CEO of the Spectacular Collection of hospitality properties in the United States, he'd needed the getaway to rejuvenate both mind and body. He was in great spirits until, at his New York layover, he checked in with the ParaSpec resort's president, Leo Stein. It was then that Sammy learned of the tragedy that had occurred earlier that morning. He felt compelled to put in an appearance, and instructed Leo to be available to meet with him at the LOL later in the day. His tone was uncharacteristically abrupt.

The architects may not have planned it that way, but Libations on the Lobby had evolved into the very essence of the Paradise Spectacular property. The LOL was situated at the building's core, but that wasn't what made it the spirit and soul of the hotel. While purporting to be a cocktail bar for friends and acquaintances to get together and relax, it served a multitude of other roles. Gamblers came alone, some to smugly count their chips, others to mitigate their losses with alcohol. Tourist groups gathered here, before setting out to see a show or tour Hoover Dam. Guests enjoyed pre-dinner cocktails or after-dinner cordials, or both. Small business meetings convened here, and there was even an eight-seat table in one corner outfitted as if it were in a conference room. Rendezvous occurred here, some innocent, others less so. Money exchanged hands, above board or under the table. Trysts began here, before moving elsewhere for privacy's sake. Eavesdropping occurred with regularity.

In fact, the LOL was so much the nucleus of the property that the VP of Food & Beverage, Ira Brickner, had assigned Charlie Champagne the task of keeping 'one ear to the grindstone.' Those were his exact words. While an unorthodox approach, to be sure, it was one of the few things Brickner had ever done that didn't rub Charlie the wrong way. She enjoyed the task and the challenges it presented. It was a fact that the bartending staff were aware of; they'd been alerted that Charlie would be hanging around serving as eyes and ears, and they willingly accepted her presence. They were, after all, on the same team.

The LOL bartenders were a diverse bunch. There were four of them, though several Banquet Operations staff had expressed their willingness to supplement the regulars if the need arose, and were put on a list. The need rarely arose, though, probably because the regulars were all top notch.

Grayson Moore was the lead guy, now in his early 50s and a jewel to have around. He was a great mixologist and a superb conversationalist, and what else can one ask for in a barkeep? Charlie and Mason had become friends with Gray and his husband, Jackie St. Nevis, a part-time event planner and a full-time day trader who raked in a quarter mil a year short selling and playing options fast and close to the vest. Amazing talent and fortitude, that guy. They enjoyed backyard barbeque foursomes and drinking champagne till it came out their ears. The Champagne Palace or Casa GrayJack; it didn't matter. Even Sunday brunch was a regular occurrence.

Lynne-Anne Tapp was 32, but most would guess her to be around 26. Abounding with energy, this half-white/half-Jamaican gal with an athlete's physique and a Miss America smile clearly merited her nickname 'Tapper.' She almost seemed to tap dance through her drink mixing routines, and that, coupled with her last name, earned her the appellation. Anyone served a drink by the bubbly Tapper was highly likely to order a second one, simply because of her outgoing nature. That's the kind of employee every employer wants to hold onto. Tapper's job was very secure, though no one in management had expressly told her so. She was a dynamo, and Charlie appreciated that trait.

Tapper and Gray obviously couldn't handle all the hours the LOL was open. The other regular staffers generally drew the less attractive shifts – meaning fewer customers, less cash transacted, less in tip revenue. The Spectacular Collection had no gratuity sharing policy in the food and beverage domain, though something along those lines was in effect for the table game dealers in the casino. Tapper and Gray netted a bundle in tips; that much was common knowledge.

One of the two other regulars was John Joseph Potter, nicknamed since birth as 'Jack' … and further nicknamed (since joining the gaming world) as 'Jackpot.' He was born on 7/7/77 in a tiny town named Dinero, Texas, and his future was virtually ordained by all such indicators. Jackpot had minimal education, minimal savoir faire, but he could mix a mean Bloody Mary – 'Dinero Style' as he fancied calling it, made with a few extra special but undisclosed 'Lone Star spices' – and his designer martinis were out of this world. Pretty decent conversation-maker, too. ParaSpec was keeping him for sure!

Rounding out the frontline four was the old guy, Artie. Art Foster was one of the original employees of the four-decades-old property – then called the 'Strip Spectacular' – and he'd had every job imaginable over his long career. Bellman, valet parker, kitchen and maintenance. Handyman with a capital 'H.' A dozen or so years ago, he'd tired of weed pulling and repairing crumbling stucco in the desert heat and had – at his wife's suggestion – enrolled in an onsite mixology class. As lady luck would have it, he'd enjoyed it and had done well … and his natural gift of gab had made him an instant success as a bartender. Artie was short and wiry, slightly hunched over at 72, but he showed no signs of slowing down or even thinking about retiring. The ParaSpec wasn't tossing him out to the wolves yet either. As a bartender, he'd proven to be a fount of gossip. Charlie loved him for this reason, among others, and occasionally brought him some homemade cookies to make sure the info he overheard didn't stay bottled up inside him.

The bartenders continually compared notes, discussing a stranger they'd seen or a conversation they'd overheard. When necessary, they passed the information on to their ally, Charlie Champagne.

By 5:30 New Year's afternoon, less than 18 hours after the place had rocked with raucous revelers, the LOL had returned to near-normalcy. Gray and Jackpot were manning the shop, and not overexerting to keep things afloat. Compared to yesterday's party surge, this was a tame day, and it afforded them time to do some tidying of table set-ups, behind-the-bar bottle layouts, and spit-polishing the myriad chrome and glass surfaces that had collected sticky fingerprints from hundreds of careless patrons.

Their conscientious efforts were well-timed, as a tall distinguished man with short-cropped curly hair that matched his charcoal Brooks Brothers suit ambled in and took a seat at the curvilinear bar, far right end. He did it with the ease of a man who'd done it a hundred times before, but Gray sincerely doubted that he had. He knew who the man was, and was trying to recall if he'd ever seen him in the flesh. Or was it only his 11-by-14 glossy that hung in the employee lounge that made his face a familiar one?

"Evening, Mr. Moore. Could you whip me up an old fashioned?"

The well-dressed man had surprised Grayson Moore by addressing him by name. Peculiar, since their prior encounters – if there'd ever even been any – eluded him. The man's manner was assertive yet affable, and Gray couldn't fault the combination.

"Of course, Mr. Stein. Would you like that original or smoked?" Gray figured if the president of the property could address him by name, he should repay the courtesy.

"I've never tried the smoked. But yes, please, I'll give it a whirl. If it's not too much trouble."

Of course not, Gray thought. And now that he'd sold the novel idea to the big boss, he desperately sought a positive outcome. The smoky old fashioned was a drink he'd only attempted a handful of times. But the master wasn't far away.

"I'll summon our in-house specialist," he said, beckoning Jackpot over and quietly conveying Stein's order. In no time, the Texan gathered his ingredients and equipment, and proceeded to create a masterpiece before the attentive eyes of his thirsty patron. As he worked, he explained that the smoke source could be a commercial infusing gun, wood chips or even rosemary or a blend of several spices. He'd chosen to use a combination of mesquite from Arizona and apple from Oregon, which he placed upon a small marble slab and hit with the flame from a miniature propane torch. Once smoldering, the drink glass was inverted over the tiny conflagration and began to extinguish it, during which time he mixed the liquid ingredients – whiskey, bitters, simple syrup and some ice – in a separate glass. Then, with a deftness that revealed his mixology know-how, the smoked glass was turned upright, the tiny fire snuffed with a damp paper towel, four fresh ice cubes placed in the smoked glass, the mixed beverage strained into it, and orange peel garnish applied – all in a matter of five seconds.

"Enjoy your drink, Mr. Stein," the mixologist said with a proud smile, gently placing it in front of his astonished-looking customer.

"I will, Mr. Potter. But perhaps only half as much as I did your showmanship."

Jackpot was beaming, because the big boss had called him by name and had seemed genuinely entertained by his mastery of the drink preparation process. The display of confidence by his co-worker/supervisor Grayson added to the glow of his special moment.

Both barmen watched as Stein took his first sip, waiting for the verdict. But suddenly, the gazes of all three were drawn to the steps that led down into the LOL from the lobby, where two people descended. Each one a familiar face, but hardly a duo seen together frequently.   Smiles covered both faces, which served to put the others at ease.

The woman did the intros, though they probably weren't necessary. Panning the group with an outstretched arm, she gestured and spoke everyone's name: "Dr. Sammy Spakisumar, Leo Stein, Grayson Moore, John J. Potter – who we all happily call 'Jackpot.'" She dispensed with the unnecessary job titles.

She neglected to identify herself in the process, but then, *everyone* knew Charlie Champagne.

After a few cordialities, the two new arrivals ordered drinks and, along with Leo Stein, retired to the large table in the back corner. The bartenders returned to their routine, which suddenly blossomed with the arrival of a half-dozen revelers headed for a Wayne Newton/Elvis Presley/Michael Jackson take-off dinner show someplace north on the Strip. They all wanted cocktails and would keep the mixologists hopping for some time.

Just as well, Charlie thought, since Grayson was a gossip hound … and by now, he'd probably made Jackpot a disciple. Whatever was about to transpire between her, Leo and Sammy did *not* need prying eyes or ears.

Though Sammy's tone had been snappish earlier when he spoke with Leo, there was no trace of consternation in his demeanor now. He was the corporate CEO, a director, a leader, a driver of actions, a decision-maker who based his decisiveness on the facts at his disposal. Right now – here at the LOL amongst trusted allies – he was merely collecting facts so that his decisions in the days ahead could be well-reasoned rather than reckless and spontaneous.

Charlie was the one with all the facts, and she dispensed them to bring Sammy and Leo up to speed. They talked briefly about what to expect from the police investigation, and she produced a pair of Lieutenant Scharffenberger's business cards, giving one to each man. "Rex seems like a competent cop, but I guess time will tell how effective he is. I'll be sure to keep you both informed if I speak to him again, which Gunnar Block has also adamantly insisted that I do."

Law enforcement in Southern Nevada has a unique organizational structure that's actually quite effective. Clark County – which is the 22nd largest in the country, larger than Connecticut and Rhode Island combined – is policed by one single agency that covers everything except the three incorporated cities of Henderson, North Las Vegas and Mesquite. It was back in the 1970s when the City of Las Vegas Police Department and the Clark County Sheriff's Department decided to merge (agreed upon by the State Legislature and Governor). Too many folks were clueless as to where they really lived and called the wrong agency to report crimes or other concerns, which caused both agencies to waste time and tax dollars. The merge proved successful and, in fact, received commendations from an independent audit conducted in 1999.

The head honcho is the Sheriff, an elected official – which tends to keep things a bit more on the up-and-up than if you have a Police Chief who's appointed and possibly party to good ol' boys cronyism. But the rank and file are called 'officer' rather than 'deputy.' And, of course, there are the special units who go wherever the need arises … from way north in the unincorporated village of Bunkerville to way south around Laughlin, a gambling mecca on the Colorado River at the southernmost tip of the state, 180 miles apart. Operating units like Violent Crimes, Crimes Against Youth and Family, SWAT and the K-9 squad deal with this spatial challenge on a regular basis.

And, lest one think everything on TV is pure fiction, there *really is* a CSI unit alive and functioning in Las Vegas Metro. They're not sworn officers, but they are sworn to do a professional job of examining, collecting, analyzing and cataloging the forensic evidence at crime scenes all over Clark County. Just like Gil Grissom, Catherine Willows, Nick Stokes, Sara Sidle et al. But Grissom was fiction; the real head guy is Mason Leroux Champagne.

Charlie's husband, Mase.

4

Yep, Mason's my loving husband! Most people, me included, call him Mase. I had a hunch it'd be him on my caller ID that New Year's Day morning, and I told him so.

"Of course you did," he said knowingly, hinting that he thought my psychic capacity – such as it was – had kicked in again. It was a power I really did possess, I had finally come to admit, though I was hesitant to give it too much weight, since it sorta came and went sporadically. I couldn't take it to the bank … nor, for that matter, the roulette or poker table.

"Making any progress?" I asked hopefully. I knew Detective Rex had informed him of the identity of the deceased many hours ago, but this was our first time talking since, and there was little time for private lamenting now. Mase had already been busy at the crime lab for much of the morning and figured himself for a long afternoon. Ben Pierce's murder had not only hit him hard emotionally, but also given him a new and perplexing assignment. There really wasn't that much trace evidence available, but he vowed to give it his best effort nonetheless.

"Not much. At two I'll be observing the autopsy. Always a fun thing," he said with decided sarcasm. "Then back to the lab, so I may be late home. But at least it'll free me up to be off tomorrow."

I knew my guy wanted desperately to be off Monday, so he could watch the bowl games that are deferred a day whenever January 1st falls on a Sunday. He was a big college pigskin fan, and would be rooting for his beloved Iowa Hawkeyes in the Outback Bowl. He'd also be following the NHL Winter Classic being played outdoors in St. Louis. Blues hosting the Blackhawks in a huge baseball stadium - crazy, huh? For sure, I'd have a tough time pulling Mase from the TV tomorrow, so I'll probably whip up some chips, dips and other goodies and join him.

A grief-stricken Stella Pierce was entrenched in a small corner table by the time I joined her, after Sammy and Leo's departure from the LOL. She was working on her second – or maybe third – dry gin martini. Who could blame her for trying to get blitzed in the wake of her husband's untimely execution 18 hours earlier?

We hugged. We shed a few tears together. We sat in silence, her hand in mine, as I awaited Jackpot's delivery of my first Crown and soda of the evening. It was after 6:00 and I had declared myself 'off duty', hence the drink. Stella ordered yet another martini.

"He was so young, so vibrant, so full of life and enthusiasm," Stella wailed in a raspy voice that told me she'd been crying for hours. "Byron and Brayden will be beside themselves."

She was referring to their two sons, aged 20 and 21, though I couldn't recall which was which. Ben had always seemed so enthusiastically involved in their school sports and academic activities. Both were now enrolled in college and seemed motivated to succeed in the business world. Byron was studying animal husbandry in his home state of Ohio while Brayden was studying at a small school in Arizona, preparing for a career as a general contractor. Understandably, Stella was worried that Ben's passing would adversely affect the boys' commitment to crafting successful futures.

Trying to console a person who's just lost their best friend, lover and life partner for an incomprehensible reason is not an easy thing to do. My attempt was half-baked, at best. Mostly we held hands, sniffled and blew our noses, and guzzled our drinks a bit too fast. I had no problem with Stella downing martinis all evening if it helped her, but I had to drive home before long. I ordered one more, but pronounced it my last. Earlier I'd had VIP Services rebook her flight back to Cleveland for midmorning on Wednesday the 4th. Ben's casket would accompany her on the flight. Ben's brother, Stephen, would meet the plane and handle the difficult arrangements on the other end.

I left my friend from Ohio at the bar, and as I walked away I glanced back at her and that old jazz classic *Stella by Starlight* by Stan Getz, Ella Fitzgerald and countless others insinuated itself in my gray matter. She was a lovely woman and I truly hoped for her full survival of this ordeal. Back in my office, I put the wraps on a few things and finalized my routine MOD report – which was the most unroutine one I had ever submitted. Murder and body parts – it wasn't easy to convey the mayhem in a corporate tone of voice.

I was transitioning my new Renegade onto the 215 when my cell chirped its generic tone. That meant it could be anyone *except* Mase, Ira or Maris. I looked at the caller ID; *Metro Det* suggested it might be important so I hit the Bluetooth switch.

I confess to a slight flutter of anxiety when I see an ID like that, seeing as how my dearest is a member of the Metro team and there's always a chance someone could be calling with bad news of some kind. Scary, when you think about it. Thankfully nothing like that had ever happened.

"Ms. Champagne? Lieutenant Scharffenberger here."

"Yes sir, how are you?"

"Not bad, just another messed up holiday. Why is it people have to commit capital crimes on—"

"I'm afraid that's your department, Detective, not mine." A tad acerbic, but I hoped it didn't come across that way.

"Yep, you're right." He laughed slightly, which was the first show of emotion I'd seen from the man I'd sat with earlier in my office. "Anyway, ma'am, I just wanted to thank you for your courtesy this morning, and let you know I may be calling on you again."

"No problem." If he was trying to soften me up, I think it was working.

"In fact, if it's OK with you, I'd sorta like to consider you my point person at the Paradise Spectacular."

"I'm flattered, but I've gotta tell you I'd be committing corporate suicide if I agreed to be your contact without running it by our security. Matter of fact, it might go over better if *you* called them. You've already met the Director, Gunnar Block," I said. He grunted in agreement, so I continued. "He's an old-school type not keen on sharing authority, but I know we're talking about a lot of back-and-forth stuff, so maybe try to make him see that having me as your point person will make his life easier. He's not totally unreasonable, and can actually be a decent guy if you don't cross him. Call the hotel main number and ask for extension 3200." I wasn't about to give him Gunnar's cell. I knew better. Only a select few, myself included, were privy to that.

"Sounds good. I'll give him a buzz. And thank you, Ms. Champagne."

"If Gunnar gives you the green light, of course you can count on my help. I'm a big supporter of law enforcement. My husband is head of the Metro CSI unit."

"Yeah, I'd kinda figured."

"We've sorta got the corner on Champagne in this town," I joked. This time I added the laugh track.

There, the ice was officially broken between us.

I took it one step farther.

"I have an idea," I said. "And just so you know, whenever I say that at home, Mason rolls his eyeballs, so feel free to do the same."

"OK," he laughed, then said, "Consider them rolled. What's your idea?"

"If we're gonna tackle this together, can we do it as Charlie and Rex? Big long last names give me the willies. Titles too."

"Deal. Except if we're in a meeting with the big guys or the media, maybe then we'd best stick with 'Detective' and 'Ma'am'. Sound reasonable?"

"Very."

He promised to text me his personal cell info, and recommended that I use it to contact him in the future.

"Nice speaking to you, Rex. I'll talk to you Wednesday."

There was a moment of silence before the perplexed detective said, "You will? About what exactly?"

"Not sure, but I know you'll be calling. Trust me, I can see it."

"Good night, Charlie."

"Night, Rex."

There I go. That psychic stuff again. If I could just harness this pesky 'gift' of mine! I mean, it's so enthralling when something I've foreseen actually materializes. I find myself feeling empowered beyond belief, like I can do no wrong, like there are no limits. But alas, there are limitations, because it's so hit-and-miss that its value is too.

Imagine if I could reliably predict when 29 is gonna hit on the roulette wheel. Now *that one* could have real value.

And imagine if I could help solve crimes!

Yeah, that's the one that really holds the most appeal for me.

It all dated back to my high school days at the Seacliff Academy. My friend – my *very best friend*, Chelsea Buckman – up and disappeared one day shortly before Christmas in our junior year. Poof, gone, nada, no clues whatsoever. The scuttlebutt around school was that she must have been a victim of some heinous kidnapping scheme, probably abducted by human traffickers to endure a miserable life of servitude. At least that was the theory put forward by the school administrators, who were reluctant to talk about it much. My classmates seemed to take it in stride, but it gnawed at me then and it still does today. We were, after all, the C-C girls – 'Cherry Pie' and 'Chickadee' – inseparable and unstoppable pals who shared everything from boy crush fantasies to pinky swear secrets to lip gloss moments.

Whatever really happened, I was convinced there was a felon or felonious network running loose, responsible for my dear friend's disappearance. I began to visualize myself as a sleuth, tracking down this criminal element and bringing him/her/them to justice. And the old Hoagy Carmichael tune *Georgia on my Mind* was refashioned as *Chelsea on my Mind* – same melody, altered words, endlessly coursing through the fabric of my brain cells.

So yeah, I was a wannabe detective with songs running through my head and crazy psychic visions consuming me every now and then. And with all that baggage, I was hiding in the shell of a Catering & Convention Services Manager.

5

Charlie again, and it's finally January 2nd.

It felt good to sleep in, if only till 8:15. It was supremely relaxing, a rarity in my busy life. Even better was that initial part of the day when a nightful of knots were magically released from my anxiety-laden body. I was now ready to tackle a day free of murder and mayhem, a day that held nothing more complex than a couple of new recipes I was gonna try out on Mase along about halftime during the Outback Bowl, which pitted his alma mater Iowa Hawkeyes against the Florida Gators, and was slated to start at 10 a.m., so we couldn't lollygag too long. First a good long stretch while we were still horizontal, then 20 minutes apiece on the treadmills (we had a matching pair), some ab crunches and free weights.

For a 43-year-old guy, my Mase is in amazing shape ... and I think it's our early morning fitness routine that's largely deserving of the credit. I'm not that shabby either, even if a few mid-30 rolls keep trying to attach themselves to my midsection. Mase works hard at it, and he keeps that body of his in tip-top shape. And mine stays firm enough to keep him firm enough for an occasional romp that leaves us both breathless with expended sexual energy. Doesn't happen as often as it once did, but it's just as good when it does happen.

It was his turn to feed the critters, so I showered and mentally reviewed the culinary challenges I planned to tackle in the immediate future. Meanwhile, Mase fed Saff and Nuts and Pest and Mess, and prepared us humans a minimal fruit compote of banana and blueberries. He'd become a gastronomic virtuoso, I was learning lately, though cat food, dog food and a few chopped-up fruits were not his main claims to fame.

I should explain that in our house, we spare extraneous syllables. The pets each have a monosyllabic nickname and they all know theirs and respond when called. Our twin kitties, now 3½, were three-month-old domestic shorthairs when they came to us 'on approval' and quickly captivated us with their antics. Our pets have always had foodie names, and since, when these guys arrived, I'd just been creating some exotic dish, the names Saffron and Nutmeg seemed perfect for them. Mase loved them … the names as well as the cats. The nicknames 'Saff' and 'Nuts' came about organically; Saffron has a lustrous orange mane and Nutmeg is a duller grayish brown, and his playful nature made the nickname Nuts a no-brainer.

The puppies came a year later, a beautiful pair of year-old Red Beagle littermates, a distribution from some overly-canined friends. I must've been cooking Italian that day, thus the names Pesto and Romesco. 'Pest' and 'Mess' followed with ease.

The Hawkeyes were tied with the Gators at the end of the first quarter, but quickly fell into mediocrity. Frustrating to watch. Mase had flipped from channel to channel, but was more than ready for my spread of Sonora Style Carnitas Enchiladas, Cheese/Onion/Olive Quesadillas, a killer salsa I'd made from scratch, and an exquisite Tomatillo & Jalapeño Guacamole Dip with warm homemade chips. We both love Mexican, and I'm learning to love making it. My friend Ramon Zintero, head chef at the hotel, has been giving me pointers and encouragement lately. Wednesdays at 9 a.m. he finds a half-hour in his schedule for me. Lucky me. And now, lucky Mase.

"Wow, this is spectacular!" he exclaimed when he saw the enormity of my offerings. "I expected maybe some bagged chips and a quickie guac."

"That's 'Spectacular' with a capital S, I'll have you know. Ramon is teaching me all sorts of tricks of his trade."

With a mouthful, Mase managed to mumble, "Wll, giff hm a tums up fum me!"

We gorged ourselves on these delicious treats because it was after 11:30 and we'd barely nibbled on our bana-berry compote. We were famished.

Later, as I was stacking dishes in the sink, Mase displayed a whole other kind of hunger that had suddenly consumed him. As he reached around me to deposit a pair of plates in the sink, I felt a familiar firmness grind into my backside. No mistaking what it was, and I was not one to squander opportunity. Impromptu frolicking was the best kind – we'd agreed on that – and it wasn't very far to the sofa. Suddenly *Afternoon Delight* by Starland Vocal Band began playing in my head. Oh yeah, how true that was!

I left dirty dishes helter-skelter, and barely managed to turn the faucet off. The TV was still on, and one of us muted it just as Mase and I joined together in one of our favorite positions of entanglement. We must've put on quite a performance, since the beagles howled their appreciation in unison with Mase.

By the time we'd regained our senses, Florida had scored another TD and Mase was about to give up on his team. But he cared little at this point. He'd just completed the ultimate act of love with the woman he cherished, and for him that was better than football any day.

I liked the way my hubby prioritized things.

My mind began wandering … drifting … digressing … to times long ago, when life was more carefree and we were both fancy-free and full of all the vigor our natural testosterone and estrogen made possible. I recalled the day

I met Mason – such a handsome hunk he was, like maybe he was a lifeguard out of uniform, or maybe a nouveau movie star I'd not yet heard about. Tall, sandy, reddish-tinged hair, muscles that said 'I will protect you' without saying 'I will overpower you.' My God, what a dream on two feet, literally right there in front of me! We met by chance at UCI's Bren Center, where our Anteaters were hosting the Cal Poly Mustangs. I was seated in Row K with three of my girlfriends when along came this group of four thirtyish men who took the empty seats in Row J directly in front of us. As luck would have it, five-foot-five me ended up with the six-foot-three guy directly in front of me. I remember spending the first half craning my neck around him at the action on the basketball court, but as an exciting rally unfolded early in the second half, I found myself standing up and actually putting my hands on the big man's shoulders. Realizing my gaffe, I immediately removed my hands but the guy turned around and gave me a smile that melted my heart. He couldn't have been nicer about it, and in fact suggested to his buddies that they switch seats with us four girls so we could all see better.

The next day, we met at the Anthill Pub for a burger, and that weekend we had our first real date at a sandcastle competition in Seal Beach – as observers, not castle builders, though we both thought it might be fun to pursue someday. Strange, talking about our future on our very first date.

Three weeks later, we spent a long weekend together at a beachside bungalow in Santa Barbara. I'd already learned that Mr. Champagne was quite a scholar, with a Masters in Chemical and Biochemical Engineering, and was currently head of the bio-chem pathology program at UCI, in addition to working towards his Ph.D. That weekend I learned that he was also a sensitive and unpretentious man who happened to be a zealous and accomplished lover. That he was nine years my senior mattered not. We were soulmates from the get-go, a union made in heaven.

The following year we both graduated – him with his doctorate in chemical forensics and me with a Master's in Hospitality Management. We rewarded ourselves with a trip to the Galapagos, where we made love on the rocks with the tortoises and blue-footed boobies watching. Two months later, we both abandoned our separate apartments and moved into a cozy loft on a Laguna Beach hillside. In those days we were paying the bills with his salary as an apprentice in the Santa Ana Police crime lab and through my concierge work at a Dana Point resort. We really had to scrape to get by, and I can recall many a heated argument over our limited finances and whose entry-level work was more important. We fought, we cried, and we made up. And we couldn't stop fretting about when our advanced levels of education would pay off in future earnings.

Ah yes, the future! The more we talked about it, the more we realized that neither one of us wanted ours to exclude the other. We wanted to live it together. So, on September 29th of 2007, we secured that togetherness by tying the knot in a river-view suite at the Flamingo Hotel in Laughlin, Nevada, and I can honestly say that neither of us has ever for a moment regretted that impulsive decision.

Well, maybe one regret hung a little heavy, and that was depriving our parents the enjoyment of sharing our nuptials. Elopement hadn't seemed like a big deal at the time, but when both of my folks died a couple of years later the guilt hit me rather hard. Strangely, too, it ignited a desire to find out who my blood relations were. That smoldered under the surface for some time, but finally, just a few months ago, I began pursuing it through one of those genealogy websites. It was fun, though I expected little in the way of new knowledge would ever come from it.

Yep, in a few months, Mase and I will be celebrating ten years of wedded bliss. How the time had flown, and oh, the memories we had!

I had to drag myself away from them and get back to my dishwasher loading and kitchen clean-up. Across the room, I could see Mase flipping channels and I knew his games were over.

"I can see the headline," he grimaced, "Gators Devour Hawkeyes."

"That bad, was it?"

"30 to 3. Held us scoreless the last three quarters. Damned amphibians!"

I empathized, but could think of no words to console. And I didn't think it was the right time to mention that gators were reptiles, not amphibians.

"When does basketball season start?" he wailed from the couch.

It was January. Hoops had long since started, which of course he knew. What he meant was: When does March Madness start? Will the Hawkeyes make it to the Select 64 and exact some vengeance? Mase could dream, but unfortunately, dreaming was all it was.

Now he was suddenly engrossed in the NHL's Winter Classic outdoor hockey game. At least it got his mind off football (and basketball) for a while.

6

The Brickner Bunch, as they called themselves, customarily converged in Philadelphia every winter. Ira Brickner, along with wife Ida and their son Edward, traveled to Ira's parents' estate in suburban Swarthmore to celebrate the winter holidays. His sister, two brothers and their families all came as well. The siblings each had a spouse, and between the four families there were eleven offspring. About half of those had flown the nest by now, but it was still the youngest generation's school break schedule that was the determinant of the time to visit the grandparents. This year Hanukkah had fortuitously fallen during that time frame, and the spacious Swarthmore home was ablaze with an abundance of menorahs every evening.

Of the middle generation, only Ira and his wife Ida had ever migrated west of the Mississippi; they'd lived a few years in Denver and the last 22 in Las Vegas. Ira was now Vice President of Food & Beverage at the Paradise Spectacular Resort Hotel and Casino, and as such, was Charlie Champagne's immediate boss.

On the morning of January 2nd, Ira and his family beat a hasty retreat back to Las Vegas. The unfortunate homicide at his workplace – the first of the year for Clark County and the first ever at a property Ira was associated with – was on Ira's mind. He silently cussed 'Blockhead,' the resort's security guy, for having the audacity to tarnish his festive holiday with the terrible news in yesterday's email.

Turbulence over Indiana gave rise to turmoil in Ira's stomach. But rather than fret, he decided to use it as an 'out' for tomorrow. His gastric distress would be the perfect excuse to keep him from putting in an appearance at Charlie's weekly staff meeting. There'd be too many questions, for which he had too few answers. He'd just call in, and keep it extra brief.

The flight smoothed out as soon as they crossed the Big Muddy River in southern Illinois. Eddie ordered a refill of his root beer, and gazed at the picturesque patchwork of Missouri and Kansas farmland. Ida worked one online crossword puzzle after another.

And Ira, in the aisle seat, dozed off with a tranquil smile playing across his face.

Susan Lenore Hart had grown up in San Diego County, and knew early on that she wanted to follow a career involving some aspect of the natural sciences. As a child, she'd collected and catalogued sand dollars and seashells, watched the swallows building nests in the La Jolla cliffs, spent hours studying the habits of the jellyfish at Torrey Pines Beach and the running grunion up in Oceanside. Suzy had an ever-curious mind. She'd attended San Diego State for a while, but as a sophomore transferred to New Mexico State at the urging of a high school friend who was very happy there. Liberation from the oppressive thumbs of her parents had played a role in her decision-making as well. Las Cruces seemed a blessed light year away from the old homestead in Carlsbad Beach, and long overdue.

She finished her studies and earned a B.S. in BioSci, then promptly enrolled in graduate classwork with no career plan yet in mind. But one day, totally unexpectedly, an opportunity popped in front of her eyes like a miraculous mirage on the horizon. It was an employment ad for a Forensic Analyst I, which would utilize her talents as a flora and fauna expert. She wasn't even sure what 'forensic analyst' meant, but it sounded good. Six weeks later she was on the road to Las Vegas, Nevada – her Master's program aborted in its infancy – driving her little Prius across the desert. She'd arrived on December 30th two years ago, and always enjoyed reminiscing about it when the New Year rolled around.

Another local, a twentysomething transplant from Idaho, had arrived in Las Vegas about the same time as Suzy Hart. He had squeaked through high school in Boise and graduated from University of Nevada, Reno, in 2015 with a C+ GPA. He was far from scholastic in traditional areas, but managed to excel in mathematics and the physical sciences. He especially enjoyed the coursework he'd taken in computer technology.

Victor Heron was a bit of a slimeball, a derogatory descriptor someone had actually used when talking to him face-to-face on the Reno campus. While he was hurt by the name-calling, he was also awakened to the truth. He *was* a slimeball, always had been and probably always would be. But since moving south and entering the working world, he had undergone a make-over, at least to his physical appearance: hair and skin treatments to reduce his oiliness, a shortened, stylized haircut, and a clean shave to erase the sparse stubble that did him no favors. He still had an angular bone structure that assured he'd never be Bradley Cooper-handsome, but for the first time in his life he didn't dread looking in the mirror.

He'd been hired as a Group Reservations Coordinator for one of the large casino hotels in town. It was a foot in the door to the incredible shiny world of Las Vegas, USA. He was empowered. The young man found Sin City to his liking, and the job appealed to his need for interaction with people from other walks of life. He was a gangly youth who'd never had much of a social life, save his one high school girl, Noreen Hurlbutt, who'd gone off to college in the dreaded East. Northwestern, in fact, which sounded good until he learned it was in Illinois. He refused to set foot east of the Rockies, having done so only once and hating the humidity and dull landscapes. So Noreen was history, which made Las Vegas that much more appealing to Victor.

Vic learned to enjoy working with people – which had thus far not been his forte – and especially relished manipulating meeting planners who relied on him for suite upgrades, reservation changes after the cut-off date, and finding connecting rooms for CEOs and their staffers in order to facilitate affairs of the heart.

He felt invincible. He enjoyed a world replete with gracious praise, generous gratuities and other abundant perks. It was so good that he found it difficult to pursue a newly-created position when it opened up 18 months later, but given his techie background and love affair with video games, it seemed right up his alley. Add to that a bit of intrigue and that the pay was nearly double his Reservations Coordinator salary; how could he not go after it?

From a field of seven candidates, Victor Heron was selected as the first-ever Social Media Sales Manager at the Swank Illusion Resort. He approached this new assignment with passion, now feeling that he'd been hand-picked to perform some very important tasks.

Yes, 'Vegas Victor' was gonna take this town by storm.

His official start date had been December 19th of 2016, but with all the holidays and such, he'd spent the first two weeks on a self-fashioned orientation tour. Floating here and there, getting to know the scope of his new playing field.

Especially enjoyable was his orientation visit to the Paradise Spectacular, where he'd been able to mix business with pleasure at the LOL as the year had flipped to 2017. That guy Gray seemed an OK dude, and he sure kept the Vod-bombs flowing.

Now that January was in full swing, he'd be getting down to brass tacks.

Detective Rex Scharffenberger had caught a big one with the Pierce murder, and he knew it would require long hours and some major fact-finding. On the surface, it looked to be random, but experience told him that wouldn't turn out to be the case. There is always a purpose, even if only in the eyes of the perpetrator. He'd spent the balance of January 1st strategizing his fact-finding efforts, and continued on the 2nd but with one eye and ear focused on the myriad college football bowl games that populated his television screen. He had no sentimental favorite teams in this year's mix, but he enjoyed the sport at the college level and couldn't entirely deny himself the pleasure. After all, he was a red-blooded American guy.

Besides, he had a hundred bucks each riding on Wisconsin, Florida, Penn State and Auburn. All to beat the point spread, nothing elaborate.

Over the years, Rex had taken a few classes in criminology – an intense two weeks at Quantico and a semester on criminal motivation from old Doc Cruz at UNLV – though most of his knowledge had been acquired on the job. The rationale behind murder was one of the topics he'd been schooled in, but after a few decades in the trenches he believed it was a bit more complex than the oft-stated and over-simplified sex-money-power triumvirate. There were hate crimes to consider, as well as those committed to eradicate a witness to another crime. There were thrill killings, mercy killings and deaths that were unintentional consequences of a lesser crime (arson, for example).

Right now he had no way of knowing how to categorize the killer of Benjamin F. Pierce of wherever-heights, Ohio. It was a daunting task that faced him.

He needed a mental break, and some sustenance. He prescribed himself a Red Baron mini-pizza, a Miller Lite and full attention to the television for at least half an hour. A highlights show on ESPN told him the Badgers and Gators were both looking good going into halftime. A tiny bright spot in the midst of his ponderings about murder. The other two games he'd wagered on were being played a bit later, so he'd have to wait for those results.

Halfway through his break, a cryptic message announced itself on his Metro cellphone. He ignored it until he was sure he'd captured the latest football updates and finished swallowing his bite of sausage and jalapeño pizza. Only then did he take a peek. The text message was unnerving, though its meaning wasn't entirely clear to Rex at the moment. It simply said *'Whodunit, copper?'*

Now what was that supposed to mean? He considered it throughout the rest of his meal and beer hiatus, and finally decided it was just a crackpot. He gave it no further thought, but didn't erase it from his phone just yet.

Now rejuvenated, Rex was able to concoct a plan of attack for this case. He could see no way of avoiding a face-to-face interview with a large percentage of the ParaSpec workers.

He would call Gunnar Block first thing in the morning and, assuming the security guy would approve of him contacting the Senior CCSM, he knew his first request of Charlie Champagne would probably be a list of all the hotel's employees arranged in some sort of time/work shift order. Was that asking too much? He didn't think so, in view of Charlie's cooperative attitude, and especially since she'd admitted to being a personal friend of the victim. She'd probably jump at the chance to make a meaningful contribution to the investigation. Her enigmatic 'trust me' the other night had made him do exactly that – *trust her* – though he couldn't put a finger on exactly what it was that instilled that confidence. But he believed she would do all she could to assist his efforts, rather than thwart them.

When January 3rd dawned, he'd be ready to hit the pavement with a game plan destined for success.

7

With the New Year's festivities – and tragedy – behind them, it was time for ParaSpec's Catering and Convention Services staff to return to the routine chaos that ruled the hospitality world during the first quarter of every year. Adding a murder to the mix would make for more turmoil than usual.

Tuesday at 10 a.m. was the staff meeting, and today's promised to be a doozie. Per custom, everyone emailed Charlie at least an hour in advance any special item they wanted to discuss in the meeting. She'd been doing it this way – *her way* – ever since she'd become the de facto group leader when the director had quit four months ago to seek greener pastures in the Bay Area. Today, it seemed, everyone had an issue, so they'd probably go on till noon. Maris was still feeling hogtied by her Dyvan group, and was asking for someone to assist in managing their fluid BEO mess. "It's like wrestling with a snake," she warned. Charlie assigned Hermie Stevenson, a good-natured young Aussie guy who had little on his plate in the immediate timeframe.

Charlie then tried to capsulize the events surrounding Ben Pierce's horrific Psycho-style murder, and the ensuing investigation by Metro PD. Everyone was eager to hear the morbid details.

Partly because of her relationship to the head of CSI, partly because she was sorta friends with the deceased and his widow, and partly because she was just so swamped with other things, Charlie designated a go-to guy for routine

Metro interface matters. Hamakuri Yamasaki – Ham or Hammy, after you got to know him – was the well-seasoned and level-headed guy who drew this duty. Expectedly, Ham jumped at the assignment. Charlie was jumping the gun, though, as if Gunnar Block had already blessed the idea, which he had not.

They were just about through with that discussion when Julie, the unit's Admin Assistant, appeared in the doorway and pointed at the speaker-phone on the conference table. "Mister B on line 3," she announced before retreating. Suddenly, they all heard static followed by their so-called leader's voice: "Charlie, everyone, Ira here. Sorry I couldn't make it to your meeting today. Long flight yesterday, still recuperating. But there's a couple o' things I wanted to share." Charlie looked around, and saw Maris rolling her eyeballs – something they both did well, and often – and which echoed her own sentiment exactly. Kinchy, the Samoan girl, and Hermie, naïve youngsters that they were, both looked as if they halfway cared what Ira had to say. Hammy was staring at his iPhone, probably checking the stock market or NBA scores. "This bedbug thing is still plaguing us. Gotta do somethin'. Any ideas, lemme know ASAP." Ira's voice was momentarily drowned out by a horrendous background roar. When it abated, he continued, "And just so you know, Sammy's got a major case of laryngitis. So the big address on Thursday is a question mark right now."

"Daftie's out on the links," Hermie observed after the brief call disconnected. "Plane on takeoff from two-five right. Unmistakable!" The gay surfer from Queensland was the team's staff jock, and golf was his most frequent choice of sport since he'd relocated to the desert. He knew of what he spoke. The Bali Hai course was the handiest one to the ParaSpec, and to Ira's Silverado-area home as well. The people gathered around the table all snickered.

Bedbugs, everyone knew, were a problem that occurred when the critters hitched a ride on an incoming guest's luggage, usually an international traveler. It happens, you treat it, case closed. The only *plague* was the negative PR that the hotel is subjected to when stories are blown out of proportion, oftentimes accompanied by 'photographic proof' posted on TripAdvisor, Yelp or another review site. When used for less-than-authentic purposes, however, these same sites became weapons against an honest business; bogus complaints accompanied by bedbug photos taken who-knows-when-or-where could damage a hotel's reputation. Ham opined, "You ask me, our revered leader oughta be onsite whipping up a good media blitz, maybe holding a news conference on this mostly-fabricated bedbug thing, maybe trying to find out who's posting this defamatory garbage about us. But no, he's playing with his balls while someone's posting crap about this hotel." He was outspoken and clearly not an Ira Brickner fan. But then, none of them were.

For her part, Charlie was more concerned to hear that the CEO had a case of laryngitis, and that it could affect the scheduling of his 'State of the Spectacular' address. She knew that Sammy wanted to do it at the earliest possible time, beating all the politicians and corporate bigwigs to the punch, so she made a note to email him and suggest the remedy Mase had used last year when he'd lost his voice just before some important court testimony; it had worked wonders.

The crew was getting into their 'round table' routine, where everyone had an opportunity to update the others on the current status of their programs, which ran the gamut in terms of size, duration and scope. Programs could range from a single 20-person professional breakfast in a small conference room to a week-long convention of an international association with several thousand attendees that included many sleeping room nights, multiple assembly rooms, luncheons and refreshment breaks, gala awards banquets with PowerPoint presentations, and live music and dancing.

Next came the file assignment exercise, in which new programs that had come on board were allocated to individual cast members; Charlie was the assigner, and it wasn't a task that made everyone happy all the time

– difficult repeat clients were never popular, but they had to be handled. Likewise, the easy-to-work-with meeting planners, who often were also generous with the gratuities, were considered favored assignments. She tried to divvy everything up as fairly as she could, in a way that didn't leave anyone feeling shortchanged.

At 10:45 a.m., Rex finally reached Gunnar Block. It was his third attempt of the morning.

"Director Block, this is Detective Lieutenant Rex Scharffenberger, Metro Homicide."

"Good morning, Detective. How can I help you?"

"I'm sure you can guess what I'm calling about."

"The Pierce case," Block seemed to grumble with irritation.

"Yes sir. I need to request your cooperation in this matter. Specifically, I need access to your employees."

"Access to employees must be cleared through this office. I need to be apprised of what you're asking of them, and what they are telling you."

"Director Block, I understand that an operation as large as your hotel needs to contain its intelligence and probably keep a lid on many things in the interest of damage control."

"Exactly."

"I'm not out to smear your hotel, Director Block. In a homicide investigation, we need to speak with and clear a lot of people. This includes the victim's acquaintances, which includes many of the staffers there at the Paradise Spectacular. They are not suspects at the moment, but it's possible someone saw or heard something that could be of help in solving the case."

"That's all well and good, Detective, but I don't have the time to—"

"I realize that. That's why I'd like you to assign someone on your staff to work with me as a go-between. So far I've only talked with a handful of your people – Charlie Champagne, Josh Wheeler, Alfredo Suarez ... those are the ones who come to mind right now – but there are literally hundreds more I need to interview."

"För helvete! *Goddamn it!* I don't have enough people—"

"Director, we're on the same side. I want to catch a killer. I'd like to suggest that Ms. Champagne assign one of her people to act in your stead. With your approval, of course. Someone who will provide you a short daily report on who we've interviewed. You're free to follow up with them as you see fit."

"You've been talking with that woman caterer already? Without my authorization?"

"She was the one who insisted that I contact you and seek your approval. She wasn't about to circumvent your departmental protocol."

The Swede took a moment, rubbed his chin pensively, and finally spoke. "Very well, Detective, you make some sense. I still insist on being kept informed about your progress."

"I will keep you in the loop, I promise you that."

The stubborn Swede acquiesced and Rex thanked him. He also reminded himself to learn the Swedish phrase for *thank you* so he could strengthen the bond that was forming between them.

He called Charlie as soon as he hung up with Block. Though he'd be happy to forego his own lunch and pounce on the opportunity immediately, he knew he couldn't assume her schedule was as flexible as his; he wouldn't chance a drive to the hotel on the faint hope that she'd be available this afternoon. It was 11:15 and his call went straight to her voicemail. "Charlie, Rex here. Just talked with your man Block and he gave in – reluctantly, I might add. You, or someone you designate, can be my point of contact, so long as we loop him in on a daily basis. You and I need to meet, and I'd love to do it this afternoon, any time after one. Call me."

8

Heading back to the 14' by 20' office I called home for more hours than I cared to think about, my phone babbled some dumb tone that told me multiple messages were inbound. Just what I needed!

Mase was the first message I listened to as I walked. Priorities, y'know. My hubby told me the Pierce autopsy and toxicology results had been released, and that they were 'intriguing.' That was his word, whatever it meant. I called him to find out, but he said he'd prefer to elucidate in person. He could swing by for a quick bite about 1:15, and I said that'd be great. Which it was. I needed a breather after the morning's big meeting. "I'll pick up some pretzels and raspberry mustard from Higgley's and meet you at the LOL."

As I hustled my buns back to my office, I listened to the remainder of my messages. My Israeli meeting planner babbling about the rabbi and the salmon – which was actually good to hear, despite her annoying manner, because I *had* forgotten to call Rabbi Schulmann. I added it to my mental checklist. Next call was a November 2016 client grumbling about his final bill – get back to ya later, buster! A cold call inquiry from an Atlanta insurance group – I saved the message for later callback. Then another, almost identical; this one from a software consortium in Austin, Houston and San Antonio. Saved that one too.

Experience has taught me that even if you put a client – or prospective one – on the back burner, you can't do it for too long or they will call your boss to complain. And that's the worst feeling imaginable, sorta like 'getting called into the principal's office' in grade school.

I determined that my next priority was to dash off a quickie email to our esteemed CEO. I felt privileged to know him on a first-name basis, and I hoped my few words would be taken as a sincere expression of concern: *'Hello again, Sammy, hope you're getting adjusted to life on this side of the globe. Sorry to hear of your laryngitis. My hubby had a bout last year right before an important event but used a combination of extreme humidity (saunas) and a strong dose of corticosteroids, and it worked great. Just a suggestion, in case it helps.'*

After that, I reached Rabbi Schulmann and reminded him that I was expecting 300 pounds of farm-raised Atlantic salmon and asked if we could please arrange for him to bless it sometime on Friday the 6th.

"As long as it's before sundown," he reminded me. We settled on 1 p.m. at the ParaSpec kitchen.

I called the insurance lady in Atlanta and promised to mail her our catering menus, sample BEOs and pricing quotes. She was looking at April or May, so I told her to try to get back to me soon so we could put a wrap on her plans by the end of the month. She was an easy-going Southern gal, nice to talk to and listen to. The Texan was more of a challenge to deal with, interrupting as I tried to explain how we did things, but I promised her the menu packet as well. Her group was looking towards October, so I didn't rush her to make a decision. Truth be told, I hoped she decided to go somewhere else, as I dreaded the barrage of questions and micromanaging that I knew would be part of her baggage. Oftentimes, first impressions tell a huge story.

Just as I thought I'd taken care of all the messages, another showed up. It must have arrived as I was listening to an earlier one. It was my new comrade, Detective Rex. I delighted in his message. He had dealt with the Blockhead and emerged victorious.

I called him back and told him that 2:00 would work best for me. That would give me plenty of time to hear whatever Mase had to tell me about the autopsy.

As the troops started heading out to lunch, Maris stopped by with an urgent look on her face. I had reached a stopping point, so I motioned for her to sit down, and waited for the latest Dyvan bombshell to be dropped.

But her expression had nothing to do with Dyvan.

"I didn't know if I should bring this up in staff, but you need to know. I learned just this morning that over New Year's one of Jameson's guys shared some info about the Pierces. He thought maybe that lieutenant oughta know what he knows."

Her husband, Jameson Kean, was the Director of VIP Services, who oversaw the crew of butlers who provide a special level of service to our high-roller suites. Director and butler, acting as a team, develop an intimate connection with all the guests, and create private dossiers on them over the years. Likes and dislikes, family highlights, stuff like that.

Maris didn't tell me the substance of Jameson's information, but I knew she was right. Rex would be eager to talk with him, and to the butler, Roberto Guanacaste.

"You did right. Detective Scharffenberger will want to speak with them both, I'm sure. As a matter of fact, Metro detectives have just gotten the go-ahead from Gunnar to interview all employees. I'm meeting with the lieutenant this afternoon, so I'll be sure to red flag their names for him.

Working through the traditional lunch period – when the other CCSMs and admins fled to eat their lunches elsewhere, gave me a chance to catch up on emails without interruption. As the troops started trickling back in, I shut down and headed out myself. Higgley's Boutiquerie was a specialty cheese and wine shop along the Spectacular Galleria. Their foodstuffs are superb, and I knew Mase enjoyed the big warm pretzels as much as I did.

I secured a choice table at the LOL and spread out the goods.

Barely a minute later, Mase and I exchanged a quick peck and he sat down across from me.

"The usual, Gray, ol' buddy," he addressed the bartender from afar, as he offered a friendly wave. Tapper, who often doubled as a server at slow times like this, soon delivered his Pacifico longneck and my tumbler of clear bubbles.

Mase had earlier said the autopsy was 'intriguing' and I was dying to learn what he'd meant. Beyond the stab wounds, what else did the M.E. have to say about Ben Pierce's death?

"His conclusion confirmed his suspicions," Mase explained as he swigged the Mexican brew straight from the bottle. "A large-bladed knife, single-edged, entered Ben's back between the fourth and fifth ribs to the left side of the spine, and then penetrated the heart."

"How awful!" I said, aghast, my expression illustrating my revulsion. But I remained curious. "But what's the intriguing part you mentioned earlier?"

Mase grimaced. "He found a high concentration of hydrocodone in Ben's system. Extraordinarily high."

"And? Where would that come from?" I was pretty ignorant in the world of drugs, or anything to do with chemicals, actually. But my hubby was a chemist, and a damn good one.

"I wondered that too. It's perfectly legal, a Schedule II prescription pain killer. My father takes Norco, which is one of its many formulations, 10 milligrams of hydro per pill. Pop takes two pills a day, three if his arthritis is really kicking up. But he's 79 and full of old age. Ben was about half as old, and he had about eight times the concentration a person would have from a single Norco tablet. Do you know if he had any pain problems worth mentioning? Has Stella said anything?"

I thought about it, but quickly realized Stella and I hadn't shared any personal health concerns – not two days ago when we'd met at the LOL, nor anytime in the past. As far as I knew, the Pierces were both perfectly healthy specimens of the human race, aged 41 and 38. They didn't seem like they would need pain relievers of the type Mase was describing. "No, not ever. But she's still here at the hotel. Should I ask her?"

Mase frowned as he thought. "Officially, no. I wouldn't even be telling you any of this stuff, but the Sergeant told me to go for it. We're curious, and it's an aberration that can't be easily explained. So if you meet with Stella again before she goes home, see what you can find out. Discreetly, of course."

Of course, I thought, with a twinge of discomfort about prying.

"Sure, I'll wheedle a bit," I told my dearest. For Mase, I'd do anything, but I wasn't relishing the assignment.

Hammy arrived in my office at 1:55, wearing his best eager-to-help-solve-a-crime face. When Rex arrived, I introduced them and we wasted no time on small talk.

"First of all, Charlie, thank you for greasing the skids with Director Block. And thank you, too, for enlisting Mr. Yamakuri here to assist with the investigation."

The Asian man chuckled, holding up a hand like a traffic cop, and saying, "It's Yamasaki, like the motorcycles. But please, Hammy is fine. My long Japanese names confuse almost everyone, sometimes even my own family."

After a group laugh, Rex got down to business. "Ok, so my people and I need to talk to virtually every property employee in the next few days, and we'll need your help to make that happen."

I freely, and perhaps carelessly, responded confidently, "We can do it, Rex." My mind was already trying to identify available rooms to provide Metro on a complimentary basis to conduct their interviews.

Charlie Champagne, purveyor of extraordinary customer service. No matter who the client or what the price.

9

He went by Jameson A. Kean, though he'd not settled on it without a bit of strife. Ironically, that was exactly what his parents had named him, but he'd tried on multiple variations during the process of growing up. He'd stuck with 'Jamie,' the family nickname, through the end of his secondary schooling, though as he matured he'd grown increasingly uncomfortable with it. Effeminate at worst, equivocal at best. 'Jamie' seemed gender-neutral, and he was all man (even at age 16) and didn't want anyone to doubt it. The fact that he'd encountered a female classmate with the same moniker had clinched it. So in his university days he'd become 'James.' But that proved to be commonplace, and he considered himself anything but. He tried 'J. Angus' in his final year at the University of Glasgow, but many folks took him for a law student.

In his last term he'd gone out pubbing at a small joint by the River Clyde, where one of his cohorts had insisted he try a very special Irish whiskey. Not being much of a hard liquor chap, J. Angus complied with a long measure of trepidation. But he was astonished by the soft smooth warmth of the golden liquid, nothing close to the biting acidity of other whiskeys to which he'd been exposed. His companion had the barman bring the bottle over so Kean could examine it. 'Jameson Irish Whiskey,' a product of Dublin.

From that moment forward, J. Angus again became Jameson A., and proudly so.

He'd done well in the two decades since graduating with a BSc in Veterinary Biosciences. While initially intending to pursue zoological research, he quickly gravitated to the equine side of things. He found appealing work at race tracks and stud farms throughout the UK and France, and eventually in the Americas … primarily in Pennsylvania, Kentucky and Ontario. Jameson found that diversification suited him and he was soon involved in caring for the personal needs of the stable owners as much as those of their steeds – 'butlering,' some called it – and he enjoyed that sort of work.

Over time, butlering became his prime focus, and he was surprised to learn that there was a market for persons with such skills in the hotel industry. And in hotels there were other doors that opened for him – server, maître d', master meat carver, sous chef and more. He evolved into one of those people who was a 'Jack of All Trades.' And surprisingly – even to himself – he mastered nearly everything he tried.

Jameson bounced around on a global tour that included Toronto, Barcelona, Key West, Cartagena, Toronto a second time, Vail and Vancouver. He enjoyed the frequent change of sights, climates and cultures and tried to assimilate into them, and valued the few fragile friendships he was able to make. Along the way he managed to acquire 20% ownership in Bourbon Barrel Stables near Lexington, and 25% of a promising young stallion named Tucky Troubadour. He saved well, invested smartly, and planned for eventualities.

In 2005 he encountered an enchanting woman – one far more captivating than the short-term flings his mobile lifestyle normally allowed him – while on holiday from his second stint in Toronto. It was January, not a nice time to be in Canada but exceedingly pleasant in the Caymans. The young lady, though an Asian miss through-and-through, was then employed at a resort in Flagstaff, also not so pleasant in winter unless you were a ski bunny. She was not that, and much preferred the warm aqua waters of the Caribbean.

Jameson Kean and Maris Ohana had hit it off splendidly on the Seven Mile Beach. For five days, they shared everything, including energizing beach walks and runs, creative dining discoveries, philosophical discussions, yoga sessions and absurdly wild sex. Within a month, she'd quit her Arizona job and joined him in chilly Toronto, then followed him to his next assignments in Colorado and British Columbia. She initially enjoyed the nomadic life-style but eventually realized it wasn't a long-term happiness solution for her. In her 13-year hospitality career she'd only worked in Honolulu (her home city), San Jose and Flagstaff. She waited tables here and there during this nomadic period with Jameson, but otherwise was not putting her Cal Poly Pomona training to much use.

As she was mulling these thoughts one day on a Sunday stroll through Vancouver's Stanley Park, trying to craft a delicate way to broach the issue with Jameson, he blindsided her with a not-so-subtle question.

"Ready to settle?"

She looked blankly at him, so he elucidated.

"Shall we settle down somewhere? I hear Las Vegas has plenty of career opps for both of us."

"Jameson Kean, are you proposing marriage to me?" asked a dumb-struck Maris.

"Bloody right I am. What say, lassie?"

"What if I need some time to think about it?"

He gave her an are-you-kidding-me squint, then softened his gaze and said, "Sure. I'll ask again tomorrow."

Maris was bubbling inside, but tried not to show it. She'd asked for time to think, so she damn well better act like she was doing some deep internal deliberation.

Two hours later, after some spirited cavorting back at their hotel, she made a bold pronouncement: "Done thinking. Answer is YES."

"Yes to settling down?" he asked.

"YES!"

"Yes to Las Vegas?"

"YES!"

"Yes to marriage?"

"YES, YES, YES, my adorable Jamie Angus!" She lunged forward and grasped him around the neck, smothering him with wet kisses.

He allowed her the nicknames. Only her. Only the future Mrs. Kean.

The 'Strip Spectacular' had opened its doors in 1977, on the east side of Las Vegas Boulevard, south of Harmon Avenue. In its initial incarnation, it consisted of seven stories with 183 sleeping rooms, three executive suites and a large free-form swimming pool. The entire first floor was consumed by a 44,000 square-foot casino ("an acre of fun" was its slogan), a 24-hour coffee shop, a dinnertime steak house, three fast-food stops, a lobby bar, 'The Spectacular Showroom' and two small meeting rooms. Its first decade saw a few additions, but by 1990 a major expansion was deemed appropriate ... and affordable, by virtue of a 1988 stock IPO which raised over $66 million. By that time, two offshoot properties in California had been spawned – the Pacifica Spectacular in Long Beach and the Seaside Spectacular in La Jolla – and the chain was renamed the Spectacular Collection, concurrent with the stock offering. The common stock was listed on the NASDAQ with the ticker symbol SCOL. The Las Vegas property received not only a major transformation, but also a new name: Paradise Spectacular Resort Hotel and Casino.

Since that initial expansion, which saw the room count explode from 183 to 912 and the casino footprint grow to three acres, there had been other significant incremental enhancements. The 'ParaSpec' of 2017 now stood 30 stories high (with twin towers) and had 2105 standard rooms, 122 mini-suites and 34 two-story loft suites. And new Spectacular properties were popping up everywhere – places like Sedona, Atlantic City, Coeur d'Alene, Scottsdale, and Baltimore had been added to the portfolio in the past few years.

In short, Spectacular was performing spectacularly, and the Vegas properties were doing a fine job of developing a loyalty base of gamblers who came back again and again and enjoyed the hell out of themselves while dropping five- or six-figure bundles in a matter of days … or even hours. A whole department called VIP Services/Casino Marketing focused on nothing but creating events to repeatedly lure these high rollers back, many of them focusing on holidays (New Year's Eve/Day, 4th of July, etc.) or major sporting events (Super Bowl, World Series, etc.). It was a game all the major casino operators played, some better than others.

Spectacular's success did not go unnoticed, either by the public or by the business community that was ever-vigilant for investing opportunities. On Wall Street, SCOL shares had been climbing steadily since the recession had given way to better times.

Mason Champagne was engrossed in a report prepared by Willis Bronx, the most junior analyst in his office, but definitely a rising star. Suzy Hart, second-in-charge now, agreed with that assessment and also agreed – albeit modestly – when Mason gave her much of the credit for nurturing the young black man's intrinsic talent. Willis had joined the CSI team just four months earlier, after attending a Metro job fair on a whim. He'd earned an Associate of Arts degree in Justice Admin from the community college in Bullhead

City, Arizona, which was his home, working his way through school driving a water taxi on the river and dealing blackjack and cashiering at the Aqua Vista Casino in Laughlin. Now enrolled in the BS program in Public Safety at the College of Southern Nevada in Henderson, the 24-year-old had been eager to become 'really employed' and acquire some on-the-job skills. Suzy had collected his preliminaries, called in her boss, and they scooped him up in a Las Vegas minute.

Willis's latest assignment was an analysis of the trace evidence that had been collected from the ParaSpec's loading dock on the morning of January 1st. When that was done, he took it upon himself to compare his findings with those of one of the lab techs who had worked in the Fascination Ballroom, especially the portion Josh Wheeler had not yet given the 'Carpet Zamboni' treatment. Interesting results, which he quickly reported to Suzy, and she to Mase.

Mase picked up the phone and called his colleague one floor up.

"Rex? Mason. We've got some interesting results on the soil samples from the crime scene. Or I guess I should say our crime scenes, since we don't know yet where the actual death occurred. Unless you've—"

"No, not a clue yet. What soil samples? You saying the crime took place outdoors?"

"No, I'm not saying that. Not necessarily, at least. You're the detective, come look for yourself."

"I'm in the middle of something. Can't you just tell me?"

"Actually, no. It's a visual that you've gotta see. Take your time, we'll keep it open till COB."

"Uh … OK, I'll try to make it down there before you shut down," Rex said before hanging up.

Mase grumbled to himself, miffed that the detective seemed to lack enthusiasm to review his team's findings and couldn't even commit to descending a single flight of stairs sometime in the next three hours.

"Rex is tied up, but he promised to hurry down as soon as he can break free from some big meeting," Mase lied, in an effort to protect his young colleagues from the detective's indifference to their hard work.

But only a few minutes later, all three 'labbies' were surprised by the animated arrival of Detective Scharffenberger and his colleague, Marisa Quiñones from the Homicide Bureau. "Our meeting broke for 10. Whatcha got, guys?"

Mase was heartened by the good faith effort of the detectives – both of them, no less – to show up sooner rather than later. He gestured to Willis, allowing him the opportunity to explain his findings to the folks who would hopefully be able to use it as a piece of their puzzle. The youngster beamed as he began.

"Lieutenant, Sergeant, here's what we've got." Pointing to a projected image from the electron microscope, Willis described what they were looking at. "On the left slide, you can see particles of sandy loam found on the loading dock, within a foot of the body's left knee, according to the chalk diagram your people drew there. On the right slide, you'll see identical soil found on the carpet of the ballroom in an area that had not yet been vacuumed by Mr. Wheeler, and which was about five feet from the location of the severed hand."

"Intriguing. Is there more?" Rex could sense the young lab tech's eagerness.

"Yes, sir, there is." He popped two more slides on the scope's tray and pointed to the image on the wall. "Here you have rosemary leaves. Ornamental rosemary, like that found in a garden, not the kitchen variety, though they both smell similar. These were found – in a rather trampled state, as you can see – within inches of, and in some cases mixed in with the sandy loam on the loading dock and the carpet."

"So, what does that tell us?" Sgt. Quiñones mused aloud before her lieutenant had a chance to ask.

Willis glanced at Mase, who gave a go-ahead nod, and then explained, "It demonstrates that someone – whoever had this particular soil and plant matter on his shoes – was both on that loading dock and also in the banquet room recently. While having both items tracked into either location tells us nothing, having them both in both locations, along with the body in one and the severed hand in the other, strongly suggests that the perpetrator was the one who tracked it from one location to the other, and that his or her shoes may still contain remnants of the soil and/or rosemary. It also gives us a clue as to his whereabouts before or even during the crime, although unfortunately this city has an abundance of ornamental rosemary, much of it likely growing in soil just like this."

Rex looked at Marisa, then turned towards Suzy and Mase. "I think this fellow's on the wrong floor. I'm looking for a rookie detective, and I think I just found him!" Turning to Willis, he said, "Good work, son. Astute observation, attention to detail – that's what it takes. We'll put this info in our hopper of leads and see where it sends us."

Scharffenberger then told Quiñones, "I've got another matter to go over with Mason," and she nodded and made her exit.

It was nearly 3:00, and a beaming Willis Bronx joined the rest of the CSI crew for a well-deserved snack in the break room.

"What's up?" Mase asked Scharffenberger.

"I just wanted to take a moment to say thanks to you and your team, but also to your wife and her crew down at the ParaSpec. Charlie's great and I really appreciate her helpful attitude."

"I'm glad to hear you two are getting along. Just don't put her in any danger, got it?"

"Got it." They fist-bumped, and Rex headed for the stairwell.

10

'Bless you, my child. Your therapies worked wonders, and I'm almost 100% now. I will be thanking you silently through every minute of tomorrow's presentation.' Early-bird Sammy Spakisumar had sent the email at 5:13 a.m., nearly an hour before I read it. That good news put an upbeat spin on my day, and I celebrated by climbing back into bed and amorously snuggling up to my just-awakening husband.

I made it out of the house by 7:00, leaving said husband to feed the furry foursome, a chore he thoroughly enjoyed.

At 9:15, I phoned Stella's room and left a message asking if she'd like to join me for a parting drink before her noon limo to the airport and 2:10 flight back to Cleveland. She returned the call quickly, and we settled on 11:00 at the LOL.

Ben and Stella were shrewd gamers, but despite that they had dropped about $42,000 on our roulette and slots in the 36 hours before Ben's untimely death. I knew that because I'd checked the records yesterday. A modest loss by some standards, but it still made them valuable customers worthy of VIP treatment.

Thinking in that vein made me wonder if Stella would continue to be invited, as a single person, to our Casino Marketing events. It was simply idle speculation, and of course not something on which I had any input, but I was curious. I made a mental note to contact Marketing to make sure they removed Ben's name from their database and changed the salutation on any future invitations.

Earlier that morning I'd felt compelled to get a dig in at my 'inferior superior' (as I liked to think of him) and composed a brief note to my boss: *'Ira – Happy to report that Sammy's voice will be in fine shape by 10:00 tomorrow morning. He told me so himself. Thought you should know! – Charlie'.*

At 9:55 I received an amusing response. *'Thanks, but let's not forget the chain of command, young lady.'*

I irritably dashed off a retort. *'Please note I said HE contacted ME. Your reprimand is misdirected.'* I knew that would infuriate old Ira, but didn't care. He knew I loathed him, and I knew he couldn't afford to lose me, since I was the strongest link in the CCS Department.

Fun and games in the old workplace.

A Bloody Mary was one of Art's signature drinks, though he called his version a Seattle Mary because he garnished it with a long green string bean instead of a celery stalk. Something he'd seen on a trip to the Pacific Northwest decades ago. He made one for Stella and I got an equally tall glass of plain ol' bubbly water on the rocks, my mid-day staple.

Stella was a lovely woman under normal circumstances – a trim and shapely brunette with a pretty Italian-featured face – but she was showing the ravaging effects of these last three days of grief. She hadn't slept well, and her makeup seemed to have been applied haphazardly. Still, she managed a genuinely warm smile when she saw me approach and she seemed almost chipper. It gave me hope that she was gonna get through this ordeal in decent shape. I also sensed she'd be strong enough to withstand a few probing questions about Ben. I approached the subject slowly, after about ten minutes of small talk.

I felt awkward and fumbled with my napkin. "Stella, there's something I'd like to ask you … but if it's none of my business, just say so." I paused and looked at her before continuing. "I'm just wondering if Ben recently had any illnesses, injuries, pain, that sorta thing."

She looked at me with wide eyes and shook her head. "Why do you ask, Charlie? I'm just ... how could you even know ...?" Her defenses were coming up alongside her curiosity.

"Stella, I'm not trying to pry, believe me. I wouldn't do that." I placed my hand gently on her forearm. "But Mase told me that Ben had a high level of a narcotic in his system. Detective Scharffenberger and the medical examiner are wondering if you can shed any light on this. Don't misunderstand – it's not an illegal substance, but there was so much of it that we wondered if there was a logical explanation."

"As opposed to foul play, you mean?" There was suddenly fire in Stella's eyes, but it was quickly doused by tears. "Don't worry, Charlie, I didn't kill the man I loved," she said sarcastically. "Ben probably overmedicated himself so he could have a pain-free New Year's Eve celebration. Last February, we were skiing in Vermont and he fell and broke his left leg in two places and his right arm as well. His arm healed poorly and continued to cause him incredible pain. It wasn't that difficult to get multiple doctors to prescribe him Lortab and Norco over the last 11 months. He was so much happier when he wasn't in pain, so I stopped questioning the legality of it all and just appreciated that he could enjoy life again, 'doped up' as he used to put it. But I knew it had gotten out of control."

She began sobbing and I was starting to cry myself, so I hugged her. She composed herself, and I apologized for my questions. But she said it actually made her feel good to share the secret with someone, even though no good would come of it. I would tell Mase and Rex, so they could eliminate that line of inquiry from the investigation and keep it private.

Thirty minutes later, Stella was smiling – almost – as the hotel limo whisked her away, a blazing sun reflecting off its rear window.

I passed by the LOL after seeing Stella off, and Artie beckoned me back in, saying he couldn't let me get away just yet. He brought me another club soda and a cola for himself, and sat where Stella had been. Jackpot had come in to double-team the bar, since they were expecting a big flurry around 3:00, when a golf outing of over 100 tournament golfers would be returning to the hotel, no doubt parched. It'd take both bartenders to keep up with the '19th Hole' role their bar would be playing. But they'd done it well before, and would no doubt do it well again. Thirsty golfers tend to go for bottled beer, which is a bartender's easiest task, and that helped a lot.

At the moment, however, Jackpot tended to the LOL's sparse clientele while Artie spilled his guts like a schoolboy. "Gotta tell you this, Miss Charlie. Been seein' a few strange faces around here lately."

Art Foster always called me 'Miss Charlie,' but with more than 30 years separating us I appreciated his fatherly style and rolled with it. "Artie," I laughed, "this is a hotel. We deal with transients. Why wouldn't the faces seem strange to you?" I found his remark genuinely enigmatic. Besides, I had specifically asked all four bartenders to stay alert at all times – Ira's orders, actually – since the bar was the lifeblood of the place, where lots of people came and went, and chattered about everything, and we needed to know any scuttlebutt that was brewing.

"Guess I phrased it poorly," clarified Artie. "I've been seeing strange faces over and over again. You know, like a guy with a funny-looking mole comes in on Sunday, then you see him again on Friday, then maybe again two weeks later. Not an employee or vendor. Not a regular barfly, like Maryland. These guys are true strangers, if you get my drift."

Indeed I did. Artie was revealing exactly the kind of intelligence that I was after. It was good to hear and bad to hear, at the same time. I decided to keep it to myself for right now – that is, not share it with Ira, in case I needed an ace to play sometime soon – and I asked Artie to stay mum as well. He said Gray had also mentioned seeing a few of these types, including 'Mr. Mole' on one occasion.

I knew the barkeeps would have their version of a staff meeting tomorrow, sometime after Sammy's speech, so I asked Artie if I could crash their little gathering and speak for five minutes.

"Sure thing," he nodded. "11:30 tomorrow in Utopia 6. Not opening up here until noon."

As I headed back towards my office, I received a text on my personal cell – I carry it as well as my ParaSpec-issued one with me everywhere I go – and it was from Suzy Hart. Since arriving in Vegas two years ago, she'd become far more than Mase's star employee. She'd also become my best friend, a relationship that began at a CSI-unit spring picnic in 2015 and had grown stronger in the year and a half since. She was all jazzed about some concert in April or May, I forget which, and she wanted me to tag along with her. Though it wasn't a group I was fond of, I figured I'd go because I enjoyed spending time with her, and because it was at an outside stage in suburban Blue Diamond Park, so the thought of being out in nature in nice weather was appealing. BYOB, picnic basket and all.

Another reason I agreed to go was because I knew her love life had been hitting some rough spots lately. She needed the camaraderie, and if her on-again-off-again boyfriend wasn't up for the task, I was glad to fill in some of the gaps.

Unavoidably, a psychic vision hit me then, and it was all about Suzy being swept off her feet by a knight in shining armor (figuratively). It got me so jazzed that I phoned her back and told her to count me in. For the concert, that was.

But Suzy was astute enough to realize I'd had one of my visions, which I'd mentioned to her in the past. But she'd never been the subject of one, and she wasn't gonna let me off the hook now, not without a little embellishment.

"Tell me!" Suzy could be giddy if the occasion called for it. This occasion did.

"I wasn't gonna mention it because, you know, my visions aren't reliable. I didn't wanna get your hopes high and have them dashed—"

"Tell me!" she demanded again.

I told her, and while it lifted her spirits I don't think was fully buying my tale of fantasy. I know I wouldn't, if I were her.

Time would tell.

11

Charlie and her team arrived twenty minutes early, thus managing to snag up-close seats in the third row, center section. True to form, Sammy showed up a few minutes early too, and by 10:03 a.m., he was standing behind the podium and ready to get down to business.

'Sammy Spectacular' was a go-getter in every sense of the word. He'd been aboard The Spectacular Collection as CEO for twenty months now, and the rank-and-file workers, middle and upper management folks, and most importantly the clientele, were seeing and feeling the change. With snow-white hair and the ruddy chocolate complexion you'd expect of an East Indian, this Stanford-educated man had Americanized himself remarkably. He was deliriously happy in his marriage to a Sri Lankan woman and together they had a trio of delightful offspring who were scholastic and athletic standouts. He'd almost outgrown the name Samir Jukala Spakisumar that his parents had given him 58 years earlier, and as a practical matter he also shunned use of the Ph.D. title he'd earned in Palo Alto. The term 'minority' meant nothing to him, as he'd totally assimilated into the culture of the good old USA.

The State of The Spectacular speech, 'SOTS' for short, had been scheduled on January 5th for good reason. Sammy wanted to beat all the politicos to the punch, something his predecessors never managed to accomplish – probably never even thought to attempt. To him, it was important to be the first horse out of the gate, to give his 'state of' address before the president, the governors and mayors of any of the states and communities he operated in. To be in front of the line is the man's nature. That's why he rises at 5 a.m. even if it's not a workday. First guy to whatever meeting he's attending, first to congratulate an employee on a stellar performance with a personal note. And first to get a good seat at every one of his 16-year-old daughter's high school softball games.

Most of the day-shift workers at the ParaSpec were assembled in the Enchantment Ballroom to hear the CEO's wisdom in person. But it was telecast live to all Spectacular properties across the nation, and also recorded for rebroadcast later, so other shifts could hear it at their workplace on company time. Refreshments would be served, of course, and here in the home-property ballroom alone that represented six BEOs, which Charlie Champagne had personally prepared. Nothing but the best for the big guy.

His obligatory welcoming remarks, couched in the context of it being the 40th anniversary of the company's founding, mentioned by name the three employees who had been on hand since Day One and the fact that a ceremony in a few months would honor their loyalty. From there, he launched into the meat of his remarks, first touching on the impressive increase in room occupancy at most of Spectacular's resorts, headlined by a considerable turnaround right here at the ParaSpec. "Ladies and Gentlemen, from where I stand, I see a company that has fully emerged from the Great Recession, and every one of you has helped to make that a reality. I thank you all deeply for your dedication."

Sammy's humility forbade him from claiming any credit. Truth was, his coming aboard in May of '15 had been a shot in the arm for all of the organization's employees. The man had even spent five whole days circulating amongst the offices, kitchens and casino pits at its two Las Vegas properties, getting to know the operation *and* its people.

He continued with generalities about the organization's mission and its positive returns to the stockholders, before moving on to ambitious growth plans. Property openings this year in Santa Rosa, Jackson Hole and Branson, next year in Galveston and Seattle. On the drawing board were projects in Pensacola, Nashville and Tucson. "And closer to home, our 'Spectacular Suites on the Boulevard,' a few miles north of where we now sit, and the 'Sports Spectacular' on West Tropicana Avenue; both those projects are moving ahead briskly and should be complete in 2018. The latter will be a diversion from our norm, with fixed components that play heavily to fans of our new NHL Golden Knights and our hopefully-soon-to-be hometown NFL Raiders. Beyond that, it will abound with sports themes of all varieties, with emphasis on the sporting event of the moment ... be it Super Bowl, World Series, The Masters, you name it.

"Ambitious? Yes! But that's what the Spectacular Collection is all about! We're gonna have a great ride together, my friends. Be proud, because you're all Spectacular components of a Spectacular team! If you have questions or comments, I welcome your input as always. You know my email address. Bless you all, and have a Spectacular day!"

Sammy's speech was more of a pep talk than an actual 'state of' address, but staff knew by now it was Sammy's style to focus on the good, put it out there like a banner waving in the sky and sing it to the heavens. Yes, there were some negatives, as there are in any business, but he saw no need to broadcast operational concerns – workforce matters, property deterioration and maintenance needs, antiquated hardware and software systems, etc. – because his underlings were fully aware of these things and kept on top of them through his firm yet sensitive management approach.

Charlie was aware of many of these issues. Mold. Crud floating in the pools. Bed bugs, real or perceived. In-room Wi-Fi that didn't work properly. Toilets that wouldn't flush. Such things had little to do with her CCS operational realm, but when it was *her* clients complaining about them to *her*, it was suddenly very much *her* concern and the issues easily became *hers*.

As they exited the venue, Charlie was delighted to see the Spectacular Farmers' Market in place, immediately adjacent. Perfect execution, she thought; her BEOs for the set-up had been followed to the letter. The SFM, as it was known, was a periodic employee perk full of fresh produce, baked goods and other items for sale at the hotel's cost. That is, extremely cheap. Though it was already crowded, she and Maris made their way in and headed for the veggie table.

"I need some potatoes and peppers," Maris remarked, as she grabbed six russets ($1.50 total) and four assorted bells ($1.00 total).

Charlie was stocking up on vine-ripened tomatoes and encouraged her friend to do the same. "They're so beautiful, and so full of lycopene. I think you need some."

"Whatever," Maris snorted, as she selected a few to placate Charlie. Charlie filled a bag with ten jumbo tomatoes, grabbed some celery and zucchini and headed for the checkout line. She had to hurry now; her meeting with the LOL bartenders was due to start in ten minutes.

Though Grayson Moore was the lead bartender, he willingly deferred to the elderly Art Foster in welcoming Charlie to their meeting. The guy may be 72 years old, but was still very much 'with it,' as he'd been all of his 40 years with the company. He was one of the three honorees Sammy had referenced in his speech.

"I told Miss Charlie I'd seen some suspicious characters at the bar lately and she wanted to come give us a few management pointers," he said, casting an outstretched arm in her direction. She'd just entered the room, not yet had a chance to sit, so instead moved to the short end of the rectangular conference table and remained standing. Gray and Artie were to her left, Tapper and Jackpot on her right. Four friendly but apprehensive faces.

"Thanks, Artie. I won't take much of your time 'cause I know you've got your own issues to chat about." Charlie reiterated what Artie had said about the guy with the mole and other strangers, and that Gray had also seen this guy as well as other suspicious individuals. "It's clear you guys have been keeping watch, and that's really great. Now I'm hoping you can document some of it. You know - make written notations – brief description of the person, the when and who he or she was with, etc. And if at all possible, see if you can manage to get a photo or two on the sly. This place is noisy enough, I think, that nobody's gonna notice the click of a cell phone camera, right?"

"Excuse me for being naïve," Tapper, the inquisitive Jamaican, said, "but what exactly are we looking for?"

"Good question. The answer is *we don't exactly know*. But intelligence gathering occurs in most businesses, not just in the high levels of government. Corporate espionage can take many forms. We here at Spectacular could be on the receiving end of one of our competitors trying to learn some of our trade secrets, or other entities could be using our premises to conduct illicit activities. What better place for any such goings-on than at a cocktail lounge where people loosen up, let their defenses down, talk a bit too loud, and even converse with strangers, right? It could also be social media types who are trying to find or fabricate ammunition to post on sites to make us look bad. Whatever is going on, we want to extinguish it." That was Ira's word, and while most of them would like to extinguish old Ira himself, they had his back on this one.

Tapper, the most computer-savvy of the bunch, volunteered to organize meeting minutes and tasks on Outlook, and they all pledged to keep their cellphones at the ready to take pictures. They also agreed to meet twice weekly from now on – Mondays and Thursdays at 10:30 – and to allow Charlie a few minutes to check in at the outset of every meeting. She left on an upbeat note, and her brain happily accepted *I Love This Bar* by Toby Keith as its latest musical invasion.

Gray opened the LOL at noon sharp, and was quickly barraged by a hoard of thirsty people. With Charlie's directive forefront in his mind he was more watchful than ever of his customer base. These folks, however, seemed genuinely in search of a tall cool one, a quick shot or a nice smooth cabernet.

A guy in a business suit ordered a Bud Light and tried to engage Gray in political discourse. It had always been a taboo topic to him, but especially since the November '16 election, when emotions ran so high no matter which side you were on. No sense getting into it with a customer who was simply dehydrated and willing to part with some cash in exchange for a cold drink. A 12-ounce draft drawn, topped off perfectly and delivered with a smile. "How about those Raiders, huh?" Gray offered, always eager to talk sports, and right now the Oakland Raiders – maybe, *hopefully*, the future Las Vegas Raiders – were two days away from their wild card game against the Texans. He preached the silver and black gospel as if he were Al Davis himself. Mr. Bud Light didn't take the bait. "Not much of a football fan, I'm afraid," he said as he walked away and found a table. Next up was a pair of ladies anxious for 'super dry' gin martinis. Gray loved a good gin martini, and made them as dry as the parched Mojave Desert the hotel was built upon: Bombay Sapphire with exactly three drops of dry vermouth. They were engrossed in their own chattering, and didn't seem much like football fans either. The fact was, all this noontime crowd wanted was a good drink served up with efficiency and courtesy. That, Grayson Moore could handle with his eyes closed.

He just wished a few more of them had Raidermania at this crucial time of the season.

Jameson Kean wasn't much into American football either, but he had a sporting mindset. Former horse handler, trainer and 25% owner of an aging stallion/stud. He had an open mind when it came to any athletic competition, especially at its climactic final stages. He shunned baseball all year long, but took in the World Series with interest. Same with basketball and March Madness, football and the Super Bowl, and so on. He happily conversed with others on the sport of the week, whatever it was. If he didn't understand it, he professed his ignorance and a willingness to learn and understand the nuances.

When Kean furtively slid onto one of the LOL's barstools and said to Gray Moore's back, "I'll have whatever Derek Carr would have," the bartender instantly knew he'd found an ally. As he turned, he realized the accented voice had come from his coworker Jameson Kean, and the two high-fived with genuine gusto.

"Actually, Carr would probably order a new fibula if he could," Gray joked, wondering if Jameson would understand the oblique reference to the Raiders' starting quarterback's debilitating injury a few weeks earlier.

To Gray's surprise, the Scotsman replied, "Bloody shame, that."

"What brings you in, my man? Not working today, are you?" Gray had taken notice of Kean's uncharacteristically casual attire, a blue ParaSpec polo and grey sweatpants. Usually he was at least partially, if not fully, attired in his three-piece business suit.

"Off until Saturday. But today I've got an interview with that detective with the long name. I'm sure you've talked to him since you were on duty that night."

That night.

Right now, at the Paradise Spectacular Resort Hotel & Casino, there was hardly a soul who didn't know what *that night* meant.

At that very moment, Scharffenberger appeared, nodding a greeting to Gray before beckoning the Director of VIP Services to join him at the high-boy table in the farthest corner of the LOL. It was out of earshot of the rest of the bar, and from any of the currently occupied tables.

An ideal interview spot, both men reckoned. Only Gray Moore would disagree, and that was because it dashed his ability to eavesdrop.

The detective took copious notes – handwritten in a pocket-size spiral notebook – and occasionally looked at the other man's phone and asked him to air drop the photos to his own phone. He was more animated than when he'd questioned Gray, and that suggested that he was being fed some really meaty info.

Oh my, how Gray wished he were a fly on the window pane beside these two men.

In less than thirty minutes, their meeting was over, as was Gray's futile peeping. The cop left a ten on the table, which amply covered two iced teas and a gratis bowl of bar snacks. They walked out together, both waving to Gray as they did, and shook hands vigorously once they were back on the lobby floor.

Gray went over to clean off the men's table, bemoaning his being *this close* to learning some really hot scuttlebutt. Returning behind the bar, he was surprised to see Lt. Scharffenberger standing there. The detective extended his hand with a small yellow piece of cardstock in it.

"Validate me?"

Gray smiled, peeled a small adhesive sticker from a roll he kept under the bar, and affixed it to the yellow parking receipt. *Saving the taxpayers a couple of bucks*, he thought appreciatively.

"There ya go," he said with his best bartender's grin.

For the head bartender, it had actually been a better than average day. He was still excited about the CEO's morning revelation of the plans for the new sports-oriented hotel. He'd spent much of the afternoon visualizing roles he might fill in that establishment.

As Maris Kean prepared to leave for the day around 4:45, she noticed an extra brown bag amongst her other purchases from the Farmers' Market. Attached was a note that said, 'Perfect for a big dinner salad tonight.' The handwriting was Charlie's, and inside the bag were six gorgeous vine-ripened tomatoes.

Maris rolled her eyes at her friend's impudence, but since she'd given no serious thought yet to the night's dinner, she decided it might be a great change of pace. Jameson would enjoy it, especially if she added some sautéed ground turkey and dressed it with a rich Roquefort. Their three daughters would buy into the idea if she topped it with some still-warm homemade polenta croutons. She could easily do it all.

She was eager to get home to hear about her husband's chat with the detective and his visit to the urologist earlier in the day.

12

I'd had a tough time masking my exhilaration all afternoon, and did a poor job of it when I bounded into the house about 6:15. Mase was already home, casually dressed and prepping snacks and pre-dinner cocktails. I threw a kiss his way and headed for the bedroom, and when I returned in my pajamas in less than five minutes, he acknowledged my energized state. "What's up, my little Cheshire Charlie?" He called me that whenever I couldn't conceal my bubbling-over emotions.

I grabbed a chip and spilled my news. "At his 'State Of' speech today, Sammy dropped a zinger." I proceeded to tell him that the West Tropicana project that was originally dubbed 'Spectacular OFF the Strip' was now being envisioned as 'Sports Spectacular.' I needed to say no more; my hubby was right there on my wavelength. Almost, anyway.

"Applying for a transfer, are you?"

"As a last resort, I suppose. I was thinking more in terms of a *promotion*. Use that advanced degree I worked so hard for, be director of something-or-other. Doesn't matter, really. I just feel so damn ready for this, I think I could direct whatever the hell they throw at me. Whaddya think, lover boy?"

"Better yet, you could be one of the Vice Presidents and then *you* can be one of the *they* you're always referring to," he winked. "You've got the smarts and the creativity and the ingenuity to be a big cog in the management wheel. You're definitely more of a leader than some VPs I can think of."

No names mentioned. None needed.

After that upbeat ending to the 5th, January became a blur ... and not a particularly pleasant one. It started on the morning of Friday the 6th, when I received an email from Stephen Pierce, Ben's older brother, informing me that his sister-in-law Stella was clinging to life in a Cleveland hospital. Apparently she'd overdosed on hydrocodone, the same drug that had been found in excessive quantities in her husband's body. *Had it been intentional?* I wondered to myself. Stephen didn't say. I also wondered about Brayden and Byron, the young men who were now bearing a horrendous double burden. How could they possibly be coping?

I couldn't think of how to respond to Stephen, but I knew I had to say something. I would dwell on it for a while. I self-imposed a 2 p.m. deadline for a response, which was 5 in Ohio.

By 8:10 that morning, Maris was in my face crying the Dyvan blues, and her sidekick Hermie had tagged along. The pharma folks were changing menus and schedules faster than Maris could crank out revisions and generate pop-up BEOs. The Banquet Operations Team and chefs were beside themselves, and adding to her woes by acting as if it was all *her* fault.

"Not the full quid, those blokes," Hermie opined, and Maris agreed heartily, as if she actually understood his Aussie jargon. I consoled them, but could do little else. They were both competent and would see this thing through. Dyvan would load in on the 10th and pull the plug on the 16th. "You're doing great, guys. Hang in there and it'll be over soon," I reassured them. Hermie departed promptly, his self-esteem boosted by my words, but Maris deliberately lagged behind, something else on her mind. Once we were alone, she squinted at me suspiciously, her hands on her hips. "OK, how'd you know?"

"Know what?" I asked, genuinely puzzled.

"Charlie, goddamn it, how the fuck did you know? How did your miracle brain snag the vibes this time?"

"What vibes? What are you talking about, Maris?"

"I'm saying that Jameson found out yesterday that he's got prostate cancer, and—"

"Oh my god, Mare, I'm so sorry. I had no idea." It was the truth. "How horrible. How bad is it?"

"No symptoms yet, but the doc says he'll need radiation. His Gleason score is 6, whatever the fuck that means, but it's not good news. Until we can start that – sometime after Spain, for sure – he says just practice a good diet. And I know you know what that means, with your obnoxious little bag of tomatoes and the note you left me yesterday."

Still stunned, I just shook my head.

"It means that somehow you knew this fucking lycopene in the tomatoes would be exactly what Dr. Whatshisface – I forget his name – would recommend for my Jameson. 'Stuff yourself with lycopene,' he told him."

I didn't consciously know *anything*, and I swore to that fact to my hysterical friend.

Then I realized that I, too, ought to be hysterical. This was a momentous happening for me. My psychic powers had gone off on their own, done their own thing. My 'gift' had been giving when I didn't even know it was gift-giving time.

Holy shit. To be honest, it was scary.

Chelsea on my Mind.

Yeah, Chelsea, it's scary as hell. Just like I know it must've been for you way back when.

After those lightning bolts to my psyche, I found forging ahead a formidable task. But forge ahead I did.

In two short weeks we'd be faced with Inauguration Day, an event that was causing many folks – perhaps most notably our own Grayson Moore – major heartburn. Gray'd been feeling the pressure coming ever since November 8th when, in his view, the unthinkable had occurred. He'd confided to me, and probably others as well, that "no way was the travesty of *that man's* coronation" gonna occur during his watch. Gray was slated to work on the 20th from opening till 8 p.m., but did not think that relinquishing his shift to someone else was enough of a resolution to his dilemma. I had no solution, but told him I'd support him when it got to the point of discussing it with Ira and Leo.

It was an impasse that had gone to the upper management think tank, but life went on down in the trenches without a plan. *What would the collective minds upstairs offer?*

I missed my own deadline, but late in the day I did fire off a short email to Stephen Pierce: *'So terribly sorry to hear the news about Stella. When you have a chance, please fill me in with more details. And please send me the hospital info so I can send flowers and a card.'* He responded within minutes and I decided to wire her a bouquet for delivery first thing tomorrow.

While I was on my phone, I got a dropdown alert to an inbound Twitter message. Someone who'd invented the tag *#whatssodamnedspectacular* had tweeted *'Sammy Unspectacular spoke for an hour yesterday. Nothing to get excited about, so far as I can see. Stay tuned.'* It wasn't the first such negative message I'd seen from this idiot, whoever he (or she) was, but I had to wonder who was claiming to have knowledge about Sammy's SOTS address. Access to the live presentation had been well gu.

under password-protection by the IT and sec

we had an internal leak – highly unlikely, I thoug.

tion by someone whose only knowledge was that Sa..

to his crew yesterday. That someone apparently wante.

within the tranquil ParaSpec trenches. Damn this person!

I went home that night with my emotions in a state of upheava..   ..a.
Inauguration day blues. Jameson's illness. Evil-minded tweets. Dyvan's
unpredictability.

So much to think about!

I checked the stalking app on my phone and saw that Mase was at
home so I dictated him a text message ala Siri that said *'Just got on 15 south.
Fix me a drink, dearest. I don't care what, just make it a double!'*

Seventeen minutes later, a gin martini was sitting on the driveway
when I pulled my blue Renegade into its spot next to Mase's Metro-issued
beige Tundra. But it wasn't just any martini. This one was served up in a
schooner glass, with six green olives, three cocktail onions, a pair of dill pickle
chips and a leafy celery stick. A double, for sure, and then some. I adored it.

And I adored the man who'd created it. Before the drink was gone, I
showed him just how much.

13

Maryland Burfurd wasn't used to the chill, and it made her cranky. *Crankier than usual*, some would quip, as if to imply she was perpetually in such a state. But Maryland was actually a laid-back and affable soul, though her sardonic wit was sometimes misconstrued as mean-spirited irritability rather than the upshot of years of hard living and the dogged tenacity that went with it.

She answered to no one, and liked it that way. The way she figured things, if you told someone what you were doing, when and where you were doing it … well, then you were accountable, and somehow less of an independent person than if you shed all the puppet strings and did exactly what your own free-thinking self decided was the right thing for you.

It was 12 degrees in Baltimore, which is where the woman found herself at forty-five minutes to midnight on the seventh day of the new year. They were calling it 2017, but aside from its numerical label she couldn't see much about it that was new. It was even colder than last January had been.

Maryland owned condos or timeshares in a half dozen places, some rather tropical, so it was a mystery why she gravitated to the frigid northeast in January. That is, unless one knew the sorry truth. Maryland's mother lived near Baltimore, and had been there all of her septuagenarian life. Every year, along about October, she laid a guilt trip on her only daughter: "If you can't make it for Thanksgiving or Christmas, at least come see your lonely old Ma when the new year rolls around." And thus Maryland, who so prided herself on her independence, succumbed annually to the age-old practice of deferring to a parent, regardless of the parent's level of rationality. In fact, there was little that was rational about Carolynn Burnside, but her daughter visited for a week this winter as she always did – usually managing to convince the nursing-home-bound woman that she'd been there a month before she moved on to visit her dear old Pa in North Carolina. He, Marlin Burfurd, was the antithesis of his long-ago common-law spouse, and Maryland thoroughly enjoyed her visits with him.

When she was not visiting Ma, she spent her time at the LOL, the Libations on the Lobby, of the plush digs her friend Charlie Champagne had arranged for her in Baltimore at the $89/night Family and Friends rate. The lobby bar used the same moniker as its flagship operation in Las Vegas, as did others in the Spectacular Collection. Many of the decorative appointments were even identical, and Maryland felt quite at home. She made mental notes to thank Charlie when she returned to Sin City, and also to write a positive TripAdvisor and Google review of the nearly-new Harbor Spectacular Hotel.

As she sipped on her second Brandy Alexander of the evening, her cellphone vibrated. An actual voice call coming in – a rarity these days – and the caller ID told her to accept it. "Charlie! I was just thinking about you. This hotel is incredible. Right on the waterfront, and the LOL is almost a carbon copy. Except the view is way better," she teased.

"Glad you're enjoying it, Maryland. Remember to post a few good reviews for us. And emphasize the specific things you like the best."

"That won't be hard. Everything is pretty … well, y'know, *spectacular!*"

Charlie told Maryland that Metro Lieutenant Scharffenberger was still waiting to interview her. "He's getting impatient."

"I keep forgetting, but I'll call him tomorrow," Maryland assured Charlie, as she wrote down the detective's cell number on the back of her napkin.

"When's your return date?" Charlie asked.

"To Vegas? Not really sure. After this I'm heading on down to see my old Pa. It's only a five-hour drive. A couple weeks there, I suppose. He's such a joy to be around compared to Ma. We'll spend a few days out at the cottage if the weather's halfway decent. I haven't been back there since Matthew, but my Pa says from a drive-by it looks be in pretty good shape. We'll meet with my contractor while we're there and get done whatever's needed. Should be rentable when the demand picks up in the spring. And ready for my annual summer pilgrimage."

Charlie complimented Maryland on how well-planned everything was. And without saying it, she thought, *not too bad for a dancer-turned-mad-am-turned-entrepreneur*. Even in the wake of Hurricane Matthew, she'd been able to think and act pragmatically.

"One thing I do know. I'll be back to the ParaSpec in time for the Super Bowl."

When they'd hung up, Maryland placed another call. It was now close to midnight, and the recipient of her call was also in the Eastern time zone, but he picked up promptly. They talked for only forty seconds, confirming plans already made. Raleigh Lofts, Unit 17, 5-ish on Thursday night. She wrote down those particulars on her napkin below the phone number for Lt. Scharffenberger.

She smiled with satisfaction as they disconnected. *She* had made the call, thus *she* remained in control. Had it been the other way around, she'd have been feeling suffocated by a lack of independent thought.

As she ordered her third and final Brandy Alexander, she folded the napkin and stuck it in her purse. The front of the napkin had a logo similar to the one used at the Vegas property, but this one was embellished with sailboats instead of mountains and contained the simple words 'Harbor Spectacular.'

She asked the bartender – who bore an uncanny resemblance to Grayson Moore – for another napkin, and she turned it over and began to write on the blank side. She needed to work on refining her schedule:

1/8-1/10: with Ma

1/11: drive to NC

1/12: to Raleigh, overnight

1/13-1/20: Chapel Hill

1/21-1/27: cottage

1/28-1/31: Chapel Hill

2/1: fly to LAS

It was loose, the only fixed points being her secret rendezvous in Raleigh and the flight home. She hoped her return to Las Vegas was early enough to miss the mass influx of bettors and partiers that always accompanied the Super Bowl, which this year was on February 5th. The game may be played in Texas but the sports books were alive and well in Nevada, and Vegas would be overrun.

By then, she'd be super relaxed after nearly four weeks in the company of dear old Pa. She invariably relished the time she spent with Marlin Burfurd, Ph.D., Professor Emeritus of Clinical Pharmacology at Duke University's School of Medicine. Wow, was that a handle! She was proud of her accomplished father, but still preferred to think of him as just plain Pa.

Dr. Burfurd had a modest three-bedroom ranch-style home that backed up to an urban park, affording him no neighbors to the rear. No human neighbors, that is, and he thoroughly relished the proximity of his mammal and avian ones. He even had a favorite blue jay family that habitually came out of the woods to collect peanuts in the shell (unsalted, of course) that he placed on his porch railing. With a lot width of nearly 200 feet, he was also well-insulated from his neighbors to the left and right, and he kept heavy vegetation along the lot lines to optimize his privacy. Maryland savored her visits here, finding it a superb respite from the bling of Las Vegas and the urban congestion of Baltimore. Even better than the time in Chapel Hill were their visits to 'the cottage,' as they called it, a two-bedroom built on stilts in Nags Head, out in the Outer Banks. Though Maryland was the legal owner, both she and her father often used it solo, and offered it for rental by the week using the VRBO online platform.

Her favorite times were those they spent together at the cottage. Fishing Albemarle Sound in an old dinghy, building bonfires in the sand, singing old time songs and cooking breakfast on a Coleman stove – these were the activities that had strengthened their bonds over the years. But those were warm weather activities, and January was a bit too inhospitable. During this coming visit, she expected they'd spend quiet time curled up in front of a roaring fire, watching classic movie DVDs, perusing family photo albums, and perhaps playing board games like Monopoly and Clue – throwbacks from her childhood. And of course, there was the cooking! While Maryland was a passable cook, in her eyes, her father was up there with some of the masters. The modernized kitchen she'd spent over $12,000 on two years ago was given quite a workout when 'Chef Marlin' visited and demonstrated his talents; his favorite was Chateaubriand, hers a more simplistic Maryland (what else?) crab cake recipe that melted in your mouth. They should have time for both on this trip.

She hoped Pa wasn't annoyed by her overnight excursion on Thursday. She'd rather have waited until later into her visit, but the man she was meeting wasn't able to change his schedule. In truth, Maryland wasn't sure she believed that and wondered if he was really just trying to wrest control of their relationship again. It wouldn't be the first time.

14

Charlie called Stella in Cleveland just before she was discharged from the hospital, to see how she was doing. They talked about the overdose that had nearly taken her life. Stella said she was just trying to ease the pain of losing Ben and thought she'd simply achieve that euphoric state she'd sometimes seen in Ben when he'd taken too many pills.

Then the talk turned to her two sons, who were both in college. Byron, 20, was a sophomore at Ohio State studying agriculture/animal husbandry. Brayden, 21, was at Arizona Western College in Yuma, in a construction management Associate of Applied Science program. It was winter break, so both were home in Shaker Heights and were devastated over the news of their father's murder. "They were planning to take some time off from school to be with me," she said, "but I told them that's not what their father would have wanted. And truthfully, it's not what I wanted. I need to get on with life, and I'm sure their wounds will heal faster if they go back and immerse themselves in their classes and their school friendships. We squabbled a bit over this, but in the end they knew their mother was right. And they both agreed to come running if I need them. But hopefully I won't. I'm strong, and so are my sons."

Charlie had never met the boys, but based on what their mother had told her of them, she knew they were resilient young men. And while she was unnerved by their seeming abandonment of their mother, it was *their* family decision and not hers to question.

"Stephen and his wife Annie are here, less than ten miles away," Stella added reassuringly, "and my sister Sandy from Pittsburgh is coming to stay for a bit and my brother Carlo is in Akron. Lots of support nearby."

The dinner that night went well, with 1207 Jewish tummies filled with tasty kosher salmon, fresh asparagus, rice pilaf and raspberry sorbet. There were a number of extra plates prepared, so Charlie managed to bring three home for a late dinner for the family. Mase commented, "Salmon's OK, but a bit overcooked. Yours with the honey mustard sauce is far superior." Charlie proudly agreed. The pets, however, scarfed eagerly and without critical commentary. Watching the kitties devour those asparagus spears like kids slurping spaghetti never failed to generate laughs.

The next morning she was taken aback by an email from the senior of the two Israeli ladies who'd been a thorn in her side for many months and especially these last two weeks. *'Our dear Charlie C: The entire program went so well, and last night's dinner went beyond our expectations. Thank you again. Check the front desk for an envelope. Regards, Golda and Sally.'*

With so many tasks on her plate, Charlie forgot all about the front desk till early afternoon. When she finally checked for messages, the clerk handed her a crisp ParaSpec envelope with five equally crisp hundred-dollar bills inside, along with Golda Razim's and Selah "Sally" Naham's business cards. What a pleasant surprise that was.

While Charlie was rejoicing in the front of the house, Maris Kean was busy in the back of the house making Day 1 of the Dyvan program the success she knew it should and could be. She and Hermie had worked their tails off all weekend to prepare for load-in on Monday, a day ahead of schedule. Trade show stuff to the Fascination Ballroom, special shipments to the

COO's penthouse suite, and on and on. In a sense, the worst was over – that is, so long as the Dyvan planners didn't start issuing a flurry of last-minute program changes.

The bulk of attendees would arrive during the day Tuesday, with the group's 'get acquainted social' event set for that evening from 6 till 9. With Hermie's help, Maris was making it all happen smoothly, and they could begin to see the light of hope. At 5 p.m. Monday she pulled her assistant aside and said, "Still agree to take over tonight for however long it takes – shouldn't be more than a few more hours – and I'll take tomorrow night by myself?"

"Are you sure you'll be OK with that? Tomorrow, I mean," the young Queenslander asked.

They'd discussed it all earlier, so Hermie was merely being polite. He knew she had two TV specials she wanted to watch tonight, one on Discovery and one on Travel, which dealt with Spanish history and Spanish beaches, respectively. And Maris knew that Hermie and his partner had an LBGTQ event they wanted to attend on Tuesday, and she didn't want him hanging around the ParaSpec waiting for a problem that would probably not occur when he could be enjoying himself with Scooter and their friends.

"I'll be OK. For sure."

On Tuesday the 10th, Detective Rex Scharffenberger flew to Cleveland, Ohio. Though he'd booked a Southwest nonstop of four hours duration, two hours of delay at the Las Vegas airport due to inclement weather over the country's midsection had made for an exhausting experience. He was not in a great mood as he checked into the Holiday Inn Express just outside Cleveland Hopkins airport. A vending machine sandwich and a mini-bottle of cabernet in his room constituted dinner. Then straight to bed. He would deal with renting a car in the morning.

Maryland Burfurd arose and packed up early, stopped in at Carolynn Burnside's nursing home in Glen Burnie, and shared one last breakfast with Ma. Cold pancakes, rubbery bacon and scorched coffee – Tranquility Bay's finest fare. They hugged, and by 9:15 a.m. Maryland had navigated her rented Mustang onto State Route 100 in the general direction of the nation's capital. She'd left early so she could take 'the back way,' a relaxing and somewhat more rural route through Charlottesville and Lynchburg. Fewer freeways and lighter traffic. The plan was to reach Pa's place in plenty of time for dinner.

Dutiful daughter notwithstanding, Maryland was rather a peculiar dame, starting with her nonconformist name, which she asserted was from being born to a woman from Annapolis. Her Tar Heel father had contributed her middle name, Carolina. Her parents had never married, and had been estranged for many years.

The weather was lovely this fine Wednesday – sunshine and approaching 50 degrees – as she wound her way south through the Virginia hills. Maryland Carolina Burfurd wondered what would be on the menu tonight, because Pa never disappointed.

She didn't think the cell signal would be very strong this far out in the boondocks, but at 2:10 p.m. her phone gave a healthy warble. It was the sound of a laughing gull, one of the happy sounds of her place in the Outer Banks. The custom ringtone meant someone was calling, but not someone on her array of regulars, all of whom had been assigned their own distinctive tones.

It was from an unfamiliar number in the familiar 702 area code.

Las Vegas was calling.

She answered it. Why the hell not?

After an adequate (and free) breakfast at his Cleveland hotel and a quick Lyft ride to the airport rental car center, Detective Lieutenant Scharffenberger was in an improved frame of mind. By 8:30 a.m., he was headed off to the offices of Great Lakes Fixtures and Plumbing Supply in the eastern suburb of Solon. It was a 40-minute drive and he found his way with no difficulty, thanks to the GPS unit built into the dash of his almost-new Kia Soul rental. The anticipated snow flurries had not yet materialized, which enhanced his positive mood.

He had a 9:30 appointment to speak with a man named Arnold Hatch, Vice President of Marketing for GLFPS. Rex had been made aware of this man's existence from a conversation he'd had the previous week with Merle Cash, one of the ParaSpec's Casino Hosts. Cash had been singled out for a second interview with Scharffenberger after the initial screening of all employees revealed he had been the Pierces' host. In the second interview, Cash had mentioned to the detective, almost off-handedly, that Mr. Hatch had been another of his charges for the New Year's weekend of events. Rex wasn't sure, but he had the impression that Hatch and Pierce, though executives in the same company, were not close friends. He aimed to dig deeper, to see if just maybe there was some bad blood between the two.

Arnold Hatch was a fit-looking mid-fifties guy with thin graying hair and a wary look on his face. He seemed nervous at the unexpected appearance of a cop from halfway across the country, asking rather personal questions.

"No, Lieutenant, I didn't socialize with Mr. Pierce while I was in Vegas. I was invited by the hotel, partied at their expense, gambled at my expense, and left."

"Partied? What exactly did that involve?"

"That's really pertinent to your investigation?"

"Could be, ya never know. Ask a hundred questions, get ninety-nine useless answers. Trouble is, ya never know which question's gonna turn up the useful answer. So, I'll ask it again: What did your so-called partying involve on New Year's Eve?"

"Other than eating too much, drinking too much Scotch whiskey, and going out to a couple of girly shows? Not much else, Lieutenant. If you lived in Ohio, you'd know that's way beyond the standard quota of excitement for a guy like me."

Rex smirked wryly. Living in Ohio looked like an exercise in boredom, on that much they apparently agreed. "No ladies?"

"What exactly are you asking, Lieutenant?"

"I'm wondering if you availed yourself of any of our fine state's vast collection of willing and talented females."

"I can't see how that pertains to your murder investigation. You're sounding a bit like the PI my second ex-wife hired to track my comings and goings a few years ago."

"So ... OK, I guess I have my answer. Have a nice day, Mr. Hatch," said Rex sarcastically, as he rose from his chair.

Rex really didn't care if Arnold Hatch had kept his pants on or not. He'd been looking for attitude, and what he'd learned was that the man had an antagonistic streak a mile deep.

As he approached the office doorway, he went halfway through it and then turned back – classic Columbo style – and said, "By the way, sir, I was just wondering. Did you and Mr. Pierce ever compete for the same position here at Great Lakes? You know, was there any professional rivalry between the two of you?"

"You've got a bit to learn, officer. Great Lakes is, and always has been, a Pierce stronghold. Ben's daddy, brother, uncles, grandpappy. They only hire folks like me because there's not quite enough of them to run the whole shebang alone. But we outsiders are limited in how high we can climb, and I'm quite sure I've already reached the top rung of my career ladder in this company."

Rex absorbed this and mumbled, "Gotcha, thanks for that. Have a wonderful day." He mock saluted Hatch, opened the door and closed it behind him.

With this new information in hand, he decided to seek out the HR department. There he learned that Ben's brother, Stephen, was one of only two Pierces currently employed in upper management, the other being Penelope Pierce, the HR Director. He also discovered that some in-laws with different surnames earned a paycheck there as well. The receptionist was unable – or unwilling – to provide details, and Rex decided there was no need to pursue this angle right now. He noted Penelope Pierce's name for a possible phone follow-up if needed later.

He put 'Penny P' in his coat pocket, with no immediate plans to chase her down. He'd already arranged to meet with Stephen Pierce, the Director of Sales and Marketing – Midwest Region, at his home later in the day, and after that he'd thankfully be returning to the more hospitable southwestern desert he called home.

Late that morning, as the promised flurries began to sweep in off Lake Erie, Rex paid a visit to Stella Pierce at her home in the fashionable suburb of Shaker Heights. It was an attractive brick two-story that backed up to tiny Green Lake. He imagined it was idyllic during the summertime when the now-snowy lawn was emerald green and the lake wasn't frozen over.

After offering his condolences, Rex quickly built a rapport with the attractive brunette widow. He was surprised to learn that she'd been hospitalized since she'd returned from Las Vegas, and even more surprised when she revealed that it was an accidental overdose of her husband's pain medication that had sent her there. It was in his cop nature to question anything called 'accidental,' but he didn't really see a point in belaboring this painful issue and causing the woman any more grief. Not now at least.

The detective had a mental list of questions aimed at assessing the health of the Pierces' marriage, but he skipped over most of them. He could sense her fragility, and understood it. They moved on to the subject of her sons, who Scharffenberger was hoping to speak with on this visit.

"I'm so sorry, Detective, but my sons are not home. My sister offered to have them come stay with her in Pittsburgh for a day or two, for a change of scenery. They'll come home tomorrow afternoon or the next … if the weather cooperates. I really worry with all the ice and snow this time of year."

Rex nodded knowingly. He grew up in New Hampshire and had vivid recollections tucked in his memory bank. "Well, I would like to talk with the boys at some point," he said. "Perhaps you could share their cellphone numbers with me and I'll catch up with them later."

Stella sighed. "I could do that, but why on earth is that necessary, Detective? They are grieving over their father's death, and surely have nothing useful to add to your investigation. They were thousands of miles away at the time. Right here in this house, as a matter of fact."

"I understand. But ma'am, it's routine to talk with all close relations of the deceased." He decided he wouldn't push it and left before he caused her any more distress.

But he did leave with both sons' cell phone numbers, a victory for him.

And Stella Pierce's assertion that her sons had been 'right here in this house' when 2017 had arrived was taken with the grain of salt it deserved. What else would a protective mother say?

15

At the Paradise Spectacular, Charlie Champagne's Wednesday was far from spectacular. The company as a whole was grappling with the issues of parking fees and resort fees, which were unrelated except for the fact that both were levies that many guests weren't expecting and which were therefore wildly unpopular.

Neither of these issues was directly related to Charlie's domain, but when her clients did the bellyaching to her, she was forced to respond as a representative of the company. Although all staff had been counseled on how to deal with such complaints, it was no fun to constantly defend these money-grabbing practices that she didn't fully agree with.

A more specific challenge, however, was creeping up. Charlie had been assigned to a committee of mid-level managers charged with planning a modest celebration of the Chinese New Year on January 28th. Top management had decided months ago to scale back from the full-blown Casino Marketing event that they'd done the prior two years with only mediocre results. The ParaSpec was not a bastion of Asian tourism, while other properties in Las Vegas certainly were, and it seemed futile to compete. But ignoring the date entirely could not and would not be done, and it was now the task of the ad hoc Lunar New Year Committee to develop a décor and event plan that was appropriate in scale and scope. Since it was the Year of the Rooster, the group quickly became known as the 'Loony Roosters.'

Charlie had been chosen co-chair of the Loony Roosters when they first convened back in September, probably because she was one of the two people who came to that kickoff meeting prepared with background research and some working concepts. Today she took full charge, as the other co-chair was out with the flu. Time was passing quickly, and they had to start moving into execution stage. She pointed at people authoritatively, making assignments, and she was good at it.

For his lunch in Ohio, Rex splurged on a corned beef sandwich so thick he had to deconstruct it and eat it with a fork. Stella Pierce had suggested the place to him, and she'd recommended well. She told him it had been one of Ben's favorites, and that she usually ordered a bowl of soup with two spoons and a fork … the second spoon to share her soup with him, and the fork to snag a few pieces of the corned beef that overflowed from his sandwich. They'd invariably both leave sufficiently sated.

As did Detective Scharffenberger on this chilly Wednesday afternoon. The soup of the day had been a satisfying zucchini/corn/farro broth, which complemented the rich sandwich nicely. He'd patted his stomach as he squeezed back into his small rental car.

Shortly after two, he found a telephone number in his pocket-sized notebook and punched in ten digits on his iPhone. It was not a number he'd ever called before. He didn't know what to expect.

"Yeah, what is it?" The voice was female, as expected. But it was gruff and rough, not at all what he'd anticipated from a lady.

"Miss Burfurd? Miss Maryland Burfurd?"

"Yeah, but I don't want whatever you're selling. And don't tell me my Social Security number is gonna self-destruct or I can't afford not to buy your solar panels. I'm not interested in—"

"Murder. Does that interest you, ma'am?"

Silence. Five seconds of it. Then finally she said, "I love a good murder. As long as I'm not the vic or the perp. Especially the vic."

Rex sniggered under his breath. "Your cop slang is impressive. Watch a lot of TV?"

"Read a lot. Harry Bosch is my hero."

Rex recognized the name as one of author Michael Connelly's protagonists. He hadn't read any of the Bosch books himself.

"Well, your Harry is fiction, but I'm his real-life counterpart. Name is Rex Scharffenberger, ma'am, Detective Lieutenant with the Las Vegas Metropolitan Police Department, Homicide Division."

"Let's cut the *ma'am* crap, ok? My name is Maryland, spelled like the state but I won't hard-ass you if you fail to pronounce the final D. Most people don't."

"Well, ma'am – I mean Maryland – I need to ask you a few questions. Face to face, not over a lousy phone connection." He apologized for the road noise: a busy intersection in downtown Cleveland, jackhammers and taxi horns competing for attention.

Maryland had her own issues: 45 mph, winding through the hills of Virginia, window half-way down.

After a shared chuckle, their rapport improved. It began by acknowledging that the 'lousy phone connection' was no fault of Apple or Samsung. They were dealing with environmental barriers at both ends.

Maryland apologized for not calling earlier. "I had your number on a napkin, but I must've lost it," she admitted, then went on to assure him that her hasty departure after January 1st had been planned and had nothing to do with that high-roller's death, which she'd read about online while waiting for her plane at McCarran. She could prove it, if need be. Sure, she'd be happy to meet with him in person when they're both back in Vegas. "Someplace nice and quiet. You know where the LOL is?" she asked.

Didn't everyone? thought Rex. "I know it," he said.

They agreed to meet there on Thursday, February 2nd. "Two in the afternoon," Maryland instructed. "Groundhog Day, Detective, but let's hope we only have to live it once."

He laughed in agreement.

The light-hearted closure with Maryland put Rex in a good mood, though he recognized it as a power play on her part.

Memories of the corned beef sandwich and soup lingered. After a restroom break and a refueling of his rental car, he was more than ready to meet with Stephen Pierce by the time 4:00 rolled around. They met, per agreement, at the Pierce home on Harborview Drive in the Edgewater neighborhood of Cleveland's near west side, which was – as the name implied – on the edge of the water. Lake Erie, a massive body of fresh water. A housekeeper answered the front door after Rex had gained driveway access through a voice-activated security system. He found his host amiable and welcoming, while professing a suitable degree of remorse over the loss of his brother and the near loss of his sister-in-law.

They sat in the so-called 'sun room' – inaptly named for the day's inhospitable weather conditions, but no doubt lovely in the spring through autumn months – and were served coffee and warm chocolate chip cookies by the housekeeper who had greeted Rex at the front door. A small flagon of brandy was included with the tray.

The woman added a measure of the brandy to her employer's cup. She looked then to Rex, who politely declined the offer.

"On the job," he explained.

"Of course. A cop, above all people, needs to keep a level head. But as for being on the job, what exactly is your job at this moment?" Stephen asked.

"My job at all times is to serve the citizens of Clark County, Nevada, as a member of the police force sworn to investigate and solve crimes. I'd like to think I do it pretty well. Sometimes it takes me to places where the weather and the people might be less hospitable than in Clark County," Rex said with a manufactured smile. He wasn't sure if he trusted this guy, but he would withhold judgment for the time being.

"Climates like Cleveland in the winter?" Stephen joked.

Rex's nodding head and scowl said it all.

Across the room a fireplace sparkled, but he wasn't sure if it was real or one of those fake ones with ceramic logs and natural gas. Too far away to tell. Not really important, he decided. Outside the weather sucked, regardless of the indoor amenities.

"And people like me?" Stephen continued.

"Mr. Pierce, so far I find you very hospitable. But I haven't asked you anything yet. If I have any reason to think you're lying, being evasive or feeding me a fat line of bullshit, that could certainly change how I perceive you, sir."

"Well then, let's get to it," Stephen Pierce said, his manner remarkably engaging.

The Keans' trip to Spain was in the latter third of January, but they were managing to make it consume the majority of the month. Preparation began on the 11th with Jameson flying to Oakland to retrieve his mother-in-law, who lived in the nearby bedroom community of Benicia. Franny Ohana disliked airports and air travel so much that her devoted son-in-law volunteered to fly up and escort her back to Vegas for a week's visit before he and her daughter escaped across the country and then across the Atlantic. She adored her Nevada family, doting especially on granddaughters Valencia, Almeria and Sevilla, and welcomed the babysitting assignment. Valencia, the eldest at eight years, two months and twenty-three days (so she would inform anyone who asked), vehemently objected to the term 'babysitter.' So Grams was just visiting to keep her and the 'little sisters' company while their parents flew to a distant land of bullfights and sunny beaches. Franny's husband – Maris' father, George – was a workaholic stockbroker who refused to divert his attention from the NYSE and NASDAQ long enough to do anything that resembled a vacation.

The night following Jameson's return with his mother-in-law, Thursday the 12th, was a slow spot in the Dyvan Pharmaceuticals program, so Maris and Jameson had chosen that night to begin their transit to the Old World lifestyle in which they were about to immerse themselves. They'd done their research. Talked to people and pored over websites. The place in Vegas to go for Spanish cuisine – genuine *Spanish*, not Mexican or Central/South American, please! – was a place called 'Badajoz' on Charleston Boulevard. They'd studied its menu from top to bottom, and had decided before even setting foot in the place every element of their celebratory repast.

They each left their work-issued cellphone at home that evening. Nothing would be allowed to interrupt their special time together.

On his late evening flight home, with an annoying plane change in Dallas, Rex pondered what Stephen had revealed – and hadn't revealed – earlier that afternoon.

It would require some digesting. And unfortunately some follow up. And even more unfortunately, the Metro Detective Bureau budget didn't allow much for out-of-state travel, so how he was going to achieve any meaningful investigative time back east was a big question mark. Frustration was engulfing him. This homicide was like no other in his eighteen-year career, and he wasn't quite sure how to approach it.

The only thing he decided was that as soon as he was airborne, he'd no longer be 'on the job.' So he ordered a beer. He enjoyed it so much that he ordered another before landing in Texas.

At Love Field, Rex found a pub that served up a 24-ounce glass of Lone Star Lager, and that, along with a jumbo order of mesquite onion rings, constituted his dinner. The corned beef sandwich was still a vivid memory.

Contented, he dozed across west Texas, New Mexico and most of Arizona. His frustrations were forgotten for the moment.

16

The past work week hadn't ended well, with two of my staffers, Hermie and Kinchy, calling in sick with what turned out to be a fear of Friday the 13th. Since I had suffered the same phobia until I was in my mid-twenties, and had only conquered it through hypnosis, I knew I had to be tolerant of such nonsense.

On Monday, I sent the duo links to a few websites on hypnotism. "It worked for me," I wrote. "Please try to be cured by Friday, the 13th of October."

By now I'd had several occasions to join the bartenders in their now-semi-weekly staff meetings. They'd made a few observations, and Jackpot had collected several good photos of a man with a spattering of moles on his right cheek; photos collected on the 7th, 10th and 12th. Today, the 16th, Gray confirmed it was the same 'Mr. Mole' he'd seen on several occasions, dating back to November or earlier. Next up for examination was a rather dorky-looking individual, a man in his 20s who sipped all day on iced teas and/or spiked energy drinks while fiddling on his cellphone and his tablet. Ate no food except the LOL's complimentary snack mix, talked to no one other than an occasional bartender. On a few occasions, he'd appeared to be making a pass at Tapper, but she brushed him off and gave a glare and a head tilt at the 'eye in the sky', which pivoted to capture the gentleman's likeness quite clearly. Sadly, the poor guy would win no beauty contests. Gray recalled he'd seen him talking with Maryland on New Year's morning after everyone else had pulled out, but had no details. He'd been seen maybe a couple of times since.

I was appreciative of the intelligence and promised to pass it up the chain. Everyone knew good old Ira Brickner was the first rung on the ladder, and the chances of a positive reaction, and perhaps even gratitude, were therefore slim. "Don't worry, I won't let this info die there," I assured my cohorts. Gunnar, Leo, they'll all hear about it." This satisfied the four bartenders and made their clandestine efforts seem worthwhile. But for some reason, lead bartender Grayson Moore seemed a bit reticent. When the others had dispersed, we sat down for a quiet one-on-one.

Turns out Gray was distraught about the approach of Inauguration Day on the 20th, just four days away. There'd been no response from above about the suggestion he'd made over a week ago. I assured him I'd follow up and get back to him tomorrow.

I scurried back to my office and enjoyed a gourmet lunch of salami, Swiss and pickle on Jewish rye, an apple and barbeque potato chips – 'gourmet' only because it was so much more than I frequently had – and I managed to make a productive afternoon of it. Phone calls and emails returned, paperwork produced and sent on its way, and appointments made. The earliest – and most urgent – of those appointments was a 3:30 today with the ParaSpec president, Leo Stein. I had an important matter to discuss with the man. I chose that time because I had an out-of-office meeting at 5 that I didn't want to be late for.

My day was coming together nicely, I thought. Far better than anticipated.

It was the MLK holiday for much of the working world, but that didn't apply in the hotel business. We worked it like any other day. Civil servants like my hubby enjoyed a paid holiday, so we used the occasion to meet at my place of business, which he enjoyed doing from time to time. We agreed on 5 o'clock – at the LOL, of course – and were pleased to see our friend Grayson Moore manning the ship. Grayson, however, was not a happy man at that moment.

His discontent became readily apparent to both of us. Mase and I stood there as he unloaded his frustration. To be perfectly honest, it was fairly entertaining, in a pathetic sorta way.

"Damn new electronics, who the hell needs 'em? All I ask is for something *not* to be shown, and they punish me with a slap in the face and *this*!" Gray gestured upward at the two technicians who were installing the second of three new HDTV monitors. The old ones were about 36 inches and at least five years old. The new ones appeared to be at least 54 inches, and were being positioned so that every table in the establishment would have a view of at least one screen (from at least one seat); previously there were several tables that had no view. Gray said, "Charlie, my friend, my dearest comrade, what the fuck is happening here? Mason, tell her to do something ..."

I decided Mase and I had been entertained enough. There were real tears in Grayson's eyes. "Calm down, Gray. Fifty minutes ago I left Leo's office, and he said he thought your concept was ingenious. He basically said that since the election was so divisive, it makes perfect sense for the ParaSpec to be diverse in our presentation of news and entertainment options for Inauguration Day." Gray listened intently, waiting for the punchline. "As you know," I continued, "many folks are eager to welcome the 45th President, and look forward to watching the festivities in D.C. Others want no part of it. As a business, we cannot take sides. Our role is to provide lodging, dining, gaming and entertainment experiences for *all* our guests. Therefore, the Ecstasy Ballroom has been set aside for the viewing of inaugural events, but these screens here at the LOL will be operated at the sole discretion of the lead bartender on duty." I beamed at him, knowing he'd be pleased.

Gray's mood changed quickly and dramatically, and for the first time ever I saw the man tongue-tied. He did a double-take. "You mean ... uh, now ... does that mean I've really got permission to show what I want on the 20th?"

"Really does. Dawn to dusk, and beyond!" I grinned at my friend, delighted to be the messenger of good tidings. "Each new TV can show anything on cable or take a feed from one of the three DVD players. You can show the same thing on all three screens, or show three different things at once. All equipment will be at ground level in your supply room, so no more ladder climbing for anyone."

"Goddamn! I love you for this, Charlie!" he exclaimed.

"As well you should, Gray. But seriously, I was just the messenger. The credit goes to Leo Stein, who refused to stick his head in the sand."

"My man, Leo," Grayson said. "Hot damn, that man is brilliant!"

Mase gestured towards a four-person high-boy and said, "Can you join us in a celebratory drink, Gray?"

"As long as it's H2O," he replied. He knew the rules, and followed them rigorously. "What'll ya have?"

This reminded me to get out my work cell and dictate a quick message to Ira, copying his secretary, Jewel, as well as Maris, Hammy and Gray: "Official notice to whom it may concern at the Paradise Spectacular: I, Charlie Champagne, am officially off duty on Monday, January 16th, as of 5 p.m. Pacific Standard Time. I will resume my duties at 7 a.m. on Tuesday, January 17th." I hit the SEND button and said, "There. Yes, Gray, a flute of Veuve Clicquot, please. A nicely chilled flute."

Gray and Mase knew that my hasty email was to officially 'sign out' for the day, so I could imbibe in something above zero proof on property. It was a trick of the trade I employed infrequently, lest anyone think of me as a lush (little did they know!).

But this seemed like a special moment for all of us.

I removed my name badge and put it in my purse. I was officially a civilian.

We finished our drinks, thanked Gray (who had comped them) and before leaving invited him and his husband, Jackie, to a cookout at our house on Saturday. We then proceeded to the rooftop Spectacular Steaks 'n' Such, where we shared some heavy-duty apps that served as our dinner. A superb finale to the evening!

Mase and I drove home in separate vehicles, obviously, and I beat him by five minutes because he had to detour to refuel and wash his Tundra. He'd been on a junket to the desert north of Moapa over the weekend and had not yet removed the filthy evidence of his adventure.

Rex phoned just as I was pulling onto our street, Stardust Circle, and apologized for being incommunicado since his return from Ohio. He'd returned late on the 11th and here it was the 16th. "Believe it or not, I learned some good stuff that I wanted to share with you, but my higher-ups had other ideas about how I should use my time." He ranted on about having to attend a mandatory – and virtually useless – two-day session on workplace harassment, and then talked about a flurry of homicides that had kept him and the rest of his team hopping all weekend. "The new year is bringin' out the crazies, I guess," he said, rattling off a list of killings that had occurred since he'd last spoken to Charlie. The latest and most mystifying – a twentysomething couple discovered in a shallow grave by a group of off-roaders in the hills east of Coyote Springs – was the case that Mase had worked on Friday and Saturday, the one that had encrusted his truck with several layers of desert mud and dust.

I was still sitting in my vehicle in the driveway when Mase pulled his now-sparkling truck in next to me. With a hand over the mouthpiece, I explained that Rex was about to start downloading the latest in his investigation of the Pierce case. Before uncovering the mouthpiece, I also asked my dearest to pour me a glass of something with bubbles in it and bring it out to the driveway. "Pretty please."

"Hola, Rex!" Mase hollered, before he scurried inside.

Rex and I had already discussed the results from his office's shotgun style questioning of more than half of the ParaSpec employees. It had produced little for all the time, effort and hubbub involved. A few of the banquet servers reported seeing Ben in the back-of-house at two distinct times, when he should logically have been out in the hallway heading to or from a restroom or drink/dessert refill station. But the accounts did not dovetail, and Rex had written them off as unreliable.

But while the New Year's event staff could be of little help, one ParaSpec employee had provided information quite useful to Detective Scharffenberger's investigation. That individual was Jameson Kean, Director of VIP Services for Mr. and Mrs. Pierce during their visit, which had begun on Wednesday the 28th of December. I had given Rex a heads-up about Jameson before they met, based on the sketchy tidbit Maris had fed me over a week ago.

"Kean informed me," Rex said, "that although the Pierce's suite has regular housekeeping service, it also includes the services of a butler, who is supervised by Kean. The butler's duties include tidying up. Collecting used bottles, glasses and food dishes, emptying trash containers, and so forth. While neatening up the desk, Roberto, the butler, couldn't help but see some rather interesting handwritten notes, likely scribbled by Mr. Pierce while listening to voicemail messages. Most of them seemed to be business-related, but a few were clearly not. I figured I'd probe the issue when I was in Ohio visiting Mrs. Pierce, but she was pretty closed-mouthed about everything.

More interesting is what I learned from the vic's brother, Stephen. He didn't personally tell me a whole lot, but visiting him revealed quite a bit."

"Like what?" I asked eagerly. This was a police matter, of course, but Rex had voluntarily launched into his little exposé and my curiosity was understandably aroused. That wanna-be detective streak in me was showing its colors.

"Like a lifestyle that's a bit beyond his means, that's what."

"I thought he was an exec at the Pierce family-owned company, just like Ben."

"He is," Rex confirmed, and I could envision that signature wry grin of his through the phone. "But Ben was a Senior VP pulling down about one-point-five mil a year, plus bonus. As a Regional Sales Director, or whatever his title is, Stephen makes about a third of that but looks like he enjoys a standard of living way beyond his means. I gotta wonder how he comes by it."

I was hooked. "Gimme a 'for instance.'"

"For instance, Charlie my friend, the man's got an enormous home with gated acreage, right on the shore of Lake Erie. Fancy wheels parked out front. Hired help, probably a live-in. Boat dock with a small dinghy to get him to downtown Lake Haven, where he keeps – get a load o' this – a 28-foot, double-mast sailboat and an Icon A5 amphibious fold-up plane sitting in the slip next to the sailboat. In a nutshell, the guy is living the high life and seems obsessed with his toys."

"Sure doesn't sound like his brother," I said.

"And he flaunts it. All you gotta do is look at that Maybach, a $200,000 vehicle, sitting in front of a four-car garage with six inches of snow on it! He's either stupid or ostentatious as hell, and I really don't think he's stupid."

Before hanging up, Rex informed me that he got the Pierce's sons' cell-phone numbers from Stella and would be calling them soon, maybe even tomorrow. "If the homicides in this county would slow down and give me a chance to do a little catch up. I finally did touch base with that Burfurd woman the other day, but it was a bad time for both of us. So I'll be meeting with her at your lobby bar on the 2nd of next month."

"Glad to hear that. I think you'll get along with Maryland."

"Hey, I see you pronounced the *d*."

"She's trained me," I told him. It was true.

"Funny. She told me it didn't matter to her."

"See, Rex. I think she likes you already."

17

It was a maiden voyage for the two nearly-identical vehicles, blasting south on Interstate 71. Beyond the Mansfield exits, they let the horses loose – all 460 of them (in each car) – and cranked it up to 98 mph. Just briefly. Could've gone waaaay more, but there was no sense tempting law enforcement this early in the trip.

Origin: Ohio.

Destination: Arizona.

The plan: Drop the red one in Columbus, the yellow one to continue on.

The route: I-71, I-70, I-44, I-40, I-17, I-10, I-8, with a few minor diversions. Cleveland to Yuma in 33 hours, so said Google Maps. Their hope was to do it in 28.

The Corvettes were up for the challenge, despite snow and ice, sleet and rain. Brayden Pierce, owner of the yellow one, was pleased to have his brother Byron along to share the driving duties. 28 hours seemed ambitious, but doable.

The pool and its adjoining snack shop/bar were closed for the winter, but that didn't stop the slender man with sharp facial features from sitting at one of the outdoor tables. He went into the adjacent LOL, ordered his drink and took it back to his table. The pretty dark-skinned server wasn't working or he'd have insisted that she deliver it to him.

Jackpot – sole barkeep at the moment – was charged with keeping tabs on everything, and he noted the presence of this young man, who'd become a fixture. Gray Moore had already nicknamed him Bird Boy. Jack made entries into his Notes app and stealthily snapped off several photographs.

Things amped up when another man joined Bird Boy. He was older, but not by much. Early to mid-thirties, perhaps. This new fellow looked vaguely familiar, and when he turned his face, a nickel-sized mole on his lower cheek became evident. That's when Jack remembered: he was watching the same man that both Gray and Artie had showed photos of at last week's meeting.

Jackpot immediately dialed Charlie Champagne. He described the scenario outside by the pool, and Charlie grabbed her cellphone and hurried to the escalator. She arrived just in time to see Mr. Mole stand, shake Bird Boy's hand and crack what looked like a smile. First time any of them had witnessed that emotion on this guy. Charlie surreptitiously took about a dozen photos herself, thanked Jackpot and returned to her duties upstairs. Mr. Mole disappeared beyond the pool, from whence he had come.

They did Indiana in a blizzard, Illinois in sleet. Missouri and Oklahoma dried out and they whizzed through them uneventfully in the dead of night.

With Byron at the wheel, they pulled off for gas and a fast-food breakfast at a Flying J near Amarillo. Dawn had broken. The weather had improved considerably, though patches of white along the roadside were evidence of the storm's recent passage through the Texas panhandle.

As soon as they were back on the road, with Brayden at the wheel now, his cellphone jingled. It was the beginning of a busy telephonic morning. By the time they'd passed Albuquerque, both young men had talked with

Charlie Champagne and their respective lady friends – one in Arizona, the other in Alabama – and Brayden had also endured a lengthy interview with Rex Scharffenberger. At its conclusion, the lieutenant said he'd also like to speak with Byron sometime soon.

"I'll tell him the next time I see him," Brayden assured the detective.

Once they'd hung up, Byron was full of questions. Listening to 12 minutes of half a conversation was frustrating. "What will you tell me next time you see me?" he asked.

"He asked why you'd snuffed out dear old Dad."

"You have a lousy sense of humor, brother dear."

"He just said he wanted to pick your brain too. The guy's thorough, I'll say that."

"Well, thanks for running interference," Byron said. "I'll have to think about what I wanna say to this dude."

"Just answer his questions, but volunteer nothing extra."

"You sound like a defense attorney."

"Just sound advice," Brayden said with a knowing smile as he maneuvered onto a ramp to old Historic Route 66. They were in Gallup, New Mexico, and he was fatigued from driving, needed a restroom and something to munch on.

And the Corvette needed a fill-up too; it was guzzling fuel like it was lemonade.

With Byron at the wheel, Brayden now relaxed and mentioned his plan to enter a big e-game tournament set for the following Sunday. It would be his first since being accepted to the Pro Division of the Regal Cavaliers, a prestigious group with a hefty price tag attached.

"You really oughta join," he urged Byron, and not for the first time. "You can afford it." They'd both received a generous monthly living allowance since starting college, and had no reason to expect it to change even with their father's death. $5000 a month covered a whole lot of extras beyond tuition, lodging, chow and condoms. Especially if you were a good money manager, as both boys were learning to be.

Byron startled his older brother then. "I already did. I was gonna surprise you."

Brayden glanced over at his sib, grinned, fist bumped him and exclaimed, "Well goddamn, bro, consider me properly surprised!"

They had just entered Arizona, the final state in their trek. But the longest, with 300 miles to Phoenix and nearly 500 to Yuma. The 'Yellow Flash' was up for the trip, as were the two freshly energized Regal Cavaliers.

Brayden was so revved up that he put in another call to his girl, Paige, to tell her that he was 'back home in Arizona' and couldn't wait to see her that evening.

'Dyvan 2017' concluded without incident on Tuesday afternoon. Everyone – client included – seemed enormously pleased. No one more so than Maris, who was simply delighted that it was *over* and she had *survived*. She had an exciting adventure in her immediate future, and just wanted to escape the hotel and the city before some calamity appeared out of nowhere and altered her plans.

It was a burnout of epic proportions and she needed relief in the worst way. The antidote was packed in her purse: two passports and two boarding passes.

She and Jameson – who was equally eager, though not coming off a super-stressed assignment like his wife – managed five hours of sleep that night. Granny Franny and the girls were all up early to see the travelers catch their 5:30 taxi ride to McCarran.

The 8:10 flight to Miami left at 8:22 that Wednesday morning. Maris Kean allowed herself a huge – and quite audible – sigh of relief. People twelve rows behind her heard it and wondered aloud about its origins. She didn't care a whit. It was her long-awaited vacation, and she'd sigh all she wanted. They ordered Bloody Marys and then Maris played word games on her phone while Jameson read an equestrian magazine. Eventually, they both dozed off.

Jameson dreamt of himself exclaiming "Olé" as he chugged down the jetway for their flight to Spain. Though he had never piloted a plane in his life, he dreamt himself in the cockpit seat of the giant Airbus, hollering, "All aboard!"

Maris's reverie was five thousand miles ahead of her husband's. She envisioned the two of them in bold-colored outfits, dancing flamenco on a stage in Seville. When she awoke, she realized it was the same vision Charlie Champagne had spoken of back on New Year's Day. Gasping, all she managed to say was, "Holy crap!"

"What's that, my love?" Jameson asked, as he opened his eyes and faced her.

She explained.

And he said, "Aye, I guess 'Holy crap' sums it up, doesn't it?"

As he sat in a craft beer pub at Phoenix Sky Harbor, Byron Pierce put in a call to the Las Vegas detective. The lieutenant had gone home for the day but a pleasant-sounding woman named Sgt. Quiñones was working late, and she seemed knowledgeable about his father's case. He answered her questions, and – as his brother had counseled – offered nothing extra. As he disconnected, he somehow felt as if he'd dodged a bullet.

He ordered another Buckeye IPA, and called his brother to report on the conversation. Brayden was pleased and doing fine, only 40 miles from Yuma. Byron then called his true love. Jill happily informed him she'd just arrived with her parents in Louisville, where they were staying overnight with her aunt. She was eager for the road trip to Columbus with her father in the morning. Weather forecast was favorable.

He told her he expected to be back at his frat house by 3:00 in the morning, ready to hook up with her by early afternoon … as soon as he was assured her daddy was on the road out of town. He had no desire to cross paths with that man any time soon.

18

Maris headed off on vacation as soon as her Dyvan group departed, and she'd emailed me from Miami on Thursday to report all was well, and to gush about the generous cash tip Dyvan had given her on the last day. I congratulated her and Hermie on a job well done. It went without saying that she'd have shared her monetary reward with him. Ingrained protocol. It got me to thinking about how different groups can be from one another. Some generous and genuinely appreciative, others much less so. And regrettably (but understandably), there was zero gratuity in store for any of the Casino Marketing events like New Year's Eve or the Super Bowl.

Oops – I mean 'Big Game.' In our business, use of the term 'Super Bowl' is prohibited because the omnipotent National Football League has it trademarked, which means it can't be used in connection with any commercial, profit-making activity ... which the casino industry obviously is. Anyway, the Super Bowl was gonna be played on February 5th, and I had a major Big Game extravaganza to produce for about 2,000 whales (an apt nickname for those high-rollers) who would be in attendance.

Happily, soon after that event wound up, Mase and I would be beachbound, off on our Playa del Carmen escape ... with solitude galore. I could hardly wait! I'd finally be able to spend my hoard of 210 pesos left over from last year's visit to Mazatlán. That impressive bankroll, at last assessment, was worth about eleven U.S. dollars. But it was burning a hole in my purse, screaming *¡Vámanos!* every time I saw it.

Now that the inauguration strife was behind us, I could breathe easier. The separation of factions at the Paradise Spectacular had been orchestrated by Grayson Moore with considerable help from the folks upstairs. The Ecstasy Ballroom had been set aside for inaugural viewing from 6 a.m. until 10 p.m., complete with snacks, sandwiches and bar service. At the LOL, Gray manned the ship – with help from Tapper – and he showed an array of personally selected DVDs: TV #1 paraded a collection of classic cooking shows, including some from Emeril Lagasse, Two Hot Tamales, Two Fat Ladies and even a few ancient Julia Child episodes. TV #2 was devoted to old sitcoms and cartoons, even though children were not a part of the LOL's customer base; Archie Bunker, Happy Days, Smurfs and Flintstones populated this lighthearted collection. Gray's favorites were on TV #3, which was the only one he could completely see from behind the bar; it showed highlights of Super Bowls XI, XV and XVIII, all of which his cherished Raiders had won.

Gray called me late in the day to report it had all been well received. He was happy as a pig in a puddle of mud.

I look forward to sleeping in on Saturday mornings. By 'sleep in' I mean 7:30, more or less. So I was less than thrilled when my cell phone blared at 6:20 on the morning of the 21st and disturbed a fantasy dream that was taking place at the LOL. Something about Suzy with a pile of $100 chips stacked neatly on the bar, and she was buying drinks for the house. I hated to wake from that one!

Turns out it was Detective Scharffenberger – Rex, to me – who apologized for the break-of-dawn phone call and then proceeded to tell me the gist of what he'd learned from the Pierces' sons during the boys' recent cross-country drive. It wasn't so much facts that troubled Rex as it was Brayden's tone of voice, and Byron's attitude when Sgt. Quiñones spoke with him. Both young men seemed to be trying to mask some long-ingrained hostility towards their parents – more Ben than Stella, it seemed – and did a poor job of conveying a true sense of mourning for their dead daddy. To me, it was disconcerting to learn that all was not as smooth in the Pierce household as I'd been led to believe since first meeting these lovely people a few years ago. I learned the twin Corvettes were less a pair of generous Christmas gifts than they were inducements to keep their rocky relationship quiet, the bribe unknown to their mother. "Daddy bribing his sons, can you imagine?" Brayden had snarled sarcastically to Rex. Byron had seemed equally bitter, and hinted that the root of their animosity was in the boys' rejection of Great Lakes Fixtures and Plumbing Supply for their future careers.

Rex then added, "Just for the record, their alibis are pretty weak, since no one can substantiate that they were really home during that entire time period. According to them, they both returned to Cleveland on December 18th and stayed there throughout the long Christmas holiday until their drive back to Arizona a few days ago. But I'm not convinced – there are some big chunks of time that are unaccounted for."

I now considered myself pretty well caught up on the official investigation. Gratified that my prodding of the boys had resulted in them speaking to the detectives, I thanked him for sharing what he'd learned. I almost found myself forgiving him for calling at such an ungodly hour.

Before we said goodbye, Rex also reminded me he had an appointment to meet Maryland when she returned from her trip back east, in about ten days. This compelled me to lay out some facts about Maryland that I felt it was important for the detective to know going in to his meeting with the one-of-a-kind Miss Burfurd. Basically, I told him the following:

- Maryland is a gruff and earthy woman in her early 50s, with a less-than-stellar repute.

- Maryland may have lived her life on the edge, but she's always leaned towards the side of lawfulness.

- Maryland is compassionate and understanding, and bends over backwards for those she cares about.

- Maryland has little use for those with whom she deeply disagrees.

- Maryland is quite wealthy, having amassed her affluence through an initial inheritance coupled with her own shrewd investing in the right things at the right time. She owns real estate here and there across the nation, including a lounge/motel/brothel in Pahrump that she's currently trying to get licensed for live entertainment and a few slot machines.

- Maryland's parents are both living back east, had never married, and are as different as night and day.

What I didn't tell Rex was that we at the ParaSpec don't know (though we are great at speculating) why Maryland likes to hang out at the LOL. Is it just the ambiance, a *Cheers*-type place where everyone knows her name? Or is she searching for male companionship, a man she can latch onto and take a bite out of? Every time I ponder that last possibility, *Maneater* by Hall & Oates hits me like the pop-up surprise of a child's jack-in-the-box.

About 10:30 that morning, I texted Grayson to make sure he and Jackie were still on for our afternoon barbeque. He assured me they were, and sounded as upbeat as he ever had. Clearly, he was still in a happy place after yesterday's turn of events.

Jackie St. Nevis was possibly a better cook than I was (and I'm not too shabby), and he'd be bringing some unidentified hot hors d'oeuvres (he loved to surprise people) to precede the spatchcocked Cornish hens and filet mignons I was prepping for Mase to grill. My guy loved to cook outside, and did a consistently fine job. Also on my docket were a big green salad, a side veggie dish and a peach chiffon pie, the latter being a creation I'd whipped up last night. Gray wasn't much of a chef, but he could sure shop for wines and champagnes to pair with every course. I was sure he'd not disappoint.

There was never a shortage of topics to chat about when the four of us got together. As expected, Gray was still raving about his new TVs and how much his client base had appreciated the escape from the pomp and ceremony that had consumed Washington and countless other places across our land yesterday. He'd managed to catch virtually all of the three Super Bowl videos, and was still exhilarated by his Raiders' conquests over the Vikings, Eagles and Redskins. He'd lived up in the Bay Area during the team's first residency in Oakland, and remained a fan after they'd moved to L.A. Talk naturally drifted to the current state of NFL football, and who'd be crowned the next champion in a couple of weeks. The two division championship games to be played tomorrow would finalize the match-up for the 51st Super Bowl on February 5th. Sadly, Gray's Raiders had been ousted from contention two weeks earlier.

A little jabbering followed about the NHL and how we were all looking forward to the new Vegas team's season that was fast approaching. Ever since his college days in the Midwest, Mase was big on the Blues, but I could foresee his new allegiance shifting to the new Golden Knights with ease. I'd always liked the Ducks since I hailed from O.C., but I too would no doubt support the new Vegas team when they arrived.

Finally shifting away from sports, Mason asked Jackie about the recent big event he'd arranged and orchestrated in Hawaii. Jackie's St. Nevis Productions, Inc. (SNPI) was a global event planning outfit, and the Hawaiian job may have been the latest, but certainly wasn't the most remote. He'd traveled to Iceland, Barbados and Costa Rica over the past few years.

The Maui job was a lavish weekend celebration hosted by a Powerball winner who'd purchased and renovated an aging waterfront inn near Kihei. The 'grand reopening-under-new-management' shindig ran from noon

Friday through Sunday midnight a week ago, had netted SNPI a handsome five-figure return, and had been a delightful change of scenery to boot!

I'd done enough chatting and listening for any decent hostess. I retrieved the birds and the beef and delivered them to Mase, who was anxious to begin grilling. We were all very hungry.

Everyone devoured zealously. There was unanimous agreement that the menu had been conceived and executed perfectly. Gray's wine selections were exquisite, as were Jackie's hors d'oeuvres.

Once we'd all sated ourselves, someone brought up the Pierce murder, and while I was not enthused about rehashing it, I offered an abbreviated update. It was difficult to convey progress, however, since Metro was actually moving quite slowly towards identification and apprehension of the murderer, and there was only so much I felt at liberty to share anyway.

19

The modern-day Maryland Carolina Burfurd carries business cards that identify her as 'Lifestyle Communicatarian,' whatever that means. It doesn't mention that she is also a jokester and prankster, but those she definitely is. To evidence that, she'd bought a few picture postcards on her current trip, and sent Grayson Moore one with a photo of the White House on it. Her timing was outrageous – it had arrived smack-dab on the 20th – with *'There's a spare crib in the Lincoln Bedroom, Grayboy. Come visit! Your faithful servant, DJT'* scrawled across the back. He fumed and tore the card to shreds.

A few days later a card with an intense hurricane scene landed in Charlie's Monday morning mail. *'My destructive cousin Matthew sends his regards!'* was all it said, but Charlie knew its source. She recalled Maryland was in the midst of a month-long swing along the east coast to visit both of her parents.

Charlie admired the older woman's fortitude. The despair of nurturing one aging parent after another had to be challenging.

She tacked the card to her wall as a reminder of the many blessings in her life.

A few bumps here and there, but at least no devastating hurricanes.

And having friends with fortitude.

Clark County Sheriff Mickey McGraw was full of positive energy this Monday. His beloved Falcons had thrashed the Packers the day before and were Super Bowl bound for the first time since '99. The nice wager he'd put on them at Aristotle's Sports Book gave him a Rocky Balboa throw-your-arms-in-the-air moment. His Georgia roots were paying off! For Big Mick, the positive mood was all he needed to launch his almost-innovative idea – 'almost' because he'd read of the concept being used twice before, once in Texas last year and another time a decade ago in Great Britain. A crime-solving task force.

He'd originally thought of making his special task force eleven people, but had scaled back to only seven. It would still fit with the 'community friendly initiative' the new Las Vegas mayor had mandated for the behemoth law enforcement agency. The phone calls he'd be making today were the initial step in the process.

Paige Lansing was growing concerned. Brayden had canceled their date on Sunday, and to her it had been a special occasion. Her sister from Utah was in Yuma, on her way to San Diego for a job interview, and had looked forward to meeting the new boyfriend. And Paige had eagerly anticipated showing him off. But Brayden had called midafternoon and said he couldn't make it, claiming to have 'suddenly come down with' a mysterious ailment he couldn't – or wouldn't – identify.

Now, on Monday, he was still short-tempered and she began to suspect that his condition had more to do with his recent fascination with e-games than anything physical. She knew he'd joined a new club, and was playing in some a high-stakes tournament soon. Or maybe it had already happened. She didn't know, and hesitated to ask.

By noon, the sheriff had talked to the two academics who would be the cornerstone of his task force idea. The two that would cause the community to hold it in high esteem. They were both acquainted with the Pierce case and each said they would consider it an honor to serve.

The final call Mickey McGraw made that day would be the most challenging. He phoned Undersheriff Lauren Gomez about 2:30 p.m. and asked her to fetch Detective Lieutenant Rex Scharffenberger. "Three o'clock, and bring your coffee mugs. This could take a while."

The toughest sell of all was coming. He refilled his own mug and waited. .

Charlie's Tuesday morning was fraught with difficulties and frustrations, and they dribbled on all day long. Her mood matched the hurricane photo tacked on her office wall.

It began even before she reached the office. A chilly downpour, coupled with a wind-ravaged umbrella that had failed to do its job. She arrived looking like a wet rat. Ira happened by the office just after she got in (remarkably early for him) and made an unappreciated joke about her appearance, which further set her off.

Her verbal response: "Yeah, a new umbrella's on my shopping list."

Her non-verbal response contained an array of expletives. Ira moved on, in the general direction of his office.

Charlie grabbed some coffee and two powdered-sugar beignets (Grayson Moore had brought in a dozen to the CCSMs, still conveying his gratitude for the new TVs and the banishment of Friday's inaugural to a faraway corner of the hotel) – which cheered her a bit. Then she opened her emails and the bottom dropped out from her already-dismal disposition. The oldest unopened message was from one of the two Israeli ladies she'd worked with earlier in the month. It was cordial, but quickly got to the point:

'*Dear Charlie: We are still telling our colleagues back home what a fine job you did for us two weeks ago. Your property is attractive and was most accommodating to our needs. I regret to inform you, however, that my colleague Sally became ill on our flight to JFK on 9 Jan, and had to be hospitalized in New York for two days before being able to continue with the trip home. The doctor in NY said it was food poisoning, most likely from spoilt meat. Further toxicology tests here at home have confirmed this.*

Our theory is that the salmon served at our 8 Jan awards banquet was the culprit. Have you received any other complaints?

Please understand we do not hold you personally responsible, but Sally's husband is rather livid and has consulted with a liability attorney. I felt compelled to warn you of the potential for litigation in the future.

Cordially, Golda Razim.'

Charlie stared at her screen in disbelief. She read the message again and decided one course of action was to forward the message to Ira Brickner and let him deal with it. Trouble was, Ira was not the type to handle it himself. He would either ignore it or delegate it, and if he was in a delegating mood it would most likely fall right back into her lap. Besides, she could actually deal with it herself, as such scenarios were not uncommon and the response always began with the complainant filling out a Security Incident Report. There was a PDF of the form residing on her computer, and she attached it to a response to the woman on the other side of the world:

'*My dear Golda: I was deeply saddened to learn of Sally's illness. I trust by now she has had a complete recovery. I have attached a copy of our in-house Security Incident Report, which is the first step in officially lodging this complaint.*

Sincerely, Charlie Champagne.'

She decided to delay sending this until 3 p.m., taking advantage of the ten-hour time differential between Las Vegas and Tel Aviv, so Golda would not see it till after Wednesday's sunrise in Israel, because Charlie had no wish to deal with a reply anytime soon. She blind-copied Ira, Leo, Sammy and the in-house legal counsel.

Charlie had spent 20 minutes on that single issue. Irritated by her lack of progress, she continued with the other emails that had accumulated overnight. Must've been two dozen of them, but most were routine or unimportant and it went quickly. She finished in 10 minutes and was ready for the daily Security Report that she always saved for last, because it often conveyed good general hotel info, and occasionally something germane to her operation. And invariably there was something worth a good chuckle or two: a drunk locked out of his room, a peeping tom report; things like that.

Today's report out of Gunnar Block's office was mostly trivia, but one item caught Charlie's eye. It was heartbreaking with a humorous edge, but the fact that it involved one of the kingpins of Kinchy's current in-house client raised a red flag for her.

A guest named Elliott Kee had been a bit tipsy at bedtime, placed his expensive watch and a wad of cash in the in-room safe and gone to bed. The next morning, his wife Harriet had reheated the prior evening's leftover tea and an explosion ensued. It was quickly determined that Mr. Kee had mistaken the microwave for the safe, and as a result his $8,000 Blancpain was in several hundred pieces and soaked with lotus blossom tea. The man's bundle of cash survived, although a bit damp. The security report said damage was confined to the microwave and its immediate area, and it seemed unlikely that the hotel would attempt to charge the guests; it was clearly an accident. It also stated that the couple seemed quite upset and accused the hotel of negligence for having insufficient warnings on the microwave.

Charlie was flabbergasted. Negligence by the hotel? Failure to warn against the perils of nuking your overpriced timepiece? Or maybe failure to label the safe as a potential instrument of destruction? She had no idea if Mr. & Mrs. Kee were rational folks or conniving types who would seize on any opportunity to file a lawsuit. She didn't know, but the matter hung heavily alongside the issue of the food-poisoned woman from Israel.

The afternoon dragged on, and after sending the email to Golda Razim and then checking on Kinchy and her group, Charlie created an excuse to leave early. She related the unfortunate watch incident to Kinchy, who then pointed out Mr. Elliott Kee and said he'd seemed to be in good spirits all day. Charlie regarded that as a good sign, but there was still an uneasiness festering within her as she headed out to the parking garage.

At least the storm had taken a break, though more was expected later in the week. But once in the garage, she was met with a dead battery – left her lights on after the morning storm, she assumed – and had to call AAA and wait for emergency road service to arrive.

She stopped on the way home to get a new umbrella. BOGOs at Walgreen's, a sale she couldn't resist.

Mason Champagne's Tuesday had been a downer as well. He was thankful for the 'Good Mood Jar' that he and Charlie kept filled with folded chits of paper with annotations of happy dates and events from their past, or things in their future worthy of joyful anticipation. The idea was for the contented spouse (in this case, Charlie) to draw a chit at random and have the troubled spouse (Mase) read it and express a happy recollection associated with it. It usually took only two to four such drawings to snap the distressed half of the duo out of their funk. It was premised, of course, on the fact that their relationship had a multitude of positive memories and promises (ergo, a jar full of chits) that could be called up to expunge the occasional negativity in one's life and turn moods rosy once again.

Thankfully, it worked. Mase hurried home, eager to be liberated from the lousy mood one of his staffers had thrust upon him late in the day. He arrived at his usual 5:45-ish, a bit surprised to see Charlie's Renegade parked in the driveway. Her schedule was more erratic than his, but she was rarely there when he rolled in. He found his wife engrossed in a cooking magazine that had come in the day's mail, sitting at the kitchen island with a nearly empty glass of pinot noir in front of her, and from the level of wine in the bottle he could tell it was her second glass. He came over and kissed her on the top of her head, but she barely responded.

Clearly, something was troubling her too. And just when he needed to lay his own troubles on her. Not an ideal scenario. Tonight the jar might be called into dual service.

He dallied in the bedroom, retrieving the Good Mood Jar from a closet shelf and strategizing their use of it. Finally returning to the kitchen in sweats and an Iowa T-shirt, he grabbed a glass and poured a generous slug of pinot from the bottle. He put his arm across her shoulders as he settled onto the stool next to her.

"Bad day, huh, babe?"

She nodded wordlessly.

"Yeah, me too."

"Really?" Charlie seemed surprised and genuinely concerned. But he was not to be sidetracked.

"Yeah, we'll get to that later," he said, as he produced the jar, removed its lid and slid it in front of her. "You know the rules here." Of course she did; she herself had created the scheme, after all.

Charlie reached into the jar and pulled out a chit, unfolding it and reading: "September 29, 2007." The rules called for saying the first thing that pops into your mind, while making eye contact with the other. "Married my dream man," she said with a smile. There was a sparkle in her lovely brown eyes.

Second card: "Lust in front of the tortoises. Who had the bottom?" She turned a little pink as she vividly recalled the scene. "You did, you chivalrous angel!" They laughed about it now as they had back then, on Espumilla Beach, since bottom was not the ideal place to be on those jagged volcanic rocks.

About to turn over the third card, Charlie halted and drilled her gaze directly into Mase's. "Let's save the rest for next time. Mission accomplished, Mr. Romantic. I feel so much better already."

Mase leaned in and gave her a warm lingering kiss. "I'm glad it worked. Wanna download?"

"Maybe later. Tell me your problem now."

Mase tried to downplay it, since he too felt much better after being reminded of their marriage in Laughlin nearly ten years ago and their sexual escapades in the Galapagos Islands years before that. "My rising star quit today, no warning, no nothing. But I'm sure—"

She looked at him with disbelief. "Whaaa … who d'you … *Suzy?*"

"No, Willis," he clarified. "About 3 o'clock, he sauntered into my office and asked if I had a minute. I said sure, thinking he was gonna divulge a technical finding in one of our working cases. In the minute I had to rationalize, I remember thinking how much I hoped for a break in the Ben Pierce case. But no such luck. He told me he was transferring within the department, and Friday would be his last day with CSI." Mase paused as he recalled the conversation. "I was stunned, but I know that young people think about upward mobility all the time, often more than their allegiance to their current unit. But here comes the shocker: Willis is destined for the homicide team, under the direction of your pal, Rex. Soon as he graduates the academy, he'll do an accelerated few months as a street cop before becoming a full-fledged gumshoe." As he spoke, Mase felt his emotions surge, despite believing only minutes ago that he was running on an even keel.

Charlie, astute wife that she was, drew a chit from the jar, unfolded it and held it up to him. "Read," she instructed.

"Resort Espectacular en la Playa."

"And?"

"It's where I'm taking my true love for a week of R&R on February 8th."

"And it's more important than Willis Bronx, Golda Razim, and everyone else in our lives. Let's not forget that!"

Mase hesitated, then broke into a broad grin, and replied, "It's not forgotten, babe. But who the heck is Golda Razim?"

"Oh my, I guess I never explained *my* crappy mood, did I?" By now she was loosened up and let it all spill freely. The ruined umbrella and getting soaked to start her day. Ira's remarks. The email and veiled threat from Golda. The Security Report detailing the Kees' bizarre watch destruction incident, which might also lead to legal headaches for the hotel. Her dead battery and the 40-minute wait for AAA to give her a charge. "But I do have some good news," she added at the end.

"I believe we're ready for some," Mase observed.

"I bought us four new umbrellas on the way home. Two for you and two for me. All for less than 20 bucks."

"Be good to have in Mexico," Mase remarked cleverly.

"We won't be needing them there. I had a vision yesterday." Charlie smirked and gave her man a great big slobbery kiss. "Eight days of pure sunshine. Trust me!"

She went back to her magazine, humming James Taylor's *Mexico* as she did. Not to be left out as he foraged in the fridge, Mase began humming right along with her.

Trust her? Of course he did.

20

January's been a helluva month so far. I'm more than ready for it to be over, but there's still a week to go.

Mase and I both recovered from our disheartening Tuesdays, thanks to the trusty Good Mood Jar and some cozy snuggling afterwards. It would take more than a few negative external influences to damage our Champagne lust-and-love affair.

Wednesday dawned clear, but I still packed my two umbrellas, one to keep in my vehicle and one in my office. You never know when the clouds will decide to burst. Mase embraced my logic and did the same with his new bumbershoots.

The day was routine until I got a call about 10:30 from my venerable friend, Rex, suggesting – no, almost demanding – that we talk. I said I had some time to talk right now but he wanted to do it in person. We settled on 1:00 at the B-L-D Spectacle, the hotel's all-hours coffee shop, and he said he was buying lunch. The last part was happy news (even though I had a comp account). I hoped the rest of our meeting would be as welcome.

I hadn't tried to guess what Rex wanted to talk about, and he seemed a tad flummoxed when he sat down at the B-L-D. His entire countenance seemed a bit altered, as if he had been stripped of a segment of his soul. I felt I'd gotten to know the detective fairly well in the 25 days since we'd first met, but suddenly I was seeing a slightly altered version of him. New and improved? Not really. Beaten down? Not that either, not quite anyway.

"Charlie, my friend, some changes are in the works. I'm still trying to make sense out of it, deciding whether it's a good thing or not."

"Spit it out, Rex. I'm a good listener and you know I'll be straight with you."

He smiled at that, seeming to find reassurance from my words. It was as if I was figuratively holding his hand.

He proceeded to explain what had occurred in Monday afternoon's meeting with his two bosses, Sheriff Mickey McGraw and Undersheriff Lauren Gomez. They had decided to form a task force to look into the baffling New Year's Eve murder at the ParaSpec.

"A task force? You mean more than you and your homicide unit?"

"Yes, more than just us." By now Rex was frowning and I could sense the consternation boiling up within him. He went on to say that 'Big Mick' had this crazy notion that he, Rex, and his crew needed some assistance to give him ideas on who offed poor old Ben Pierce and where that perpetrator might be found. He'd never heard of such a wacko idea, despite the boss man's contention that he'd read about instances where it'd been used successfully. Rex opined, and I couldn't help but agree, that it sounded like an outgrowth of the LV Mayor's 'community friendly' focus for Metro.

Despite his misgivings, I had to admit – to myself, initially – that maybe the idea had some merit. But I kept my mouth shut and let him continue his rant.

"He tried to enlist a few of his old law enforcement colleagues – retirees, all of them – but they were all lukewarm to the idea, so he turned towards academia. There he found success. He's got two lined up who are bursting at the seams with crime-fighting enthusiasm. Or so the big man says."

"Bosses can be frustrating sometimes," I empathized. "I think you know my situation here. Just bite the bullet and create your own work-arounds, that's what I do."

"Sounds good on paper, but I'm not sure how I can *work around* this one. Wanna hear the details of my charge?"

I told him I did, and I listened intently, like a shrink with a patient on my proverbial couch, trying to catch subtleties and undercurrents in Rex's account.

"Mickey's thinking a seven-person task force. Me, as chairman. And you, dear lady, as vice-chair." My eyebrows arched at that, but I managed to hold my tongue. "Your security man, Gunnar Block, and someone else from the hotel that you select. That's six now, counting the two from the colleges. I need one more to make it the odd number he's set on."

I found an opening and said, "First of all, I'm stunned and scared and honored all at once, but I guess honored will overrule. Of course I'll serve, because what occurred on January 1st was an affront to both me personally and to my hotel. I'm sure Gunnar would be delighted to be included – insistent upon it, actually – and I think I'll enlist my man Hammy, if that's OK with you," I said. "He'd be happy to be involved, and would be devoted to the cause."

Now came the delicate part, and I had to word it carefully. "I have one more thought, a specific person who might just do a bang up job for you – for *us*, for *our* task force – as the seventh member. And that is Willis Bronx. I realize he's still in my husband's shop for the near term, and will then be attending the Academy before officially becoming a beat cop and part of your homicide team. But there's no reason he can't serve as a useful part of our team, assuming we'll be meeting in the evenings. I've met the kid; he's young and energetic, insightful and—"

"Fantastic idea, Charlie!" Rex bellowed. It was the happiest I seen him since he'd sat down.

Our lunches finally arrived; a BLT for Rex, a Cobb salad for me. Two iced teas.

When we'd finished, Rex arose and said he had to hurry back to his office. He remained in a jovial mood, much more so than when he sat down a half-hour earlier. "You're making the impossible seem almost possible, my friend," he said gratefully.

I liked making people's 'impossibles' possible. It's one of the reasons I got into the business I'm in. And if truth be known, I was liking this task force idea. Community service of a new sort for Charlie Champagne.

Chelsea on my Mind.

Yeah girl, maybe a task force back in the day could have saved you. So sad, my heart weeps.

After lunch I approached Hammy and he bought in without hesitation, as I knew he would. If he weren't such a super caterer, I suspect he would have chosen to be some kind of investigator. I had to hope that he didn't find this mission too enthralling, or I'd have a ship-jumping subordinate like Mase had with Willis.

Speaking of Willis, another challenge was to sell him on this assignment – which he'd likely love and do well at – without him feeling his promotion to Detective Trainee was being diverted or sidetracked. Rex managed that, and had enlisted Mase's input. The three huddled late that afternoon, and all came out of it happy as clams at high tide.

Before the week was out, Rex was pretty well accepting of the new approach, as he became more convinced that it could provide some valuable help while in no way eroding his authority. And he'd had no problem convincing Gunnar Block of the important role he'd be able to play, and how well the assignment would look on his résumé. He jumped at it, as had the others. And OK, I'll admit it, I was right there with everyone else – eager to don my deerstalker hat and do what I could.

By Saturday the 28th, my focus was totally redirected. The efforts of the Loony Roosters committee were about to kick off the Lunar New Year. Festive red decorations were in place, and special hors d'oeuvres were being served at all of our restaurants, including an abbreviated menu at the LOL (which normally had no food service). Chinese traditions were being followed as closely as possible.

Although the ParaSpec didn't attempt to compete with the hotels that specifically catered to the overseas Asian markets, we had done a bit of local advertising. Our Marketing Department had even blitzed California's biggest cities with some promos. So our festivities were pretty well attended and our sleeping room occupancy was at 92 percent. That had to make Leo happy!

The highlight of the day was the dragon that meandered its way through the public areas on the lobby level and out onto the patio and pool deck. This display lasted about 15 minutes – or so it had on its trial runs a few days earlier – and was scheduled to begin every two hours from 11 a.m. until 9 p.m. The dragon consisted of 12 people tethered together and covered with a long red printed fabric that hung to their ankles; they were volunteers from various departments, mostly kitchen workers and valets, who were between 5'6" and 5'9". Eight men and four women, whose only requirement other than their physical height was that they could prance around hunched over for 15 consecutive minutes. The leader was allowed to stand a bit straighter and was the only one who had a view of where they were going; his 11 followers simply spent 15 long minutes watching the floor in front of their feet. You couldn't help but admire their tenacity.

I witnessed the 11 a.m. and 1 p.m. runs of the dragon, the second time following it from the front desk through the casino and in and out of the LOL. I saw Tapper and Artie at the LOL, also enjoying the show, and

I waved from afar. Tapper gave me a wide smile and a thumbs up, and I returned the gesture.

By late afternoon I packed up and headed home. I'd had enough of Saturday catch-up, and I had plans for the evening. Mase and I had a quick bite of take-out red pork tamales from Doña Maria's, enough to tide us over but not so much that we were too stuffed to eat more if the opportunity presented itself. And it just might.

As it happened, Mase and Suzy and I planned to do a variation on a dine-around. More like a smorgasbord of Year of the Rooster revelries, celebrated in several hotels in the heart of the Las Vegas valley. Scoping out the competition, if you will. Intelligence-gathering (as opposed to its more radical cousin, corporate espionage). First and foremost, I wanted to get a look at the décor and entertainment these places were serving up to their guests. Second, I wanted to taste whatever themed food and drink concoctions were being offered. I would be idea grabbing, nothing more. Hence the important distinction between intelligence and espionage. My two comrades would be helping to gather intelligence by virtue of their oohs, aahs and facial expressions.

Long story short, we hit three less-than-impressive establishments. They all, it seemed, had placed marginal emphasis on the Chinese holiday – even less than the ParaSpec had – and by 9 p.m. we were ready to pack it in. We retrieved the Renegade and headed back to Suzy's place to drop her off.

On the way, we were forced to the curb by a fire engine rushing south to a point somewhere beyond us; Mase, who was driving, handled the situation with aplomb while Suzy and I remained locked in girl gab. That is, until a snorting sound erupted from my cellphone. A news alert, I suspected; they arrived several times an hour, and weren't usually worth interrupting our nattering. But minutes later when I finally peeked at the drop-down, my jaw dropped and I blurted, "Holy shit!" Mase and Suzy looked alarmed as I turned the phone towards them so they could read the headline: 'Fire at the ParaSpec.'

21

I was back down at the office bright and early Sunday, the 29th. January still hadn't released me from duty. In this business, the calendar cuts you little slack; you worked when you had to.

My sleep the night before had been sketchy, as I tossed about with horrific fiery dreams that looked like the MGM in 1980 or the Monte Carlo in 2008, possibly worse. In truth, the blaring headline the night before had been wildly sensationalized.

I got there early and found time to make a pot of coffee, sit down and review the happenings of the past twelve hours. The TV news we watched last night told all there was to tell. In 30 seconds, it showed our Lunar New Year's dragon dancing through the casino, with fire engulfing the last two dancers in the procession. "And in our final story," the Fox 5 reporter had said, "The Year of the Fire Rooster arrived with unexpected irreverence at the Paradise Spectacular Resort tonight. Two valet parkers, who began the night at the rear end of the dragon, quickly transformed their serpentine wiggling into a frantic drop-and-roll routine that smothered the flames, thus sparing the resort significant damages or the need to evacuate."

I'd appreciated the station's attempt to inject a bit of levity into a serious report.

It was 7:12 when the coffee was ready and I poured myself a welcome cup. I would have an hour or more to myself before anyone else showed up, and I decided to work on menu design for the Hearts and Diamonds Ball. That was an annual Casino Marketing event held on the Saturday night nearest to (usually before) Valentine's Day; this year it would be the 11th of February. In addition to the customary high rollers – this time from the Las Vegas region only – the invitation list also included local dignitaries and the ParaSpec's four Employee of the Quarter (EOQ) winners from the previous calendar year. It was a fancy-schmancy dinner with a musical ensemble on hand for entertainment and dancing afterwards. The CCS team's primary charge was the food and beverage execution, since a musical group called the Spectaculeers (their bass player was Sammy's nephew) had already been booked, and door prizes had been arranged and donated by an outside planning firm (owned by Leo's daughter-in-law). My assignment was to create a food shopping list for the head chef to use in ordering.

I sincerely hoped the event went well, but I wouldn't be on site to oversee it. I planned to be soaking up the culture and cuisine of Playa del Carmen with Mase on that night. Maybe I'd pick up some south-of-the-border V-Day ideas so we can give next year's Hearts and Diamonds Ball a bit of an international flair.

This year's event was being left in Maris' capable hands. I had no worries.

In addition, our very own Hammy Yamasaki would surely be in attendance, since he was the third-quarter recipient of the EOQ award. Well deserved, I might add. I looked forward to his report on the function, and I was expecting Maris to give me the scoop on Hammy's date; we knew next to nothing about his love life.

Ira Brickner popped in, displaying 'his royal assholiness' (one of his several adjectival nicknames) as usual. We were exactly seven days out from the 'Big Game Spectacular' as he pranced into my office at 10:20 a.m. and demanded to know if I'd begun working on the tailgate menu, the halftime menu, and had I arranged the cadre of 27 Lady Gaga look-alike servers, 27 male servers, the 18 portable bars with 36 bartenders in football jerseys, the extra portable bars by the betting stations, the betting stations themselves, and the floor set-up plans for Enchantment and Fascination Ballrooms and the Shangri La al fresco terrace.

"No prob, Ira," I informed him smugly. He looked mildly stunned, so I elucidated. "Every one of those things, plus the approved Fire Marshal plan, has been wrapped up tight as a drum since mid-November, with the exception of the Gaga servers. Seems a dozen of them were playing elf at the North Pole for your Christmas Eve epic, but we signed them on as soon as Santa gave them their releases. All 27 are ready to go."

I regularly delighted in squelching Ira's criticisms, suggestions or any other crap he came up with, but never more than this time. By now, if you were him, wouldn't you be asking yourself: *Just what the hell am I contributing to this organization?* But Ira wasn't that self-reflective, because he was as clueless as he was useless. The higher-ups might need him to keep them informed (though I doubt he did a decent job of even that, given his frequent absences), but I certainly didn't need him micromanaging me.

There was no way the Big Game Spectacular would not be a rousing success, regardless of whether New England or Atlanta prevailed on the field. And it would happen in spite of – rather than because of – the so-called leadership of Ira Brickner.

On Monday morning, the Sheriff's task force was the top local news item. Mickey McGraw got behind the microphone at the news conference his people had arranged. All the TV stations were present, and several radio stations, as well. All the CCSMs huddled around and watched on our office's 27-inch monitor. I cranked up the volume and we listened to Sheriff McGraw speak.

"After consultation with the elected and administrative officials of the entities to which Metro answers, we have decided to form a task force to investigate the murder of a man who was visiting our community with his wife, and welcoming in the New Year at the Paradise Spectacular Resort. The victim, Benjamin Pierce, from Ohio, died at the hotel on New Year's Eve. Unfortunately, we have so far been unable to close the case. Our lead detective, Lieutenant Rex Scharffenberger, will remain in charge of the investigation and will draw upon the task force as an additional resource in tracking down the many leads we have and ultimately apprehending the perpetrator."

As expected, McGraw was full of generalities, making it sound as if the task force's formation had been a group decision by his office and the 'elected and administrative officials' that he referenced. Everything was *we*, rather than *I*. I seriously doubted that he'd consulted with anyone, because he was not answerable to anyone. No one but the voters who'd elected him twice and were likely to do so again in November. And, less directly, of course, to the mayor of the largest city in Metro's domain, who had been the originator of the community friendliness concept.

Before long, McGraw turned the mic over to Rex, who added a bit of rah-rah support for the task force. But I knew he still wasn't enamored of the concept, and I admired his show of enthusiasm, given his apprehension. I wondered if he was going to talk about the makeup of the task force, but he did not. For that I was grateful, as I really didn't want my name splashed all over the 5 o'clock news for all of Southern Nevada to hear.

After the broadcast, I shared with my assembled staff that I was to be Rex's co-chair, and that Hammy would also be a member. In the interest of completeness, I added that our Director of Security, Gunnar Block, would also be joining the task force.

The only other thing Rex had said was that the kickoff meeting of the task force would be Wednesday evening of this week, the 1st of February.

Quite a rushed schedule.

But hey, you don't hear Charlie Champagne complaining.

22

'New Month, New Approach' asserted the banner atop the front page of Wednesday's *Las Vegas Review-Journal*. February's first issue arrived with this proclamation of hope, along with a slew of photos and abbreviated biographies.

The formation of the first-ever Clark County Violent Crimes Task Force, convened to investigate the January 1st murder of Ben Pierce of Shaker Heights, Ohio, was being championed with great fanfare. A photo of Pierce accompanied the photos of the seven task force members.

Charlie recognized the photos of herself, Hammy and Gunnar as the standard headshots provided by the Spectacular HR Department. Hers and Rex's were 50% larger than the others, since they were chair and vice-chair. She quickly perused the photos of the two from academia – the only ones she didn't know – and read their one-paragraph bios. She had no idea that Dr. Cruz, the criminologist, and Dr. Grigio, the psychology professor, were such heavyweights in their fields. Their presence would certainly add to the task force's significance.

Though not pictured, Metro Sgt. Shelly Lee was mentioned as an assistant from Sheriff McGraw's office who would serve as the task force's recording secretary. Rex had already mentioned Sgt. Lee to Charlie; he viewed her as Mickey McGraw's leash on the task force that McGraw had created but was not a part of. Rex therefore regarded Lee with trepidation, but Charlie decided she'd give her the benefit of the doubt and would try to befriend her early on. It was the old sugar vs. vinegar premise that she'd successfully employed throughout her professional career.

The article mentioned that the group's kick-off meeting would be that very evening, Wednesday the 1st, but said it was not open to the general public. The time and location of the gathering were not disclosed, and would not be revealed to anyone who phoned the Metro offices.

Charlie and Mase had been having coffee and a quick bowl of yogurt with honey and raspberries before heading off to their respective offices, but both had been more engrossed than usual in their reading. Mase rose and Charlie offered him a quick glance at the front page, since he'd been reading sports and comics during breakfast. "No time. Gotta run. I'll read the office copy when I get a chance."

"Just so you remember what's happening tonight. I probably won't be home earlier than 9. If you miss me too much, you can admire my photo on the front page."

Mason chuckled, kissed her and headed out to his truck. But in five minutes, she was in his ear on his cellphone. "Forgot to ask if you know this woman, Shelly Lee."

"Big Sarge Shell? Sure, everyone at Metro knows her. Most people wish they didn't."

Charlie moaned, knowing that was a bad sign for her plan to get on the good side of Lee.

Maryland Burfurd was up early, well before the sun, and kissed Pa on the forehead without waking him. They'd said their goodbyes the night before. She was out on the front walk at 4 a.m. when the Uber sedan arrived to transport her to the airport 20 miles away. Her flight out of Raleigh-Durham departed on time at 6:30 Eastern and she was on the ground in Las Vegas by 10:20 Pacific, even with a 90-minute plane change in Kansas City.

Her time spent with Pa – and yes, even Ma – had been relaxing and gratifying, but Maryland was always pleased to return to the city she now regarded as home. When she deplaned, she stopped at a sundries shop for some much-needed eye drops and caught a glimpse of the newspapers on display: *NYT, WaPo, LAT, WSJ* and of course the local *LVRJ*. The latter's bold headline and large array of photos caught her attention. Most noticeably, her friend Charlie and the cop she was scheduled to meet with tomorrow.

She bought the paper, and read the lead piece during her second Uber ride of the day. By the time she reached her Torre Elegante condo on Koval Lane, she'd finished the article and felt relatively well-versed on recent happenings related to the murder. Knowing that she had left the city a month ago, when the Pierce murder had just occurred, she was a bit surprised to see that it was still fresh news. She would, of course, answer the detective's questions, but she doubted she had anything to offer that would be of any help.

Still, the prospective meeting with the detective intrigued her. After all, she'd spent most of her life sizing up men in one way or another, for one purpose or another. Rex Scharffenberger was definitely a man she planned to evaluate as a professional, as a social acquaintance, or – who knows? – even as a potential relationship interest. For Maryland, relationships came in all shapes, sizes and intensities, and no one should be ruled out of any option until she deemed it necessary.

Yes indeed, she was looking forward to finally meeting this lieutenant with the four-syllable surname.

The task force was meeting at Fire Station 112 in the southeast sector of the valley, not far from the UNLV campus. Attendees had been provided the location the night before, and were requested not to share it with anyone else.

In his email broadcast, Sheriff McGraw had informed the others that *'It is NOT a public meeting, in the legal sense, as no public policy issues will be considered, recommended or voted upon. As a task force participant you are a volunteer member of my staff. And I again extend my heartfelt thanks for your assistance as we work together to bring to justice the perpetrator of this crime.'*

Lieutenant Scharffenberger echoed these sentiments in his welcoming remarks, and asked everyone to give a brief introduction of themselves and to explain why they wanted to help, and – more insightfully, perhaps – *how* they expected to contribute. In truth, everyone had been solicited to join, but all seemed perfectly willing to do their civic duty.

Charlie was especially impressed by the two she knew nothing about: Dr. Roscoe Max Cruz, head of the Criminology Department at UNLV, and Dr. Chloe P. Grigio from CSN, the valley's multi-campus community college. Cruz was renowned for his studies of criminal motivation and provocation, and had over three decades of teaching and research under his belt. Grigio was considered an expert in the field of human pathology with an emphasis on psychotic deviations and had many publications to her credit.

It had been naïve to expect more from a kickoff meeting than introductions and a reiteration of their assignment, so Charlie was pleased when Rex shared a thumb-drive that he said might be helpful to all of the task force members. He cautioned everyone that, although they weren't legally bound to keep its contents confidential, it would best serve their mission if they did so. "Especially avoid those media vultures who are sure to attack when you least expect it," he added wryly.

Rex wrapped up with an announcement that the plan was to hold task force meetings on a weekly basis, every Wednesday evening. "But," he added, "we have to deviate slightly from that for our next two gatherings, since our vice-chair, Ms. Champagne, will be out of town. So let's go with Tuesday the 7th and Thursday the 16th, if that works for everyone." No one objected, so it was cast in stone.

"Thank you all," Charlie said to the group. "I think if I'd cancelled one more vacation, my husband would be your prime suspect in another murder."

Jameson Kean was gearing up for another big weekend. As Director of VIP Services, his workload had peaks and valleys that corresponded with the scheduling of Casino Marketing events. The Big Game extravaganza was one of the hotel's largest draws of the year, and came close on the heels of the multi-day NYE/NYD event only five weeks earlier. He juggled a lot of people during the winter months, and had to use care to separate the two events in his mind; some people were attendees of both and had differing requirements for each.

On this Wednesday afternoon, he had assembled his entire butlering staff and gave them the final rundown on person counts, room assignments and their individual assignments. He opened the meeting up for discussion, but little was said. The butlers all seemed content with their duties. When the meeting broke, however, one young man remained behind.

"Mr. Kean," he said politely, "I have no problem with *who* you assigned me to, but I'm hoping these couples are not staying in the same suite where the Pierces stayed in December."

"Of course, Bobby. I understand that you felt close to them and would like to avoid the constant reminder of what happened to Mr. Pierce. Let me look at the list again." Jameson pulled a spreadsheet from the blue folder in front of him, paged through it and looked up with a smile. "The folks I've got you down for have four suites: two in the Amazing Tower, and the other two in the Wonderful Wing. As I recall, Stella and Ben … uh, I mean the Pierces, were in the Awesome Tower for their New Year's visit."

"That's right," Roberto Guanacaste nodded. "Thank you so much, sir." He left the director's office with a smile on his face and a bounce in his step.

With Bobby G's departure, Jameson put the wraps on things and departed as quickly as he could. Maris had promised a dinner treat, but wouldn't say what it was. He loved it when she did that; her 'Wednesday wonders' were always enticing and delicious. This would be her first culinary foray since their return from Spain, so question marks had been dancing in his head all afternoon.

Because he had a number of outside business endeavors, Jameson kept a box at one of the many private mailbox outfits that dotted every community in the country these days. His was on Bonanza Road east of the 515, right on the way home. He stopped there about 5:30, emptied the contents of his box, and dropped off a 6" x 9" envelope marked only with the initials 'B.P.' He resumed his homeward trek, with a stop at a liquor superstore to acquire some Angostura aromatic bitters and blue Curaçao for tonight's special concoction. He and Maris surprised each other like this twice a week. Maris did the food and he did the special pre-meal beverages on Wednesdays; on Sundays they reversed their roles.

Charlie expected the thumb drive Rex had distributed to be perfunctory blather and not much else. Still, she wasted little time in checking it out shortly after arriving home.

She was wrong. The little electronic device contained a copy of the official police reports from Officer Ainsworth, Sgt. Quiñones, and Lt. Scharffenberger, as well as press releases from the Sheriff. It even included a couple of reports from the CSI team – *led by a guy whose last name matched hers, no less!* – regarding soils, rosemary leaves, tire marks, fabric samples and dried blood samples.

Most fascinating was a detailed timeline of events from 6 p.m. on the 31st of December until 6 a.m. on the 1st of January, a 12-hour span that encompassed the lead-up to and aftermath of the crime. Within that timeframe were multiple entries that had been developed from the differing investigative paths; it appeared to be a tool that could help identify opportunities for criminal skullduggery.

Mason Champagne had to wave a reheated plate of Kung Pao Chicken beneath his wife's nose to jar her loose from her analysis of the timeline. She got the hint and came to the table. It was 9:20, and he'd reheated a complete take-out meal from Fong Kong, their favorite Chinese eatery, and complemented it with a nice Sauvignon Blanc from Argentina.

"I think I'm really gonna enjoy this challenge," she said to her husband as she struggled to capture an elusive chunk of white meat between her chopsticks.

"Looks like Rex provided you with some good backgrounding," he said, in reference to the spreadsheet she'd been inspecting moments earlier.

"I'll say! I never thought that he and Marisa would go so far for the task force, but if every member studies it as diligently as I plan to, there's bound to be some helpful leads, theories, solutions, whatever, coming out of that collection of brainpower."

Charlie paused to add some soy sauce to her spring roll, then added, "That is, unless we get sabotaged by your friend 'Big Sarge.'"

Mase laughed, swallowed some rice and said, "Shelly? She has absolutely no bedside manner, as you may have learned for yourself, but she's really pretty benign. She'll go back and give Big Mick her impressions of everyone, or everything and anything that's discussed, but I don't think sabotage is part of her playbook. She just likes to give the impression that she's in charge."

"Rex did a good job of taking charge," Charlie said.

"Glad to hear that."

"And I actually think I may have made a little connection with Sgt. Lee after all. Wanna guess why?"

"I can't possibly. Tell me."

"You, my dearest. She realized that my husband was the esteemed Dr. Mason Champagne who headed up Metro's crime lab. She actually called you 'doctor' repeatedly, so I'd say she's impressed with you and hopefully – by osmosis or whatever – me as well. We spent several minutes chatting about you – *us*, I should say – starting way back at that Anteaters game where you and your buddies traded your seats with short ladies behind you. Our Laguna Beach bungalow, Laughlin wedding, the works."

"The works?"

"Well almost. I left out the lust on the rocks and assorted other indiscretions." She grinned and poked him in the ribs, and their lips met. A moment was all it took to ignite things.

"Keep that thought!" he insisted, handing her the finale to their meals before leading her off to their master suite.

In bed, they opened their fortune cookies.

Hers read: *'You will solve a great mystery within thirty days.'*

His read: *'You are your better half's better half.'*

After those thought-provoking messages, a round of 'assorted other indiscretions' seemed appropriate. And most certainly inevitable.

23

Channel 8 reported that, in Pennsylvania, a certain furry critter had predicted six more weeks of winter, but the local weather lady came on with the short-term forecast for Las Vegas. Partly sunny, reaching the upper 60s. Maryland Burfurd absorbed that information as she considered her wardrobe options for the day.

At 2 p.m. she'd be meeting the police detective at the LOL, but she planned to get there a few hours early so she could rub elbows with some friends and have lunch at the 'B-L-D Spectacle' on their al fresco terrace. Their Cobb salad was delightful, and eating it on the sunny patio would be a special treat for a winter day. She pondered the correct wine pairing: Sauvignon Blanc or Unoaked Chardonnay?

Maryland settled on a new outfit – snug black slacks with a lively red print blouse, low cut but not glaringly so – that she'd picked up during her side trip to Raleigh last week. She thought it conveyed her personality and her mood well. A small touch-up with an iron was needed after its cross-country travels inside her luggage.

She had earlier called for her car, a blue Saab convertible, to be washed and detailed for her. January's dust and grime were gone when it was brought around at 10:30. With the temperature still in the 50s, she opted to keep the top up. Maybe on the way home she'd let her hair down to blow in the wind.

Rex approached the meeting with Maryland with much less anticipation. In his mind, she was just another lead to follow – a very loose end, actually – but one he mustn't overlook. He felt quite certain this Burfurd woman was not a potential suspect, especially after discussing her with Charlie, but it was possible she had seen or heard something.

Since he was in a casino environment, he used the opportunity to place a few wagers on the Patriots; a straight win bet against the point spread, and a couple of proposition bets involving running backs and yardage gained. He wasn't quite sure he understood them fully, but his teenaged son, Russell, could certainly decipher them. Something to follow on Sunday alongside the game itself. Earlier in the week, he'd bought eight $10 squares in one of those 100-square grids that circulated in his office; four squares with his name, the other four with 'Russ S' written in. He planned to watch the game with his son; they lived under the same roof but their busy schedules allowed for little quality father-son time.

Rex arrived at 2 p.m. sharp, and Jackpot directed him to the 'young lady' seated by the window overlooking the patio. He reckoned that 'young' was a bit of a stretch, but the woman was certainly far from old. Right around his age, he guessed, and likely a bit better preserved than he was. She was gazing into a cellphone and had a half-empty glass in front of her. Something creamy and classy, by the looks of it.

"Ms. Burfurd?" he said, his approach not intentionally stealthy but definitely catching her by surprise. He recognized that as proof of the hypnotic appeal of smart phone apps.

"Yes, oh my, yes!" she was clearly startled, and seemingly embarrassed at being caught doing a big online crossword puzzle. "You must be Lieutenant Schafter … Scarffen …"

"Rex will do fine," he said with a smile and an outstretched hand. Her hand was soft but her shake was firm. He liked the combination, though he'd never given it any thought before. "And if it's OK with you, I'll just call you Maryland … with a' D' on the end, of course."

His recall and attention to detail pleased her. He sat opposite her and suddenly Tapper appeared. Rex ordered an Arnold Palmer and offered to refresh Maryland's drink, which she declined.

"So you want to chat with me in case I'm the key to your unsolved case? Or maybe I'm a 'suspect'? Is that it, Rex?"

"Not at all, Maryland. I just—"

"Now, I'll admit it does look suspicious. Man gets wasted at just past midnight. And I, who was nearby at the time, suddenly hightail it outta town nine hours later. But there are a few things wrong with that theory." Rex opened his mouth to speak, but she held up a finger. "First off, I had a ticket on American Flight 416, Seat 7A, that I'd purchased the day after Thanksgiving last year. Second, I had a mini-suite at the Harbor Spectacular Hotel in Baltimore that had been reserved for me in mid-December by my friend Charlie Champagne, who got me a fantastic rate. Third, I'm not at all good with a knife. I've never carved a turkey, can barely manage a tender steak, and sure as hell wouldn't know how or where to stab a man to death … or, God forbid, how to separate his hand from his arm. The very thought revolts me. Fourth, I'm just a frail little thing. Can you really see my 130 pounds stabbing a man, dragging him out of sight, and dismembering him?"

Rex listened patiently, and couldn't suppress a smirk. When she'd finished, he leaned in, looked at her solemnly and said, "Ms. Burfurd, you've never been a suspect, so put your mind at ease. You are merely a 'person of interest' as we say in the crime-solving business."

"I see. Well, Rex, you say that as if it's a bad thing. In *my* business, a person of interest is someone to get to know better. Y'know what I mean, Rex?" She all but winked at him.

Rex flushed ever so slightly. "Yeah, I think I do."

Maryland sat up straighter, as if she were a schoolchild directed to pay closer attention. "So what is it you wanted to ask me about then?"

"Well, if you could just give me a rundown on all your comings and goings from the time you arrived at the Paradise Spectacular on New Year's Eve until you left, I'd appreciate it."

And that she did, for the next 20 minutes. Beginning with her walk and monorail ride to the ParaSpec, dinner at the B-L-D, a brief stroll amongst the revelers out on the Strip, and finally her 11:45 p.m. arrival at the same table at which they were now seated, reserved for her ahead of time. "I thought maybe I could see the fireworks out of this window, but I was wrong. The TVs gave a much better view." After the ball dropped, it was chit chat with an awkward-looking, pointy-faced loner who loved spiked energy drinks and playing games on his phone. "Crazy dude, he was. Now, I play solitaire by myself, which is kinda tame, but this guy was competing against a live person somewhere in Southeast Asia, using real money. He'd get real pissed if he lost a round and overjoyed when he won." She seemed to find his behavior amusing but was unable to provide a name for the young man.

"So you never left the lobby level?" the detective asked.

"Nope. Sat here all evening, except for a couple of trips around the corner to powder my nose," she added with a hint of flirtatiousness.

Inevitably, Rex's eyes were drawn to Maryland's nose, even though she'd repeated the well-worn euphemism that had little to do with that body part. "You know where the Fascination Ballroom is located?" he asked.

"Upstairs on the Mezzanine, I think. Which is really just the second floor; why not call it the second floor?" she mused.

"Good point. You ready for another drink?" asked Rex.

"Sure. Brandy Alexander, shaved chocolate on the top. Jackpot knows how I like it."

"Never went up to the Mezzanine level?" He waved at Tapper to come over. "Never got curious and went up to peek at the high-rollers' party?"

"Not interested in that kinda folly."

"Never paid a visit to Charlie Champagne, whose office is on the Mezzanine?"

"Why would I? I knew that party was her shindig and she'd have a dozen irons in the fire. I was sorta hoping for a drop-in from her, but it never happened. She was a busy bee, and all her action was upstairs."

"Who was tending bar that night?"

"Grayson Moore, all by himself at the end. This girl Tapper – not sure of her full and proper name – was there until around 1 a.m."

Just then Tapper arrived with the drink Jackpot had carefully crafted. Maryland thanked her and took a welcome sip. Rex said, "Did you know that during Prohibition Punxsutawney Phil threatened to impose *60 weeks of winter* if he didn't get some booze?"

"You sure jump around," Maryland observed with amusement.

"Keeps the subject off balance. A time-tested interrogation technique."

"Well, mister detective, I'd say you've got your technique down pat … but this old gal's not lost her balance."

"I noticed. You're one of my better subjects lately."

"Should I take that as a compliment?"

"Sure, if you like."

The 'Yellow Flash' sped north, embracing the freedom its driver had allowed it. It wasn't quite like Ohio-to-Arizona in under 30 hours, but it was good times nonetheless. Those fuel injectors needed a good workout, and the wide-open desert produced attractive driving conditions: dry, flat, and minimal traffic interference.

There was no passenger on this jaunt, but this one was all business. He stopped at a gas station in Searchlight, a tiny Nevada outpost, to fill the Corvette's tank and empty his own. Silently, he cussed that second coffee he'd bought as he left Yuma four hours ago.

In another hour he'd be safely ensconced in the Trail's End Motor Lodge on East Harmon, and that would be after detouring to the mailbox and picking up the envelope, the all-important envelope. Trail's End was a small and inconspicuous place, free parking, monorail close. Byron would taxi there from McCarran, arriving 5:30-ish. Then they'd put their heads together while downing a few brews to get loose.

As for the game on Sunday, who really gave a shit? Not him. He was much less an NFL fan than a NHL (Go Penguins!) or NBA (Go Cavs!) devotee, but he disliked sports dynasties and that's what New England was beginning to look like. Ergo, for this one anyway, he'd muster up a 'Go Falcons!' attitude. Maybe the size 2XL 'Matt Ryan' shirt Byron was bringing him would help build his support for the underdogs from Georgia. Couldn't hurt.

24

I awoke to the feel of Mase nuzzling my neck, then sticking his cellphone in my face and whispering, "Next week at this time." On the screen was a drone-shot video of Resort Espectacular en la Playa, the plush digs we'd booked for seven nights, beginning Wednesday. Three days from now ... hard to believe! OK, I admit we were initially drawn to the place by its name – though it's definitely *not* a part of my employer's burgeoning empire – but after giving it the once-over it looked like the perfect getaway spot for us to unwind from the turmoil that had been January. We'd splurged on a villa with a private infinity pool, hot tub and al fresco shower, to make sure February was an improvement.

But it was now Super Bowl Sunday, and Big Game Day duty called. Time to drag my reluctant ass outta the sack, into the shower and down to the office.

Our Big Game doings weren't slated to start till around noon. I landed in my office around 10:30ish, to make sure there were no snafus in our multi-faceted function. The last two years had not run as smoothly as I'd have liked, and it was my objective to be glitch-free this time around.

Imagine that – smooth sailing through a Casino Marketing event attended by nearly 2000 well-heeled folks from all across the country. I mean, this would be a tremendous corporate shot in the arm, worthy of priceless publicity from Portland, Maine to Portland, Oregon.

Hammy had volunteered to be on hand to help me out, so long as I let him wear his Aaron Rodgers jersey; he was still smarting over the Packers' loss to the Falcons two weeks earlier. I didn't care what he wore, and in fact I thought the idea might have benefits if I needed staff to infiltrate the ocean of jerseyed-up whales during the day's events. I knew he wouldn't be the only dissenter from the two competing teams. Attendees would be a strange mix of street clothes and football garb, so I knew Hammy would blend right in. He'd be my culinary eyes and ears, because I really needed to keep a watch on both the quality and quantity that flowed from kitchen to the various banquet sites, where my high rollers were rolling. Gotta give 'em quality stuff, and gotta keep from running out.

One star of our show was the 'Shrimpetizers,' an Aussie recipe that Hermie Stevenson's aunt used to make when she worked as a caterer in Brisbane. Grilled large crustaceans with a spot of creamy risotto, chopped cilantro and julienned jalapeno, wrapped up in a warm-and-wet nori leaf sprinkled with garlicky/oniony spices. A Down Under take on sushi … sorta. Hammy tried one, told me it was scrumptious and promised to bring me one. "Fill up a plate. I'm starved!" I told him. Ten minutes later he delivered two, along with a couple of crispy phyllo cups filled with Boston baked beans and a pair of Georgia pecan praline cupcakes, both in keeping with the regional rivalries involved in today's football matchup. After all that, my hunger was satiated. Temporarily.

Soon afterward, I set out on a facilities check. It was almost 2 p.m. and folks were arriving in droves and picking the choice seats with a view of their favored big screen. Truthfully, with 16 flying big screens in each of the ballrooms, and a multitude of 48" to 70" monitors scattered around, there was no shortage of viewing opportunities. The open-air deck off the Shangri La was an attractive change of pace, and had its share of guests enjoying the 60+ temperature and soft breezes. Setting up the video and audio outdoors proved a bit of a challenge, but our IT and AV teams had done a dry run under similar conditions on Thursday afternoon. No stone unturned.

About half of the tables on the Shangri La balcony had 'RESERVED' signs placed on them, as the Director of VIP Services had been instructed by upper management to preserve certain of the most desirable seating for the upper echelon of the hotel's 'SpectaculaCard' holders. I suspected that he, the Director, took it upon himself to add a few of his own favored clients to that elite group. It was no concern of mine, though it seemed a tad presumptuous.

Indoors, the video feeds were clear but the audio needed a bit of tweaking so that Joe Buck and Troy Aikman could be heard but were not shouting. This, too, had been checked out a few days earlier, but the techs were at the ready to beef up the volume after the rooms filled with hundreds of jabbering people. They also knew they'd probably have to subdue the sound during halftime so that Lady Gaga's show would be entertaining but not overpowering. The last two years had taught us the value of planning ahead.

The gaming stations in the foyer were well populated, with frenzied pigskin bettors making straight wagers on the game's outcome, as well as a host of proposition bets. Would Brady or Ryan end up with a better passing percentage? How many field goals would be scored by the two teams combined? Would the halftime score be more or less than half of the total score? I found the whole concept rather mind-boggling, but of course wagering was the lifeblood of our establishment and had to be encouraged.

The foodstuffs were the lifeblood of *my* part of the production, and so I made it a point to promote consumption. The offerings were many, and I tasted a few as I made the rounds. Nothing fell short of exquisite. When I ran into my Mr. Yamasaki snagging a bite, I offered a thumbs up and asked him to capture everything on his cellphone. I was doing likewise. I noticed a number of guests doing the same – tasting and picturing – and I found myself hoping some of those photos ended up with favorable comments on TripAdvisor or Yelp.

Specially-printed paper napkins with a likeness of our handsome high-rise towers had been ordered by the thousands, and were emblazoned with a customized message:

BIG GAME SPECTACULAR

February 5, 2017

Paradise Spectacular Resort and Casino

Las Vegas, Nevada

Ira would shit a brick at the incredible competence of his team if he'd had the moxie to show up. Which he didn't. He was conveniently out of town so he wouldn't have to visit and personally applaud his staff. He was better at criticizing than praising.

But I had no intention of letting him off the hook; our best photos of every delicacy would be made into 8"x10" glossies, placed in a binder and put on his desk by the end of the day. And I would add a Post-It message strongly suggesting that a personal note of thanks to the chefs, bartenders, IT staff and others for their devotion and creativity would be a wise use of his time.

We'll see how well that works out. He returns tomorrow morning.

Around 3:30 I stopped by the LOL and saw Gray and Artie, both their gazes trained on a monitor, where former President and Mrs. Bush were arriving on the field in a golf cart for the coin toss. Most eyes, in fact, were on this heart-warming scene. Falcons won the toss, but strategically deferred their choice to the beginning of the second half. I wasn't well studied in the nuances of football, but to me this sounded like it might have been a wise move; not spending something of value as soon as you get it sorta corresponds with my philosophy of life. Keep it in your back pocket (or your purse, like my prized 210 pesos) until you really need it.

The bar was offering some special themed drinks that they had created themselves in their own little in-house contest, two of which had been imported into the repertoire of the banquet room bars – that's how good they were! Tapper had created her 'Georgia Sunrise', which was a Tequila Sunrise with peach nectar and peach schnapps replacing the traditional orange juice, and peach pecan whiskey instead of tequila. Jackpot's concoction was a piece of complex workmanship and ingenuity, a 'Bloody Boston Harbor.' It began with a traditional Bloody Mary base, with the addition of clam juice and a dash of baked bean syrup, and a long wooden skewer threaded with alternating baked beans and clam nuggets, capped with a chunk of succulent lobster meat at each end. The banquet bars were offering both these delicacies, and I would later learn they flew off the bars like crazy.

Neither Gray nor Artie seemed bothered by having been 'outmixed' by Tapper and Jackpot, and the two of them were working the LOL during game time. Gray was chief, decked out in a Raiders jersey with 'PLUNKETT' and '16' on it while Artie, in a vintage L.A. Rams pullover with '85' and 'YOUNGBLOOD' plastered across his back, assisted. They were a pair of reminiscing relics, living in the past, but I couldn't help but love 'em both!

The squad of servers for the Mezzanine Level high-roller event were either Lady Gaga look-alikes (27 of them) or gentlemen (27 of them too) bedecked in a wide array of football jerseys, some Big Game players, others currently active NFL players, and a few dredged up from history, like my two favorite barkeeps had done. No one person was conspicuous by virtue of his attire.

Things were well under control and I was trying not to let my feelings escalate into euphoria. The entire program – *my program*, I kept reminding myself

– was a resounding success. There had been no glitches thus far, and I could not imagine one occurring that would dampen my spirits. My menu of delicacies was far more exciting than the scoreless first quarter of the football game, and I only wished Mase were here to enjoy some of them with me. I was planning to bring some home after it was all over.

If there were any leftovers ... I was beginning to have doubts.

I returned to my office to get off my feet, and found some flat shoes stashed under my desk, useful for my next venture onto the floor. Heels sucked at any time, but especially when there was no need to fancy up. Like today. For the moment, I kept my feet shoeless and propped on my desk, and speed-dialed my hubby.

"Exciting game, huh?" he opened, sarcasm dripping. He was an expert at that. No *Hello* or *Hi honey, how are you?* But he was right; a few minutes into the second quarter and the scoreboard still said zip to zip. Thus far, exciting was *not* the word for this contest.

"Yeah, and I love you too."

"Everything going OK at *the Super Big Bowl Game Spectacular?*" Mase loved to ridicule the league's possessiveness of their event's name.

"Actually, my spirits are flying pretty high right now. For the first time ever, a Casino Marketing event is running like a well-oiled machine."

"Thanks all to you, no doubt."

"What, you don't think I called to tell you how good a job absentee Ira did on this showcase event? I just wish I could share some of it with you."

"I could drop by."

That sounded appealing, but I knew I couldn't devote any significant time to him. And it was too far to drive for an exotic drink or two. "You stay put. I'll snag you some goodies if there are any left. In the meantime, eat well and don't forget to watch Lady Gaga," I joked.

"Yum and yuck," Mase said, respectively. For dinner, I'd left him a batch of the same fancy enchiladas I'd whipped up back on January 2nd, which elicited the 'yum,' and I knew his taste in music was way too countrified to enjoy Gaga. Hence the 'yuck.'

"Love you, sweets!" I told him.

"Even more!"

And then, without warning, Lady Gaga's *Born This Way* situated itself in my gray matter.

I, for one, would enjoy the hell out of her halftime show.

Things were looking up for the underdog Atlanta Falcons. It was only their second trip to the Super Bowl in its 51 years of existence (and *their* 51 years of existence). They hadn't won the first time, but with the score at 21-3 as the third quarter began, their fan base was becoming giddy and boisterous.

The two banquet rooms were not segregated by team affiliation, but the Shangri La Terrace had inexplicably evolved into an Atlanta stronghold, by maybe a 3 to 1 ratio. And it was there that everyone's reverie was suddenly shattered by an inexplicably loud noise and a burst of electronic light. Initial reports were rather sketchy, but it sounded ominous.

I heard about it immediately, thanks to the Security Department walkie-talkie that sat near my elbow. I carried it everywhere on a day like today. In a rare moment of relaxation, I'd been composing a quick email to Suzy, asking if she'd enjoyed the halftime spectacle as much as I had. Shocked, I jumped up, pushed the SEND key in mid-sentence, and bolted.

Damn! In a split second, I saw my perfect day turning to shit.

25

Seventeen-year-old Russell Scharffenberger was relishing a full day with his pop, a rarity these days. Even though they lived under the same roof, their lives were both so busy and their schedules so fluid, that they saw little of each other. Today was especially choice, since it involved father-son bonding over their favorite sport, football. Russ was a senior, a good student who'd opted for a stint in the military after graduation, where he would focus on weapon systems telemetry.

His father had been reared in New Hampshire and was a follower of pro sports from the Boston area for as long as he could remember. Celtics, Red Sox, Bruins ... and of course the Patriots. There was no doubt about his favorite in today's game, and young Russ cheered alongside his dad for his dad's team. During the regular season, the youngster who'd been raised in the West was a fan of the Denver Broncos and Arizona Cardinals, but neither team had made it to the playoffs this season.

Halfway into the fourth quarter of Super Bowl LI, Russ was returning from the kitchen with a fresh Sprite for himself and a Heineken for his dad, plus a new bag of white cheddar popcorn, when the unthinkable happened: Rex's work cellphone chirped. He answered it, but only after mulling the idea of tossing the phone off his third-floor balcony. It could not be good news. His cheery demeanor – the product of a Patriot TD and two-point conversion moments earlier – instantly faded as he listened to the dispatcher's voice on the other end. With the score now 20 to 28, Patriots trailing but exhibiting great momentum. Six minutes remaining, the game seemed potentially within reach. But alas, duty demanded he turn his back on it. And on his son.

"Russ, my boy, hate to do this to you. Hate to do it to *me* too. I gotta run. Something's happened at one of the big casinos."

The boy looked at him expectantly.

"Two DBs, and one guess who's gotta go. Record the rest of the game for me, will ya? There's a pizza in the freezer, and leftover chicken in the fridge. No telling when I'll be back."

"Got it, Pop. Good luck."

Russ Scharffenberger knew how to roll with the crap his father wallowed in. He knew what a DB was in cop lingo, as he'd been down this road before. It was why his chosen vocation was a field where he wouldn't be likely to encounter any dead bodies.

Charlie wished to hell it had just been an electrical problem, but the Paradise Spectacular wasn't gonna get off that easy.

By the time she reached the Shangri La, chaos had erupted. The SL ballroom itself was not part of the Big Game event, and was set up for a Monday morning Rotary breakfast. But there was an uncluttered 20-foot passageway along the south edge that gave the high rollers access to and from the 60' by 120' terrace beyond. It was open air, with a pergola 16 feet up that provided some shade, as did the mature grapevine that was intertwined among its crossbeams. A few potted shrubs added to the ambience that made it one of the hotel's most prized venues for small to medium gatherings. An eastern exposure made it ideal for late afternoon events, especially during the warmer months.

Right now, that ambience sucked. Folks were scurrying off the balcony in droves, most along the ballroom passageway – through which Charlie Champagne was trying to swim upstream – while the more daring were leaping over the short perimeter wall onto the plaza four feet below.

At the exit onto the terrace she could see Gunnar Block standing guard. The Security Director was not her favorite person, for sure, but she felt they'd developed a bit more mutual respect and tolerance since last month's scuffle over Rex's attempt to bypass Gunnar and work directly with Charlie. As a result of that conflict, Charlie had come to appreciate Gunnar's ability to grasp the big picture and make rational security decisions.

Would he bar her from entering the terrace to get a first-hand look at what was happening? She'd find out as soon as she could navigate the oncoming tide of panicked humans. No small task.

Instead of denying Charlie passage, Block pulled her aside and cupped a hand to her ear as he explained. "There was an explosion at one of the big screens, and that's what people are running from. Most of them, at least. There are a few who understand the reality of the tragedy that has occurred."

Charlie, looking puzzled, said, "Which is?"

"Two men have collapsed. They appear to have been drugged. EMTs are on the way, but it may be too late."

Charlie stared blankly at Gunnar for a long moment as she processed what he'd told her. Weak-kneed and pale, she muttered, "Oh shit."

"Shit, indeed." Gunnar let her pass, but admonished her to let his officers keep control and to not ask too many questions.

The two victims were quickly confirmed as being 'dead' rather than 'ill.' It wasn't rocket science, and one of Gunnar's men was confident in making the pronouncement.

Victim 1 was a black male in an Atlanta jersey #2 (quarterback Matt Ryan) who had slumped over in his stool, head falling onto the table and knocking over what was left of his designer drink, a Georgia Sunrise. The tablecloth was soaked in orange liquid, and the man's tablemates had all dispersed and left him behind.

Victim 2 was an Asian male in a New England jersey #12 (quarterback Tom Brady) who was found in a similar slouched position at his two-person tall boy table about forty feet from Victim 1. In front of him were the remnants of a Bloody Boston Harbor drink, still in the glass. His table appeared to have been shared with no one else, as no evidence of other drinks could be seen.

Security was doing a capable job of shunting the other customers past the two casualties. Four uniformed Metro officers, who had been on routine patrol along the Strip, arrived within five minutes; the detectives would take a bit longer.

Detective Rex Scharffenberger was in a dreadful mood, as one would expect of a lifelong Patriots fan who'd been dragged away from what might be a comeback for the history books. But he was a professional who knew when he'd signed on as a Homicide Detective that he'd encounter situations that weren't to his liking, both with regard to substance or timing. This one sucked on both counts.

He ran Code 3 along the 215 and 15 freeways, all the way, even after exiting onto eastbound Flamingo. Though he turned the AM radio up full bore to try to catch the end of the last quarter, the siren drowned out most of it.

After reaching the hotel balcony, he tried to keep an ear towards a telecast in an adjacent room, but it was futile. Too far away, too much hubbub. He had a task, and that had to remain his top priority. His only priority.

The first fatality was an advertising company owner named Michael Swann, 44, from Hoover, Alabama, whose firm was headquartered in nearby Birmingham. He had satellite offices in Nashville and Jacksonville. He and his 42-year-old wife Ruth Anne were frequent guests of the Paradise Spectacular, due to their penchant for gaming and their longtime history of visiting the Big Easy Spectacular in New Orleans. The Swanns had been married 21 years, attended Meadowbrook AME Church regularly and had produced a trio of fine young Christian students. Two were 'tweens' at home and Jill, the oldest, was a sophomore, studying international commerce at Ohio State.

Detective Scharffenberger had learned most of that from Officer Rob Ainsworth, the uniform who'd interviewed Mrs. Swann, but she embellished when he finally got to her. She was in tears, but coherent. He learned that the Swanns had shared the table with their fellow high-rollers, Tommy and Margie Jo Stallworth of St. Augustine, Florida. She explained that Margie Jo was her sister, and that Margie Jo and her husband Tommy both worked at Michael's satellite office in Jacksonville, where Tommy was branch office manager.

Ruth Anne Swann confirmed that the two men had been drinking the specialty Georgia Sunrise drinks while she and Margie Jo were drinking white wine. She had been seated to her husband's right, with her sister directly across from her. They'd all heard and seen the big monitor (the one they'd been watching) explode and had instinctively run from the room, and it wasn't until she was off the balcony that she realized Michael wasn't right behind her. She'd tried to go back, but security had stopped her. Panic set in about then, but another security person – a man named Block – had escorted her to a seat at one of the empty tables in the Shangri La Ballroom and asked a server to bring her water and a cool wet towel.

The second victim was a software developer from Pacifica, California. The body was being guarded by a Metro uniform and the female hotel security guard who had discovered him 'dozing' at his table. Rex was able to learn little from them, other than his name, age and address. All this was evident from papers found in the man's wallet. Adam Honshu was 33, and was CEO and Chief of Product Development at Twixxter Gaming Systems in Sunnyvale.

Adam's social security number began with a zero, so Rex knew he was a transplanted easterner. He would have to find someone else to fill in answers to a lot of the questions he had.

The primary question was whether Mr. Honshu had died of natural causes – which seemed unlikely, given his age and that there was a second dead guy nearby – or was the victim of foul play. The same question would have to be asked regarding Mr. Swann, lying lifeless a few tables to the north. Rex figured the M.E. would provide some answers when he arrived. He hoped the doc wasn't as big a football fan as he was, because that would mean he'd be in just as foul a mood.

Scharffenberger left the crime scene in capable hands and headed for the ParaSpec's front desk. On the way, he pulled out his cellphone and speed dialed his comrade from the Metro CSI unit.

"Mase, Rex here. Got a pair here that need you and your team ASAP."

"OK, I can mobilize and roust a couple of the others. Gimme the particulars."

"Your wife's place again. And at the high-roller party again, too."

"Oh, bloody shit!"

"Déjà vu all over again, huh? Sorry to do this to you. Y'know, the game and all."

"Not to worry. We'll be there in 25 or 30. I'll round up Suzy and my new guy."

"Thanks. Hey, how's the game goin'? Had to drag myself away."

"Two minute warning. Pats are marching. Edelman and Amendola, what a pair of receivers! They're on the 21, but it's still an 8-point game."

"Thanks. I'll try to catch a peek somehow."

Rex reached the front desk, identified himself, and asked the clerk for his supervisor. Before long, a bespectacled, attractive young woman appeared. "Tindra Block," she said, extending a hand. Rex shook it, showed his badge and gave her a business card. "You can call me Rex," he said, lately becoming used to offering such a casual greeting.

"How may I help you, Detective?"

"That's an unusual name, Tindra. I like it. Is it—?" he began.

"Swedish or Finnish, not really sure. I have one parent of each."

"Well, Tindra, I'm afraid there's been an incident in your Shangri La Ballroom. The terrace, to be exact. Two men have died while watching the game."

Block raised her hand to her mouth, stifling a gasp. It seemed from her reaction that news of the deaths – now nearly an hour old – had not yet reached the front of the hotel. That was a consolation, Rex thought, albeit a small one, in this afternoon of horrific events. Keeping the mayhem controlled was always an important consideration in conducting an effective investigation.

"I need some information about one of your guests. A Mr. Adam Honshu. Was he sharing—?"

"Adam? Oh my god, was he one of the—?"

"Yes, ma'am, I'm afraid so. Were you and Mr. Honshu acquainted?"

"Yes. I mean no, not really. Just barely. I mean I ... well, we—"

This conversation needed to be moved along, Rex could see that. The woman was looking over both shoulders as she hemmed and hawed and blurted non-committal gibberish.

"Do you have an office, Tindra? Someplace we can talk a bit more privately?" He smiled sympathetically.

"I came to you to ask about Mr. Honshu's rooming arrangements, who he was with, if anyone, questions like that," Rex explained to Tindra after they were ensconced in her private little office, door closed. "But since it appears you're personally acquainted with the man, suppose you tell me what you know about him and we'll go from there."

"Oh geez, lemme see. I met Adam two nights ago – Friday – when my girlfriend Amy asked me to join her for a drink with these guys she'd just met. She said they were 'a couple of Asian hunks.'" She blushed.

"OK, and Amy's last name and whereabouts?"

"Boutella. Amy Boutella, my best friend. She's a server at the 'B-L-D Spectacle,' our 24/7 diner. Works the morning and noontime shift, 6 a.m. to 2 p.m. Anyway, these two guys, Adam and Aaron, started flirting with her over breakfast Friday, and suggested meeting up later in the day. She agreed and said she'd bring a friend. There's no way she would've gone alone to meet two unknown guys on the prowl, so she called me."

"And so you and Ms. Boutella met these two men. Where, when, and what can you tell me about them?"

"We met at the LOL – that's our Libations on the Lobby bar, right over there by the entrance." She pointed, and Rex nodded impatiently. He knew where it was. "Turned out they were cousins, computer nerds from California. Nerds in the sense that they were brainiacs, owned a startup company in that Silicon Valley area around San Jose. But they weren't the nerdy coke-bottle-glasses type of guys, just smart-guy geeks who owned a business of game apps that were selling like Amy's breakfast hotcakes. I mean, they seemed like pretty cool guys."

"What else can you tell me about this Friday rendezvous? I need to know everything you remember about it."

"OK, OK." She dabbed her eyes. "It was about 8 o'clock, and I found Amy at a hi-boy table for four in the LOL, and I sat next to her. She told me to move opposite her; that way the guys could sit in between both of us. We ordered drinks. Chardonnay for me. Vodka and soda, splash of cran for Amy."

"A Rose Kennedy," Rex mused.

"Huh?"

"That's called a Rose Kennedy cocktail. My mother grew up on Cape Cod and used to love 'em. Sorry to digress, go ahead."

He realized that Tindra was so young she probably didn't even recognize the name, much less the fact that Rose Kennedy was the Cape Cod matriarch who'd mothered our nation's 35th president 100 years ago. He regretted his pointless excursion into trivia-land.

Tindra Block resumed her memory recall, saying that the two young men had joined them about 8:20. They'd apologized for being late but gave no reason. Adam sat to her right, Aaron to her left. Each ordered a Dos Equis Lager. Their small talk was meaningless banter, largely focused on the upcoming Super Bowl game. Tindra had explained to the men how they, as hotel employees, were required to refer to it as the 'Big Game,' and everyone got a chuckle out of that. But Adam had said he understood, since he was a businessman and knew how valuable a company's trademarks could be. She repeated to Rex what Adam had told her. "He said something like, 'You've gotta choose your business names, logos and whatever else carefully, and then protect it all with trademarks and copyrights. Anyone infringes, you climb all over their ass.'"

"Smart," Rex observed.

"Yeah, he seemed pretty smart," she smiled sadly. "He said he'd chosen his company's name, Twixxter, and all its products very carefully. He didn't want it to be confused with Twister, that party game, ya know? Didn't want to be confused with Twix, the candy bar, either. But he did want to give the impression that there were, like, risqué elements, which is why he used the 'xx' buried within the name. I remember wondering to myself if that was why they were both drinking Dos Equis. Anyway, it was interesting, at least to me," she shrugged. "It was a fun conversation and he seemed like a nice guy."

"Sure," Rex nodded solemnly. "Now tell me about his friend Aaron."

Tindra reminded him that they were cousins, not just friends. "He was a bit more laid back, not quite as serious as Adam seemed to be. He worked for the same company, I think as the head money guy. Yeah, that's it; Aaron was CFO and Adam was the top guy, the CEO. I think they both made a lot of money, and they were here for the high rollers' Big Game party."

"Is Aaron's last name Honshu as well?"

"Yes. Their fathers are brothers. They grew up near Boston, where both their fathers taught some kind of high-brow science stuff at M.I.T. They said they were only children, so they were raised kinda like brothers. Said they restored a couple of old mansions in Cambridge when they were students and then flipped them for a bunch of cash, which is how they got the money to start Twixxter."

Before Rex took leave of Tindra Block, he learned that Adam and Aaron Honshu had shared a two-bedroom suite in the all-suites Elegant Tower, one that had two separate entrances from the exterior hall. Quite convenient for the private pairings that followed, which the young woman owned up to with considerable reticence. She was 24 and fairly intelligent, but talked more like 14 now and then. "Oh, I'm gonna be in so much trouble! I've slept with a guest, violated company policy on a bunch of counts, and my daddy's gonna be furious!"

Rex suddenly put two and two together and looked at the worried girl. He wrote something in his small spiral notebook. "Your father?" he prompted.

"Yeah, he sorta runs this place. Well, maybe not exactly *runs* it. But close, he's a honcho."

Of course, as in Gunnar Block, Rex reckoned. "Yes, I believe we're acquainted, your daddy and me."

26

It was nearly 9 p.m. when Rex Scharffenberger returned to his condo in Henderson. Russell was now studying his trigonometry text in preparation for an exam later in the week. Seeing the boy so industriously engrossed reminded Rex that despite the depravity and sin that exists in this world – evidenced today by two senseless murders within his domain – the important things in life remained intact. He couldn't suppress the smile that came to his face when he saw the son who was making him so proud lately. Rex eagerly looked forward to watching him grow as the young man prepared to head off in service to his country, a bittersweet moment that was coming all too soon.

Later, as he was reading the newspaper at the kitchen table and munching on some reheated pizza that Russ hadn't polished off, one of his cellphones chirped with an incoming text. Like so many modern professionals, Rex was burdened with both a personal and business phone, but the ringtones Russ had helped him set up told him which was which. Rex was always impressed with his son's technical know-how.

It was the business phone sounding off now, and his heart sank in expectation of another gruesome callout. Luckily, the caller ID was an unfamiliar number, so there would be no more dead bodies for the time being. Probably a robocaller selling something, he thought, though those usually landed during the day. He pushed it aside till he finished the article he was reading about the Celtics' recent victory over the Warriors. 110-93, a nice rout. It took him less than a minute to read and left him in a good mood. It was a good day in Beantown, what with that game and the incredible Patriots overtime win in the Super Bowl.

But suddenly his mood vanished. "Son of a bitch!" he yelled.

He tried not to subject his son to a lot of foul language, but sometimes the cop in him came out when he was upset. Like now. The text message Rex was staring at was short and nonspecific, but for him it carried a clear and ominous message.

'Do you see a pattern, Detective?'

Charlie returned to Stardust Circle even later than Rex had reached his own homestead. She found Mase reclined in front of the flat-screen TV with a Tampa Bay Zoo show on, and a Grisham novel opened atop his newspaper-covered lap. It was hard to tell which form of media had most recently held his attention. Before he had dozed off, that is.

Her movements awakened him as she plopped her beleaguered body on the end of the purple couch nearest his blue recliner.

"You eat something?" she asked.

"Leftover lasagna and a quickie Caesars I whipped up."

"Any left for a beat-up old broad?"

"Nope. But plenty for the most wonderful Senior CCSM around. Sangiovese to go with?"

The thought of a refreshing glass of the hearty red cheered her. "Sangiovese right now sounds even better. Pour me a glass while you reheat and dish up, will you?"

"Will do. Stay put and rest your bod."

Mase disappeared, returning a minute later with a winery glass containing at least nine ounces of her miracle cure. The glass and the wine both came from a favorite spot of theirs in Oregon. He placed it on the end table as she dug in her purse for her work cellphone. There were several messages, but one in particular jumped out at her.

Suddenly, a cry the likes of which Mason Champagne had rarely heard – and never from his wife – permeated their 2400 square-foot home. He immediately came running. She showed him the phone message as she sat slack-jawed, shuddering.

He failed to comprehend its meaning, so she enlightened him. Someone out there was taunting her, and it had everything to do with the day's dreadful happenings at the ParaSpec. What else could it possibly mean?

'Do you see a pattern, lassie?'

Mase insisted that she eat what he'd prepared. She had to be famished, in need of some protein and carbs after a long and trying day with no sustenance other than her taste-testings with Hammy early in the day. Lasagna with meat sauce to the rescue. He sat at the table with her, gnawing on a chunk of garlic bread and enjoying his own glass of the red.

The food helped immensely, and a second glass of the wine helped even more. Charlie was beginning to unwind. She was ready to discuss the 'pattern' to which the texter might be referring. They left the clutter of dishes and harshness of the kitchen lighting, returning to the living room's comfortable couch. Side by side, cozy, calming.

To Charlie it was obvious. "This bozo, whoever he is, must be talking about the two deaths today. That's the pattern I see, if you can call it that. And he's being disrespectful too, calling me a 'lassie' as if he knows me. What do you see?"

Mase chose his words carefully. "What I see is more ominous, I'm afraid. The pattern I see – and I think this entered my mind when Scharffenberger called me this afternoon to request my team's workup of the scene – is the similarity of today's events and those surrounding Ben Pierce's death. As Rex put it: *'Your wife's place again. Just like New Year's, and it's at the high roller party again. It's déjà vu all over again.'* I've been troubled by it ever since he said it, and there definitely *is* a pattern. Several repeating similarities, beyond the obvious location of your hotel. It's a Casino Marketing-sponsored event. It's a Charlie Champagne-orchestrated event. And it's the first Sunday of the month."

"Oh no, you're right!"

"And here's the scariest pattern of all," Mase continued, "You now have a single death in the first month and a double death in the second month. Kinda makes you wonder what'll happen in March, doesn't it?"

27

I finally fell asleep about 3 a.m., and felt better when morning came. As I watched Mase shower and shave, I silently thanked the gods for giving me such a strong and brilliant man as my life partner. His tenderness and understanding had carried me past yet another rough spot.

Now, as we said goodbye for the day, he simply touched my cheek tenderly and said, "Good luck," as we hopped into our respective vehicles. He knew that I knew what he meant and that there was no need to mention the brand new hurdle of last night's message. Not one to dilly dally, he backed out and was down to the exit from the Stardust Circle cul-de-sac before I had my seatbelt fastened and my Bluetooth speaker engaged.

Mase's *good luck* wish was in regard to my planned phone call with Rex about the cryptic text message that had rocked my world last night. I intended to find a quiet spot in the hotel's surface parking lot to call him, but as soon as I'd gotten on I-15, Rex called me.

"Good morning, Rex!" I answered hands-free. "I was gonna call you in ten minutes. What's up, my friend?"

"I got a strange text last night, and I wanted to fill you in before the whole world hears about it and tries to analyze it."

Oh shit, I thought, but I decided to hear him out before sharing my news. Traffic was doing its usual slowdown as I approached the 215 beltway interchange, and I had to concentrate on the hulking semi to my right, the herky-jerky cab in front of me and whatever it was Rex was about to unload.

"Tell me," I said, but I was wondering why he'd chosen me to hear his revelation before others in his life, his chain of command, or his actual inner circle. As I pondered that, the stupid taxi in my lane slammed on his brakes and my Renegade was suddenly within five feet of his bumper.

"Some creep dropped me a text that said '*Do you see a pattern, Detective?*' Short and sweet, kinda to the point," he mused, unaware of the roadway danger that I had just barely escaped.

"And do you?" I asked, my calm belying the tension of the moment. I was curious to find out if he'd drawn conclusions similar to mine or Mase's.

"What? See a pattern? Maybe, but not sure. There are a number of possibilities. Thought I'd bounce things off of you first, Charlie, before I followed up on it."

I had my opening and I took it. "Actually I *do* see a pattern, and I say that because I received a nearly identical text last night too, Rex. I've had time to think about it and I've been worried sick ever since, especially since Mase had some ideas about it." I explained what Mase and I had talked about last night.

"Listen Charlie, I know your work phone's like a third arm for you, but I'm gonna ask that you relinquish it for a few hours so we can try to trace that text. I can send a uniform by to pick it up around 8:30, if that's OK. I'll do my best to get it back to you before noon."

I wasn't thrilled with the idea, but I understood the need. There was no proprietary or personal information on the phone, but it'd be a bloody nuisance to be without it for even a few hours. "I'll be in my office by then," I assured Rex, and as soon as I reached ParaSpec parking, I composed an out-of-office message that alerted voice callers, texters and emailers that my phone was unavailable until 1 p.m. No reason given.

I was correct about being besieged by my staff and others who wanted to hear all about the deaths of the two high-roller football fans the day before, so I quickly scrawled a message on a blank sheet of paper that said *'DO NOT DISTURB – Return here for a quick stand-up meeting at 9 a.m. sharp.'* I taped it on the outside of my door and retreated inside. I felt like a celebrity avoiding the paparazzi.

I got to work on emails via my PC for a change. My first stop was the daily security report, which I normally check out from home first thing in the morning. Today there'd been a bit too much on my mind to think about it. There were no unusual guestroom issues, thank goodness, but a lot of entries that had something or other to do with the two Big Game deaths. Near the end, I suddenly bolted upright as a report from Gunnar Block himself snagged my full attention. *'For the record: Director Block received a mysterious text message on his hotel-issued phone at 2350 hours 5 Feb. Director will notify Metro detective of this occurrence at earliest opportunity on 6 Feb.'*

I jumped on the land-line phone on my desk and dialed 3200. Gunnar's assistant answered, and said he'd just stepped out for coffee.

"Got his cellphone with him?"

"I imagine so. I think he's married to it."

I thanked her and called him on his cell. He answered in half a ring, confirming his assistant's remark about his relationship with the phone.

"Gunnar, I just read the Security Report blurb about the text message you received last night. The lieutenant and I each received a text too, a few hours earlier than yours. Seems like whoever sent them was having some fun at our expense, using little nicknames for us. I was 'lassie' and Rex was 'copper.'

"Mine said 'Do you see a pattern, Big Swede?'" This person know us? He is the killer, you think, or just a peanut gallery lunatic getting his jollies?"

"Your guess is as good as mine. Anyway, Rex is sending an officer down to pick up my phone. They'll be here any minute. They'll probably want yours as well, if you're willing to part with it?"

The 'Big Swede' laughed. "Normally, I'd say no way. But today I have a root canal at 10:30, and the phone just brings me grief. Dentist is plenty grief for one day."

"Thanks. I'll have the officer swing by your office after he picks mine up."

I called Rex and shared Gunnar's news, telling him to have his officer retrieve Gunnar's phone as well as mine.

Returning to my emails, I was deeply engrossed until a knock sounded on my door and Hammy's voice said, "A cop out here to arrest you for being anti-social, Charlie!"

"Send him in," I said, smiling at Hammy's cheeky attempt at humor.

The door opened and a familiar face entered.

"Welcome, Officer Robin," I said, handing my beloved cellphone to the uniformed cop, who placed it in an evidence bag already labeled with my name and today's date. I then directed him to Gunnar's office.

"OK. Have a nice day, Miss Charlie."

As he left, I saw the crowd gathering outside my office. It was three minutes to nine. Almost time to face them and regurgitate in detail all that had happened the day before.

The worst part was having to relive the terror myself. How the thrill of the creative drinks and artfully displayed and delicious foods, along with the excitement and overall good spirits of the crowd, combined with a suspenseful fourth quarter of the biggest football event of the year had all evaporated in an instant. The exploding flat screen was at the heart of that instant, but instead of being the problem, it quickly transformed into the precursor of the catastrophic problem: the two dead bodies that remained behind after everyone else evacuated the Shangri La Terrace. Hammy, who'd been on-site with me, added a few of his own details.

Ninety minutes later, Rex called. "Hey, Charlie. Thanks for the phones. I'm having the lab take a look at all three in case there's anything we can learn. Mase's colleague Suzy picked them up a half hour ago; always happy for a reason to see her." I was secretly intrigued by this comment. He then went on with the real reason for his call; to change the time for the next task force from tomorrow evening to tomorrow noon, and he wanted to hold it at the ParaSpec. "We are in crisis mode now, Charlie," he said, with an urgency that was out of character for laid back Rex. He reminded me that the original rescheduling from Wednesday to Tuesday had been to accommodate my vacation, so I 'owed' him this one.

Despite his imperious tone, I found no reason to argue. I really hadn't relished going to a night meeting just before an early flight out, so perhaps this was a blessing. I found an available meeting room and reserved it, did a BEO for water service and box lunches – sandwich, chips and apple – enough for 12 people. A few extras just in case.

By 11:30, Rex had broadcast an email invite to an 'urgent' task force meeting at the Paradise Spectacular Resort tomorrow at noon sharp. "Please look for a message from the Vice-Chair, Ms. Champagne, with details and directions."

That was my cue, so I 'replied all' that we'd meet at the Nirvana 4 Meeting Room on the Mezzanine Level, and said a box lunch would be provided. Bring your parking voucher and we'll validate, I assured them, though it wasn't clear who'd be footing the bill for this little event. I hadn't asked and Rex hadn't brought it up.

Oh well, details …

Officer Ainsworth returned my phone about 12:30 as I was snacking on a yogurt and some baby carrots. A typical lunch for the harried executive, especially since I'd finally managed to get tightfisted Ira to approve my budget request for a mini-fridge. I thanked Rob and he left, presumably on his way to Gunnar's office down the hall.

The phone's return was well-timed; within a few minutes it was sounding *The Autumn Wind,* the ringtone for my favorite Raiders fan.

"Hi Gray, what's up?"

He was whispering. "Hey Charlie, come see who's here at the LOL. Approach with stealth!" he warned.

I adopted my well-practiced guileful advance to the LOL. I'd done this before, at the bartender's behest, whenever he'd witnessed a celeb or some wacky activity. Gray's the kinda guy you gotta humor. What I saw this time, however, was Ira Brickner in deep conversation with Maryland Burfurd. An unexpected duo, to be sure. Grayson sidled up to me, and confessed to being mystified. "Didn't even know they knew each other."

"Maryland knows almost everyone," I replied softly, but I, too, was a bit puzzled.

When it looked like they'd finished speaking, Ira put his hands on hers in a comforting way, and flashed a short smile, the kind I'd never before seen on my boss.

By 5 o'clock, that same man had lost any semblance of a smile. Acting very boss-like, he appeared in my office doorway, umbrella and briefcase in hand, obviously homeward bound. It was the first he'd talked to me since his return from wherever he'd been over the weekend. He asked nothing about how our program had gone, failed to acknowledge the fancy photo album Hammy had assembled for him, and made no mention of the pair of deaths that had occurred on our turf. Instead he interrogated me about the task force … once again. Last week, when he'd read about it in the newspaper, he'd acted disgruntled at being left out when so many others at the ParaSpec were included. Apparently he was still steamed.

"You'd have to ask Rex. I didn't populate the group, Ira." I spoke as curtly as he'd spoken to me. He looked at me, bewildered, and I wondered if he'd ever even met the lieutenant face-to-face.

Now wasn't the right time – but there'd never be one – so I blurted out, "You do recall I'll be O-O-O for a week starting on Wednesday." It was a statement, but inflected as if a question. I was sure he'd forgotten. "Actually eight consecutive days. Returning the 16th."

"Out of office? What for?"

"A well-deserved vacation, that's what for. Maris Kean will handle things just fine."

"Damn it, Charlie. That's a long time. Just be sure to keep your cellphone handy in case we have an—"

"My work cell will be off – that's O-F-F – for the duration of my O-O-O. I've already cleared it with Sammy." I was beginning to enjoy this back-and-forth repartee.

"Sammy? C'mon, Charlie. Why do you have to go around me, ignoring the chain of command?"

"Because the chain was broken, Ira. Leo was in Seattle visiting his daughter and new grandson, and you were off swinging your golf clubs in some far-off corner of the country with *your* cellphone turned off. Sammy was the only upper management available."

Brooding silence hung heavy for a moment, then he asked in an almost frail voice, "Where are you headed?"

"Mexico. And if it makes you feel any better, Ira, the cellphone coverage down there is lousy. You'd have difficulty reaching me even if I did turn on my phone." I smiled sweetly.

28

By five minutes past noon on Tuesday, everyone had arrived and selected a box lunch that appealed to them. Roasted turkey seemed to be winning out, as it often did with a random mix of people. Charlie, of course, knew this and had planned accordingly. She had also had her assistant Julie make and set out name tags, so folks easily found their assigned spots. The placements were arbitrary, per Charlie's instruction.

Second meeting, second welcome by the Sheriff himself. One might wonder if Mickey McGraw really planned to allow the task force to operate and deliberate autonomously. Apparently sensing such worries, the big man sought to dispel them. "Greetings, folks, and thank you again for your dedicated service. I'm here today to request that you, as a committee, accept an additional component to your original assignment. As you all know by now, two men died this past Sunday as they participated in a Casino Marketing event in this hotel, the same place Mr. Pierce was killed on New Year's Day. This, as well as other factors Lt. Scharffenberger will discuss with you in a moment, leads us to the inescapable conclusion that the crimes are likely related. Thus, their investigations must be intertwined as well. While this may initially seem like an added burden, it might give you additional clues that will make the job easier. Again, I thank you for your participation, and

I'd like to add a special thanks to Ms. Champagne for making this room and lunch available on such short notice."

Once the sheriff had left, Rex elaborated on the connection between the two crimes – January 1st and February 5th – that Sheriff McGraw had alluded to, highlighting the mysterious text messages that had been received by himself, Ms. Champagne and Chief Block. While the nearly identical content of the texts had suggested it, analysis of the call history on the three cellphones had confirmed that they had all originated from the same prepaid mobile phone. "You've probably heard the term 'burner phones' because they're essentially untraceable. The user purchases them with a prepaid number of minutes on them, no identification needed, and when they've used up the minutes or no longer want the phone, they toss 'em in the trash. If used for illicit purposes, like this one seems to have been, they are often physically destroyed first. So we have no chance of recovering the phone, but we do know the number and that it was purchased in a convenience market on West Sahara Avenue in early December of last year. That's about all we know, unfortunately."

"Any other call history on it?" Hammy Yamasaki asked.

"Good question. But the answer, regrettably, is no. Only the three text messages sent to us within over a couple of hours on Sunday night."

The ominous implications of the messages were then discussed. Same hotel. Casino Marketing event orchestrated by Charlie Champagne. First Sunday. One in January, two in February.

The psychology professor, Dr. Grigio, said, "It sounds like we need to resolve this before the month is up." No one disagreed with her.

Next, Rex introduced the subject of the finger and what it meant.

"*Fuck you*' is what it's saying," Rex said, spreading his arms as if it was super obvious. "In case that's offensive to anyone here, from now on let's just say *FU*'. OK with everyone?" All agreed.

"The big questions are who's that message directed to, and who's sending it?" he stated flatly.

Dr. Cruz showed no reluctance to offer his views. "It could be a message from the victim – it's his hand, after all – as interpreted and choreographed by the killer, using some perverse rationale," he began. "But more likely it's a message from the killer, using the hand of his victim as a medium with shock value. He has a message to the world, or to some segment of the world, or to a specific group, or to an individual, and he figures – however twisted it may seem – that using a severed hand is more effective than writing a letter or taking out an advertisement on the radio, whatever. Of course, he's 100% correct in supposing that. We, as a community and as individuals, are duly shocked, and we react just as we are doing here in this room today: trying to make some sense out of it."

"OK," Rex said, "so let's brainstorm a bit. Assuming Dr. Cruz has correctly theorized that it's a message from the killer, who might he – or she – be sending an FU message to?

"The victim's wife?"

"One or both of his sons?"

"Other family members?"

"Work associates?"

"Workplace competition?"

The input came so fast, it was impossible to tell the sources. But that was irrelevant; the ice was broken on the topic, and it showed the people had put on their thinking caps. Rex was pleased, and gestured to Sgt. Lee to make an entry on her whiteboard. "Just write FAMILY MEMBER and WORK ASSOCIATE for now," he instructed Lee. Turning to his colleagues, "Who else?"

Now they seemed stumped. The *'FU'* message, they reckoned, could have been directed at almost anyone who – in the killer's twisted mind – was deserving of his scorn. Without knowing the perp's identity, further refinement of this line of thought was impossible.

Gunnar had been thinking and posed a corollary question to further muddy the waters: Did the killer even know Pierce, or was here merely a handy human being who happened to be in the right place at the wrong time, and whose hand looked ripe for the picking? "Not likely, but as investigators shouldn't we be looking at all possible angles?" he posed.

From there, the group delved into the relationship between the three victims, if in fact there was one. The rookie detective, Willis Bronx, expressed an eagerness to examine that aspect and report back to the group at its next meeting. Sgt. Lee made a notation to that effect, thus casting it in concrete.

Dr. Cruz promised a report on the way in which serial killers – everyone hated to hear that term come into play, but there was no escaping it – choose their victims and their manner of displaying their handiwork.

The other educator, Dr. Grigio, promised a brief treatise on the motivating factors behind what she termed 'exhibitionism killings.' While serial killings were relatively rare, they often involved some form of display that conveyed a message.

Charlie and Rex were encouraged by the eagerness of the task force members. It substantiated the notion that everyone is a sleuth at heart. Rex doled out a few more assignments before adjourning the meeting at 2:20 p.m., but Charlie was given none since she was beach-bound in the morning, and fully deserved the week off with nothing important to think about.

"I doubt I can force it from my mind entirely," she lamented aloud. "Ben Pierce was a friend and it was my event where it happened. There's a certain level of personal responsibility I can't seem to shed."

Rex reminded the group that the next meeting would be on Thursday the 16th at 7 p.m. Location to be disclosed in an email just prior.

Charlie was pleased that the meeting had been as concise as it had been, wrapping up well under her anticipated three hours. It bode well for an earlier than expected arrival home, and to a better night's sleep before their pair of flights, the first to Houston and then a continuation on to Cancún.

Most of her afternoon was devoted to preparation for a week's absence from the office. She had several programs on which she had to bring Maris up to speed, and they'd set aside an hour from 4 to 5 to put their heads together. The Hearts and Diamonds Ball on the 11th was the only one of Charlie's functions actually occurring during her absence. But in the foreseeable future she also had a Rotary/Kiwanis joint meeting later in February, with lunch and speakers, a four-day traffic engineers group beginning March 5th, and then a Casino Marketing multi-day event for the first two rounds of March Madness in the middle of the month. She expected none of these to pose problems, but Maris was briefed anyway.

"Don't worry," she told Charlie. "Jameson has to go back east for a few days, so I'll have lots of time to devote to work. Especially the Ball this weekend. I'll be onsite, and I hear that a couple of our own will be attending," she added mysteriously.

Charlie's eyebrows arched. "Care to elaborate?"

"Well, I guess it's not a secret. Kinchy told me today that Hammy asked her to go." Hammy was one of four ParaSpec employees who were given an invitation to the event as a result of earning an Employee of the Quarter (EOQ) award in 2016.

Charlie beamed. "How nice! I feel even better about the event now," she admitted. "The latest head count is 211, by the way. Funny how it just happens to match the date. So, where's Jameson headed, not that it's any of my business?"

"I think he said Toronto. He's got a few irons in the fire back there, y'know, as well as in Kentucky and … gee, I can't keep it all straight."

"And you don't need to. Just be glad he's raking in a few extra bucks to fund those elaborate vacations you guys thrive on."

Maris scrunched up her nose and giggled. She was already looking forward to Scotland and Ireland in July. Charlie had given her the green light on that trip two days after she'd returned from Spain.

Victor Heron had developed a routine, albeit a loosely fashioned one. He popped into the LOL no less than twice a week, interspersing those stops with visits to other properties where the landscape also seemed ripe. As Social Media Sales Manager for the Swank Illusion Resort, he spent 80 percent of his time on the go – 'in the field' as the common vernacular went – visiting one establishment or another. He was ostensibly charged with developing marketing relationships with other businesses – restaurants, retail outlets, service providers and so forth – and he carried with him a briefcase packed with blank business contracts, brochures and shiny business cards. He knew what to do with these tools, and he produced acceptably. But back when he'd been promoted to the position, he'd had a private meeting with none other than Billy Swank himself. The big man had given Vic some verbal instruction on special features of the new job.

The young man was duly impressed. *Sure, Mr. Swank, you can count on Vegas Victor to do some dirty work for you, and sure, Mr. Swank, I understand there'll be some under-the-table bonuses from time to time.*

Too impressed, perhaps. His head tended to swell as he allowed himself a jazzed-up self-image. He forgot that beneath the new job, the clandestine assignments and the promise of lofty responsibilities lurked a man whose underpinnings were still laced with slime. Unavoidably, the slime oozed to the surface from time to time, causing him and others substantial embarrassment.

On Tuesday afternoon, Vic approached the LOL's pretty dark-skinned bartender/server with an unusual amount of straightforwardness.

Embarrassment ensued when he allowed himself, as he was ordering refill number two of his spiked energy drink, to brazenly ask the young lady to be his date for the upcoming Hearts and Diamonds Ball. Never mind that the function was not open to the general public, he went right for the kill and received – not unexpectedly – an unequivocal brush-off. But at least the young lady was kind-mannered about it as she informed him that (a) the event was for invited guests only, (b) she *was* among the invited but she *already had* a date, and (c) she wasn't allowed to fraternize with her customers anyway.

Duly chastened, Vic vanished before his new drink arrived. Tapper was mildly surprised, though nothing about this guy who the other barkeeps called 'Bird Boy' was really alarming. A creepy schmuck, for sure, but she happily noticed that he'd left a pair of twenties next to his empty glass; at $8 per drink, his tab was $24 plus tax, so he had stuck true to form as far as tipping went. She'd cleared about $14 in exchange for her part of the embarrassment, of which he'd suffered the lion's share.

Wow, thank you for that, Mister Victor! she thought, and meant it. He may have been an undateable entity, but he wasn't a total disaster.

But despite the painless ending to a potentially awkward situation, and the nice monetary reward, the lady from the West Indies was uneasy. When she returned to the bar, she figured it out. She hadn't been totally truthful in what she told her would-be suitor. Her (a) and (c) points were clearly stated and were the whole truth. Argument (b), however, was flawed, and it wasn't the part about her being among the invitees to the Ball. That much was true … as another of the four EOQ winners, she and a date were automatic invitees to the gala event.

What was untrue – and indeed lamentable at this late juncture – was that she already had a date for the gala affair. In fact, she had none, and was beside herself with worry over that situation.

That evening, Rex Scharffenberger received a jingle on his Metro-issued cellphone. He was casually watching a college hoops game from somewhere in the South, though not paying close attention. A half-empty bottle of Amstel sat on the side table where the phone was making its noise.

Once again, the caller ID revealed a number that was not familiar to him. The text message, however, carried a snide tone that was all too familiar.

'Is your task force helping, copper?'

Damn, this jackass was back to his taunting. What was the purpose, if not to goad and provoke the detective and his team?

His team. He instantly wondered if they – specifically, Charlie and Gunnar – had also received a message tonight, as they had on Sunday. His good judgment overruled his curiosity, especially in the case of Charlie. He wasn't about to put a cloud over her vacation by checking in with her. In the morning, he would touch base with Gunnar to see if he'd been contacted again.

He'd also have the lab folks trace the number that had called him, for whatever that was worth. Probably very little, just like last time. The biggest upside to that idea was that with Mase off on his Mexican trip, Rex would have a surefire reason to interact with CSI's second in command. Every time he saw Suzy Hart, his hormones did a bit of a dance.

29

¡Buenos días, amigos!

Some would call it 'hump day,' but for Mase and me it was 'Wonderful Wednesday.' It felt sooo good to be escaping the grind and, most specifically, the pressures of the killings that had occurred at the ParaSpec. Being a CSI guy, Mase was sorta used to death and all its trappings, but it was new territory for me. And even though I was slightly enamored by the idea of having an important seat on the sheriff's task force, I was happy to leave all thought of it behind for a week.

By 10:30 a.m. Las Vegas time, we were sitting in a pub in Houston's Hobby airport, resetting our virtual watches to 12:30 and trying to find something light to tide us over till our early dinner. We had reservations at the resort's flagship steakhouse for 6 p.m., but that was only 3 back home.

Gene Autry, the Singing Cowboy from ages ago, had recorded *South of the Border (Down Mexico Way)* before my parents were even born. But that didn't keep the persistent chorus from replaying through my mind all morning long. The urge to put the USA in my rearview for a few days was powerful!

As we'd promised ourselves, our work cellphones were safely stashed in our suitcases, and would stay there for the duration. Sometimes I wondered why we even brought them with us. We were getting reacquainted with our personal phones. I was Facebooking, and texting Suzy and Maris (the latter with strict instructions to discuss nothing workwise). Mase was reading sports news on the ESPN app. Top story (to his way of thinking): his Iowa Hawkeyes were heading north to play Minnesota's Golden Gophers tonight.

Our second flight went without incident, as did our private shuttle to the resort. The cozy thatched-roof bungalow was charming, with a spacious front porch that was closer to the ocean than the length of our eleven-house cul-de-sac back home. I could think of no way to improve upon it.

Dinner was pretty good, but to be honest Mase can grill a steak better and I can make a superior tiramisu. The whipped potatoes and steamed veggies were typical restaurant fare – edible but unexciting. But those shortcomings were outweighed by the incredible setting in which we found ourselves. It was an individual palapa about ten feet in diameter, with our table for two situated in the center on a single pole imbedded in below-the-sand concrete. With the nearest neighboring palapa a good 20 feet away, it was truly a private experience. The only distraction was the haunting refrain of a mariachi band that was either elsewhere on property or somewhere down the beach. But to its credit, it did put the brain brakes on Mr. Autry's tune, which was by now becoming a bit much.

There was no floor, only the beautiful fine sand, and a notation on the menu invited us to feel free to remove our shoes and enjoy the sensation of fine dining with bare feet squishing in the sand. Fortuitously, we had worn flip-flops so we did just that.

Suddenly, the stiff potatoes and overcooked broccoli seemed much tastier. And the flickering candle on our table made the tiramisu much more romantic than any version I'd ever prepared. Our timing was perfect too (because Mase had researched it in advance, of course); with sunset coming at 6:41 p.m., our meal began in daylight and ended after dark. The sunset was behind us, since Playa del Carmen is on a southeast facing shoreline, but we were still treated to a smattering of pinkish-orangeish puffs all over the eastern sky. This place was certainly living up to its auspicious name, *Resort Espectacular.*

We returned to our room, after each enjoying a 'Mayan Chocolate' nightcap at an al fresco lounge along the way. The final drinks sent us off to dreamland, and put creative thoughts in our heads.

That first half-day was just a preamble to a wonderfully relaxing week. We approached it with no great forethought, as there was plenty to keep us occupied.

On Thursday morning we talked about starting a Kahlua pairing blog, inspired by the prior night's final drink. "Why not?" I wondered aloud. "There are a zillion possibilities! We're both full of ideas. We're both good photographers and good writers."

Mase was on board immediately. "And good taste testers for each other's creations. Let's do it!"

Mase's mood took a hit when he discovered Iowa had been trounced by Minnesota the night before, 101 to 89. "How in the hell do you lose by 12 points in double overtime? Tied after regulation. Tied after first overtime. It was a real squeaker … until all of a sudden our guys fold and give it away in the last five minutes. What a pisser!"

Later we frolicked in the pool, took an overly long siesta and had a relaxed meal at the seaside taquito stand just before it closed for the day. The Hawkeyes' basketball misfortune was long lost in a litany of pleasures.

By Friday, I found myself occasionally thinking about things north of the border, specifically the Hearts and Diamonds Ball at the ParaSpec. "It's just cocktails, dinner and dancing," Mase wisely counseled. "A straightforward task for Maris, you said so yourself last week. What could possibly go wrong?" That's the part that had me concerned. It seemed like lately *something* always went wrong.

We moved on to brighter thoughts. We found the swim-up bar, ordered some jalapeno poppers and Mexican-style spring rolls to go with our *cantinera's* Kahlua-based concoction. Walked the beach a mile north, then U-turned and jogged back. I found myself using muscles that had been long neglected, but it felt good later on. A healthy kinda good.

Next day, Saturday, the big event was again on my mind, but then I recalled my final conversation with Maris. She'd said that since Jameson would be gone somewhere for the weekend that she'd likely get a sitter for her kids and stay the night at the hotel.

No hurries, no worries.

That was nice ... for Maris.

Crazy me, I still worried.

30

Determined to prove his worth, young Willis Bronx wasted no time. He'd already perused every item on the thumb drive his new boss had distributed at the first task force meeting. He'd made himself a 'must do' list of unanswered questions, needed clarifications, and gaps that begged for explanation. He'd done all that even before the second meeting, the one at noon on the 7th that had added the Super Bowl deaths to the mix. At that one he'd volunteered to do some probing into relationships, to see if there was a connection between the Pierce, Swann and Honshu men or their families. The more he explored, the more new questions arose.

Before he left the hotel that Tuesday, Willis managed to make contact with both Jameson Kean and Roberto 'Bobby G' Guanacaste. He learned nothing new about the Pierce case, but he did discover that Bobby G had not only been the Pierces' butler in December/January but also the Swanns' butler in February. And Adam and Alex Honshu's deluxe two-bedroom suite had been served by Bobby G as well.

Thankfully, Willis' training session at the police academy was abbreviated that Wednesday, so he arrived at the ParaSpec a few minutes past noon. He followed up with the butler, learned little new, and moved on to speak with Tindra Block and Amy Boutella, the two young ladies who had succumbed to the Honshu men's charms on February 3rd. Nothing new from them either, but he felt good covering all the bases. Good detective work, he told himself. Next it was on to the reputed LOL bar with hopes of encountering some of the bartending staff who had been working during either or both of the ill-fated events. He was in luck; Grayson Moore, who was on duty and in charge for both, welcomed the detective, and said he'd be glad to help out even though he'd already talked with Willis' lieutenant at least twice. Gray told Willis that yes, the pretty Jamaican over there was with him on New Year's, but that 'our senior citizen, Art Foster' was his back-up during the Big Game. Artie would be coming on at 3 p.m. tomorrow afternoon. After a few minutes of mostly-unremarkable chit chat, Gray called his co-worker over and made the introductions.

"Please, just call me Tapper," she smiled at Willis. Gray had used her full legal name, and was scurrying back to the bar to handle some arriving customers.

Willis was struck by her charm and self-assurance as they went through her recollections of what had transpired at the LOL in the afternoon and evening, and especially the late night portion until she went off duty at 1 a.m. She explained that business had been brisk until about 10 p.m., when it dropped off more than usual for a Saturday night. She attributed this to people heading off to New Year's Eve parties here at the ParaSpec, at other hotels or joining the throng out on the Boulevard. By the time the old year had drawn to a close there were only a half dozen or so in the bar. She listed them for Willis: Maryland Burfurd, a regular; a tourist couple from Calgary; two businessmen from Wichita; and a strange young man who had become an erratic regular, and who she only knew as Vic.

When he had all the information he thought she could provide, Willis tossed out one last thought. "One of the questions I've been asking people is if they're worried about what might happen at the Valentine's event coming up this weekend. You know, because of the similarities to these other events?"

"The Hearts and Diamonds Ball? No, actually it hadn't occurred to me ... but then I'm a barkeep, not a detective. Do you think something might happen?"

"Well ... I guess I have to be concerned, but it helps to hear from—"

"I have an idea, Detective," she said with an impulsive sparkle highlighting her voice as well as her eyes. "Do you like off-the-wall daring ideas from people you hardly know?" she asked.

Willis stammered, not knowing what to say. Finally he admitted, "First of all, I'm not actually a detective yet, just a member of the task force. But to answer your question: sure, why not? I like bold and daring ideas."

"How would *you*, Detective Bronx," Tapper went on, discounting the correction to his title, "like to be *my* date for the Hearts and Diamonds Ball? Then you can keep a close eye on things, first hand, and you won't have to go around asking questions after the fact. I mean, as long as you don't completely ignore your date," she winked flirtatiously. "How about it, Detective?"

Willis' smile was the most profound grin he could ever recall having. It was, of course, an involuntary reaction to the 'off-the-wall daring idea' this lovely creature had just suggested.

"Call me Willis, and yes, I'd be delighted to be your date." His calm demeanor belied the exhilaration inside him and he hoped she couldn't tell he was blushing. "All in the name of justice, of course." They smiled knowingly at each other.

The following morning (and the one after it) the aspiring detective was in his office by 5:30 a.m. Armed with a battery of contact phone numbers, he placed calls to Ohio, North Carolina and Alabama, all of them three hours further into the day than Nevada was. He may have ruffled a few feathers, but he also learned a lot. The calls to California, Arizona and Utah he fit into his lunch hour or mid-afternoon break. Locally, he managed to chat in person with Ms. Burfurd at her Torre Elegante condo. He'd also hoped to talk with Charlie's boss, Ira Brickner, at the hotel, but he hadn't been in when he'd visited earlier in the week, and now on Friday was told the man was gone for an extended weekend trip.

So be it. Enough for one week for the nascent gumshoe. He went home to his golf-course-fronting studio in Summerlin and became 'just plain Willis' again. He popped a Bud Light and tuned into WGN which was having a binge day of old *Hawaii 5-0* and *CSI Miami* episodes. He was a cop-show aficionado, but right now his mind was more focused on his dazzling date for the Hearts and Diamonds Ball than on crime-busting in some tropical waterfront setting.

At the first show's end, he went to his closet and made sure his new blue pinstripe was ready for a romantic evening out. *He* certainly was.

When Jill Swann had sympathized with Byron Pierce over the loss of his father, she had no idea the tables would turn, and so quickly. But here she was being held and consoled by him over the tragic loss of her own father. Circumstances all too similar – the city, the hotel, the fact that it occurred at a high-roller shindig – made both deaths more mystifying, but did not dull her pain one iota.

She'd admired Byron for his resilience after his father's death and hoped that by next month she would be in as good a shape as he seemed to be. Right now, she doubted it. Her father had meant the world to her. Perhaps more than Ben had ever meant to Byron. She didn't know, and that was irrelevant anyway.

What was relevant was that her true love was comforting her now as they waited at the Columbus airport for her flight to Birmingham, just as he had been ever since she'd gotten the awful news on Sunday. She knew it wasn't that easy for him because of her father's condemnation of their interracial romance, but Byron had admitted to having a similar issue with his own father.

It was all a bit too complex for Jill to unravel, so she didn't try.

Bobby Guanacaste was enjoying the trust his boss had been showing him lately. First it was the promotion back in November from Butler to Senior Butler; he remembered telling his dear mama that he really had much to be grateful for that Thanksgiving. But there were two other Senior Butlers on Jameson Kean's staff, so Bobby G was the 'juniorest' of the seniors. That's why he'd been surprised – and thrilled – when Mr. Kean had solicited his help with the Hearts and Diamonds Ball this month.

"I have out of town business this weekend, so I'll be leaving it all in your capable hands," he'd told Bobby. Now it was Thursday the 9th, mid-morning, and the time had come to transfer responsibility.

Jameson introduced Bobby G to the small windowless area with a full-height chain-link front door wide enough for a fork lift. Officially called the Liquor Room, it had long ago been dubbed the 'Booze Closet' by everyone from Leo on down. It was located within the labyrinth of the back-of-house area, convenient by freight elevator to the meeting and banquet facilities one floor up, as well as the kitchen and the LOL. Liquors, wines and beers were stored here, some refrigerated but mostly not. It was under lock and key, of course, with very few keys in circulation. Jameson was one of the fortunate few.

He explained how the Booze Closet was arranged and accessed. It required both a brass key and a thumb print reading, and Jameson told him they'd use Bobby's thumbprint that he'd given when he'd been hired. "I will give you my copy of the metal key before I leave tomorrow."

Next they stopped at the LOL, where Jackpot and Artie were manning the fort. It was the first Bobby'd met either of them, and he was glad to learn that Jackpot would be on duty on Saturday evening. Grayson, the lead bartender with whom Bobby was already acquainted, would also be on. "If you have an unusual request not on the portables – a high-end whiskey, a rare liqueur – it's often easier to come get a bottle from these guys than bother with the closet," Jameson explained.

"Got it," Bobby said, nodding confidently. "See you Saturday, Jack. Pleasure to meet you, Artie." They all waved cordially at one another.

Maryland was just settling down after the rigors of her month-long trip back east, followed by a lighthearted verbal sparring session with Lt. Rex and a Super Bowl watch party at a friend's manor in Rancho Heights. She was looking forward to some low-key routine relaxation for the weeks to come.

Routine relaxation. Her definition of the term included sleeping in till 8:30 or beyond, coffee and crullers in the den – or on the lanai if the weather was agreeable – along with a good book, a short nap, a bubble bath and finally a Brandy Alexander (or two) before an evening out on the town. Some nights to the Illusion, but more often than not to her favorite spot, the ParaSpec's LOL. She'd usually grab a light bite while she was out. Uber was her preferred transport mode, so there'd be no need to ration her alcohol intake and no worries about taking her Saab out amongst the nighttime crazies on the Strip.

But this Thursday morning, Maryland's routine was sent reeling. She received the call she never wanted to receive, although the news was not as dire as it could have been. On the phone was the woman who'd lived next door to Marlin Burfurd in Chapel Hill for nearly 20 years. Long ago they'd made a pact to look out for each other, which included calling for EMTs and notifying family members if necessary. This morning, the woman called to inform Maryland that her Pa had just been picked up by an ambulance and taken to the hospital, suffering from a cardiac occlusion. He was in and out of consciousness, but his diagnosis was 'serious.'

It was the first time the neighborly accord had come into play for medical reasons, and it had served its purpose well. Within 30 minutes Maryland was packing a suitcase and making an online reservation on Southwest Airlines. One-way this time, since she had no idea when she'd be coming back. She normally flew American, since she could select her seat, but they had no non-stops – or even one-stops – that would get her to North Carolina *today.*

Her plane was departing at 1:30 so there was no time to dawdle. She finished packing and called for a 10:45 pick-up. On the short trek, she composed and sent a quick note to her friend Charlie Champagne: *'Just so you know, Pa has taken a turn for the worse, and is in the ICU at Duke University Hospital. I'll be staying at his place in Chapel Hill for a week or two, maybe longer.'*

After check-in and TSA security check, she found a restaurant/bar near her gate and ordered a Brandy Alexander and Caesar salad. She retrieved her phone, opened up the recent message to Charlie, and copy/pasted it into a new email. She added *'Visitors welcome and encouraged'* to the content, and entered the address of the recipient. She pressed SEND just as the drink appeared in front of her.

It wasn't as good as Jackpot's rendition, but very few were.

31

A flock of 24 lovebirds served as mood-setting décor for the Hearts and Diamonds Ball. It had been Charlie's idea, with final arrangements by Maris. Housed in four cages around the ballroom, they suddenly became a liability when one of the cage doors accidentally swung open and its six birds were on the loose, fluttering about the huge room. Fortunately, the dinner was over and the dessert was underway. The birds showed a fondness for the Pecan Rum Crumble that Charlie and the pastry chef had laboriously created weeks earlier.

Fortunately for the 11 inconvenienced diners who'd had their crumbles sampled or pooped upon, there was a surplus in the kitchen, and within minutes each was delivered a replacement dessert along with a small envelope containing a note of apology and a notice that their casino reward card had just been given a $100 boost.

Damage control at work, Maris Kean at the helm. She called Rainbow Fur, Feather and Fin Rentals, the rental birds' owners, to round them up. Then she called the Southern Nevada Health District to get an inspection after a quick cleanup was made by kitchen and housekeeping staffs. Order was restored within 60 minutes, and most of the people who had been eager to party at the start of the evening filed back into Fascination 3 & 4 and continued the festivities as if nothing had happened.

Then Maris appeared in the flesh, standing on a small riser in front of a curtain with a mic in her hand. She wore a salmon-colored business suit, very handsome but nothing to compete with the many elegant gowns around the ballroom. She apologized for the 'lovebird incident' and proceeded with introducing the invited dignitaries and the ParaSpec's four Employee of the Quarter winners from 2016:

- Hamakuri Yamasaki, Catering and Conventions Services Manager. Hammy's date was his co-worker and fellow Pacific Islander, the charming Kinishi 'Kinchy' Loatonga. Kinchy, who was pushing six feet and 180 pounds, had selected a peachy-pink gown that made her look glamorous alongside her tuxedo-clad companion.

- Tindra Block, Front Desk Supervisor. Tindra's date was a forgettable young motorcycle mechanic from her apartment complex who probably had no idea that eight days earlier his date had been passionately entangled with one of the hotel's recent Big Game casualties. Their attire was dressy, but not elaborate.

- Alfredo Suarez, Senior Banquet Server. Alf's date was his wife of 13 years, Consuelo, who rarely got to go anywhere – let alone dress up really nice – due to the duties of motherhood. With the Christmas Eve arrival of twin boys, their brood now totaled five! Their story received a standing ovation.

- Lynne-Anne Tapp, Bartender II at the Libations on the Lobby Bar. Tapper's date was a dapper young police academy student and aspiring detective with Metro Police.

There was no sartorial award to be presented, but if there had been, it might well have gone to Tapper's date, Willis Bronx. He'd gone to the trouble to ask about Tapper's dress fabric and color, and then found a matching lapel-pocket hankie – white satin, with accents that matched his elegant navy suit. Tapper had been pleasantly astonished.

The door prizes were next. Maris enlisted her helper, Hermie Stevenson, to draw winning ticket stubs and dole out a half-dozen prizes. Fittingly, an elegant heart-cut diamond jewelry set of necklace, earrings and bracelet was the grand prize, which went to a flamboyant local attorney who frequented the Spectacular Pit while his socialite wife played the $5 slots; she shrieked when her husband's name was called.

From there, the event segued to spirited dancing to the music of 'our very own Spectaculeers,' as Maris described them when a dramatic kabuki drop behind her revealed a 7-piece musical ensemble at the ready. The guests soon filled the 24'-by-48' parquet floor.

In fact, the music could be heard well beyond the walls of Fascination 3 & 4, permeating the whole Mezzanine level. It did not cheer everyone whose ears it reached. Victor Heron sat in a wing-back chair in the hallway, trying to appear inconspicuous but failing miserably due to his UNR sweatsuit and scuffed-up Nikes. The music did nothing for him, other than mess with his concentration during the elimination round of the video game *'Death to the Crimson Planet'* that he was playing against a chap up in Manitoba.

Suddenly the music stopped, which broke his train of self-deprecating thoughts, and the night took an upturn. There, exiting the ballroom, came lovely Tapper and her dashing date. Vic glumly realized that he was no comparison to this guy, but the knowledge strangely offered him a measure of satisfaction. She had *not* been lying to him just to brush him off. She *did* have a date, and he was – by all appearances – quite a catch.

As soon as the couple was out of sight, heading for the restrooms with a throng of others it seemed, he arose and moseyed on.

He went back to the LOL, of course, his usual stompin' grounds when hanging at the ParaSpec Resort. Pretty busy by now, and his usual table by the window was occupied. That was an irritant to the angular-faced man, but he coped. He recognized a few people who had departed the Ball a few minutes earlier, including the fortyish couple who were sitting at 'his' table. The two-person table next to it was open, so he sat down and caught the eye of Jackpot, who was waiting tables in addition to tending bar. The usual Vodbomb and snack mix were soon delivered, and he nibbled and sipped.

Results of *'Death to the Crimson Planet'* were in, and he had ended up in fourth place after an exceptionally poor showing against the player from Winnipeg. Damned Canuck! Momentarily disheartened, he let the emotion slide and instead stole a glance at the woman who was seated in 'his' seat. It wasn't his first glance, as she was easy to look at for a woman on the upside of forty. This time she caught his eye and offered a weak smile in his direction. It was his opening.

"Those birds poop in your pudding?" he asked her.

"I beg your pardon?"

"I saw those parakeets – lovebirds someone called them – flying all over the ballroom. Just trying to get your reaction."

"What? Surely *you* weren't in there." She cast a derisive look at his sweatshirt and beat-up sneakers.

"I wasn't, no. But sometimes I just like to get a peek at the upper crust, y'know. So are you worried about the bird flu after that?"

The woman's husband could no longer hold his tongue. "Young man, I don't know what you want, but please—"

Vic interrupted, "Hey, just asking a friendly question. I thought it was kinda funny, but I wondered if people in there felt differently."

"It was clearly an accident, and no one was harmed," the man replied, his irritation barely held in check.

Victor punched a few buttons on his cellphone, and abruptly looked back at the couple, smiling. "Understood. Have a nice evening." He arose and picked up his drink, then looked directly at the woman. "That's my favorite seat you're in. Enjoy it."

He moved on, found another couple from the Ball and began chatting them up. Their faces went from affable to annoyed in a matter of 30 seconds. Victor excused himself and made a few more keystrokes on his phone.

After one more similar encounter, Victor's antagonistic behavior got the attention of Grayson Moore from behind the bar. He recognized the offender as the weird guy who often comes in and sits by the window, minding his own business but never without his ever-present cellphone or tablet. He'd been bothersome at times, but never disrespectful. Tonight it seems he'd gone over the line, and Gray had no choice but to call Security. He was surprised when Gunnar Block himself answered.

"We have a disruptive guest who needs to be watched," he informed the Director of Security.

"I'll send M.O. up now. He's dressed up tonight, so he'll blend with the Ball crowd."

"Good, thanks. M.O.'s your best man." Gray turned back to a customer who had ordered four Corona Lights but kept one eye on Victor and the other on the lookout for M.O. Multi-tasking at its best.

With the beers uncapped and sent on their way, Gray found a slack moment to check in with his social media sites. It was one of his self-assigned duties, keeping tabs on what's going on locally. Made him a better conversationalist, thus a better bartender and a more informed guy all around. He first went to Facebook, then pulled up Instagram. There he saw a disturbing post from a poster he'd seen maybe once or twice before. Now @vvofreno was hitting close to home: '*DANGER: Birds loose at Paradise Spectacular spreading disease and feathers. Lovebirds at Hearts & Diamonds Ball were observed flying above diners, perching on dessert plates and joining the party. They couldn't find any bird potties so they improvised. Health District is on the way.*'

Another posting from the same individual, a dozen minutes later, was more scathing, and hit closer to home. *'Hotel president Leo-something is at home relaxing, and his event manager Charlie-something is beaching it in Mexico. So who's minding the farm at the ParaSpec? Maybe they assigned one of the LOL bartenders?'*

Mario Ochoa, known to all as M.O., appeared just in time. Gray was hot under the collar by now and had turned the mixology and bottle opening over to Jackpot, who was fast becoming overwhelmed. So be it. Gray *had to* talk with M.O.

"M.O. my man, you're lookin' spiffy!" Gray exchanged a fist bump with the bulky Hispanic whose appearance told everyone *'No nonsense, señor,'* even through the fancy duds. At an even six feet, with 18" biceps packed into the specially-tailored suit jacket, he was not to be overlooked. A hush came over the packed LOL room as his presence became noticed. Gray lowered his voice, and explained his concerns. "The guy with the schnozz over there," he pointed with his thumb, "he's approaching the customers – the ones just outta the Ball – asking them about the lovebird incident and inciting their negative emotions. He's a semi-regular here, but a creepy one for sure." Then he showed M.O. the two Instagram posts and suggested that the same guy was probably the author.

Ochoa approached the alleged offender, who was again absorbed with his device. "Excuse me, sir," he said, "we've had several complaints about your interactions with some of the other guests." M.O. was as cool as he was imposing. He had an audience, but he remained the unruffled security guy determined to keep order.

"Me? I can't imagine why." Victor offered M.O. an expression of feigned surprise. "I suppose I just don't speak in the language of the upper crust. For which I humbly apologize. Poor guy from the wrong side of the tracks in Boise, y'know how it is," he winked smarmily.

Unimpressed with the bullshit attitude of this guy, M.O. stiffened. "No sir, I *don't* know how it is. I'm going to have to ask you to leave the hotel."

"I'm not leaving yet, sir. I paid for a drink and I intend to finish it." Vic thrust the vodka concoction high in the air to make his point.

"Then it looks like you'll be finishing it in my holding tank."

"Your *what?*" Vic's voice became louder. "Are you arresting me?"

"Call it whatever you want, buster. I'm removing you from this bar, and I'll do so forcibly if I have to."

"No wonder this place is a hotbed of death and crime! Look at how you treat your customers!" Then even louder, he shouted at the mesmerized patrons, "Someone video this. Somebody post it!"

Grasping his subject by the arm, M.O. spoke sternly, "Sir, lower your voice and come with—"

Vic turned abruptly in the direction of Grayson, who was 20 feet away pouring a draft beer while keeping an eye on the action. "Hey there, bartender, I'll have another murder!" Impressed with his own impudence, Vic began to guffaw even as M.O. tightened his grip and began to haul him from the LOL. He continued to repeat the refrain even after he was out of sight.

While the upscale crowd was mostly appalled by Victor's impertinence, a few found it entertaining. They jumped on the bandwagon as soon as Vegas Victor was dragged from the premises towards the hotel's detention area. One man walked up to the bar and slapped down a ten-spot in front of Grayson, saying, "Bartender, I'll have another murder," and laughed almost as annoyingly as Victor had. Another jokester followed suit over at Jackpot's end of the bar, saying, "Bartender, I'll have another murder too," as he put down a twenty and began chortling. Before long, several others joined the merriment and a chant began:

"Bartender, I'll have another murder. Bartender, I'll have another murder. Bartender, I'll have—"

And then: "Shut the hell up, you morons!" The voice resonated convincingly, bringing the chorus to an abrupt halt and effectively shutting down all conversation in the LOL. "This is a respectable establishment catering to respectable guests. You wanna act like fools, take your childish act down the street to Piggy's Pool Hall or some other place. Either that or we call that security guard back up here and you can go join that first idiot."

There was a brief silence, followed by a smattering of grateful applause.

The tall man in the blue pinstripe suit continued. "And by the way, murder is no joke. The fact that three have occurred in this hotel in the last six weeks is shocking, and of great concern to many in this community. The Metro police have even formed a task force to investigate. The least you folks can do is show some respect and decency." He stopped, then took a deep breath and said, "Enjoy the rest of your evening."

Who was this mystery man? most everyone wondered. A management guy with the hotel, or maybe the Spectacular Collection's corporate team. That was the consensus.

But Bobby Guanacaste, who'd just happened on the scene as it was unfolding, recognized him at once. And he now had quite a tale to tell his boss on Monday, when he was reporting the details of the Ball. He grabbed the bottle of Maker's Mark he had come for and bolted from the LOL as unobtrusively as possible.

The lovely lady in the white satin gown was mightily impressed. She turned to her date, saying softly, "You knocked 'em dead, man. Let's go back to the Ball. I feel a dance coming on."

Early Sunday morning, Jameson Kean texted his wife back in Las Vegas. *'I'm through in Toronto, heading to Lexington about 11 (Eastern). Love you, and see you tomorrow!'*

An hour later he sent another text, to a different addressee. *'At YYZ, heading to CLE on the noon AC shuttle. See you soon, and looking forward.'* He knew the recipient would comprehend his abbreviations.

Six hours later, he was wishing he'd not made that extra stop. Going straight to Kentucky would've been so much less complicated. Why'd she have to be so damned pissy all of a sudden? It wasn't as if *he* was the only one responsible for their little problem. If it takes two to tango, as they say, then it sure as hell takes two to create an out-of-wedlock child. And to engage in a long-standing affair of the flesh, for that matter.

Willis Bronx's weekend had been extraordinary: the date of a lifetime on Saturday – with more Tapper in his future looking likely – and a relaxing Sunday lounging about his townhouse, doing some cooking (his secret hobby), and watching some more good detective shows. Today's fare included back-to-back Hercule Poirot movies, followed by an evening of *Murdoch Mysteries* on PBS. With the first movie he enjoyed his homemade chicken pot pie and decided it wasn't bad for a first attempt. He packed the leftovers in his work-day lunch bag and stuck them in the refrigerator.

Next morning, after transferring his lunch bag to the Detective Division's break room fridge, Willis booted up his PC. It was 6:15 a.m. on Monday and he was eager to get started on the analytic methodology that had been dancing in his head off and on since he'd left the office on Friday.

His 'SS Tool' – Sleuthing Spreadsheet Tool – was taking shape by 7:00, when Rex arrived. Along the left edge – the y-axis in mathematical terms – was a column to put names, the names of every person remotely connected to the victims and/or their premature deaths. Along the top – the x-axis – were headings for attributes such as motive, opportunity, alibi and others. Rex came over, took a quick look and made an encouraging remark to his rising star.

Four minutes later, Rex was in his corner office, howling so loud that Willis could hear it from fifty feet away. The young man jumped up and hurried to see what the problem was. Had there been others present, a stampede might have ensued, but it was so early that only Willis was in the squad room to respond.

Rex was seated in his swivel chair, and looked to be in good health. That part was a relief to Willis, who had feared a slip and fall. Instead, his boss just looked enraged and pointed at the screen of his cellphone. Willis leaned close and read the short message. *'Lucky for you, lieutenant. No deaths at the Ball. I do hope you didn't feel left out.'*

"Put *that* in your stinking spreadsheet, man!" Rex bellowed.

32

By Sunday, our trip was about half done, and I still had my treasured stash of 210 pesos. We hadn't spent a thing, since the resort was all-inclusive, and hadn't even been off site except for our Friday venture up the beach on foot. So this would be a day for shopping. Gifts for back home folks, a few indulgences for ourselves too. Blouses, scarves, footwear for me. Huaraches and a tri-fold leather wallet for Mase. Vanilla and mini-bottles of habanero sauce; we stock up on these every trip to Mexico. And while I'm always on the lookout for jewelry, I decided to wait till I could bargain with a beach vendor, where I could get a better deal; that little pleasure I'd save for tomorrow or Tuesday.

We dined that evening at a cute spot called La Cocina Latinoamericana on Calle Quinta (aka *5th Avenue*) that offered a hodge-podge of Latin American foods. In ignorance, we ordered the sampler plate, served family style, and I must say this family of two left very satiated. Stuffed is more like it. This was definitely worth straying from our all-inclusive resort. I must've snapped twenty photos!

On Monday morning we were still full, so we ordered room service; a fruit plate to share and a pot of coffee. Quiet beach time next – we preferred the mornings when the sun was less intense and the person density was also less – then back to our unit's shady deck, where I worked on research for our

'Kahluatini' blog (my cutesy working title) while Mase studied self-publishing options. This is the closest to 'work' we'll get on the whole trip. Entirely in relaxed mode, nary a care in the world. I never made it back to the beach to look for jewelry, but there's always *mañana*; the vendors never take a day off. We played some online games together, then dabbled our feet in the plunge pool, ordered room service again, and went to bed early. Funny how doing so little still makes one dozy.

Tuesday was our last full day, and we planned to make the most of it. Bountiful buffet breakfast, then a short walk along the beach, to the south this time. After returning to the resort, Mase plopped into a form-fitting fiberglass chair with a Grisham paperback he'd read before but was happily revisiting; he found a roving waiter and ordered a cold Pacifico. My man, happy as a chip full of guacamole! And yours truly set out with a fistful of U.S. ones, fives and tens, plus my small hoard of pesos. I got myself some beautiful silver earring/necklace sets and a bunch of bracelets. And voilà, all my pesos went for a cute silver comedy/tragedy mask set of earrings and necklace for my dear friend Suzy. I knew she'd think them perfect for attending the Shakespearian plays she often enjoyed.

For our farewell dinner at the Resort Espectacular, we chose the upscale Italian place, Amore Mio. Superb food on a craggy cliff-hugging patio with crashing surf below. The ambiance was rounded out by a mellifluous guy in the background, singing something about the stars and *pasta fazool*. What a romantic way to end our trip.

Of course … it was Valentine's Day!

Back to our room, started our packing, but quickly succumbed to urge for some last-chance Valentine frolicking on our lovely king-size. The rest of the packing could wait!

It seemed like just a few days ago we were reveling in 'Wonderful Wednesday,' but sadly a whole week had already flown by. With no reason to linger, we finished packing and left our lovely bungalow. We breakfasted on calamari and eggs at the Cancún airport and settled into our A & B (shady side) seats on the two-and-a-half-hour flight to Houston. Mase looked out the window and/or snoozed, while I read an e-book on my iPad.

Hours later we arrived home and unpacked our luggage. Predictably, we went first for the purposefully-neglected work cellphones and directly to our email accounts. As a CCSM of long standing, I knew my email would have been blowing up all week long with messages from clients, but I was hardly braced for what I found.

Mase found no calamities awaiting him, but he could read the distress on my face.

"Trouble, sweetheart?"

"Plenty!" I exclaimed. First, I related the almost-week-old message about Maryland's father and her need to return to North Carolina again. And then came worse news, for me personally: the Hearts and Diamonds Ball problems. There were emails from Maris, Hammy, Kinchy and Gunnar, plus the official Security Reports of Sunday and Monday mornings.

Most interesting of the emails was Hammy's, which detailed a minor uprising at the LOL during the Ball, one that ended with some rowdy customers causing a ruckus. It ended with the instigator being hauled off by one of Gunnar's guys and placed in his brig to await Metro's intervention. The Sunday Security Report also referenced this incident, saying that Officer Ochoa had interceded and left the scene with the offender, a local named Victor Heron, in handcuffs, but had not witnessed the ensuing disturbance.

Back at work Thursday for the first time in more than a week, I sequestered myself with Maris and Hammy. I had to get the complete scoop on what had transpired at the Hearts and Diamonds Ball. Maris took the lead on the lovebird incident, including her quick rescue efforts with replacement desserts and gaming credits to soothe those directly impacted. She had not been at the LOL when the brouhaha occurred, but Hammy had and picked up where Maris left off. "Guy is one of those weird regulars you and the bar folks have mentioned. Long beak of a nose, sloppy dresser. Turns out he works for Swank Illusion, and is probably a corporate spy of some sort. Gunnar kept him overnight, then turned him over to a pair of Metro uniforms for a trip downtown on Sunday morning. That's the last I heard."

"What about this chant he started?" That part of the story had really caught my eye.

"Well, as the guy's being cuffed by M.O., he looks directly at Gray Moore and says 'Bartender, I'll have another murder!' and after he's carted off, a few other drunken fools start in with the same line. Slapping money on the bar and saying the same thing. It becomes a chant, like you'd see at a street rally. Five or six guys chiming in, but fortunately it was a mostly-elite crowd, so the troublemakers were a minority and easily nipped in the bud. Would you like to guess who was responsible for restoring order?"

"No, I don't wanna *guess*. Tell me."

Hammy read my no-nonsense face and continued, "None other than our task-force cohort, Willis Bronx. And get this: Mr. Bronx was dapper as could be, and his date to the Ball was our own Tapper. She was an EOQ winner like me, you'll recall. Boy, does she clean up nice and purty! And I must say that Willis seems to have a bright future in peacekeeping."

I was amazed, encouraged and emboldened by all this. Having people like Hammy and Maris on my staff, and resources like Willis working in the wings, made my task as manager of a diverse batch of human beings much easier.

My improved mood soured later in the afternoon when Maris came to me almost in tears, lamenting about Jameson acting peculiar lately. All of a sudden he has to go back to Kentucky *again this weekend* (after just going the previous weekend in connection with the Toronto trip). Something more about the horse-breeding farm on which they're trying to conclude the sale. "He says to be patient, that it will be very lucrative … but I'm just so tired of it."

I empathized – that was about all I could do – and reminded her about Mase's and my BBQ invitation for the upcoming Monday holiday. Now more than ever she needed a recreational diversion.

It was nearly 6 p.m. I returned my thoughts to my current challenges, packed up and headed to the third task force gathering, which was taking place in an hour. We were returning to Fire Station #112 for this one.

33

The task force meeting did not disappoint, either in length or substance. Rex called it to order at 7:07, and welcomed back the well-tanned and relaxed vice-chair. They quickly got down to business.

Gunnar Block spoke about the close look he and a few members of his staff had taken at the weapons used in the three killings. They referred to the autopsy reports. How to administer a fast-acting lethal dose of poison to the drinks was the tricky issue, but logistically it must have been done by the server; no one earlier in the drink production chain could have done it because the victims had apparently not been randomly chosen – how else could proper delivery be assured? Therefore it must have been in an already-liquefied form rather than a powder or capsule that would've taken longer to be mixed in without adverse taste. A small hand-held vial – or rather two vials as there'd have been no time for painstaking measurement. The perpetrator, therefore, had to be a Lady Gaga lookalike or a male server dressed in an NFL team jersey, something that wouldn't have been too conspicuous – best bet was a Patriot or Falcon jersey, but there were plenty of others seen that day as well – Manning, Brees, even a few non-quarterbacks. Anyway, a woman transforming herself into a counterfeit Gaga seemed far less probable than a man passing himself off as a server in a football jersey.

This strongly suggested that the perp was a man. Likely just one, since Swann and Honshu were seated close enough to each other to be served by the same person, but *not* close enough to be part of a single serving tray of drinks. But the two died at close to the same time – conveniently coinciding with the electrical diversion – so they had to have been served close to each other (within one or two server trips, i.e., less than about five minutes apart).

The New Year's killing also appeared to be the handiwork of a man. Overpowering 190-pound Ben Pierce and dragging his body behind the stack of pallets did not seem to be something a woman could achieve. The use of the knife also suggested a perp of significant stature, since Pierce stood about six feet tall.

Hammy spoke next, and credited Gunnar for helping. "We looked through the evidence of the device that made the TV screen 'explode'. Metro officers found a jerry-rigged surge producer in the electrical room where the power source to the TV was located. We checked with the Engineering Department and there was no record of maintenance callouts to that room for 48 hours before the explosion, which means it was a simple device that the guy placed in advance, and planned to abandon after it did its job. It could easily have been hooked to a timer, but no evidence of that was recovered. There was, however, a radio frequency receiver, and their theory is now that it was controlled by a remote, hand-held transmitter.

"Metro confirmed that they have the receiver device and that it was crudely built as opposed to off-the-shelf from an electronics store. The signaling device was not found, either in the electrical room or anywhere else on site.

"The room was locked and there was no forced entry, so we're still trying to figure out how the killer got in." Hammy looked around at the others before continuing, secretly enjoying his newly visible role.

"We believe the Super Bowl killing was committed by a lone male in a football jersey who had a remote-controlled surge device to cause the diversion of the television exploding a short time after the drinks were delivered. We think he may have been standing watch and activated the remote when he saw the two victims beginning to look drowsy or confused." Hammy stopped and took a deep breath, then went on.

"As for the New Year's murder, we think it was probably done by someone who lured Ben Pierce to the loading dock and was already waiting there with the weapon, a rather sizeable knife from what the coroner's report suggests. He must also have had with him the tools to cut off Pierce's hand, along with washcloths, rubber bands, et cetera. We have no idea how he managed to get the fist into the ballroom and hide it under one of the tables where it wouldn't be found for over two more hours.

"The question of how Pierce was lured to the loading dock at a few minutes – 15 to 20 was their best estimate – after midnight on January 1st was more perplexing. It's possible he got a call or text to get him there, but his cellphone showed no calls had been received. Was he meeting someone he knew? A family member? Someone else he was acquainted with? Or could it be someone who was threatening him in some way – apparently Bobby Guanacaste and Jameson Kean found notes in the Pierce suite a day or two earlier that could suggest blackmail. A family member seems unlikely, since Mrs. Pierce was in the ballroom with him when he told her he was going to the restroom, and from everything we've read, both their sons were in Ohio.

"All this made us wonder what Mrs. Pierce was doing during that time? Our best guess is she must've been engrossed in conversation with some of the other high rollers and didn't realize her husband was gone. It's also possible that Pierce told his wife he was retiring for the evening, but then why did she tell the police that he'd simply gone to the restroom? Did she just forget because she'd had one too many?" Hammy closed his notebook and sat back with a confident expression.

Next came the report from the two academics, and the sociologist took the lead. She distributed a six-page printed document to everyone, plus a thumb-drive copy for Sgt. Lee so she wouldn't have to retype all or part for her minutes. The self-assured professor was quick to give equal credit to her criminologist partner, as she reported that their in-depth analysis had focused on the mindset of the perpetrator. "If we are to assume that the same evil mind acted in both the January and February instances, then we have an ego-maniac on our hands. The man – again, we are assuming gender at this point – loves to show off in front of a captive audience. Had he simply wished to eliminate these three victims, there are many less dramatic ways of doing so. Instead, he puts his subjects on display, for others to see as they die … or find shortly after they die." She concluded by saying, "It's almost as if he is taunting the authorities to identify and capture him. And the anonymous text messages received by some of you folks back up our assessment of his mindset. We are most definitely dealing with an arrogant person."

Willis Bronx had brought with him a mountain of notes. He was not as well organized as the professor duo, but full of great content. He reported on making phone calls to verify information – or in some case learn new facts – from family members and associates of all three victims, plus others whose input he thought might be valuable.

"Fifty-three phone calls to eight or nine states, a few follow up texts and I think I have some good info. Most importantly, there definitely is a connection between the men who were killed. In several ways. One, Pierce's younger son Byron is dating Swann's eldest daughter Jilliana, both students at Ohio State." There was an almost inaudible gasp around the room. "He's white and she's black, and the interracial dating didn't set well with either of their fathers, though it was fine with both mothers. The widows told me that Ben had called Jilliana a 'jungle bunny' and Michael had called Byron a 'honky' and a 'fucking cracker.' Also, these two families apparently had met before, at a Big Easy Spectacular high-roller marketing event in New Orleans a few years back. Families in tow on that one. That's when the two lovebirds – high school seniors at the time – met and hit it off, and the boy convinced her to try for admission to OSU so they could continue their relationship.

"I also spoke with Aaron Honshu, and found out that he and his late cousin, Adam Honshu, were in an electronic games club known as The Regal Cavaliers, who competed in e-games with each other and with members of other such clubs all over the world. Other members of that club's Pro Division, where big money was involved, included both Byron and Brayden Pierce. In the Amateur Division of that group I also found a man named Victor Heron, a Las Vegas local who spends a lot of time hanging around the ParaSpec Hotel's LOL bar. Heron – being an 'Amateur' only means he can't afford to play for big bucks – is apparently a major devotee of these e-games, and has an international bloc of followers."

Willis then began reading off his list of bullet points: "I also found out some additional information that may or may not have relevance to these cases."

- Two nights before the Super Bowl – Friday the 3rd – the two Honshu cousins had a wild night of sex with a pair of young ladies who are both employees of the ParaSpec.

- The two Honshu cousins had also been guests at the New Year's Eve high-roller event where Ben Pierce died, but I didn't find any evidence that they and the Pierces knew each other.

- Ben Pierce's brother, Stephen, has an ongoing business partnership with another ParaSpec employee, an executive named Jameson Kean. Stephen Pierce was reluctant to discuss details, but I gather they operate an import-export business out of both Cleveland and Toronto.

- This same Mr. Kean apparently used to date Ben Pierce's widow, Stella. This was way back, but my source – Stephen Pierce again – couldn't remember if it was before or after she married Ben. Possibly both. He also mentioned that Kean and his brother had been acquainted back then, casually only. A friendship never formed.

- Ben Pierce was well insured. His sons, Brayden and Byron, are each beneficiaries of a $500,000 policy, and his wife Stella is named in a $4 million policy.

- I visited the LOL bar at the ParaSpec and spoke with both bartenders who'd been on duty on New Year's Eve/morning. They gave me a few names of customers who were present, including Maryland Burfurd. She was cooperative, but had nothing helpful to add. Though she was at the LOL into the wee hours on January 1st, she didn't see or hear anything unusual. She left town immediately after the murder, but her trip had been planned well in advance and I don't think she's a suspect.

- Victor Heron was the last of those LOL customers I could locate. He was a challenge to talk with. I learned through other sources that he's employed by a competing resort as a Social Media Sales Manager. His role seems to include defaming other properties, such as the Paradise Spectacular, through various social media platforms. On the personal side, he's a diehard e-gamer, and most of his interests seem to be along the lines of murder, death and destruction. Even while we were talking, he was playing something with someone he called 'a bad-ass newbie from Arid-zony.' A very odd guy. I should also mention that Heron was being disruptive at the LOL bar the night of the Hearts and Diamonds Ball last weekend; Chief Block sent a security guard to haul him off but not until after he'd started a bit of a scene. I happened to be there and managed to calm things down a bit."

In closing, Willis brought up the 'SS Tool,' his giant sleuthing spreadsheet, which was still a work in progress. He projected the partially complete version onto the conference room wall and promised completion by the next meeting.

"Does that mean we'll have a bead on our bad guy by then?" the sociology prof asked.

"Probably not 100%. But we should have a good short list that we can focus on. I think we all need to be aware that next week we'll be able to identify specific suspects by name, so it's important that we maintain strict secrecy of our location, as Lieutenant Scharffenberger has repeatedly reminded us." Everyone nodded solemnly.

Charlie was a shaken by many of Willis's revelations … Jameson's involvement with all the Pierces years ago, especially Stella … the connection between Ben Pierce's son and Michael Swann's daughter … the link between the Pierce sons and the Honshu cousins. It was all troubling to her, but she tried not to show it outwardly.

Everyone else seemed to have bought into the notion that a solution was near. For that reason, the mood was upbeat as they dispersed.

Rex wasn't so certain, but he was buoyed by the enthusiasm of his troops. He and Charlie walked out together and he said, "See you next Wednesday, if not before."

"Before," she said. "Don't forget the cookout on Monday. Our house, 2 o'clock."

He flashed a thumbs up and nodded, grateful for the reminder. "Monday it is."

34

I was on an upper of sorts early Friday, the result of the productive task force meeting the previous night, followed by some good food and snuggles with my sweetie.

But there were still some issues nagging at me. I tried to push Maryland's and Maris's problems out of my mind, and was fairly successful at doing so. They were, after all, grown women who should be able to deal with their own problems; I was a friend, not a confessor.

But late in the day, a new weight was heaped upon me. Ira Brickner had been stricken by a serious – though not fatal – heart attack while traveling back east. Apparently, while I was in Mexico and with the Hearts and Diamonds Ball only a few days away, he had abruptly pulled up stakes and headed east, telling everyone that there'd been a family emergency.

Like many others, I had no love for Ira, but hearing this news was disturbing on multiple levels. First, though I was sorry to hear of his health problem, I couldn't help but wonder what it would mean for me from a workload standpoint; more work with no additional compensation was what I feared. But second, and more difficult to come to grips with, was the fact that I learned this troubling news from – *of all people* – Maryland Burfurd, who was not the least bit hesitant to confess that they had been in a state of undress and arousal at the time Ira's heart gave out. I was dumbfounded, to say the least. Maryland, my friend, and Ira, my nemesis of a boss, had been carrying on a sexual tryst on the other side of the country!

Then it began, gradually. I heard the music creeping into my head, screaming its persistent chorus. Demi Lovato's *Heart Attack* was replacing the nameless mariachi strains that had saturated my grey matter since we'd landed in the Cancún airport nine days ago. Much as I loved Mexico, it was about time!

It was 4:40 on Friday afternoon, and I made a hasty decision to keep the news under wraps. For a while at least. I packed up and headed out a tad early, and while in the parking garage I composed an email to Sammy Spakisumar and Leo Stein, giving them the barest of facts. I avoided the specifics of *how* I knew Ira had been stricken, only that he had been transported to expert care at the ICU at Duke University Hospital in Durham, North Carolina.

Yes, that's right. Ira was now in the same facility Pa had been admitted to a week earlier. Pa, Marilyn had informed me, had been shipped upstairs to a regular private room by now. That was the only ray of light in all of this.

My email to Sammy and Leo informed them – and this was 100% truthful – that I'd be unavailable for discussion until later, since Mase and I had tickets that evening to a theatrical production at the Smith Center for the Performing Arts. I confided all the details to Mase when I got home. Already, after less than 60 hours back on American soil, my nerves were frazzled.

Leo called me in to the office on Saturday. He wanted me to take over a few of Ira's duties until he was able to return. I said sure, but wasn't thrilled; Ira never did the job properly in the first place. How should I do them: the painstakingly correct way or Ira's haphazard way?

The ParaSpec was in an uproar once news of Ira's heart attack and infidelity reached our end of the country. I had become the official 'source' for updates – not a role I relished.

Publically, Leo said "no comment" when asked what Ira was doing in North Carolina while he was presumably visiting a sick family member in Connecticut. Ira's brother-in-law had recently had open-heart surgery and was recovering at the Yale University Hospital. But it was unknown whether or not Ira's trip had actually included a visit to see this recuperating relative.

A new hashtag, *#bartenderillhaveanothermurder*, reared its ugly head along about now, or at least I'd just now learned of it. I suspected that malicious guy Victor, who had coined the phrase and was supposedly an employee of our competitor, the Swank Illusion. Not only that, Facebook, Twitter and Instagram were all brimming over with negative postings about the ParaSpec and its slipshod management (Leo and Sammy), its operational team (Gunnar and his guys, the bartenders and me), and of course the still fresh topic of the H&D Ball and its lovebirds on the loose.

I groaned aloud, then went to *#smithcenterreviews*, just for somewhere to go. The reviews of the Peter Pan-themed show we'd seen last night were pretty good and matched Mase's and my take on it. Best of all, it was light-hearted and took my mind away from all that negative drivel about my hotel.

I went home about 2 p.m., fixed myself a toddy and sat by a nice fire. Mase was working a crime scene, a murder last night in a Primm hotel. *Glad to see crimes happening in other hotels for a change*, I thought a little grimly. It was raining and in the low fifties, a dreary day, so I began planning our little Presidents' Day cookout with friends. The storm should be history by then, so I opened a blank iPhone note as my grocery list.

Mase arrived about 90 minutes later, filthy and exhausted. The job down south had involved trudging through the bowels of the hotel, which were muddy and spider-infested. He showered before joining me in front of the fire.

Suzy Hart – by now a friend close enough to come early and help out – arrived at 1:40 p.m. on Monday, Presidents' Day holiday. Sunny and 64 degrees was darn good for February in these parts. The outdoor BBQ at 1521 Stardust Circle would go on!

Mase brought the gas grill up to full heat, and Suzy and I finished setting the patio picnic table for eight. As we did so, I couldn't help thinking how much simpler eight was than nine would've been. I kept the thought to myself. *No disrespect, Jameson Kean. I know you're working hard to provide for your family. Please don't disappoint them.*

The others were told 2:00, and would prove to be remarkably prompt.

Maris Kean arrived at 2:03, with a bakery cheesecake and gooey blueberry sauce, along with her three daughters, Valencia, Almeria and Sevilla. Val, as she preferred being called, was now eight years, four months and three days old (as she made a point of sharing with everyone), while her sisters Alma and Sevvy were six and four. The trio of girls were attired in swimwear and by 2:06 were happily frolicking in our 80-degree pool. We'd specially heated it for the occasion, and we'd see the results in next month's gas bill.

Our final guest, Rex Scharffenberger, arrived at 2:08 and was wearing a fashionable ensemble of khaki cargo shorts and a green-on-yellow-on-orange Hawaiian shirt. I'd never seen him in anything but a business suit, and I daresay Mase probably hadn't either. He looked relaxed for a change, and I felt happy for him. He greeted everyone warmly, and handed me a half case of Scharffenberger wines – three pinot noirs and three brut rosé bubblies.

"Holy crap, Rex! I'm flabbergasted!" I blurted out.

He laughed. "Just a little something to show my appreciation for your help with the task force and everything else lately."

Then, turning to our other guests, he said, "Suzy, what a pleasant surprise. And I recognize you, Maris, though I think you escaped our employee interviews, since you were off duty on New Year's Eve."

"Yes, lucky me!" Maris exclaimed with relief.

"But your husband, I recall, had some helpful information about the Pierces, which you encouraged him to share. Thank you for that."

"Hey, c'mon now," Mase interjected. "No work talk. We're here to relax and get away from all that."

Rex looked over at the pool and saw Val doing a cannonball. "Looks like your girls are doin' just that. And I agree, we should too."

Suddenly there it was again: *Chelsea on my Mind.*

Hey, I remember doin' cannonballs with you, C-girl. We were what, 11 or 12? Down at the Huntington Beach muni pool, all summer long.

Suzy, who was the biggest wine aficionada of the group, raved about the pinot noir and asked the obvious question of Rex. "Are you related to this wine-making family?"

"Not sure, actually. Maryland Burfurd asked me the same thing. I had no clue but her question got me wondering. So one recent weekend when I needed a break, I hopped a plane to Oakland, rented a car and drove up to Mendocino County. Two-hour drive, a needed change of pace for me. Anyway, I talked with folks at the winery, showed them my bona fide ID … but learned virtually nothing. The winery had been taken over by a conglomerate back in '04 and none of the current employees had ever had any contact with the guy who founded it in 1981. I ordered a couple of cases anyway, just to have at home as conversation starters, and because they'd tasted good to me." He grinned as everyone laughed. "But it's funny how one thing leads to another – this got me interested in my lineage, something I never gave much thought to before. I signed up with one of those ancestry-tracing websites when I got home and I'm beginning to get a few trickles of information back. The uncles and cousins and grandparents I knew back east, others in Canada, Germany and Austria. No tie-in with the winery guy yet, but it's fascinating anyway."

I was growing super excited by now. First and foremost, I guess, because we'd stumbled on a topic that pulled Rex completely out of his cop shell, which I sensed didn't happen very easily or often. He needed it, as he'd admitted, and I could see that Suzy was thoroughly captivated by his story and his enthusiasm.

The second reason I was enthralled was that I, too, had finally (back in October) enrolled in a DNA-tracing program through an online site called *whoireallyam.com*. It was feeding me some intriguing things I'd never known about my heritage, with more results popping up almost weekly. In fact, I'd talked it up so much that Hammy and Maryland had also signed up. I'd tried to get Suzy on board, but she seemed less motivated. Maybe Rex's experience would change that.

"Have any of you ever thought about doing this? Suzy, how about you?" Rex was reading my mind, it seemed, trying to draw her into this non-Metro aspect of his world. I already knew he was a bit smitten with her, so if we could move that along a bit today, Mase and I were all for it.

"Mom, I'm hungry!" It was four-year-old Sevvy voicing what most of us were probably feeling by now. Mase and I arose and dispersed, he to the grill and me to the kitchen to gather stuff to take out to him. Maris sensed I'd need some assistance, and also felt like it was the right time to leave the other two alone. Maybe Suzy would open up and share some family background with the detective who was trying hard not to act like a detective for once.

In less than 30 minutes, the feast was laid out and ready to eat. Comfort food, nothing fancy. We had an exceptionally long picnic table with benches along both sides. Plenty of room for all eight of us.

Once the meal was over (except for dessert), Suzy and I cleared the dishes while Mase and Rex cleaned up the grill and its surrounds. Maris pulled the cheesecake from the fridge and began divvying it up onto the eight paper (thank goodness!) plates I'd laid out, along with eight plastic (thank goodness!) forks. Blueberry topping for all, even a squirt of Reddi-Wip for the kids (and anyone else who wanted it). Halfway through her task, her phone jingled, but she let it go to voicemail since her fingers were sticky.

Suzy and I, meanwhile, were chatting at the sink. She said she'd told Rex the idea of tracing her ancestry had never appealed to her, since she and her parents had never been close.

"All the more reason," I said. "You may not like *them* so much, but somewhere in your tree there've gotta be some nice people to cultivate a relationship with."

"Yeah, that's about what Rex said too."

"Smart guy. You two seem to be hitting it off pretty well," I smiled, trying to hide my excitement.

She smiled a smile of true joy. "Yeah, I think we are. If that was your plan in inviting us both, then I think—"

"Jeez, what a fucking idiot!" It was Maris, frowning at her phone after having listened to and read the transcription of the voicemail that had recorded while she was dishing up dessert.

"What's wrong?" I asked, as Suzy and I both turned to Maris, alarmed. I hadn't heard Maris use such strong language since that pesky Dyvan group had messed with her life over a month ago.

"Jameson's what's wrong. He's getting so absent-minded lately. Now he's gone and left his windbreaker in his rental car in Lexington and they called me because I'm listed as an alternate number on his Hertz account. His phone's unreachable at the moment. I guess he's already in the air."

"So they'll mail it, right? I had that happen with a pair of snow boots I left in a car in Salt Lake once. Where'd you say this rental place was?"

"Lexington, Kentucky, where he owns a share of that horse breeding farm. Only 20 percent, I think, but it's side income that's been going straight into the girls' education fund. But now the majority owners have a purchase offer they can't refuse, and Jameson has no choice but to follow along and collect his share."

"That's great. I think you told me this the other day. But are you sure of the details? You said last week he was flying to Cincinnati, then driving to Lexington, which is about an hour away."

Maris furrowed her brow. "Hmm, you're right, now that I think about it."

"Lemme see your phone," I insisted, my hand outstretched and my concern mounting.

Maris handed it over, and I accessed the 'recents' and saw what I hoped I wouldn't. "Do you know Lexington's area code?"

"Not offhand."

"Me neither. But it sure isn't 310."

Maris looked befuddled. "Do I have a problem, Charlie?"

"You might," I admitted nervously.

I really wanted to talk with Mase or Rex about this. But they were outside. So I winged it like a seasoned investigator, rather than as a friend and coworker of the woman next to me.

Her iPhone was still in my hand, so I quickly made a screen shot of the message transcript and sent it to my own phone, and then I found the 'forward' icon and sent the audio part of the message to myself as well. I retrieved my own phone from the countertop and confirmed that the photo and audio message had come through. Then, almost apologetically, I handed Maris' phone back to her, holding it as if it were now a lump of radioactive material.

"I copied it. Just to be on the safe side."

Dumbfounded, I tried to decipher what it all meant. I said I needed some time to think, then walked away from the sink and plopped on the purple couch, alone, trying to come to a conclusion that was less ugly than my initial supposition.

I couldn't find a better answer. Those three uppercase letters – the airport code – and the three digits – the matching area code – kept screaming at me, and I started to cry. They were tears for my good friend Maris Kean and her children, whose lives were about to be torn to shreds.

A half-hour later, I took Maris aside and explained to her what I'd concluded the message from Hertz had really meant. It was a difficult moment for both of us.

35

Stella Pierce had pulled the slider back to let the rhythmic sound of the surf inside. It was supposed to be relaxing, but it wasn't working. Too many things were gnawing at her from within, and she felt helpless to escape. Jameson had left in a huff yesterday after a couple of difficult days in which he'd tried – and failed – to atone for their dreadful rendezvous in Ohio a week earlier. She was fed up, finished with him, and had told him so.

What she really needed was a familiar and friendly face, and those were few and far between these days. She went to the minibar and found a Bloody Mary in a can. Not gourmet, but it would do. She needed it to relax the tension. As she poured it into a glass, the answer suddenly came to her. Why had she not thought of it earlier?

Hoping she wasn't too late, she punched her elder son's number into her phone. Brayden answered immediately, listened to her plea, and said, "I'll be there by 2, Mom. That's 1 your time."

The Bloody Mary was soothing her anxieties. She fixed another and awaited her son's arrival.

The Catering & Convention Services staff meeting went on as usual on Tuesday at 10 a.m. Maris was not present, but her absence was not problematic. Predictably, Ira Brickner's heart attack and infidelity were the hot topics of the morning. Also not surprisingly, there was no castigation of Maryland, who everyone regarded as 'a likeable old gal'. Charlie, especially, had a soft spot for the woman she regarded as a friend.

Most weren't personally acquainted with Ida Brickner, the socialite wife on whom Ira was cheating, but they seemed sympathetic nonetheless. Charlie had met the woman a few times and had formulated no opinion; her disdain for Ira did not automatically translate to support for someone Ira had wronged. Mainly, she wanted to get beyond the issue and start assigning new convention groups that they had to serve in the next few months.

"Were you chilly on your flight home?" Maris asked her husband. After avoiding confrontation last night, and after getting the girls off to school this morning, it was time for reckoning with Jameson.

"Uh … no, why do you ask that?" he asked curiously.

"Because you left your windbreaker in your rental car. They called me."

"Oh, I hadn't noticed. Is that what's upsetting you, honey?"

"Don't you fuckin' *honey* me, Jameson Kean! Not till I get a few answers. Straight answers."

"Answers to what?"

She put her phone in front of him, displaying the screen grab of yesterday's voicemail message. "Read it out loud."

He did so: "'*Hello, Mr. Kean. This is Linda at the Hertz Rental Center at LAX International Airport, advising you that we found a jacket in the rear seat of the Classic Thunderbird you returned earlier this afternoon. We will be forwarding that to the Las Vegas address we have on file for you unless we hear from you by noon tomorrow. Have a nice day, sir.*'"

"LAX?"

"Maris, it's a phonetic translation. The lady was saying L-E-X. I told you I was going to Lexington to conclude the stable sale."

"The same Lexington that is 80 miles from the Cincinnati airport, which is where you said you were flying into and renting your car? You even mentioned looking forward to that peaceful drive through the countryside again. Trouble is, you weren't anywhere near Kentucky on this trip, were you?"

"Honey, I can explain, plea—"

"No bullshit, Angus!" The old nickname surfaced. Sometimes used endearingly, other times for the exact opposite. "I've got plenty of proof that you weren't where you said you were."

"What are you talking about?"

"It's right there in front of you, you deceitful bastard!" She pointed out the Hertz representative's phone number atop the phone call transcription. "Three. One. Zero. 310 area code, my shifty husband! Santa Monica, Beverly Hills, Catalina and ... oh yeah, Los Angeles International Airport, also known as L-A-X. *Not L-E-X.*"

"I can explai—"

"Please do, but don't bullshit me. If it's a girlfriend in Beverly Hills, tell me ... 'cause I've got connections who can and will follow up."

She stared at him in silence for a long moment, almost half a minute. He studied the tabletop, the maple frosting crumbs on it. "Not Beverly Hills," he finally said softly, "Malibu."

Jameson confessed then, barebones but factual. But it *was* a confession. Yes, a lady he'd known for some time, had an off-and-on relationship with for some time, not very often, and it wouldn't happen again. "But I've never stopped loving you, Maris, and every time we saw each other I realized I was more in love with you than ever. That's what I told her yesterday, and that's why we've both decided to call it quits. Forever." He held his arms out towards her, as if inviting her for a consoling hug.

She'd have none of that!

While a tiny portion of her *wanted* to believe what he said – and time would tell, of course, if there was any truth to it – she was so consumed with rage that she let him have it with both barrels.

"Sounds like baloney to me, Angus. Unadulterated crap. Just get your cheatin' ass outta here and go to work. I've had it with you for ... well, uh, *for a while*," she stammered, as tears trickled down her cheeks.

The pressure on Willis Bronx – self-imposed to some degree – drove him to visit the boss on Tuesday around noon to request some more time. Specifically, he sought to postpone the next task force meeting by 24 hours, reminding him that the previous one had also been on a Thursday. "And if we're lucky, we may even be able to make that our last meeting," Willis added mysteriously. Rex was intrigued and liked that idea. He would call Charlie and get her agreement, and then ask Sgt. Lee to notify the other members by email.

Brayden made it through the maze of unfamiliar Los Angeles freeways with ease. He stuck with Interstate 10, which took him straight through to Santa Monica, then dramatically transitioned through a short curving tunnel onto a coastal highway situated a hundred yards from the shimmering blue Pacific.

The yellow Corvette hadn't hiccupped in 300 miles and it only had 12 more to go. He picked up his cellphone as soon as the ocean entered his view. "Almost there, Mom!" he announced when she answered.

Stella called the Malibu Breakers' room service and ordered them lunch. She knew her son would be famished after his long drive. The goodies were delivered and placed on the table on the ocean-fronting balcony, so perfectly timed that Brayden and the room service lady nearly collided in the doorway to room 8 of the quaint seaside lodge.

An hour passed, all the niceties dispensed with, no more topics to kick around. But the young man remained curious about one thing.

"So what brings you to Malibu, Mom? Just had enough of icy Ohio for one winter?"

Stella laughed lightly and agreed, pleased that her son had opened the door to what still had to be discussed. "Maybe enough of Ohio *forever* ... but that's another story for another time. Actually, I was meeting someone. Someone you don't know and probably should never know."

"Gee, this sounds melodramatic." Innocent young Brayden seemingly hadn't a clue.

She paused, collecting herself, and finally spit it out.

"I have a confession to make, son, and it's one I should have made years ago. But the time never seemed right, and you were so young and didn't need the confusion it could cause. But now you're old enough to drive, to vote, to drink, so you're certainly old enough to know the truth. And now that your dad is gone, it's—"

"Spill it, Mom. I'm a big boy. An adult, like you just said."

She looked him directly in the eyes, those big blue eyes that were nothing like her greenish hazel ones or Ben's intensely brown ones. "Ben Pierce was not your father, Brayden."

She continued talking, but her son was remarkably unfazed. "Interesting, Mom. Interesting news indeed. But is it OK if I still call Ben 'Dad'? I mean, y'know, when I'm talking *about* him."

"Of course it is, honey." Stella was perplexed by her son's reaction but said nothing.

There was a long silence. Brayden looked out at the waves for which the little resort had been named. Stella studied him, and he could sense her gaze.

"Anything else?" he queried curtly.

She took a deep breath and added, "You have three half-sisters, aged 4, 6 and 8." She smiled sadly.

"And a brother, aged 20, who just got demoted to half-brother. I don't think I'll tell him, though. Or have you already?"

"No, of course not."

"Is Dad – Ben, I mean – Byron's real father?"

"Of course," she blurted quickly. And unconvincingly.

"Are you going to tell me this man's name?"

"I will if you promise not to contact him. He is out of my life now, and he shouldn't be a part of yours either."

"Isn't that for me to decide?"

"Maybe, under normal circumstances, but everything about this mess is far from normal. He made some ... well, startling revelations to me last week, things that I can't possibly overlook."

Brayden tossed up his arms in exasperation. "OK, mother dearest. I defer to your judgment. I really don't wanna know more. I'm gonna go on loving the memory of Ben Pierce like a father, despite our occasional differences, and to hell with this other guy who boinked my mama back before I had any say in the matter. Now, can we talk about something else?"

He knew there was nothing to be gained by further upsetting his mother. She seemed to be heading towards her breaking point, and he didn't want to deal with her in such a state. He shut up, looked out across the blue water and envisioned all the trophy-sized marlins waiting to be caught. He walked out onto the balcony and enjoyed a little solitude.

After ten minutes, Stella found her voice again and called from inside.

"Are you following your beloved Penguins still?"

"Are you kidding, Mom?" Brayden turned and went back inside. He was pleased by the 'something else' his mom chose to talk about. "We're defending the Stanley Cup and ready to make it two in a row! With Crosby's scoring – he just passed 1000 career goals, y'know – and Fleury deflecting the enemy pucks so well, things are looking fantastic with less than two months to go!"

Stella was only mildly interested in hockey, but she was relieved her son was now thinking about something other than the distasteful details of her marital shenanigans. The rest of their visit stayed focused on his school life, his girlfriend Paige, his brother, and how she was coping with winter on the shores of Lake Erie. This was her last one there, she claimed, not for the first time.

Later, they ordered room-service pizza, salad, wine and ice cream. Housekeeping provided an extra blanket for son's stayover on mom's comfy couch. They agreed that Brayden would drop his mother at the airport as he left town in the morning.

Stella decided the day had gone pretty well, considering. Better than some in her recent past.

For Brayden, it'd been an eye opener, although some of the 'news' was less new to him than he'd let on. He knew who the mystery man was and had even spoken with him in the past. Mom's drama was a draining experience. He was anxious to get back to the comforts of Yuma: his studies and his steady girl.

36

The hullabaloo over Ira's heart attack, and his now-exposed relationship with Maryland Burfurd, made it hard to concentrate on other things on Tuesday. But I did my best, diving headlong into stuff as soon as we put our staff meeting behind us. I had snacks in my mini-fridge that would serve as my lunch.

I put some time into analyzing RSVPs for the upcoming March Madness multi-day Casino Marketing event. This was not a pleasurable task, since that event would require me to interact with the Director of VIP Services, and right now Jameson Kean was riding high atop my personal shit list. I didn't know who or what in the Los Angeles area he was involved with, but he was injecting grief into the life of my dear friend Maris. I was pretty good at not letting personal feelings get in the way of my professional activities, but this guy had stepped over the line.

At about 2:30, my work phone rang and I saw that it was Rex. He had nothing personal to say, despite the enjoyable day we'd shared in my backyard the day before. All business, he asked if I was OK with shifting the task force meeting from tomorrow to Thursday. I readily agreed. There was no rush, and if Willis thought he'd be able to give us better results with some added time, so much the better.

Coincidentally, my personal iPhone cackled as I was on the phone with Rex. Suzy had sent a bubbly text thanking Mase and me for a great cookout and for our matchmaking efforts. She raved: *'After we left your place, Rex took me to Wizard's Lookout for a drink, and he started talking about us (just him and me) going on a winery tour someday! I tried to keep my cool, but I don't think I succeeded very well.* ☺*'*

I took a break and nuked a cup of tomato bisque, which I sipped while I read the rest of my incoming messages. Nothing else on the personal one but the ParaSpec phone was abounding with routine jibber-jabber and a few noteworthy items. Leo had written a broadcast email clarification and update on the Ira situation, which many had heard only in bits and pieces so far. It was a good job, given the touchiness of the *where* and *why* details, and he didn't go near the *who* Ira was with and *what* they were doing when his heart failed. Leo had his faults, but he was a diplomatic and articulate leader. Another broadcast email came from Ramon Zintero, the Resort's Executive Chef, whose plea was titled *'Anyone has seen my baby?'* Ramon was less articulate in English than Leo, but he still managed to convey his message in detail; his 'baby' was a chef's knife with an 8" taper-ground blade, 2¼" heel depth, forged brass-tungsten spine/tang/flush rivets, with 'RPZ' initials engraved in the end cap. *'Please return. Sentimental value. I offer nice reward to honest person who find and return my baby that's missing since New Year Eve. My other knifes not do job as good.'* Ramon covered all the bases, transmitting his appeal to everyone from CEO Sammy to the laundry room to Ira, who was lying in a North Carolina sickbed.

Holy cow! Was this the murder weapon? Why had Ramon waited seven weeks to tell anyone it was missing? Hadn't the police ever asked the chef if he was missing any knives? This information threw a slew of new questions into the mix. For sure, I'd be calling Rex first thing tomorrow to churn through it with him.

As I finished going through the rest of my inbox, my personal iPhone chirped again. I normally keep it muted and stashed in my purse while at work, but it was still sitting out after I'd read Suzy's text. I decided to have a look, and was so glad that I did. It was an email from *whoireallyam.com* that listed some really interesting findings, and a long list of people with whom I might share some genes and chromosomes. Intriguing! I told myself I'd wade through it thoroughly at home, but waiting till then was gonna be a challenge.

Later, on the way home, I experienced a vision so strong that I had to pull my Renegade to the curb of Buffalo Drive until it subsided. It was shadowy and imprecise, but it was big-time stuff and I was spellbound. I wish it came with a replay button. I felt sure it was instigated by the ancestral musing I'd been doing since I'd read that tantalizing email hours ago.

I sat at the curb for a full ten minutes. Literally. In that time I tried twice to resume the drive home, but felt I lacked the capacity. Heart racing, short gaspy breaths, lack of muscular coordination. Finally, on the third try I merged back into the slow lane. It was only four miles to home. A few moments later, though, Stella Pierce called, and answering it was a given. So I pulled back to the curb, put it in park and turned my flashers back on. Stella probed for info about the task force, specifically when and where the next meeting would be. I told her it had just been changed from tomorrow to the following night, and that it was gonna be held at my hotel. I told her it was a closed meeting, not open to the public.

"I need to speak to the group, Charlie. I'm not just *public*, I'm the bereaved widow of one of your victims and I guarantee what I have to say will interest all of you."

"I'll talk to Rex and—"

"Never mind then, I can call that detective fella myself." I could feel her exasperation, and it pained me. The poor woman had gone through so much, but before I could empathize, Stella shifted her focus. "Can you just get me a room at your hotel? Tomorrow and Thursday is all, then it's back to peaceful Ohio for me. To hell with Nevada, to hell with the rest of the friggin' world. A nice room but not a big suite or anything that has a butler or is overseen by that asshat VIP guy of yours. I need be incognito to *everyone* but you, Charlie."

"Maybe the Spectacular at the Convention Center would be a better choice," I said, mentioning our non-gaming sister property a few miles farther north.

"No, I really like your place. I just wanna lay low, OK?"

"OK, sure Stella. Whatever you say. I'll need your charge card to reserve."

Stella rattled off 16 memorized digits and an expiration date. I quickly scribbled it on the back of an old envelope I'd pulled from my purse. "Name on the card?"

"B. F. Pierce. But can you just book me in under an assumed name?"

"Whatever you say. What would that name be?" By now I was tired of trying to separate truth from fiction. *A name, Stel, any name. I just wanna cover the last few miles to home.*

"S. Perkins, how's that?" she said.

"That's fine. Call my office number when you get in, S," I said with a hint of sarcasm.

At the moment all I could think of was getting home to Mase, two adorable kitties, two adoring doggies. A pick-me-up martini. And a mouth-watering dinner of linguine al pomodoro, garlicky baguette, Mediterranean salad and old vine zinfandel.

I wasn't disappointed by any of those eagerly anticipated pleasures. And when I told Mase about my fascinating communication from the genealogy site, he told me to go hibernate in my office area and he'd take care of dinner cleanup.

I was even more appreciative of him when he brought me a mini-drum-stick (the ice cream variety) after I was 40 minutes deep into my 'project.' He said he was going to watch the Lakers whip the collective asses of the Spurs.

Three hours later, my mind was so overwhelmed with names, dates and facts that I had to quit. The TV had gone from NBA basketball to the 11 o'clock news. I zapped the set off, nudged Mase awake, and we trudged up the stairs like zombies. Kitties following, doggies remaining downstairs on guard duty.

Not for the first time, I caught myself singing Crosby, Stills, Nash & Young's *Our House* as we climbed those 15 steps.

The routine. We lived it and we loved it, all six of us.

But it was a toss-and-turn night for me. My strained conversation with Stella kept eating at me, and all the genealogical facts and dates I'd dug up and analyzed were not conducive to slumber. Mase was dead to the world as I slithered from the bed about 1:15 a.m. and went downstairs. I poured myself a glass of milk, fell into the blue recliner and covered up with a fluffy blanket. Pest and Mess soon came over to curl up on the floor near my feet.

My mind was racing and so was my heart. I tried to exorcise those extraneous issues and focus instead on the tranquility that sleep would bring, if I could only allow it to take over my brain.

Shakily, I placed my milk glass on the side table before I lost the strength to hold on to it. I stroked a dog's head and rubbed behind her ears as I found the remote and gradually reclined the seat back. My heart rate must've been 120, but all I could do was lie there motionless awaiting the return of normalcy. I thought about pleasant things – everything from white puffy cloud formations to freshly-baked cookies – focusing intently on them, forcing all the heavy stuff into obscurity.

It was neither quick nor easy, but it ultimately worked. I dozed, and it was after 3 a.m. when I crept up the stairs as quietly as I'd descended them two hours earlier. Mase had shifted sides, but was deep in REM sleep and I resumed my place without disturbing him.

Peaceful sleep came quickly this time.

But it sure didn't last long. Maryland called about 5:45. It was Wednesday, and despite my wild night of many visions and minimal sleep, I was glad to be rousted out of the sack early.

I'd planned to call her sometime during the day anyway, so this was good timing. My head was still abuzz with all of last night's reading, researching and speculating. I had some questions for Maryland, and hoped I could learn something from a heart-to-heart chat. However, she had another agenda, and she quickly launched into a medical rundown of her two recovering patients.

I tuned out most of the Ira info. I wished she had a different point of contact to disseminate his status reports to, but I knew that was asking too much. I couldn't just say, "Tell it to Ida," now, could I? I'd once considered it, ever so briefly, but my self-control prevailed.

On the other hand, I took a sincere interest in the details of Pa's recovery. Maryland said he was continuing to improve and navigate better; he could go to the bathroom without assistance, and was even seen carousing the halls putting the make on the pretty nurses or searching the used food trays for uneaten desserts. There was a good chance he'd be released early next week. That positive news gave me a measure of peace.

I told her I had to run, that I had a big agenda for the day. I also shared that tomorrow I had another task force committee meeting, and that we'd hopefully soon be done with our deliberation and detection efforts. Maybe, in fact, as soon as tomorrow's meeting.

Maryland said, "Gee, am I still a suspect?"

"No, silly, you never were."

"How about a 'person of interest'? Rex taught me that term," she joked.

"No, not that either. You're just someone who's lucky enough to be on the other side of the country when the shit starts flying!"

Maryland laughed.

And I never got around to asking *my* questions.

37

Tindra Block received a call from Charlie Champagne about 9:00 Wednesday morning. It was not unusual for the CCS staff to contact the Front Desk to make a special request on behalf of an inbound guest, usually a meeting planner or group executive. Charlie's request today was a bit different; the special guest was a personal friend who was traveling under an assumed name and wished to remain anonymous after her arrival.

Awkward, yes, but Tindra had long ago learned to comply without questioning. Thus it was that 'S. Perkins' was assured her anonymity. Tindra assured Charlie that all three clerks would be alerted, and that someone would escort Ms. Perkins to her room after check-in.

It was Jameson's first visit to a shrink. Yesterday morning he'd promised Maris, as they sought to patch up their fractured relationship, that he'd give it an honest try. It was not a hollow assurance. Jameson Kean genuinely wanted their marriage to get back on track. Ten years was a big investment for both of them. Three lovely girls had come into the world because of their devotion to each other.

If only he could control his animalistic urge for Stella Pierce, who'd been Stella Occhipinti when they'd first met, when they fell in lust, when together they parented an infant who was born months after she'd become a Pierce. *Brayden Pierce, a tolerable name … but Brayden Kean would have fit even better*, he'd always thought. Though the child was a Pierce from the get-go, he had many features derived from his mother's Sicilian heritage. Occhipinti meant 'beautiful eyes', and the young boy and Stella had shared that most dominant feature.

The Spectacular Collection had a confidential employee assistance program for things like substance abuse, anxiety, depression counseling. Jameson was lucky and managed to get an appointment with less than 24 hours' notice, due to a cancellation. In his allotted 50 minutes, he admitted that he'd been having an affair with someone for many years. "Through all 22 years of her marriage, and even through the 10 years of my own marriage to a woman I love very much and have had three lovely daughters with. What's wrong with me, doc?" he asked the psychologist.

The doctor smiled pleasantly. "Mr. Kean, it's called polyamorous love, and it's not as uncommon as you might expect. Loving two individuals, desiring them sexually even, is not alien to the nature of our species. The issue here is all psychological, as it generates a profound emotional dissonance that usually leaves one or more parties to the complex relationship feeling injured. Emotionally wounded to the core."

"OK, so what can be done about it?"

The shrink mentioned a pair of medications that she would prescribe, but added that success would require some environmental and behavioral changes on his part. "You need to make some hard choices and commit to them. Seriously."

Jameson sighed, "Good advice, doc. I've made my choice. Just hope it's not too late."

From the airport, Brayden's path of least resistance was a right turn thru the Sepulveda tunnel, a sweeping right turn onto the 105, followed by another right onto the 405, which an hour later blended gently into the 5 down in Orange County. His mom was probably at her gate already, and frankly he was happy to have left her and her intrigue behind.

But some of the drama doggedly clung to him, like it or not.

He couldn't shake those abhorrent terms she'd described with the word '*half*.' He was not going to demote Byron to *half-brother* – it would be a lie, and she knew it was – nor would he embrace the notion of having three pre-pubescent *half-sisters*.

Further along, he noticed he was entering Oceanside. He knew the city, since it was where he'd gone with his Arizona Western roommate this past Thanksgiving. It made him remember that hot San Diego State coed – his roomie's cousin – who he'd nailed to the mattress a couple of times on that trip.

That line of thinking put him into a new funk, as he realized his conduct had been no better than his mother's or – heaven forbid – that man who had sired him more than two decades ago. He suddenly loathed himself for having disrespected the relationship of trust he supposedly shared with Paige Lansing in Yuma.

Worst of all was the loathing he suddenly felt for Jameson Kean, his biological father, who had apparently passed on his dishonorable traits to his offspring. He vowed to rise above that type of behavior.

Later that day, Bobby Guanacaste came to Jameson, wondering why the rookie detective was still nosing around in his area. Kean's response was that if his nose was clean he should have no worries.

"Whaddya mean, *if?* You know I'm clean!" exclaimed Bobby.

"Well then, *show it!*"

At that point, Bobby began to worry, even though he had no reason to. What was different now? His boss had always been so supportive, but lately he'd been edgy and irritable like never before. Besides, what's a missing case of Monarch Grove Cabernet have to do with those homicide cases? Aren't those what that cop is supposed to be investigating?

38

Though I was scheduled to meet with all the bartenders on Thursday, I stopped in unannounced on Wednesday as I was passing by around noon. All were present except Jackpot – pretty good for a random drop-in. I suggested there was no further need for me to attend their meetings, since the appearance of strange people showing up at the LOL had dropped to near zero with the banishment of Victor Heron after the Hearts and Diamonds Ball brouhaha.

We all agreed on that ... but just as we did, Gray observed Mr. Mole walking in. The younger Mr. Mole, that is. At some point in the past we'd determined there were definitely two men with moles on their right cheek and neck, both very similar in size and placement. We – the three bartenders and I – watched in silence as he sat. The guy looked familiar to me, and I don't just mean from the surveillance activities the bartenders and I had been engaged in; I'd seen him *somewhere else*, in a totally different context. Or maybe just a *photo* of him. Not sure where or when. It was mystifying and a little unsettling.

Tapper exited our huddled group to take the man's order, and soon popped two Pabst longnecks and delivered them along with two glasses. She returned to her station behind the bar so as not to blow our cover. Mr. Mole was obviously waiting for someone.

Three minutes later I could barely believe my eyes. I was suddenly less than fifty feet from my good friend, Suzy Hart, though she didn't see me. I was clustered at the back table with Grayson and Arty, and she'd seated herself at the small table opposite young Mr. Mole, and her expression was stern. She wasn't exuding the typical Suzy effervescence today.

They were too far away for me to hear what was being said, so I figured they'd be unable to hear me either. In hushed tones, I explained to my tablemates who she was but that I had no idea why she'd be rendezvousing with our mystery man. We all watched and remained as quiet as possible. I was in no particular hurry, but I had developed a thirst. Gray caught Tapper's attention, called her over and ordered us three club sodas. I told her that Mr. Mole's guest was a friend of mine, and that any eavesdropping she could manage would be appreciated.

She grinned as she accepted the challenge. "Consider it done." Wink.

After a few more minutes, another familiar face appeared. A woman, older and sporting a tennis tan, with some major redness around her eyes. She'd been crying. She found a table near the entrance and sat, and I wasn't sure if she was just catching her breath or settling in for a drink. I looked at my two colleagues and whispered, "It's Ida Brickner." In my mind, I heard Patsy Cline's mournful rendition of *Your Cheatin' Heart* (though if Mase shared my knack, I'm sure he'd have heard the original version as written and crooned by Hank Williams!). Was Ida hurting the way Patsy and Hank once had?

In a few minutes, when Tapper returned with our club sodas, I clued her in. "Another situation for you to monitor." I gestured discreetly towards Ida with my thumb.

She grinned again, and reminded us she's been dating a detective lately. "I think he's rubbing off on me." Another wink. Winking was Tapper's forte.

Suddenly, *Chelsea on my Mind* popped into my head. I remembered how my high school chum had also been one to freely dispense with the winks. It was part of what I loved about her.

If ever a day was a manifestation of the catch-phrase '*It's all happening at the bar*', it was today. Unfortunately I had to cut out before anything more occurred. When I left at 12:30, I used the exit from behind the bar that led to the back of the house to avoid being seen. Suzy was still deep in conversation with Mr. Mole – they looked somber – and Ida was talking almost silently on her cellphone. She too appeared resolute. I'd have to stop by later to get a report from Tapper on her eavesdropping efforts.

I left because I got a call from Tindra Block telling me that 'S. Perkins' had arrived, checked in, and was currently being escorted by her bellman Tony directly to Room 8118. Tindra told me she'd taken the liberty of ordering fresh flowers and a fruit basket to be delivered to the room an hour ago, and I thanked her for her attention to detail.

When I got to her room about ten minutes later, I found the incognito Ms. Perkins looking far from the Mrs. Pierce I was familiar with. A spiky red wig with matching rose-hued glasses. Four-inch sling-back heels that matched the wig, red and pointy. The rest of the outfit was a strange composite of black and white ... trendy, I supposed, but rather outlandish for my tastes. "Do you like my new look, dearie? The 'S' is for 'Star,' by the way, and I think it fits perfectly!"

She could see that I wasn't a fan of the look, and seemed almost disappointed.

The room itself was a step down from the usual for Stella Pierce ... but then, at the moment she was Star instead of Stella. It was a small one-bedroom suite and I was sure she would cope. Excusing herself briefly, Star doffed the wig and shades, and ran a quick brush through her own brunette locks. Voilà, she was now my friend Stella again.

She dropped onto the couch and motioned for me to do the same. "It's been a crazy few days!" she exclaimed, without explaining herself.

"Long flight?" I asked as I sat.

"Oh, hell no. Only an hour, but it was what came before that."

"An hour? Why'd I think you were escaping the chilly winter back east?"

"Oh I am, I am. But I've been nearly a week in California. Three days in La Jolla, three in Malibu. My god, I'd forgotten how I love the ocean. Lake Erie just can't compare!"

I had to laugh at that, a picture of a barren slick of ice coming to mind.

"My boy came up for a day. He's going to school in Yuma, y'know."

"No, I didn't know," I lied. Truthfully, I *did* know, since that information was part of the fact set that Rex had collected and Willis had no doubt reexamined in greater depth.

"Ben bought both boys a new Corvette for Christmas, and Bray just loves to drive his whenever he can escape his studies. So he took a little 'pleasure drive' of 300 miles to come see his mama yesterday. Can you imagine? Stayed the night with me, dropped me at LAX this morning. Getting in that car of his and being whisked away so sleek and fast … I'd swear I was Jane Jetson heading for the spaceport."

We small talked a bit longer. She brought me up to date on her other son who was happily entrenched in his agricultural curriculum at Ohio State and had an African-American girl he was wildly in love with. "Ben didn't approve, but I think it's just fine. We are living in a different social climate than when I was their age." She didn't mention that the girl's father, who was also very opposed to the interracial relationship, had been murdered just as Ben had. Same hotel (*my* hotel!) and very possibly by the same person.

I wondered for a moment if Stella was aware of that unlikely 'coincidence'.

Time to change direction.

"So what brings you here again so soon? I doubt it's our lovely ocean." I was sidestepping what she'd told me last night on the phone, making her go through it again. Maybe I'd misunderstood. I hoped I had.

Stella's face took on an expression I'd not seen on her before. "It's your little task force, I told you that. You and that Lieutenant Rex, and the others. I've got some information that will be of great interest to your group. As I told you, I want to address the task force at the meeting tomorrow night."

"We are a closed group. But I'd be glad to hear what you have to share, and pass it along."

"I could've done that by phone or email."

"Yes, Stella, you could have."

A long pause. Stella picked up the room service menu and perused it, but clearly without purpose. She turned, looked sternly at me and said, "I need someone in my corner, Charlie. Are you gonna be it … or not?"

"In your corner? Of course I am. We've known each other for several years now, and I share your sadness over Ben's death. But Stella, I'm operating within a committee appointed by the Sheriff, the chief law enforcement officer of Clark County. I do not call the shots and I cannot just escort you into the group because I'm in your corner or you're in mine."

"I know who killed Ben," she said bluntly.

"I do too," I shot back impulsively.

Stella looked flabbergasted, and I must have looked about the same. I had actually said those three words … and I meant them. My psychic visions had clarified what I was beginning to suspect anyway, and I was now admitting that to someone other than myself.

We gazed at each other for a good five seconds before I rose and broke the silence. "I'll see you later, Stella. Order yourself some food, take a nap, relax in a bubble bath, watch TV, whatever. Just sit tight in this room, and I'll be back at seven-ish, when we can talk and plan for tomorrow. Heavy talk, but if we do it tonight then tomorrow will be more relaxing."

Giving her no chance to counter my instructions, I quickly turned and left the room.

The past 24 hours had been as chaotic a period as I can ever recall experiencing. My brain cells felt exhausted, my emotions ripped to shreds. It was as if everything was reaching the culmination point concurrently, issues that were unrelated except for the fact that they were incredibly important to me, issues that may define the rest of my life from this day forward.

I needed to bring my husband aboard. Until now, I had thought my visions had to stay private, that it was just the way one played this peculiar 'gift or affliction' game.

I was wrong.

Now, more than at any other time, I needed Mason Champagne at my side. And with what I'd just said to Stella Pierce, the need felt more urgent. It was high time to get my moral support guy involved. I called him and asked if he could escape his office early and join me for a quick bite at the B-L-D Spectacle at 5:30.

Suzy called and said she'd been at the ParaSpec earlier but hadn't had time to stop in for a visit because she had to hurry back to work. I told her I'd seen her with 'Mr. Mole' at the LOL, because I'd been there hanging out with the barkeeps. This opened the door for Suzy to share her story of regret. 'Mr. Mole' was Donnie Soul, her boyfriend, who worked for Billy Swank, owner of the Swank Illusion and a few smaller hotels in the area, and that forced Suzy to make the break. She'd learned too much – some of it from me – that told her Swank's ethics were minimal and his business practices were shady. Dumping Donnie was therefore a given, and not all that difficult. I remembered the scene I'd witnessed at the LOL and decided it may not have been pleasant but she had handled herself well.

Suzy added how opportune it was that this occurred just as Rex was entering her life. I could feel her big joyous grin through the phone lines.

"Good luck with that, girl," I said with sincerity. She was overdue for some luck in love.

I then realized that I must've seen a photo of them together on some social media site, which would explain why he'd looked familiar to me at the LOL. Mystery solved, albeit a miniscule one. I wished the bigger mysteries would be so easy.

Next I called Rex and made a case for allowing Stella to come speak to the task force. I must have been persuasive because he readily replied, "Sure, why the hell not?" I think he might have been swayed when I told him she was *absolutely convinced* who had killed her husband. I doubt, however, that he was *absolutely convinced* or he'd be on her doorstep right away to get the story from her.

And no, I didn't bother to add my own belief that her conclusion was correct; I couldn't see how a psychic vision would help matters.

Mase was waiting at the entrance to the B-L-D Spectacle when I arrived at 5:36. Being late wasn't my norm, but this wasn't a normal day. The hostess led us to a quiet table far in the back, where we could talk without whispering. I'd had enough of that for one day. She handed us menus, but both Mase and I knew what we wanted. The B-L-D's patty melts were thick and juicy, covered the full extent of the rye bread, and their medium-rare delivered Mase's desired level of pinkness. The side of onion rings were also first-rate.

I ordered a tuna salad on whole wheat with extra pickles, then launched into my spiel, looking him straight in the eyes. "Mason, dearest, I've left you out of much of the recent turmoil in my life in an attempt to protect you from things that I thought I could and should handle myself. You have your own life, your own career, and you really don't need my burdens as well. But I've recently realized that I think they're too big for me to handle alone. I need to unload and share the weight."

Mase looked both shocked and surprised as he said, "I'm all ears." A favorite Mase expression, but he always meant it.

I took a deep breath and began. "Since Monday of this week – when we were having our little backyard party – two enormous events have taken place. They are unrelated except for the fact that both impact me tremendously. With all sorts of little offshoots that complicate and confuse things even more, my mind is overwhelmed with sensations and reactions."

Mase's wordless gaze urged me to continue.

"Remember the ancestry site that I signed up for last fall? Well, I received the third round of results this week and got some very startling news. I'll get to the details in a moment, but first let me switch gears. The second major event that has clobbered me is that the killer of Ben Pierce and the other two men has come to light, and will be announced at tomorrow's task force meeting." I went on to explain that Stella was back at the hotel, lying low and incognito, and wanted to attend the meeting with me. "Of course, she cannot attend unless Rex gives his OK, and I have my doubts he'll go for it. More likely he'll want to chat with her one-on-one."

"She's not the killer, is she?"

"No, not a chance. She was scrutinized closely by the committee, especially Willis. Boy, you lost a jewel when he left the CSI!"

"Don't I know," Mase groaned. "Ok, so I assume you can't tell me who the killer is until the committee meets, but tell me about the ancestry stuff."

"*This* you are not going to believe," I prefaced, just before spilling the one inescapable conclusion I was still having difficulty accepting.

Now I knew my parents' marriage hadn't been smooth sailing, with its roughest spots occurring back in the late '70s and early '80s, their first decade together. The crux of their problem was Mama's difficulty with conception, and how to deal with it. They both desperately wanted a child, but when it came to how to make it happen, they were divided. And stubborn. She favored adoption – even to the point of adopting a child from Korea or Nigeria or who-knows-where – but Père, as I've always called my French-born daddy, was not convinced. He expressed fears and pessimism over adopting, foreign child or otherwise. Too many unknowns. He had other ideas. Together they saw doctors and more doctors, and tried one conception strategy after another.

Obviously, they'd eventually found success (to wit: yours truly), and it was only a few months before they'd died that I learned that I had been adopted after all. They'd finally decided it was time for me to know the details, and we – Mase and I – had made plans to travel to O.C. to see them and hear it all face-to-face. Tragically, the brushfire that consumed their home and killed them both occurred a week before we were to visit, and we found ourselves headed to California for a far different reason than originally planned. And, of course, I never learned the long-withheld nitty-gritties of my coming to be a member of the Chardonnay household.

I next explained to Mase the one astonishing reality that my psychic powers had dropped in my lap earlier today. When I told him my hunch, his jaw dropped.

At long last he was giving my powers of clairvoyance their due respect.

I then returned to my original topic and told him these powers had definitely given me a big boost in identifying the ParaSpec's triple killer, and that Stella's independent conclusion had simply validated it. We had zero doubt. But I refused to let even Mase in on that particular secret. He understood and didn't prod.

Later, after sending Mase on his way – four hungry pets at home, y'know – and closing down my office for the day, I returned to Stella's room and we chatted over a bottle of Chandon Brut and the hors d'oeuvres tray she'd ordered. She did most of the eating; it'd be her dinner, I imagine. I was still full from my tuna sandwich, but I happily shared her bubbly. I told her of my unexpected callback from Lt. Scharffenberger just 20 minutes earlier, and his surprise decision to permit her to attend the meeting tomorrow night. She was delighted.

"I managed a half-hour nap, and I made some calls home," she explained. One of the calls, she added casually, had been to Byron. "I just saw Brayden, and that made me so lonely for my youngest," she admitted. "He's coming to see me. Soon, very soon."

As peculiar as that sounded, she did not elaborate. And I did not ask, fearing where it might lead. Instead, we moved on and made plans for a relaxing excursion together away from the hotel the following day … spa treatments at another property, lunch, whatever. She thought it was a good idea, and was pleased to leave the details to me.

I told her I'd stop by and pick her up about 9:30 in the morning.

On my way home, I emailed Hammy and told him I'd be out of the office most of the day, so would he please plan to be in charge. Maris was still on the edge emotionally, and there was no assurance she'd even be around. I had full faith in Hammy.

I can't remember the last time I impulsively took one of those days they call PTO.

39

Willis Bronx was in early Thursday morning, putting the finishing touches on his PowerPoint presentation showing the evolution of his 'SS Tool' into what he was now calling the 'Criminal Extraction Technique.' That was more apropos to its actual function, as it takes a vast population which, at the outset, is virtually certain to include the actual perpetrator. That was the key: spread the net far and wide and let the tool toss out, over multiple iterations, the 99-plus percent who are not viable candidates. The screening attributes used were vital to getting a proper result, and he'd spent a great deal of time honing these questions and answering them as they applied to over 900 initial possibilities. Some questions were simple 'yes' and 'no' while others were weighted zero through five.

The fact that three different deaths were being investigated made the process more intricate than originally expected. Though there were many similarities and connections between the victims, there was no proof that the crimes were related.

Further complicating matters was the ever-present possibility of a hired killer. That could skew the importance of the 'opportunity' and 'alibi' attributes. Rex had already counseled him about that aspect of police work in general, especially felony crimes against persons.

A handful of names had risen to the top on all three murders. Willis became convinced there was a lone killer, and that he/she was on this list. He had his 'favorite,' but felt it was his role on the task force to present a short list and let the group work on narrowing it to one. If they strayed from his chosen one, he'd try to coerce them back to what he saw as the correct track … or he'd allow himself to be convinced of another choice. He kept an open mind.

The entire presentation had been honed to 11 slides, a manageable size. He sent a quick text to Charlie Champagne to make sure the meeting room was projector-and-screen ready, and she promptly replied that it was. Charlie did not share the room name with him, per Rex's edict.

Byron Pierce had been anticipating Thursday's daylong excursion to a working farm in Shelby County, 40 miles west of the OSU campus in Columbus. It was the prized activity in the prized class of his entire sophomore curriculum in the animal husbandry degree program.

But that was before his mother had called on Wednesday afternoon, sounding down and out, talking about how she'd just seen his brother and wouldn't it be nice to see both her boys in one week. He remembered his pledge when he'd returned to school a month ago to be at her beck and call whenever he was needed.

"Sure, Mom, I can be up in time for dinner. Want me to grab some of Giuseppe's cacciatore for us?" he'd asked, mentioning her favorite bistro in Shaker Heights. His favorite too, and he was already looking forward to it.

That's when she'd informed him she was in Las Vegas.

Despite seeing his field trip evaporate, he agreed like the good son he'd always been. By 11 the next morning, his classmates were ankle-deep in cow dung and he was boarding a 737 commuter jet to Chicago, with a connection to Las Vegas.

Charlie popped into her office just past 9 a.m., but it was not much more than a quick stop to touch base. She had confidence all would run smoothly in her absence.

"See you tonight at the task force," she told Hammy. "Expect the email notice from Sergeant Lee around 4."

From there she was off to fetch Stella. They had planned an enjoyable day of escape from the horrid truth that would be revealed at the meeting that evening. Charlie'd decided a ride in the open countryside would be symbolic of escape, so she piloted the Renegade down Highway 160, over a short mountain range into the rural community of Pahrump. A 60-mile trip, but it went quickly with pleasant talk along the way. Trying to put aside the seriousness of matters to be handled later in the day. They had an early lunch at one of the small wineries the town boasted, shared a delightful chocolatey dessert and headed back to an off-Strip resort in time for their 1:30 massage and facial appointments.

Back to the ParaSpec by 4:30, where they parted and promised to meet at the LOL at 6 sharp. From there they'd walk to the B-L-D and grab a quick meal – Stella was tired of room service! – before heading to the task force at 7. She planned to revert to her 'Star Perkins' persona for the meal, but would remove the wig and brush out her natural hair once she was in the meeting room. Charlie approved the precautionary approach.

Roberto Guanacaste snuck an unauthorized break on the oil-stained concrete by the loading dock, an inconspicuous spot where he could grab a quick cigarette. Five minutes or less, and he always disposed of his dead butt before leaving. He was allotted one 15-minute break in the afternoon, but sometimes when he was tense, one smoke just wasn't enough. Today it was the fault of his direct supervisor. The big man, Jameson Kean, was on edge, on the verge of coming down on him for no reason whatsoever.

It had been that way for the last couple of weeks, now that he th... about it. Mr. Kean hadn't been himself. Bitchy and cranky were two wo... that came to Bobby G's mind, although a few less flattering ones in *españo*... also suggested themselves.

The Corvette pulled into a familiar gas stop in Searchlight. Second time this month. Brayden could see he had plenty of time to spare. Byron's flight from Chicago Midway was scheduled to arrive at 5:40 p.m., and the latest update indicated it was right on time.

He paid for his gas, then fed three quarters into a slot machine and walked away with 80 quarters. *Wow – no wonder Mom likes these one-armed bandits so much!* he thought, with an unexpected smile.

He sent a quick text to his brother to refresh him on how to maneuver Las Vegas's airport: *'Find Level 1, a.k.a. baggage claim. Walk out the north door. Yellow Flash at the yellow curb. Can't miss it!'*

Just yesterday, Byron had related the pleading tone of their mother's voice. Otherwise Brayden wouldn't even be doing this. He'd just lost the better part of two days visiting dear old Mom in Malibu, but like his brother he was committed to helping her through her difficult days. And who knows, maybe together they could cover some of their own dirty tracks while they were together. Ohio son plus Arizona son made for a coordinated brotherly approach.

Charlie managed a productive late afternoon hour at her computer. By 5:30, she was ready to hang it up for the evening and encouraged Hermie and Kinchy to head on home. The fewer people around during the meeting in the hotel the better. Hammy remained, of course, and they talked for a few minutes before Charlie announced that she had a 6 o'clock meeting at the LOL and had better be on her way. She did not mention who she was meeting. "I'll see you at the task force," she said, and he nodded.

As Director of VIP Services, Jameson Kean was accustomed to doing a daily perusal of the hotel's check-in report. It was a habit by now, and one that occasionally bore valuable fruit. Usually it was to find a dignitary of some kind, befriend the person, and thus build goodwill and perhaps earn a handsome gratuity. It only took a couple of minutes each day.

Yesterday his efforts had turned up a curious check-in that he'd thought deserved a deeper look. The name 'S. Perkins' gave no suggestion as to gender, which piqued intrigue in itself, so he looked at the payment details and saw another non-gendered name attached to a Visa card. However, the name on the card was telling, despite its being initials as well.

Let's get this all straight, he'd pondered long and hard ... 'S. Perkins' was paying for his/her room using a card issued to 'B. F. Pierce.' Could that possibly be the late Benjamin Francis Pierce, whose wife was known to travel with monogrammed luggage bearing the letters 'S.P.'?

Kean wasn't prone to conclusion-jumping. But sometimes it was unavoidable.

It had nagged at him all Wednesday night, and when Maris asked what was wrong, he sidestepped the issue with a phony story about a demanding client in one of the suites. By Thursday morning he'd developed a plan, and he'd spent the rest of the day detailing it.

Charlie arrived at the LOL at 5:55 and set herself up at a nice window spot for her meeting with Stella. Tapper was running tables while Jackpot was manning the bar. Not very busy yet. Small talk between Charlie and Tapper soon had the young Caribbean asking whether the task force meeting was being held at the hotel tonight.

"Yes, but no further details. Please don't ask," Charlie said gently.

Tapper avowed no interest in the meeting itself, but asked if Charlie would please send Willis to see her here at the bar when the meeting was over. "I just can't get enough of that sweet boy!"

Charlie smiled, thinking of the matchmaking role she'd been playing with Suzy and Rex ... and now facilitating Tapper and Willis too. It gave her a needed dose of warm fuzzies.

But her smile faded when she realized it was 6:10 and Stella hadn't yet arrived. More precisely, the gaudy 'S. Perkins' had not shown herself.

Hmmm ...

Stella had napped for thirty minutes, taken a leisurely shower and spent more time than she normally would on her hair. She prepared it for an easy brush-out at the meeting after discarding the unruly red spikes and tinted eyeglasses. It was 5:40 and she was seated at the small vanity, adding some finishing touches. She was wrapped in a pink velour robe – her own, not the hotel's – without a stitch on underneath. Hurrying to get ready so she could get to the LOL by 6:00.

There was a rap at the door.

"Who is it?" she asked, rising and approaching the door.

"Room service for S. Perkins," came the reply. It was a rich baritone.

The cart was filled with her favorites. Tasty edibles like goat cheese-filled wontons, soft pretzel bites with a tangy mustard-apricot sauce, and flaky apple tarts. All kept pleasantly warm under a steam canopy – 110 degrees according to the digital meat thermometer that was doing duty as a pastry thermometer. Alongside the food was a brass ice vessel with a chilled magnum of Bollinger Brut and two frosty flutes.

The fellow pushing the cart had made a hurried effort to disguise himself. Hurried but effective; tinted glasses and a stick-on bushy mustache made instantaneous recognition unlikely and, yes, it got him through the door. He looked for all the world like a room service attendant, right down to the white satin gloves.

The sequence of events thoroughly stunned Stella. This room service guy waltzed right into her room, delivering an order she hadn't requested, but he seemed so determined and self-assured. He was handsome, too, and she felt the inexorable stirring of attraction. *Shame on me*, she thought ever so briefly.

That was before he swiped a hand across his face, removing the shades and Tom Selleck-mustache in one fluid movement. Her recognition was instantaneous and incredulous, though her slack jaw failed to form any words other than, "Jameson! I thought—"

"You act surprised, my love. I'm the one who should be surprised. After Malibu, you made it clear we were done. Washed up, *kaput* forever. Back to Ohio for you. But I guess you didn't mean it. You're trailing me like a magnet, Stel—no, I mean, S. Hey, what's that S stand for, anyway? Sally? Sonja?"

"Star, if it's any of your business." There was a definite edge to her reply.

"My hotel, of course it's my business." He turned and began uncorking the huge bottle of upscale bubbly. Stella watched in silent fascination as she recognized a sudden thirst for something cold, wet and intoxicating. "What I wanna know is what you're here for, Star Perkins, if not for me. Never get enough of the ol' jackhammer, do ya?" His resurrection of a term she'd used more than once to describe his style of lovemaking wasn't helping matters. Her face flushed as the animal magnetism began to kick in, even as she tried to fend it off.

Cork popped, flutes filled and a toast proclaimed: "To us, our magnificent past and our glorious future."

She accepted the glass, but blurted indignantly, "Glorious, my ass!"

"Oh, indeed it is," he quipped, as his eyes moved south, though her robe revealed nothing.

"What I meant was *future, my ass.'* There is no future for us, Jameson Kean!"

"Oh, lassie, such a defeatist attitude. Now that dear old Ben is no longer with—"

"Yeah, he's gone. You handled that nice and neatly all by yourself. You told me yo—"

"Was anything but neat, my love. A knife is not the cleanest of options, even for a master carver like myself. You never told me how you wanted—"

Stella overrode his blathering again. "You were so much neater with the pair at the Super Bowl event. Or do you deny—?"

"Experience teaches," he said sarcastically, making no attempt to deny her indictment. His attention then turned to the cartful of delicacies in front of them. He checked the temperature, seemed pleased at the result and stuck the thermometer in his vest pocket.

Stella noticed and giggled at that. "A meat thermometer for pastries. How gauche."

"You know I'm a meat guy at heart. I don't even own a *baking* thermometer."

"I guess if it works, it works."

"I'm sure it will work," he said, immediately regretting his choice of the future tense. But she was oblivious. Her focus was now on the food, and her attention to detail was already weakening.

"You still haven't told me why you're here, Stel … I mean, Star," he said as he filled a small plate and extended it towards her.

"My friend Charlie Champagne. She invited me," she lied, while she also ignored his fumbling with what to call her. "I'm going to a meeting with her tonight."

"A meeting? My goodness, whatever for?"

"I have information she and some others need to know."

By 6:20, Charlie's nervousness at the LOL had amped up. So much so that she called Tapper over and said, "Bring me three fingers of gin on the rocks, but make it look like a glass of water." Tapper complied without question. At 6:25 Charlie called Stella's room but again got no answer.

"I'm gonna look for my friend, Stella. If she shows up here, have her sit tight and gimme a buzz on my cell."

Tapper didn't know the whole story, but she recalled the woman Charlie had mentioned. The New Year's widow. She said she'd keep a close lookout.

Stella suddenly gave her visitor a cool stare. "Hey, why am I telling you this? You, of all people!"

"I wondered that too, my sweet. But let's forget about the meeting for now." He reached over to touch her, and this time she didn't recoil. She welcomed his strong hand, and returned the touch with one of her own. The champagne, the culinary delicacies, the flesh-on-flesh contact … it was all working in concert to dissolve her resolve.

"Oh no, my glass is empty already," she said, in an almost bashful whisper.

Jameson to the rescue, quick to top off her flute. His own as well, though he'd drunk hardly any of his first glassful.

A few minutes later, the robe was on the floor in a heap, and Stella was succumbing to the oft-plied charms of the lothario from Scotland/Ontario/

who-knows-where-else. All she knew was that she loved what he offered, and she was suddenly eager for more of it before her chances ran out.

"Lady's choice," he said, as they crossed the few feet to the bed. "It could be our last time together."

A contemplative look came over her face, but for only the briefest of moments. She climbed onto the bed, up on elbows and knees, presenting her delicious derriere for his inspection and assault.

He knew she'd select that configuration if given the choice. It was exactly why he'd given her the choice.

"Our last time? Don't say that! I know it's true, but must you say it aloud?"

If Jameson responded, she didn't hear his words. He was so much better than Ben had ever been. *Was it sacrilege to say that, to even think it?* She'd been plagued by that question for decades, literally, and didn't expect an answer to pop up now ... or ever. She just reveled in the sensations this Scottish lover of hers could produce. Extreme bliss was the monarch, but it was the parade of princely side spectacles that helped make it such a unique package. Twitching. Fleeting bursts of pain transforming to rapture. Bright flashes of colored light, then darkness, then more light, and finally a private fireworks show inside her head.

Today was no different, perhaps because of the worry that it might be their last.

For sure, it would be a whopper. The sideshows were enormous. The intense feeling in her chest was wonderful, though more powerful than most she'd encountered, a shade more discomfort. That was all right ... this was a coupling for the record books. She understood that much and relished it.

The pleasure grew exponentially. The pain grew too, almost to the point of agony. The shrieking had begun, though she wasn't really sure when it had. She felt an oozing warmth – a new twist on things – but it just amplified the sensation of being swept away. The rockets in her brain were becoming cataclysmic. Bright lights, then darkness, then explosive orgasming coupled with the anguish of pain in her chest, her head, even her toes. But most of all, her chest.

And then the commotion of phenomena ebbed, slowly, as they always did. First the vocalization, then the sharp neural aspects. The pyrotechnics show in her mind gave way to dark spells, the once-enormous brocades and chrysanthemums becoming a faltering array of unimpressive willows, colorless and shallow.

She knew – if she'd had the capacity to think rationally at that point – that she often blacked out for a moment after a stupendous sex session. This one was going to be like that … yet different, as well.

Yes, perhaps a lot different.

The phone rang, but Stella didn't hear it.

Jameson, dressed again and now departing, wished her sweet dreams. She didn't hear that either.

40

I left Tapper in a proverbial cloud of dust, on a desperate mission to find Stella. She was 25 minutes late for our rendezvous at the LOL, and I could think of no plausible benign reason for her tardiness. None of the other possibilities were encouraging.

The first place I checked was the B-L-D, where I'd mentioned we could grab a quick bite before the task force meeting. Perhaps she'd misunderstood and was waiting for me there instead. But no dice. She wasn't there and I'd wasted the better part of five minutes. I headed to Stella's room in the Wonderful Wing, a good long walk that I hiked at a brisk pace. I called the room a second time – again getting no answer – and then texted Rex and told him my 'Star' guest was AWOL. He said he'd delay 10 or 15 minutes, but couldn't justify making the rest of the members sit on their thumbs any longer than that. I concurred, and told him I'd update him as soon as I could.

The furtive slug of gin I'd had back at the LOL was kicking in, and it was a lifesaver. Without it, I'm sure my jangled nerves would've gotten the best of me. But now I was Charlie the super sleuth, on my way to solve a mystery that was as perplexing as any I'd ever known.

It was 6:38 when I reached room 8118.

I knocked, but there was no answer. I was not surprised.

I called Gunnar to order a 'room check,' which is when a person with a master key opens the room to make sure the occupant is OK and not suffering from a fall or a medical episode. I said it was urgent, and in a matter of moments Mario Ochoa from Security arrived with his key. After repeating the ritual of knocking and loudly announcing our presence, he inserted it and stood aside to allow me entry.

I proceeded into the room, M.O. following closely behind. There I discovered a nightmare. "Stella!" I shrieked. If not for the oversized *hombre* close behind me, I'd surely have collapsed onto the floor. M.O. supported me and helped me confront the scene that we faced.

"My God, what's happened to you?" It was a stupid question, I realized, especially since she appeared incapable of answering.

"You know the lady?" he asked, rather stupidly as well. Of course I knew her, but I'd never seen her naked, and most certainly had never seen her lying face down in a pool of her own blood. Her head was turned to the side, facing us, and I thought I saw a flicker of a response to our voices. I bent down over her, and detected an eyelash flutter and a slight exhalation. With that breath came a sound, a single fricative push that was barely discernable. We watched closely, and the sound was repeated, this time a little louder and with a little more desperation behind it. At first I thought it was a '*ch*' or '*sh*' sound, but M.O. suggested maybe it was a '*j*' instead. An English '*j*' rather than a Spanish '*j*', he clarified. I decided he was right when poor Stella uttered it a third and final time, this with a distinctive long '*a*' vowel sound attached.

M.O. was already on the phone, ordering someone to call for a bus – which I found strange, but I was too preoccupied with Stella to voice my curiosity. He then made a few additional calls, all brief and to the point.

I wasn't a rocket scientist, but it didn't take one to put it all together. I understood that Stella had been identifying the person who'd done this to her, and those few repeated sounds were sufficient. It was the person she and

I had both concluded was Ben's killer … as well as the one who'd likely poisoned the pair of Big Game fans a month later. I capsulized my conclusions for M.O., and asked him to have his fellow security guys attempt to locate and apprehend this evil man. There was a good chance he was still somewhere on our property.

Returning my attention to Stella, I could see that her condition was not improving. In fact, her mouth remained in the long *'a'* configuration, but no breath was pushing the vowel sound further outward.

M.O. attempted CPR on her, but it proved futile. Alas, Stella had passed to the other side. A tear formed in the corner of my eye, then another.

M.O. joined me in this sad realization, putting his fingers to her carotid to confirm, and offering me a slight nod. He reached down and retrieved her pink robe from the floor and gently placed it over her, shielding her lifeless form from further public scrutiny. Reinforcements would soon arrive, and the poor woman deserved this tiny measure of decorum before they descended and began their clinical assessment.

I smiled gratefully at M.O., though smiling hardly fit the situation, and I then found myself laying my tear-stained face upon his massive shoulder. I could hear *Angel* by Sarah McLachlan as my tears dampened his shirt. Having him there with me was a great comfort at this horrendous time.

There was no time for sustained weeping. I phoned Rex, who by now I figured must be at or very near the Utopia Boardroom, the small and little-known meeting room I'd selected for this week's task force gathering. It was tucked in a back corner of the Mezzanine level, fully-equipped with state-of-the-art technology – my primary reason for choosing it – so Willis' PowerPoint show and Rex's desire for an interactive whiteboard with printing capacity would be satisfied.

I caught him just as he was arriving and hanging up his rain-soaked trench coat. Our lovely desert was apparently getting a shot of unexpected moisture; it was news to me since I hadn't poked my head outside since well before noon. As I advised Rex of the dreadful turn of events, I found myself wondering if the rain shower was Mother Nature's way of crying for my departed friend Stella. It seemed so appropriate, and reminded me of the long-ago day when my beloved grandma had passed away and a sunny California day abruptly turned dismal and drippy. I often thought about that when a surprise shower materialized out of the blue.

The clock hadn't reached 7 yet, so Rex had a few minutes to act before calling the meeting to order and ... *doing what?* I couldn't imagine how he was going to handle things in light of the latest happenings.

M.O. was now on the phone with Gunnar, who I guessed was probably also at the Utopia by now – he was notoriously early for task force meetings – and asking him to mobilize every staffer he could. Though he realized it was a job for the *real police*, i.e., Metro, he wanted a piece of the pie for their in-house security team as well. I was sure Gunnar would share that perspective.

My place wasn't here with Stella's body and the crowd that would soon drop in on room 8118. I thanked Mario Ochoa, and left him in charge of the grim situation. "Gotta run to meet with the Metro lieutenant and the task force meeting," I said as I rushed out the door.

I punched in Mase's cell as I waited for the elevator. He'd be devastated by the news, but he'd asked to be kept in the loop on any major happenings, and I needed to hear his comforting voice anyway.

41

A veteran cop, particularly one who's ridden the homicide beat for a number of years, is rarely alarmed when death rears its ugly head. But the story Charlie Champagne had just laid upon Rex Scharffenberger shocked him to his core. Though Charlie had told him of Stella's surprise return to the hotel at which her husband had been murdered just 53 days earlier, he hardly expected that she, too, would become the victim of foul play.

Surprise did not hogtie his natural instincts. He was immediately on the horn to Metro command, requesting detective reinforcements (Marisa Quiñones and her latest protégé), the coroner, a CSI team and all the field uniforms that could be rounded up within ten minutes. Preferably a sergeant somewhere in the mix, to act as coordinating strawboss. He was anticipating a property-wide manhunt.

Rex was doing this as he was also trying to induce an orderly assemblage of the task force members. It was ten minutes to 7, and they were starting to trickle in. Sgt. Shelly Lee, who'd accompanied him, was taking charge. She had already put the name placards in place around the U-shaped arrangement of meeting tables. Willis was pacing, wishing his dog-and-pony show could proceed.

Charlie arrived, noticeably winded. Rex approached her and they huddled a few feet away from the doorway, where they could talk freely.

As succinctly as possible, Charlie related the details she'd skipped over in her hasty call from Stella's room. She'd found Stella a few breaths away from death, but the dying woman had mouthed enough of a name to identify her assailant. M.O. could attest to this. Charlie also explained that in their earlier discussions, she and Stella had each confided their own independent conclusions that the same person was responsible for Ben Pierce's death on New Year's Day.

Charlie disappeared nearly as quickly as she'd arrived. She told Rex to proceed without her and to offer a plausible reason for her absence. "Not sure where I'm headed, but I don't have anything to contribute here. I'll call you soon."

With that, she was off at a trot, though still unsure of her destination. She knew the man was roaming the halls of this huge hotel, which had an infinite number of potential hiding spots; what an uplifting thought that was. Her work phone chirped again – the second time since leaving Room 8118 – and then her personal phone began its characteristic rumbling vibration. She ignored both phones, though she knew she'd have to reckon with them before long.

The clock had ticked past 7, with Rex making no attempt to bring the meeting to order. He called Quiñones and dispatched her directly to Room 8118 to assume charge of the crime scene, while he established himself as operation commander right there in the task force meeting room. Temporarily only, he hoped.

Willis was showing his frustration, and several of the others present began chatting him up and picking his brain. He eagerly fired up his PowerPoint show but kept the overhead display off. They talked softly and looked at the laptop's changing images with interest. None of them – Willis included – knew what Rex and Charlie did, so they were busy speculating about the various possibilities.

Rex was oblivious to the conversations in the room, as he was busy barking instructions and answering questions on both his cellphone and a radio handset. The gist of his orders: 'Put the hotel on lockdown.'

Charlie's work phone chirped three more times, which only heightened the stress that was building within her. Soon she'd *have to* stop to check all those messages.

Jameson was quickly learning about the lockdown. He saw uniforms at the main entry and at the LOL exit to the swimming pool patio. He wasn't ready to depart the property quite yet anyway, but now he had a better grasp of the challenge he'd be facing when the time came.

He knew of a secret passage to the loading dock area. At least he assumed it was still his secret. He headed to his office – where he hoped no one would think to look for him – and planned about five minutes of critical work before he attempted to flee.

Soon he was printing out a previously-composed email to Roberto Guanacaste. Created and dated six days earlier, he silently cussed himself for not having printed it earlier … but then, it wasn't the sort of thing one wanted to leave lying around where prying eyes could see it. Maybe keeping it electronically buried had been a smart decision after all.

Now the intent was exactly the opposite: to leave it lying around where other eyes could discover, read and absorb its message. It was damning evidence, or so he thought. It spoke of Bobby's 'careless loss' of Jameson's cherished meat thermometer, a graduation gift from TARMA, the Toronto Academy of Red Meat Arts, many years ago. He buried the one-page missive in Bobby G's in-box, which was conveniently an inch or more deep with obsolete papers.

Next, he changed out of his room service attire, which he hung neatly in the closet, and returned to his usual business suit. The white satin gloves were removed and hastily stashed in his left front trouser pocket.

It was time to head for his escape route. He felt an ebullient air as he left, thinking that he'd successfully covered his tracks and directed the guilt elsewhere.

Though Charlie wasn't sure where she was headed, she was out of breath. She was standing near a bench on the Mezzanine level and she forced herself to stop and grab some air. It was a good time to check those accumulated emails, texts and voicemails that were piling up.

Suzy had texted that she was on her way down to the ParaSpec but it was unfortunately a CSI-business visit. A dead body in one of the rooms. Mase had sent her in his stead in order to avoid any conflict of interest (and this was before Mase had learned from Charlie who the victim was). She said she probably wouldn't hook up with Charlie on this occasion, but they could compare notes in the morning.

There was a call with a 216 area code ID that intrigued her. It turned out to be Byron Pierce, who was clearly distraught. No preliminaries or niceties. "Miss Charlie, is my mother there? I need to talk to her *now*! Have her call me at this number. Please hurry!" This was perplexing, but obviously too late to act upon. It wasn't her place to give the boy the awful news about his mom – and certainly not right now – so she archived the voicemail and moved on to the next.

The next was a doozy, a totally unexpected one. Ida Brickner had called and rambled for nearly three minutes, saying four significant things. This one she had to archive, for sure. Ida told Charlie that (a) she and Ira were patching up their life together, (b) Ira was not going to return to the ParaSpec but was instead going to retire from full-time work and would be a part-time consultant to the Spectacular Collection, with emphasis on its newer East-coast properties, (c) they would soon move from Las Vegas to somewhere in the Philadelphia area where his aging parents lived, and (d) Ira would be recommending to Leo and Sammy that she, Charlie, be appointed to the position of Vice President of Food & Beverage at ParaSpec, rather than doing an industrywide search that would certainly produce no finer candidate.

Charlie was dumbstruck, and had wanted to give that one a second listen before moving on, but there was no time. A torrent of conflicting emotions flooded through her mind.

Now she was down to the simple text messages.

Mase had written, with essentially the same news Suzy had. He wished her luck and that she'd make it home by midnight.

A text from Maryland said she had some info she wanted to talk over regarding the ancestry research they were both embroiled in lately.

Rex had written, but it too was old news by now.

A new call went to voicemail just as she closed out Rex's text. It was Maris, sounding perplexed and enraged at the same time. "Charlie, *what the fuck* is going on? I've got this kid calling me asking for his father, claims he lives here. I think he's confused as hell 'cause it's that Byron Pierce kid. I told him his father had been killed on New Year's, and that I was very sorry about that but please don't call my house again. He got pissed and hung up on me, which was good 'cause I was about to hang up on him! It really upset me, Charlie! I had to cry on someone's shoulder. Sorry I chose yours."

Charlie was unnerved by this as well. What was that crazy Pierce boy up to?

Bobby G returned from a stint in the Awesome Tower where he had two VIP clients for whom he was butlering. He nearly ran into his boss as he was leaving, but managed to duck into an alcove just as Jameson pulled the door shut. Jameson headed in the opposite direction and didn't see him. The last time the two had talked, the air was tense and tempers nearly flared. Bobby wanted to avoid any more of that until his boss had calmed down from whatever was bothering him lately.

But he was tuckered out. He decided to sit and relax for a few minutes, have a soda, and check emails and his hard-copy in-box. But before he forgot, he retrieved his trusty box cutter from his desk drawer and placed it in its slot in his custom utility belt; ready for his next assignment, which would involve opening several cases of wine.

As Byron watched the long shadows on the peaks of southern Colorado, he removed his earbuds and looked for a flight attendant. Another beer would be nice before they landed. He mentally recapped the messaging he'd accomplished during his three-hour stopover in Chicago.

He'd left a voicemail for Charlie Champagne. That was probably a dumb thing to do.

He'd talked to the lady who was married to his and Brayden's blood daddy. That was probably even stupider.

He'd spent 30 minutes chatting with Jilliana. Now *that* was pure delight, though it made him wish he'd be in her arms tonight rather than off on this wild-goose escapade in the desert.

And finally, he'd texted his sibling, reminding him that he desperately needed assistance and emotional support on the Nevada end. *'I'm counting on you, Bray. Remember, we're in this thing together.'*

What a day it had been. He found himself wishing – and not for the first time – that he'd visited the 'Farm of the 21st Century' in Shelby County instead of embarking on this lark of his mother's creation.

The Medical Examiner was just leaving Room 8118 as Suzy Hart and the newest CSI trainee arrived. She was training him just as Mase had trained her a few years back, and this promised to be just as bloody as her first call-out was.

"What've we got tonight?" Suzy inquired.

"Strange one," the M.E. said. "Death by meat thermometer, it appears. Won't know for sure till we do the autopsy in the morning."

"Dr. Champagne or I will want to observe. Send us the particulars please."

Although now anti-climactic, Rex was the only one to know that it was, so he told Willis to proceed with his presentation. He'd put so much work into it, and it was a great display of his cyber-knowledge wrapped into a genuine police investigative application. The task force members watched with spellbound attention as he moved rapidly through his comprehensive process towards his culmination slide that was titled 'The Four/Five Most Likely.' It listed the following names, in alphabetical order by surname:

- Roberto Guanacaste

- Jameson Kean

- Brayden Pierce and/or Byron Pierce

- Stella Pierce (if by contract)

And just then, Charlie erupted into the room, apologizing breathlessly. She glanced at the screen and said, "Excellent work, Willis. You've got the correct man up there – the lieutenant knows which one it is – and I'm sorry to say he's struck again. That's why I came back … this man is running loose in the hotel. It's not my call, but I'd strongly suggest the task force adjourn. The hotel's on lockdown till this perp is apprehended, so you'll have to blend in and stay occupied till it's lifted. Or, if anyone chooses to stay overnight, we can accommodate you – at no charge, of course – far away from the action and drama."

Rex chimed in, asking Gunnar to help him relocate his command post to a spot closer to the heart of the hotel. Gunnar said he knew just the spot.

Then he said, "Charlie why don't you take over—?"

But she was half-way out the door already. There was no keeping Charlie Champagne still when her brain was going a mile a minute.

The valet parker was a new guy, still enamored by the sometimes-elegant automobiles he was often called upon to park. So it was when the yellow Corvette Grand Sport with Ohio tags rolled in. Two young men emerged, and the driver handed him a twenty.

"Park her where she won't get dinged, *mi amigo*," he directed.

"Will you be staying the night, sir?"

"No. Couple hours max. Don't ya think, bro?"

The passenger simply gave an assured thumbs up and nodded.

The valet was pleased to hear that. He was already hoping for a second chance to drive the 'vette and maybe another nice tip from the generous driver.

Charlie had just gotten off a brief call with Mase, who by now was so concerned that he'd decided to shoot on up to the ParaSpec. Unofficial capacity, of course, not to interfere with Suzy and Mike, nor to even make his presence known to Rex or Marisa. But dammit, his wife was running through the halls of her hotel, and a murderer was on the loose! He *did* have a bit of a vested interest in what was going on up there.

She'd tried to talk him out of it, but realized she wouldn't prevail. He was coming.

Back to the matter at hand: the quest for Jameson Kean. She remained in open radio contact with M.O., in case either one happened across their fugitive. There was no letting up; she knew so many of the hotel's ins and outs, places it would take forever to educate the police personnel about. M.O. knew most of them too, and probably others she wasn't aware of.

And she had a few hunches. No premonitions just yet, but sometimes her hunches were pretty darn good.

The lockdown remained in effect. The young men who had arrived in the Corvette were allowed in, but were advised that they may be unable to leave when they wished, as there was a temporary lockdown due to an 'internal hotel issue.'

There were hundreds of registered guests and the authorities had decided early on that it was unreasonable to deny ingress to the property. The warning the Pierce boys had received was given to all arriving guests.

They agreed to the condition and headed straight for the LOL to unwind. They spotted two open bar stools and were welcomed by the captivating smile of an alluring mixologist.

In his inbox, Bobby G encountered the paper copy of an email that was allegedly sent to him almost a week ago.

He'd never seen it before, and he'd certainly not printed it out and stuck it in his inbox. It was scandalous and full of fabricated facts. His hateful boss was trying to pin something on him. Why on earth would he want to steal someone else's keepsake meat thermometer?

Suddenly supercharged, Roberto thrust open the office door and started to head ... where? He didn't even know. But he needed to be out looking for Mr. Kean so he could confront him about the phony memorandum.

That's when he spotted the attractive catering lady running along a hallway that intersected his about a hundred feet away. Instinctively, he decided to follow.

And that's when he heard a rare but not unprecedented public announcement, one that went throughout the entire hotel like those annoying captain's messages on the cruise ship he'd once worked on.

Charlie stopped so she could listen to the broadcast message. The speaker was Gunnar Block. *'Attention, Jameson Kean. We know you are on property, and we demand you come forth and surrender yourself. You cannot escape, and your continued evasion can only lead to serious consequences. Please approach any uniformed Metro officer to turn yourself in peacefully.'*

Bobby G had listened halfheartedly, but he had not stopped running and nearly collided with the catering lady. He was astounded to learn that his boss was a fugitive in some criminal action, something far bigger than creating and planting an incriminating phony email message. He stood there, mesmerized for a moment, before continuing his foot pursuit of the catering lady, who was way ahead of him again.

The two Pierce boys slugged down their Coors Light drafts and tipped their server well. Their preoccupation with her charm and beauty, coupled with a loud cheer from a rambunctious foursome as Colorado pulled ahead of San Jose late in the third period, caused them to miss the name – *Jameson Kean* – on the public address announcement, so they remained oblivious as to who was causing the unusual security activity in the hotel. No matter to them, as their agenda was only to pay the requested visit to good old Mom.

The quick beers had taken the edge off the two uptight young men. Brayden had recently had a sizeable dose of Mom-drama, but it was a first for his brother from Ohio.

They opted to first check out the loading dock where their father – *stepfather, whatever the hell Ben had actually been* – was killed and butchered on New Year's morning. Kinda morbid, but sometimes curiosity outweighed good sense. Especially at their age.

Turns out the loading dock was off limits, due to the crazy manhunt that was underway. Oh well, time to see Mom anyway.

Charlie was back at it, heading towards the 'back of house,' the vast behind-the-scenes empire that is really the lifeblood of any hotel. Offices. Kitchen. Food and beverage storage. Laundry. HVAC equipment. Electrical and mechanical. Trash processing. Water purification. And on and on and on.

It was here that Jameson would most likely feel comfortable, and would know of secret hiding spots or passages. But Charlie wasn't dumb, nor was she a tenderfoot; this was her hotel as much as it was his, and she vowed not to be outwitted or outmaneuvered.

So she kept running, vaguely aware of someone behind her. The young man who'd nearly collided with her moments ago, most likely. Not a concern. He undoubtedly had his own important destination.

Rex and Gunnar, by now a team, were hurriedly moving on to new quarters. Gunnar's Security Department had a conference room with all the technological bells and whistles one could want. To those remaining in the Utopia Boardroom, Rex managed a hasty proclamation, seeming out of duty as much as anything else: "Thank you all for your service in the pursuit of justice."

Dr. Cruz smiled and gave a mock salute, while Dr. Grigio nodded appreciatively; the lieutenant's parting words had reached the right ears and were clearly valued.

Charlie was running for her life!

The depth and tempo of the footsteps behind her had changed. Loud and heavy, sounding full of authority, experience and age. It was no longer the young guy she'd been trailed by earlier.

At the juncture of two corridors, Charlie executed a sharp left and took the opportunity to glance behind her. It was none other than Jameson, and the bastard was gaining on her! She zigged again, hoping he would zag, but no luck. He remained close behind in her wake.

This crazed man was no longer the loving husband of her friend Maris. Just a few short weeks ago the pair had enjoyed a splendid trip to Spain, where they'd married a decade ago. It had been a glorious trip, full of fun, food and frolic. Now, he'd somehow transformed into a madman, a person motivated by who-knows-what.

She kept running. Zigging, then zagging, and then – dammit, there went her left shoe as she turned a sharp corner and hooked its heel on a sewer cleanout plug. Can't run with only one shoe, she discovered quickly, so the other one was tossed aside too. Damn, they were Gucci knockoffs, and still pretty new. She hoped she'd see them again.

Barefoot now, she had a bit more trouble turning corners. The next left went towards the loading dock where all the foodstuffs entered the property. Familiar territory for Charlie. She slipped making the turn, and that's when her backwards gaze fell upon the bright glistening object in Jameson's right hand.

The Scot had abandoned any notion of avoiding detection or covering his evidentiary trail. By now it had become a brutal quest for survival.

He would escape ... or not. And that was it.

The knife gave him a sense of power, of intensity, of dominance that should carry him through this ordeal. It was time to launch his offensive, beginning with this *glaikit hoore* who thought she was so invincible. She was a petite thing, be easy to carve up like a goddamned holiday goose.

Charlie abruptly encountered a wall, a jog in the route she'd forgotten about, and it momentarily stunned her. Jameson closed the gap even more, and – worst of all – the knife he was brandishing looked bigger, sharper and shinier than it had moments earlier. He began to raise it above his head in a deadly attack stance.

She had crumbled to the floor and was essentially cornered. She had no defense left in her, other than a barrage of words: "Is that the knife you cut off Ben Pierce's hand with, you son of a bitch? Right here on this very loading dock!"

"Which body part shall I remove from you, my pretty lass? Aah, I see it now – that exquisite little foot with the ruby-painted nails. *Per-fec-tissimo!*"

A noise grabbed her attention then, and it wasn't from her would-be attacker. Beyond him, she spotted the younger man who'd earlier been in her wake. She didn't know his name, but he was clearly one of Jameson's squad of butlers. He was charging towards them, seemingly bent upon intervention.

Jameson turned then, hollering, "Bobby, keep out of this!" The knife was still poised above Charlie, who was now a quaking heap upon the floor. Her blood was racing, almost inviting the knife to slice into an artery and stop its surging flow.

But Bobby refused to be cast aside, instead redoubling his determination to save the catering lady and, ultimately, himself and his reputation.

Jameson's hand cocked back behind a bent elbow, poised for a deadly thrust at this do-gooder female who stood in the way of his escape to freedom. She would be easy carving and he wished he had the luxury of time to sever her foot, as he'd threatened. But Bobby G was an unanticipated glitch, and now there would be no time for frivolous exhibitionism.

He turned back towards Charlie, readying for the strike. In so doing, he missed the appearance of the young butler's secreted weapon. But Charlie saw it, admired its metallic glint and marveled at the speed at which it traversed the twenty feet that separated the young man from Jameson.

It was the box cutter – blade extended fully, tossed with the apparent deftness of a master knife thrower.

As the knife flew, so too did Bobby's enraged words. "You set me up, *hijo de puta!*"

Though he would later say that he'd never used the box cutter for anything but cutting open boxes, Bobby's target – Jameson Kean – was a formidable hulk, and hard to miss. The knife failed to reach the critical mass of the man's torso but was nonetheless remarkably effective. It reached flesh in his upper thigh, and caused a major eruption of bright red blood. Jameson fell to the ground with a grunt and a resounding thud, his carving knife flying out of his hand and sliding across the floor.

Charlie was astonished as she witnessed the crimson spectacle, a few feet from her, and it was then she realized exactly what she was seeing. The box cutter had severed the femoral artery in Jameson's left leg. Charlie remembered from some long-ago first aid class that this was a serious breach that needed prompt attention by a trained EMT.

She pulled out her phone and called 9-1-1, though part of her felt the creep deserved to bleed out.

Just then, Brayden and Byron Pierce happened upon the scene. To Charlie, their appearance defied logic – one of her crazy visions, perhaps – but she was too fatigued to figure it out. Or ask about it.

"Be useful, fellas," she directed immediately. "Apply hard pressure on the artery to stem the blood flow. A bus is on the way."

Bobby stood, breathless, watching in shock as the boys did what they were told. Charlie felt mildly smug, giving orders to these brat kids *and* dropping her vocabulary's newest word on them.

M.O. had explained earlier that 'bus' was cop talk for 'ambulance.'

42

Reckoning time. So much has happened, I barely know where to begin, where to focus my myriad thoughts.

It's definitely been a watershed time in my life. How could all of this occur in such a short span of time? I'm still working to grasp the full measure of its width, breadth and depth. There's hardly a facet of my existence that hasn't been mightily altered since 2017 showed its face.

Mase, of course, is the exception. Nothing was altered about my stalwart guy, my rock, my ever-ready shoulder to lean on and ear to sob into. He's kept me afloat through all of it, not the least of which was last night when he rushed to the ParaSpec, worried for my safety. A good thing, too, because I was in no condition to drive home after having a gigantic chef's knife poised a few feet from several of my bodily organs. I was still trembling hours afterwards.

Mase fed and wined me but without the usual frills. He knew I needed time alone more than anything, so he gave me space. The clock had just flipped past midnight.

Funny, how this man I just happened to encounter at a college basketball game could be so insightful, intuitive, and caring about this woman he just happened to encounter at a college basketball game. In the decade since we'd done that mutual encountering, he'd learned every little thing there was to know about what made me tick.

I was where I was ... well, because he loved me, and as that thought struck me, so too did *Because You Loved Me* by Celine Dion. She sang my thoughts precisely, and I couldn't – didn't even want to – get them out of my head.

I went off by myself knowing full well that my privacy would be respected for as long as I needed it. Because Mase gave me wings and made me fly.

I retired to my cozy home office and proceeded to welcome Friday the 24th of February all by myself. There was much to digest from Thursday the 23rd, I reckoned, as I sunk into the plush maroon loveseat and tossed a velour throw over my legs. I'd brought with me my last glass of wine from dinner. It was a nice light viognier from France, since I couldn't abide the sight of any more red liquid at the moment.

My sanctum – 'the Charlie Castle,' we called it – was where I could fully unwind. My fortress of solitude. Fully equipped with a top-of-the-line laptop, printer/copier, speakers, the works ... but I needed none of that right now. I could reach a pad of paper and a pen if I needed it, but I wouldn't. There was a well-stocked mini-fridge, in case the wine ran dry. It might, as I had a ton to absorb and come to terms with. Saffron and Nutmeg had snuck in the room as the door was closing, and quickly cuddled up on my lap, purring contentedly.

On the side table where I placed my glass was taped a small piece of paper. I immediately recognized it ... another example of Mase's thoughtful handiwork. It was the fortune that had been in my cookie back on February 1st.

'You will solve a great mystery within thirty days.'

Yeah, how 'bout that! Who'd'a thunk?

Though I'd been in phone contact with Leo Stein earlier in the evening – and he'd passed my reports on to Sammy Spakisumar – I felt I owed them both a final reporting. As I'd done after each of the previous task force meetings, I delivered it via email. I kept it brief and tried to downplay the seriousness of the terrifying ordeal I'd gone through. Factual, but not overly emotional.

With that taken care of, I moved on to other things. My brain was awash with questions and confusion. I hardly knew where to start.

The easy stuff first is always a safe bet. Ida Brickner, bless her heart, had courageously dumped her broken soul into a three-minute monologue and had made my day in more ways than one. On a normal day, her call would have been a chart-topper, worthy of celebration. Ira was stepping down! But even better, he was all but handing me his position. Leo, not known for creative problem-solving, would almost certainly take Ira's recommendation and offer me the promotion.

Future VP or not, several other items of which I was immensely proud were falling to me this fine day. I had helped – to some incalculable extent (and I wasn't about to try to calculate it!) – bring four murder investigations to a conclusion. It was tragic that it had come at the expense of dear Stella's life, but one had to concede she'd more or less brought it upon herself with her hedonistic lifestyle. I'd mostly known Jameson through work, but there'd been a few occasions when the four of us had socialized, and I felt I knew him fairly well from my many private conversations with Maris. I felt deeply sorry for her, and even more so for those three sweet daughters of theirs.

It wasn't clear yet how and why – or even *if* – Jameson figured into the deaths of Michael Swann and Adam Honshu on Big Game Sunday. The connection seemed likely, given the linguistic content of some of the mysterious messages the perp had sent to me, Rex and Gunnar over the past eight weeks, but there was no motive that I could see. Bobby Guanacaste, I suspected, would likely have some revelations that will help Metro in putting all the pieces together.

To that end, there would be a final debriefing meeting in the morning, and I was invited. I'm sure I'd learn more that would clarify matters, including the extent to which the Pierce sons or others might be implicated in any of these crimes. I was hoping to gain more insight into the motivation for the murders, for they all seemed so senseless.

While it'd be nice to credit my investigative prowess for my contributions, I actually owed much of the credit to my clairvoyant powers. And lately I'd been having not only premonitions, but also a number of 'postmonitions' (which I eventually Googled and found to be a real concept, given credibility by some in the psychiatric community), in which I could see not into the future, but into *the past*. An outlandish idea, I know, but these new experiences were vivid and quite realistic to me. Some of them were even downright scary.

Envision a scene with a butcher's knife in a man's hand, blood dripping from the blade far more abundantly than if it were merely carving up a side of beef. Though his face was not in sight, the general physique of the knife-wielder was that of Jameson Kean. Another showed a man wearing a football jersey serving drinks, and again the build was that of Jameson Kean's, but his face was not visible. The jersey had an indistinguishable numeral but the word across its back was GLASGOW. A final postmonition that my mind-trap recalled now was even stranger ... a speeding yellow sports car with drops of blood and vials of a light-golden liquid spewing from its dual exhaust pipes, somewhere out in the barren desert. This last one defied a neat explanation, but it seemed to implicate the two Pierce sons in *something*, though I'd not yet been privy to a motive that might fit their involvement. Not for the Big Game ones, and even less so for dear ol' Dad's murder. If I was a betting person – which I'm not, except for an occasional visit to a local roulette wheel – I'd say money was at the bottom of it. Probably big money, knowing the Pierces.

Can you see why I'm a basket case?

Anyway, these psychic moments – all pummeling me within the past few days, mind you – coupled with what I had learned from the task force deliberations and finally through my first-hand experience earlier this evening – undeniably suggest that Jameson Kean had killed Ben Pierce, Michael Swann and Adam Honshu. And now, of course, poor Stella Pierce as well.

Again, my feelings of sorrow focused on Maris and her children. What a terrible burden for them all to bear. I guess the only bright side was that she'd managed to escape being one of his victims.

I decided I'd done enough. I was delighted to have contributed, but was more than ready to relinquish my investigative stripes and return to pure hotel work. Rex, Marisa and Willis can carry on from here.

But let's not forget the other benefit of my sleuthing abilities. After all, it was my exploratory inclination that had me stumbling upon long-secreted facts that were far more significant to me personally than who killed whom under my employer's roof.

My involvement with my genealogy results and the *whoireallyam. com* site, has been ramping up these last few weeks. The leads were coming fast and furious, some from the website in the form of concrete, followable names, and some from that wrinkled-up generator of premonitions (and now postmonitions!) that lived inside my skull.

What was most significant, I thought, was that whopper of a postmonition that I had seen this past Tuesday when I had to pull to the side of the road. It had replayed itself twice since, and each time my excitement had grown. It was by far the clearest and most specific of those backward looks I'd yet been handed. Also – and this I considered noteworthy – the oldest in terms of age of the retro look-back. It was a flashback to the summer of 1984, when my dear parents were discussing what to name their unborn child.

My mother, Emma (whom I'd called Mama), and my father, Edouard (Père), had once considered the name Olympia, after the Los Angeles Summer Olympics that were held that summer before my birth. They lived in the greater L.A. area then – as they did until their passing a dozen years ago – and everything Olympic was in vogue. But Olympia suddenly felt overdone to them and they sought other solutions. One day Père, who was a consummate follower of French history, announced that he had the solution. "Charlemagne," he told Mama, "sounds regal and aristocratic, as indeed our child deserves, but we needn't burden her with that on a daily basis. We can call her 'Charlie' for short. Fun, playful, tomboyish perhaps." Remarkably, Mama bought in to the unusual proposition without argument. She did have a rebellious streak in her, and it probably didn't hurt that she had a favorite uncle named Charlie.

My hunch had been festering since Tuesday, possibly even before then. At the center of it, believe it or not, was my friend Maryland Burfurd. Why, one may wonder? I wasn't certain myself, but I think it started when I first got a 'match' on *whoireallyam.com* that told me I had a third or fourth cousin named Evangeline Beaufort, though no details as to her age or whereabouts was included. Evangeline, whose surname was close to but not the same as Burfurd, hadn't built a 'searchable family tree.' I felt encouraged, yet stymied.

Maryland's message from several hours back added fuel to my fire. That she'd even bought into the *whoireallyam.com* process a couple of months ago amazed me, and the fact that she was now wanting to 'talk over' some of the results with me was surprising, to say the least.

I wasn't sure how I felt about that. Much about the woman was unorthodox and cheeky, so far removed from conventionality that I wasn't entirely sure that I wanted to swap stories. On the other hand, she had a down-to-earth authenticity that was hard to find in people these days. I relished that, whether it was in an acquaintance, a friend or – *dare I even think it?* – a blood relative.

Suddenly I had to know more, and I felt Maryland had answers. Had she, too, gotten a 'hit' from this Evangeline woman?

There was one way to find out.

I called her, but dumb me was so keyed up that I totally lost sight of the fact that it was somewhere past 3:30 in the morning where she was. I knew she was a night owl, like me, but this was ridiculous. After a single ring, I decided to hang up quickly and hold off till the sun was up in North Carolina.

Apparently I wasn't quick enough.

"Aah, my little primrose," her voice warbled, as full of verve as it often was at the stroke of high noon. She often had a fun name for me, a whole host of them in her back pocket it seemed.

"Sorry for the hour. I didn't think about—"

"Balderdash. I knew you'd call before long."

Like I said, Maryland was as eccentric as they come. I decided not to debate time zone and sleep patterns with her. And here *I* was the one who was supposedly psychic, but *she* knew I'd call. Maybe the ability was contagious.

Anyway, I posed my question about the mysterious Evangeline Beaufort. Had she ever heard of her? I knew it was a longshot.

"Aah, my great-aunt Geelie! Yes, yes, of course! Oh my, what a lovely lady. She passed away back in … well, I guess it must be the late-nineties. And she was in *her* late-nineties too!" added Maryland with a chuckle. "Yeah, she was born in 1899 and always bragged that the whole 20th century was gonna be *her* century. Funny old gal."

I asked about the surname discrepancy, and Maryland was quick with an answer.

"I think some of Aunt Geelie's nephews moved to the South and wanted to assimilate. Decided they wanted to be rednecks like everyone else, I guess. Beaufort sounded too aristocratic, can you imagine? One of them fellas was Gramps, my Pa's Pa. He used to say. 'Y'all come down here to Dixie, ya best become yo'self a Burfurd.'"

"So you're originally from the South, Maryland?" I was surprised that I hadn't known that.

"Born in Maryland – of course – and that's technically the South. Mason-Dixon Line, y'know, forms the north edge of the state, slave states versus free states, all those historic considerations. My Pa lived in both Carolinas and Virginia for a spell, and I bounced from one parent's home to the other. So yeah, I'm a southerner, but I've lived all across the country over the years. I even lived with Aunt Geelie for a couple of years in her pretty little Chicago apartment, where she was some kinda freelance editor. Finished up my high school years there. But wanderlust grabbed me as soon as I graduated, and I was off, heading west again. Texas, Arizona, and finally a decade or more in the Golden State, north, south, all around. I loved it all: Sausalito, Morro Bay, San Diego, Orange County, Long—"

"Orange County? When?"

"Let me think – yeah, I think it was early to mid '80s. I knew some very good people there, did them some special favors. And they rewarded me well." Her voice was vibrant as she recalled old memories.

Holy cow, I thought silently. My thoughts and emotions were ablaze.

Finally, I found words.

"I wonder why you never told me this before."

"I wonder why you never asked, my rosebud," she replied.

Thousands of miles separated us, but I swear I could see the characteristic smirk I knew was playing across her lips as she spoke those last words.

And then the line went dead.

Apropos, I thought, for what else was left to say at that juncture? It was a time to let it all soak in, perhaps for both of us. I got the sense that Maryland was learning new things right along with me. Had Aunt Geelie been the key that opened the door to the truth? It seemed so.

Three minutes later my phone beeped, and I thought it must be her. That the abrupt disconnection had not been intentional after all.

It wasn't Maryland, however, but rather the bank at which Mase and I had our personal checking and short-term savings accounts. An automated message from the bank said that an electronic deposit had been received through the 'clearXchange' financial service. The identity of the payer wasn't divulged, but with minimal analysis I was able to put two and two together.

The amount of the anonymous deposit was $1,012.84.

It was all making sense now, and the confirmation brought a tear to the corner of each eye. A wispy smile curled across my lips as the tears began to flow in earnest.

My birth date, you see, is 10/12/84.

The phone rang again and the ID told me it was Maryland. I stared at it for a few seconds before picking it up. When I did, I said the words I'd yearned to say for a long time.

"Hi, Mom."

43

Friday dawned, and though I'd had little sleep in terms of hours, I felt well rested. There was something very soothing about fitting an important piece into your hereditary puzzle. Maryland Burfurd was that piece.

I moved slowly, as I had nowhere to be right away. I was about to take my second unscheduled PTO day in a row, absolutely unprecedented. The big summit meeting at Metro was scheduled for 11 a.m., allowing me plenty of time to get ready.

Mase displayed a mixture of moods this morning. Overall, he remained jubilant that things had turned out so well for me yesterday – learning my natural mother's identity, hearing about Ira's plans to step down, and most of all surviving my encounter with a homicidal maniac in such a heroic fashion. He couldn't quit fawning over me, telling me how glad he was that I was OK and everything was working out.

But beneath it all was a sullen component, and I eventually figured out that the prospect of observing Stella's autopsy was eating at him. No surprise there. I knew he'd observed dozens of these somber events; as a CSI, he had an interest in most autopsies where the death was due to foul play or suspicious circumstances. To have a person you consider a friend on the receiving end of the knife made the experience especially grim.

The autopsy was set for 10:00, but I tried to put it out of my mind. It wasn't easy for me to think about either.

Metro headquarters was on MLK Boulevard near downtown, so I gave myself a full hour to negotiate the 17-mile trip. You just never know about traffic in this region. As it turned out, I arrived about 20 minutes early. Enough time to sit and think about poor Mase, watching the M.E. slice Stella into pieces.

I hurried inside, eager to fill my head with new images and new faces to look at.

The conference room was large and modern, with a long oval table that had nine plush chairs along each of its two long sides, plus one at each end; a total of 20. Name placards were in place at a few spots clustered around one end, and I recognized them as the handiwork of Sgt. Shelly Lee. Rex would occupy the head of the table, flanked by Sgt. Lee, who would take notes just as she'd done for the task force, and Sgt. Quiñones, the Detective Division's second in charge. The only other persons whose name cards I could see belonged to Willis Bronx, with Gunnar Block and myself representing the Paradise Spectacular Resort.

I was first to arrive, took my seat, and used the moment of downtime to check messages on my two phones. There'd been a symphony of sounds playing during my drive from home up to Metro.

Work phone first. Always.

There was just one call, and it was from Leo – that, in itself, was a rarity – and he spoke of a strange call his office had received from a 'mystery woman back east somewhere' who said I'd want to talk with her, but wouldn't recognize her by name. Now if that isn't puzzling as all get out! Why call Leo, not me direct? Why not leave a number to call back?

My personal phone had an even more enigmatic voicemail message. Female voice, faint and distant sounding, garbled words until the end: '...

I've missed you so. Chickadee will buzz you again later." Caller ID said 242 area, wherever the heck that was. My wheels started turning, fast and furiously …

There were another two messages on that phone, but I never got to them, as I was promptly joined by Sgt. Lee. I put both phones in my purse, and we made idle small talk as the others trickled in.

Reminiscent of our first two task force meetings, Sheriff Mickey McGraw – with no name identifier, and no seat either – made a brief appearance at the beginning to welcome us and to congratulate us on a job well done. He turned the meeting over to Rex and promptly departed to his next glad-handing opportunity. There was no doubt that the efficient solution of these multiple crimes using the task force method that was 'his baby' would serve him well in the upcoming election. Typical political distortion, but not something for those of us in the room to dwell upon.

Chickadee? It meant something … but what?

Rex began with a concise statement of facts as things currently stood. "Jameson Kean is recovering from surgery at Chaparral Hospital and will be charged with two counts of first degree murder – those of Ben Pierce and Stella Pierce – and two counts of accessory to first degree murder – those of Michael Swann and Adam Honshu. The two Pierce boys, Brayden and Byron, are in custody and will be charged with one count each of first degree murder, and one count of accessory to murder. I'll let our Detective Trainee, Mr. Bronx, explain the details of how and why we feel these charges are appropriate."

"Thanks, Lieutenant," said Willis, standing. He glanced around, making eye contact with everyone before beginning. "In a nutshell, folks, Jameson and his two out-of-wedlock sons were not the strangers one might assume. We have it on good authority that they've been communicating with regularity for years. It's not entirely clear how long the boys have known they were his sons, not Ben's, but it's been at least five or more years. You see, Jameson

Kean and Stephen Pierce, Ben's brother, had a business going; imports and exports going both ways between the U.S. and Canada. Specifically between Cleveland, Ohio, and Toronto, Ontario. Partly legal, partly illegal, we think, but we are not investigating those issues 'cause it's way beyond our jurisdiction and has nothing to do with homicide here in Nevada. We've already notified the Feds."

Chickadee ... Chickadee ... oh God, I get it now, Chickadee! Chickadee is Chelsea, my long-lost comrade and half of the C-C Girls of Newport Beach! But why? How?

"The fact that a quarter kilo – about nine ounces – of fentanyl, a powerful and potentially deadly narcotic, was included in one of their recent Canada-to-U.S. shipments caught our eye when I did my investigating a few weeks ago. But since fentanyl does have legitimate purposes, we wrote it off as inconsequential back then. Now, we have reason to think otherwise.

"Anyway, remember, Ben is not happy that his son is dating a black girl, so after Ben is gone, Byron is relieved that an obstacle to his romance with girlfriend Jill has been eliminated. It gets him thinking. Once he figures out that Jameson was the one who executed his pop, he approaches Jameson and basically says, 'I know you did it, so how about snuffing my girlfriend's dad, Michael Swann, too?' Swann, after all, is equally unhappy that his daughter is dating outside her race, so for Byron it seems like a perfect opportunity to eliminate the only remaining obstacle. Byron learns from Jill that her father will be at the Big Game extravaganza at the ParaSpec on Feb 5th. Jameson agrees, but he has a price: $100K. Byron agrees, figuring he'll pay from proceeds of the $500K life insurance he knows Ben left him.

"Brother Brayden gets wind of all this and decides he wants to be part of this 'murder game' too. Morbid kinda thinking, isn't it, to call it a game? Jameson goes along, for another $100K. And Brayden just happens to have the perfect target in mind. A Californian named 'Adam H' had recently taken him and several other players for $10K each, and then had the audacity to boast about it to his social platform followers, saying that he and his cuz were gonna take all that dough he'd just won to Vegas and double or triple it at the ParaSpec's Big Game event. Brayden, who is still fuming over his loss, is suddenly thrilled that he had it within his power to have this jerk exterminated."

Fascinating tale, Willis, I thought, *but it's hard to concentrate. I've suddenly got Chelsea on my Mind.*

The detective-trainee continued, relating his tale in the present tense, which somehow made it seem more real, less a historic recounting. "With minimal effort, because of his position at the hotel, Jameson is able to ascertain the precise identity of Adam H, and he assigns him and his cousin, Aaron, to a specific upgraded table on the Shangri La Terrace, in relatively close proximity to the one he assigns to Michael and Ruth Anne Swann and their friends, the Stallworths. Then, during the days just before the Big Game, Kean becomes familiar with both Adam's and Michael's appearance (by visiting them in their rooms as a welcoming gesture from the Director of VIP Services – pretty clever, huh?) so he would be sure to administer his poison to the *correct* Asian man and the *correct* African-American man. He even takes a few surreptitious photos of both on his phone, just to be sure he didn't screw up.

"The glitch is that Jameson now realizes he wouldn't be able to be the drink server to these people because he'd likely be recognized. He tells the Pierce boys that he had done the arranging of seats and the sabotaging of the electronics room, but they would have to administer the poison themselves. Never ones to balk at a challenge, the boys agree – enthusiastically, even – then make quick plans for jerseyfied costumes. They also realize they'd have to switch targets since Byron is already known to Swann. For their trouble, they price-bicker Jameson down to $75K apiece."

"Wait a minute," Sgt. Quiñones interrupted. "How on earth have you been able to uncover this amazing level of detail so quickly?"

Chelsea on my Mind. Sorry Willis, I just can't help it.

"Wasn't easy, I'll tell you," Willis replied. "The lieutenant and I pressed both these kids long into the night, and about 2:30 this morning, Byron finally cracked. That was when he learned for the first time that Jameson had killed their mother too. He snapped then, broke down in tears, told us the whole sordid history, beginning when he and Brayden first became aware of the love and lust triangle that had been going on in their home for many years. Their first clue had actually come back when they were pre-teens and spotted Jameson at their Ohio home when Ben was off on a business trip to Washington."

Marisa, who was a seasoned interrogator, looked rather impressed.

I know I was. Even through the blur that Chelsea was imposing on my vision.

"Anyway, the big day comes," Willis continued methodically, "and the Pierces are dressed in the jerseys Byron had acquired before leaving Columbus. One Ryan and one Brady, so as to optimize their blend-in-ability. Jerseys by Byron, poisons prepped by Brayden, glass vials and fentanyl product provided by Jameson, who'd acquired it from the boys' Uncle Stephen ... that was the deal. Brayden had excelled in his past chemistry studies and has no trouble converting the potent white powder into a clear and tasteless liquid that would zonk their two subjects quickly and efficiently. And permanently.

"So instead of 27 male servers, there are 29 ... but no one's keeping track anyway. Jameson is in charge of personnel deployment, among many other things, so he'd be the only one counting. Shortly after the second half of the game begins, the guys break open the poison vials, dumped the contents into the victims' drinks and deliver them. Byron to Honshu, Brayden to Swann, plus unaltered drinks to Aaron, Ruth Anne, Tommy and Margie Jo. Great care is used to make sure the wrong persons are not poisoned; Byron pointed out Brayden's target for him and they both carefully studied

Jameson's photo of Adam Honshu. About three minutes later, after the vics' fourth or fifth sips – with noticeable incapacitation beginning to set in – Brayden, the designated 'beeper keeper,' sends a silent signal that causes the power surge to TV monitor #19, which is the one they were all watching. Predictably, the Shangri La Terrace quickly empties of all of its panic-stricken partiers. All, that is, except the two who are by now incapable of moving.

"Mission accomplished, and without a hiccup. The two Pierce boys disappear into the night, and now there are once more only 27 servers. But again, who's counting?

"And as a final point, Jameson's motivation in last night's killing of his lover, Stella, became obvious. She knew too much, though that was his own fault. He'd apparently let it slip – on that quickie trip to Toronto/Cleveland/Lexington a week before Malibu, we suspect – that he was behind Ben's death, and she was preparing to blab that to the Sheriff's task force. In his view, she had to be silenced." Willis took a deep breath and sat down.

"Quite a tale," Gunnar remarked on behalf of everyone in the room. It was the first thing he'd said, and I could tell he was impressed with the thoroughness of the young investigator. Then he turned to me and said, "I am sad for the woman I know works for you, who is married to this murdering madman. I hear they have some nice children too."

"Yes, three lovely daughters, all under ten. Old enough to know their father will no longer be a part of the family, but too young to fully comprehend the *why* of it all."

"The *why* is always the toughest part on those who are innocent bystanders to horrific crimes like this," Rex said pointedly. It was a philosophical side he didn't often display.

I viewed this as my opening to insert a crumb of positive news. "Maris Kean messaged me earlier this morning, saying she and her girls will be gone until further notice. Her parents live in Benicia, California, and she's hoping to find work up in that area so she can forget as much of this horror story as quickly as possible. The Spectacular Collection has an established property in Napa and a new one in Santa Rosa is scheduled to open in April of this year. I told her I'd give her a strong recommendation at either one, or any other property she might choose up there. She really is a model employee that any property would be lucky to have. I'll be sorry to lose her from my team."

"That's good news," Quiñones observed, and several others nodded their agreement.

"And she's a class act, too," I added. "Despite all she's been through with this evil man, she asked me to make sure he was given proper treatment for his prostate cancer during his incarceration. Can you imagine?"

No one said a thing. What was there to say?

And while they were silently absorbing that tidbit, my mind was racing elsewhere. *Chelsea on my Mind. Oh wow, girl … Chickadee, could it possibly be?*

It seemed as if everything had been covered and we all had other places we needed to be, workloads we had to tackle. I found myself dawdling, though, waiting for a chance to speak alone to Rex. It was a sort of bittersweet parting, as we wouldn't have much need to see each other from here on out.

"Well, this is it, Rex," I began. "An awful series of events we've been through, but in every tragedy there's a bit of a silver lining. I've really enjoyed working with you, Marisa and Willis. New acquaintances have turned into new friends. That's a big plus for me."

"For me too," he said simply. I could tell he was uneasy being placed in an emotionally vulnerable situation. But I could read his thoughts on his face.

"Well, you have a nice weekend," I told him in parting, "Got anything planned?"

"Low key this weekend, but really looking forward to the next one."

"Oh yeah?" I asked, hoping he'd share. By now, I was used to having to pry stuff outta him.

Rex gave Willis a glance, looked back at me and said, "That young man and I have plans."

"Really? I wasn't aware you two socialized."

Rex chuckled, looked again at his young protégé across the room and said, "Actually it's not just us two ... it's *four of us.* Suzy and Tapper are joining us for a weekend of wine tasting over in Temecula."

I could hardly contain my pleasure upon hearing this. What marvelous news! But I quickly drew my face into a serious knot. "But really, Rex, dare you leave this hotbed of crime? After all, it will be *the first Sunday of a new month.*"

We both guffawed at that, and then – compulsively and unexpectedly – shared a great big body hug that spoke volumes.

It was over. But for some it was just beginning.